KT-502-159

HOSTILE INTENT

CLIVE EGLETON

Hodder & Stoughton
LONDON SYDNEY AUCKLAND

British Library Cataloguing in Publication Data
Egleton, Clive
  Hostile intent.
  I. Title
  823.914 [F]

ISBN 0-340-58413-0

Published by Hodder and Stoughton,
a division of Hodder and Stoughton Ltd,
Mill Road, Dunton Green, Sevenoaks, Kent TN13 2YA
Editorial Office: 47 Bedford Square, London WC1B 3DP

Typeset by Hewer Text Composition Services, Edinburgh
Printed in Great Britain by Mackays of Chatham PLC, Chatham, Kent

This book is for Carol and her late husband, Chris, with love and admiration

CHAPTER I

THE MERCEDES 280E had seen better days. The last word in luxury when it had rolled off the production line in 1975, the limousine had clearly taken a battering over the next sixteen years and now looked overdue for the scrapheap. Rust had attacked the body to such an extent that the door sills had been practically eaten away. The chrome too was pockmarked with hundreds of tiny holes and large scabs of it had flaked off the fenders to expose the bare metal underneath. The coachwork itself was several shades of white where someone had used a brush to touch it up, but there was nothing amateurish about the swastikas which had replaced the chromium beading on the door panels.

Whittle first saw the vehicle as he drove down the hill into Dresden. It was parked by the kerbside with the bonnet raised and clouds of steam escaping from the radiator, which the driver was ineffectually fanning with a peak cap. There were three other neo-Nazis with him, brutal-looking young men in jeans and leather bomber jackets who reminded Whittle of the bunch of skinheads he had tangled with outside the Stamford Bridge Stadium in Walham Green back in November. As he drove past the Mercedes, one of the would-be stormtroopers ran out into the road and tried to flag him down. As far as Whittle was concerned, there were four very good and highly visible reasons for not stopping; instinctively swerving to the left to avoid the skinhead, he flattened the accelerator and roared on down the hill. Although the Trabant saloon he had borrowed from the boilerman at the Mission House in Potsdam was incapable of doing more than sixty-two miles an hour, the two-cylinder, two-stroke, air-cooled engine made a noise loud enough to suggest that it had enough power to break through the sound barrier.

A warning sign on the outskirts of Dresden Neustadt checked his headlong flight; conforming to the speed limit, Whittle filtered into Antonstrasse at the bottom of the hill and crossed the Elbe by the Marien Bridge. The moment he approached the Hauptbahnhof in the old town, he knew Galina Kutuzova had picked the wrong night to meet him in Dresden. The four Nazis he had encountered shortly after leaving the autobahn had only been a tiny sample of what was to come. The Chief of Staff had said nothing about a National Socialist rally at the briefing but there were at least two hundred party members milling about in the Leninplatz at the top of Pragerstrasse and it wasn't necessary to possess a Mensa intellect to realise that they were looking for trouble. Poles, gypsies, migrant workers from Turkey; they weren't too fussy about the nationality of their intended victims. Like the Jews in Hitler's Third Reich, they were simply convenient scapegoats for the economic ills of the former German Democratic Republic.

There were very few policemen in evidence and he wondered if the authorities were hoping for inclement weather. There was nothing like a cloudburst to take the heat out of a potentially explosive situation but although it had been a lousy spring thus far, the clear blue sky suggested that this was going to be one of the very few evenings when umbrellas could be safely left at home. Much as Whittle wanted to get out of Dresden before things turned ugly, he had the safety and wellbeing of others to consider.

He turned left, made another left turn on Budapesterstrasse and circled back to the Hauptbahnhof. Pat Norman was using the Wartburg belonging to the administrative warrant officer; the second time around, he spotted the burly sergeant parked between two ubiquitous Trabants approximately a hundred yards up the road from the railway station. Whittle changed down, kept his eyes open for a vacant space at the kerbside and was lucky enough to find one almost directly opposite the main entrance.

Galina Kutuzova had arranged to meet him at seven o'clock outside the Hauptbahnhof. He was in the right place at the right time but he doubted if she would keep the rendezvous. Chances were that Galina had taken one look at the neo-Nazi rabble and had gone straight back to Potsdam. Whittle decided he would give her exactly five minutes leeway before doing the same.

But Starshii Leitenant Galina Kutuzova of the GRU had

not returned to base. Right on time, she emerged from the Hauptbahnhof and walked briskly towards the car, a tall, dark-haired girl with angular features and a figure that a lot of young women of her age would envy. If Galina ever left the Soviet Union for the West as she claimed she intended to do, Whittle thought a reputable model agency might well take her on, provided she managed to shed a few pounds. He leaned across the adjoining seat to open the door for her but she beat him to it and almost tumbled into the car.

"Let's get out of here," she said breathlessly. "These Hitlerite people make me nervous."

"I'm not exactly crazy about them either." Whittle fired the engine into life, then checked in the rear-view mirror to make sure the road behind him was clear before he pulled out from the kerb. "Fortunately, they are few in number," he added.

"Yeah? How would you know, Robert? You have been counting them?"

English was Galina's second language and she spoke it with a marked American accent as did most of the Russian Intelligence officers who had graduated from the Smolny Institute. She was also fluent in French, though he sometimes wondered what a Parisian would make of her dialect.

"Where are we going?" she asked.

"I thought we might take a run out to the castle at Pillnitz," Whittle told her.

"No, that's too far, we'll go to the park here in town."

Her voice was crisp and decisive leaving him in no doubt that it was an order, not a suggestion. All the same, he tried to dissuade her.

"I thought you wanted to give the stormtroopers a wide berth?"

"If you don't want to go to the Volkspark, you can always drop me off here."

Whittle stretched his mouth in what passed for a smile. "I was only thinking of you," he said.

Pat Norman was expecting him to drive out to Pillnitz but this wasn't the first time Galina had thrown a spanner in the works at the last moment. It wasn't the first time the sergeant had covered his back either and he was an experienced enough operator to cope with the change of plan.

3

Whittle turned into the Leninplatz again. There were more Nazi thugs in evidence now than there had been ten minutes ago and some of them were in paramilitary uniform. For the most part, the mob surged along the sidewalk, jostling passers-by, but one particularly determined group insisted on marching in the middle of the road regardless of the traffic. Whittle sounded the horn, then swerved, narrowly missing a standard-bearer carrying a blood-red banner emblazoned with a black swastika on a white roundel. A dozen angry faces turned on him, spitting abuse, clenched fists hammered the roof and someone booted the rear wing, smashing the nearside tail light.

"Do something," Galina said nervously.

"I'm trying to," Whittle told her.

After what seemed an eternity, the road ahead was suddenly clear; putting his foot down, he rapidly drew away from the mob. When he looked in the rear-view mirror, there was no sign of the Wartburg saloon that Sergeant Norman was driving.

"Who's following us, Robert?"

"No one."

"You sound disappointed."

"There's something wrong with your hearing then." Whittle continued on Leningraderstrasse as far as Pirnaischerplatz, then turned right and headed towards the Volkspark. "Were you aware that the Nazis were holding a rally in Dresden this evening?" he asked casually.

"Do you think I would have come here if I'd known that?"

"No, I guess it was a pretty stupid question. What puzzles me is why we hadn't heard a whisper either."

"Perhaps the Police President was hoping the organisers would call it off?"

"That could only be called wishful thinking." Whittle found a parking space in front of the exhibition hall by the botanical gardens and switched off the engine. "Does this place meet with your approval?" he asked.

"It'll do."

"Okay, so what have you got for me?"

"The question is, what have you got for me, Robert? I haven't been paid for the last lot of information yet."

Whittle sighed, reached inside his sports jacket for the envelope containing six hundred Deutschmarks in denominations of

4

twenties and handed it to Galina. "Better count it to make sure it's all there," he said.

"Haven't you forgotten something?"

"I'm afraid the British passport you asked for is stuck somewhere in the pipeline."

"That's what you told me the last time we met."

"Well, it happens to be true. What makes you think our Home Office is any more efficient than your Ministry of Internal Affairs? Civil servants are the same the world over, they all move at a snail's pace."

Whittle could lie with the best of them when he had to. The Foreign and Commonwealth Office were handling the passport application and he suspected they were deliberately dragging their feet. Perestroika and glasnost might be all the rage with the politicians but as far as the Intelligence community were concerned, Starshii Leitenant Galina Kutuzova of the GRU was a valuable source of information on the current state of morale in the Red Army. As such, they weren't anxious to lose her in a hurry. Give the Starshii Leitenant a British passport and you wouldn't see her for dust, which he had been told was the theory in London. Whittle had also been told that it was up to him to keep Galina sweet which meant buying her the odd present from time to time.

"I've got a little something for you," he said and reached for the small packet on the back seat.

The little something was three pairs of one-size tights made by Aristoc which the wife of one of his colleagues had purchased for him from the NAAFI shop in Berlin. Underwear, cigarettes, perfume, lipstick, make-up, eye shadow and casettes were equally acceptable and it never ceased to amaze him that such modest gifts could give her so much pleasure.

"I hope you like them."

"They're perfect." Galina stuffed the tights into her cheap, plastic handbag, then twisted round and kissed him, her mouth open, her tongue lightly flicking his lips before she drew back. "You couldn't have given me a nicer present," she breathed.

"Good, I'm glad I've made you happy." He smiled. "Now what have you got for me?"

"Let's go for a walk. I could use a breath of fresh air, it is stifling in here."

5

The temperature had scarcely touched seventy Fahrenheit all day and the car hadn't been standing out in the sun, but Whittle didn't argue with her. Galina was a valuable source and had to be humoured. That was something he had learned from his predecessor at BRIXMIS, the army's terminology for the British Military Mission in what had formerly been the Soviet Zone. Officially, BRIXMIS had ceased to exist shortly after the Wall had come down when, almost overnight, the Mission had become the Arms Control Unit, North West Europe. They were, however, still doing much the same job.

Alighting from the Trabant saloon, he waited for Galina to get out, then locked all four doors. There was still no sign of Sergeant Norman but there was nothing he could do about that.

"Which way do you want to go?" he asked.

Galina didn't say anything, merely linked arms and keeping parallel with the miniature railway, led him towards the zoo in the southwest corner of the park. A little while later, a fun train of six open cars hauled by a model steam locomotive passed them heading in the opposite direction.

"Colonel General Alexei Ivanovich Fedyanin, the commander of 6 Guards Tank Army is to be replaced by Vitali Ilyich Lobanov," she announced suddenly.

"When is this going to happen?"

"Monday the third of June, ten days from now."

"Do you have any idea why Fedyanin is being relieved?"

"It's said that the High Command is displeased with him because he has failed to maintain discipline."

Whittle thought it carried a ring of truth. There had been numerous instances of young conscripts selling their Kalashnikov assault rifles for Deutschmarks. And on the Kurfürstendamm, you could go to a shop specialising in military regalia and kit yourself out as an Efreitor, or senior soldier, in a motor rifle, artillery, tank or engineer battalion.

"And what's the unofficial reason?"

"Vitali Ilyich Lobanov is a former chief of the Spetsnaz; Moscow wants him in place to supervise the final withdrawal of all Soviet forces in East Germany."

The Spetsnaz was the equivalent of the Special Air Service with the difference that it was thirty thousand strong and dwarfed both the SAS and the US Army's Special Operational Force.

6

"Interesting," Whittle said, his voice neutral. "What happens to Colonel General Fedyanin?"

Galina hugged his arm and smiled up at him, aping the other courting couples in the park. "Oh, he's being retired, put out to grass as you people would say."

Fedyanin was a former paratrooper who had made a name for himself in Afghanistan, a theatre of operations which had proved a graveyard for so many reputations. Only fifty-three years old, he was a young man compared with the majority of Soviet generals. At Headquarters 1st British Corps, Fedyanin was widely regarded as a very innovative commander whose star was definitely in the ascendant. There was even a school of thought that saw him as a future Minister of Defence.

"We all reckoned he was going to the top," Whittle said thoughtfully.

"So did we, Robert, but it seems he's out of favour with the General Secretary of the Central Committee of the Communist Party."

"We're talking about Mikhail Gorbachev?"

"He's the only General Secretary we've got as far as I am aware."

"What set them at each other's throats?"

"Who knows?" Galina shrugged. "I'm only a junior officer in the GRU, the Colonel General doesn't take me into his confidence."

"But you are well connected and you hear things . . ."

"Perhaps."

"We would pay a great deal of money for hard evidence of a rift between Gorbachev and the Red Army."

"You would need to, life is becoming very difficult for me."

"Are you in trouble?" Whittle asked her quietly.

"My superiors are saying that ours is a very one-sided arrangement. They complain that the information you give me in return is of very little value."

Galina had a point. Much of the stuff he had given her was so low-grade that it didn't even merit the security classification of Restricted. "I'll have a word with the Head of Mission and see what we can do about that." Whittle reached inside his jacket and took out two sheets of A4 that had been folded in half and half again. "Meantime, this may be of interest to your superiors."

7

"What is it?"

"Some notes on the projected reduction of our army. The paper lists those cavalry and infantry regiments which will either be amalgamated or disbanded altogether. The proposals have caused a lot of bitterness and could have far-reaching political implications."

"I'll take your word for it." Galina looked back over her shoulder, then stopped and turned to face him. "Listen, I'll be in touch. Okay?"

"You're leaving?" Whittle said in amazement.

"Yes, this is where we go our separate ways. A colleague is waiting for me at the Freilichtheater."

They had reached the tip of the Carolasee beyond the zoo; the theatre was situated at the far end of the lake approximately six hundred yards away. That the Russians observed the same procedures didn't surprise him; what he did find odd was that Galina's minder should be way out in front instead of watching her back.

"Look after yourself, Robert," she said and planted one of her wet kisses on his mouth, then left him to walk along the lakeside.

Whittle was tempted to follow her at a distance but on second thoughts he decided against it and slowly made his way back to the car park. Now that he had a chance to examine the Trabant in detail, the damage to the bodywork was more extensive than he had supposed. It wasn't just a question of replacing a broken tail-light assembly; there was a dent in the wing the size of a football and someone had made a yard long scratch on the boot with a sharp instrument. The boilerman was going to be pretty unhappy when he saw what had happened to his pride and joy; the fact that the army would foot the repair bill was unlikely to give him much consolation.

Whittle unlocked the door, got in behind the wheel, started the engine and drove out of the parking lot.

For some unaccountable reason, he actually got as far as the Stübelalle before the tilt switch detonated the five pounds of Semtex that had been anchored to the chassis directly beneath his seat. The blast practically severed Whittle's right leg above the kneecap and amputated his left foot; metal fragments, bits of upholstery, horsehair and part of a spring penetrated deep into the spleen and lumbar region of his back. The windscreen blew out, the roof buckled and the boot sprang open; a few seconds later, fuel from the ruptured tank dripped on to the hot silencer and exploded.

Eyewitness reports led the pathologist who performed the autopsy to assume that Whittle was dead before the flames started to consume him. The cyclist whom he was overtaking when the bomb exploded succumbed to his injuries on the way to hospital.

The subsequent murder investigation by the Kriminalpolizei sucked in the Bundesnachrichtendienst Intelligence Service and was of considerable interest to the British Security Service Organisation in Bonn. Headquarters Berlin convened a Board of Inquiry which adjourned after finding that Captain Robert Steven Whittle of the Intelligence Corps had been on duty at the time of his death. The Board then reassembled six weeks later to consider the case report submitted by the Special Investigation Branch of the Royal Military Police whose information was largely derived from the Kripo. Both Rhine Army and the German authorities were unable to say which terrorist organisation had been responsible for the incident.

The Foreign and Commonwealth Office experienced no such difficulty and instructed Century House to ensure the investigating officers reached a conclusion that was in line with their own thinking. The man the Secret Intelligence Service selected for this delicate task was Peter Ashton, a thirty-three-year-old middle-ranking desk officer of proven reliability.

CHAPTER 2

THE MAJORITY of SIS entrants recruited at university came from Oxbridge; Ashton was different, he had read German and Russian at Nottingham and had been admitted to Century House by the back door. A member of the University Officer Training Corps, he joined 23 Special Air Service Regiment in the Territorial Army when he was taken on by British Aerospace as a technical author and translator after graduating from Nottingham with a good upper second. Bored to tears by the work he was doing, Ashton volunteered for a nine-month tour of duty with the regular army's Special Patrol Unit in Northern Ireland, a move that cost him his job.

Back in civilian life again, he found temporary employment teaching Russian to mature students at a night school funded by the London Borough of Camden. Fifteen men and women had enrolled for the course in the September; by the following March the numbers attending had dwindled to two. One month later, the Argentinians invaded and captured the Falkland Islands which spared him the embarrassment of being informed that his contract would not be renewed. Still a part-time soldier with 23 SAS he volunteered for active duty and travelled south with the task force. As a supernumerary officer with D Squadron of 22 SAS he took part in the raid on Pebble Island when eleven Pucura ground attack aircraft and a fuel dump had been destroyed. In the latter stages of the campaign, he and two signallers operated behind enemy lines directing counterbattery fire on to the artillery supporting the Argentinian positions on Mount Longdon. The exploit led to a Mention in Despatches to go with the one he had been awarded for undercover work on the streets of Belfast.

The Falklands War over, Ashton was attracted by the idea of a career in the regular army, but there was no permanent officer cadre in the SAS and if he joined an infantry or a cavalry regiment, contemporaries in his age group would have a minimum of five years seniority over him. The problem of what to do with the rest of his working life was solved for him by Headquarters Special Forces. A word in the right ear at Century House led to a covert approach by the SIS soon after he had returned from the South Atlantic. It became overt after the first informal interview and on the sixth of September 1982 he found himself on an induction course at the training school outside Petersfield.

Ashton spent the next two years as a junior desk officer in London while learning the ropes and followed this with a three-year stint at Government Communications Headquarters in Cheltenham. He was then posted to South West Africa charged with assessing the extent of Soviet military involvement in Angola, a task which he was signally well-equipped to handle. To date, he had never served in an embassy and his face was therefore not known to the KGB. It was this fact, as well as his previous military experience, which made him the front runner when Century House had been told to look into the Whittle affair.

He flew into Berlin-Tegel, a municipal airport that would have to grow a lot if the city was to become the capital of a united Germany. After a cursory check at passport control, Ashton collected his overnight bag from the carousel, opted for the Nothing to Declare channel at Customs and walked out into the arrivals hall. He looked for someone holding up a sign for Ashton and saw Headquarters Berlin had sent a young captain to meet him whose immaculate appearance in shirtsleeve order made him somewhat conspicuous.

"I'm Ashton," he told him.

"Catford, David Catford," the officer said and shook hands with him. "I've got a staff car and driver outside."

The staff car was a black Ford Cortina with a left-hand drive. It was not the kind of limousine that was sent to meet VIPs which at least was in harmony with the low profile Ashton wanted to keep. Catford was also the soul of discretion; all the way out to Headquarters Berlin at the Olympic Stadium he made small talk, treating him as though he was a civil servant from the finance branch of the Ministry of Defence. After the Wall had come down, a small army of officials had descended on Berlin to discuss the thinning out and ultimate withdrawal of the garrison; as far as the staff car driver was concerned, Ashton was just one more bowler hat from Whitehall. The only jarring note was Catford's choice of dress, but he had an explanation for that.

"Sorry about the uniform," he said breezily as they left the car park and walked towards the office block, "but there's no point wearing civilian clothes. The Soviets have a mugshot of every officer serving at Headquarters Berlin and they've got their snoopers at the airport. That's why we didn't want to treat you differently from any other visitor from London."

"Right."

"We've also arranged for you to stay in the officers' mess. That's the usual procedure."

"Well, don't let it worry you, the overnight bag is purely for emergencies." Ashton smiled. "With any luck, I can finish my business in time to catch the evening flight out."

"Colonel Earley and the principal witness are on hand," Catford informed him. "They're waiting in the office we have set aside for you."

Lieutenant Colonel Richard Earley had joined the Arms Control Unit when it had been known as BRIXMIS. As Chief of Staff in those days, he had been responsible for Intelligence-gathering operations; now he was simply the coordinator of liaison duties. The principal witness was Sergeant Patrick Norman who had been Whittle's backup when he had been murdered.

Earley was a very experienced forty-two-year-old infantryman. Before departing for Berlin, Ashton had obtained a copy of his record of service and had noted that he had actually completed a tour of duty with BRIXMIS when a captain. The Military Secretary's branch at Stanmore had also made his confidential report book available and while Earley had never commanded his regiment, it was apparent that he was regarded as an extremely competent operator by his superiors. The only derogatory remark was the assertion that he had a short fuse and did not suffer fools gladly.

Although Ashton was half an inch under six feet, Earley towered over him, his height accentuated by a lean frame. His almost hungry-looking appearance made Ashton feel he needed to go on a diet even though he was well-proportioned and had tipped the scales at a hundred and seventy pounds at the time of the annual checkup a month ago.

"How do you want to play this?" Earley asked him after they had shaken hands.

"Where's Sergeant Norman?"

"Waiting in the office next door."

"Well, suppose you and I talk things over first before I see him?"

"That's fine by me. What do you want to know?"

"This would have been your second tour with BRIXMIS, if they hadn't changed the name." Ashton smiled. "Tell me about the old days and what the unit did before its charter was revised."

"BRIXMIS was established in Potsdam soon after the war; the Russian equivalent, SOXMIS was, and still is, located at Bunde in our Zone, though it too now has a different name. I think the original idea was that each of the four powers – Britain, France, the United States and the USSR – should be able to satisfy themselves that the other side wasn't secretly rearming the Germans. Then after the Cold War really got started with the Berlin blockade in '48, we were tasked with monitoring the build-up of Soviet forces in East Germany. Of course, all this happened before I was even born so I can only speak with authority from the late sixties onward when I first came on the scene, which is when we really got down to the business of spying."

There had been nothing clandestine about the way they had operated. They had always been in uniform and had driven around in military vehicles when observing the 6th Guards Tank Army on manoeuvres. But they had been issued with sophisticated cameras and infrared to photograph the latest Soviet equipment.

"We would go after their FROG missiles and the T72 main battle tank which was just coming off the production line," Earley continued. "Naturally, they weren't too happy about this and sometimes they got pretty heated about it."

"How heated?"

"They would try to run you off the road with one of their armoured personnel carriers or give you a nasty sideswipe with something heavier, like a twenty-five-ton 152mm self-propelled gun. You could get hurt. In fact, a few years back, the Yanks had one of their observers shot dead by an overzealous infantryman."

"But that was before the Wall came down," Ashton said.

"Oh yes, it's all sweetness and light these days. 'Won't you come into my parlour and see all these lovely tanks we're sending back to Russia?' Hell, we're actually on first name terms with our GRU watchdogs in Potsdam."

"This was the cell Starshii Leitenant Galina Kutuzova belonged to?"

"Until she conveniently disappeared after Bob Whittle was killed," Earley said grimly.

"According to the Russians, she's gone AWOL – deserted."

"If you believe that, you'll believe anything."

Ashton leaned back in his chair and turned his head towards the window to look at the Olympic Stadium across the football and hockey fields from the Headquarters block. Earley had made it clear that he didn't trust the Russians and believed that anyone who didn't agree with him was a fool.

"What did you think of Whittle?" he asked.

"Young Bob would never have set the world on fire but he was a good average officer, the sort you can rely on."

"Didn't he recruit Galina Kutuzova?"

"No, that was down to a cavalryman called Simon Younger of the 3rd Carabineers. Whittle took her over when Simon went back to his regiment. Matter of fact, I wanted someone else to handle Galina but there was a lot of lobbying by the Intelligence Corps who thought their man should be her case officer." Earley smiled derisively. "It was the hoary old argument of the professional versus the gifted amateur."

The men with the Latin tag, "*Manui Dat Cognito Vires*", on their regimental cap badge had won the day; officers like Whittle were given a different cap badge before they joined the Arms Control Unit. The subterfuge included a generous allowance to buy the appropriate mess kit, service dress buttons and other items peculiar to their new identity. Whittle had disported himself as a captain in the Royal Corps of Transport.

"Did the Russians know he was in the Intelligence Corps?" Ashton asked.

"Of course they did. The Army List isn't a classified document and you don't have to be a cat burglar to lay your hands on a copy. They looked him up in a back number and got his whole life history from the day he left Sandhurst as a second lieutenant. My opposite number in the GRU thought it was one hell of a joke."

Ashton could understand his amusement. Such inanities were

more commonplace within the worldwide Intelligence community than outsiders might suppose. An obsession with secrecy did not always go hand in hand with common sense, and that applied to the KGB and the GRU as well as the British Intelligence Services.

"Did Galina's superiors know she was meeting Whittle surreptitiously?"

"Bob didn't think they were being followed, neither did his minder."

"But you wouldn't put money on it?" Ashton suggested.

"No."

"Do you mind telling me why?"

Earley took time out to light a cigarette. Ashton had noticed that pipe smokers did much the same thing when they were forced into a corner and needed a breathing space to collect their thoughts. They, of course, had more props to play with and it could take them for ever to fill a bowl with tobacco.

"We are used to doing things out in the open," Earley said finally. "The Russians knew what we were up to and did their best to stop us but we usually got past their roadblocks, took the pictures we wanted and then got out of the area. We don't have the resources for covert operations. The Treasury won't give us the money to buy a Trabant, never mind a Wartburg. Whenever Bob Whittle had to meet Galina in Dresden, Leipzig, Chemnitz or wherever, he was forced to borrow the car belonging to the German boilerman. Have you ever heard anything quite so ridiculous?"

"Nothing surprises me in this game."

"You want to hear another joke? Galina wanted cash on the nail for her information so we got approval to overspend our secret imprest account provided, said the financial watchdogs, that we got her to sign a petty cash receipt voucher for every payment." Earley stared at the glowing ember on his cigarette. "Gorbachev may be looking to the West with a begging bowl but the GRU aren't short of a bob or two and they've got a whole fleet of unmarked cars. I reckon they wouldn't have had too much trouble shadowing Whittle without him being aware of it."

"With Sergeant Norman watching his back?"

"I think you should make up your mind about that after you have spoken to him."

"Maybe I should," said Ashton. "Where did you say he was?"

"Next door. Mind if I sit in on your tête-à-tête?"

Ashton would have preferred to question the NCO head to head without anyone else being present but there was no point in putting Earley's nose out of joint if he hoped to make him see things the Foreign Office way. "Not a bit," he said, smiling.

"Good." Earley stubbed out his cigarette and stood up. "I'll give him a shout."

Sergeant Patrick Norman was a twenty-six-year-old combat engineer whose burly figure suggested he was quite capable of demolishing a house without the aid of explosives. For someone who appeared to be potentially lethal, the sergeant had, however, an extremely affable manner and a dry sense of humour.

"There's not a lot I can tell you about that particular evening in Dresden," he said. "I was quietly sitting there in the Wartburg minding my own business when this crowd of skinheads descended on the car and started to take it to bits. I got out to discuss the matter with them politely and the next thing I knew was when I woke up in hospital and there was this rather severe Fräulein in a starched uniform bending over me. I asked her where I was and she stuck a thermometer in my mouth."

Ashton had seen a copy of the report by the Special Investigation Branch of the RMP and had also read the statement Norman had made to the Kripo. For obvious security reasons, the sergeant had said nothing about Whittle and had given the German police a cock and bull story when they'd asked him what he was doing in Dresden. The SIB report was informative if only because he had been able to be more frank with them but even so, the investigation raised more questions than it answered.

"When exactly were you attacked?" he asked.

"About five minutes after Captain Whittle arrived at the Hauptbahnhof and parked a hundred yards or so down the street from me."

"Were you told there was going to be a National Socialist rally in Dresden that evening?"

"Of course he wasn't," Earley said impatiently. "I didn't know there was going to be one myself until after the event."

"Was that a deliberate oversight by the German authorities?"

Earley hesitated. "No, I think it was a cock-up. The Police

President of Dresden got it wrong; the rally was organised by the local branch and he evidently thought the numbers attending would be under a hundred, so the military authorities were not advised."

Ashton believed he knew why the older man had hesitated before answering his question. Once the possibility of a cock-up had been accepted, the conspiracy theory, which was Earley's hobbyhorse, ceased to hold up.

"Who else was attacked besides you?" he asked, turning to Norman again.

"No one. These six thugs suddenly appeared from nowhere and descended on the car. I had my eyes on another bunch farther down the road and they must have come up behind me."

"And they waded into you as soon as you got out of the car?"

"That's about the size of it," Norman agreed.

"No words were exchanged?"

"Well, one of them called me an English pig and I was about to return the compliment when he head-butted me in the face and the lights went out."

"You were sitting in a German car with German registration plates – how did he know you were English?"

"Search me."

"Did you swear at him?"

"I never got the chance."

"What about your hair?" Ashton persisted. "Was it cut short back and sides?"

"No, collar length, same as it is now."

The Foreign Office wanted to believe that the skinheads had singled Norman out because his hairstyle had given him away, but that theory too was beginning to look decidedly shaky. It wasn't helped by the medical report attached to the SIB proceedings either. The head-butt had opened a gash above the sergeant's right eye that had needed eight stitches and he'd also had a couple of ribs cracked, but all things considered, he had got off pretty lightly. If they had wanted to, his assailants could have kicked him to death as he lay there unconscious in the road. As it was, they had gone to town on the Wartburg instead, slashing all four tyres and ripping the leads from the distributor cap to immobilise the vehicle completely.

"How long were you paired off with Captain Whittle?"

The sudden change of direction caught Norman off guard and he instinctively looked to Earley as if hoping for guidance before he answered the question.

"Not quite three months. I used to work with Captain Younger until he left us on the twenty-eighth of February."

"So you've been on every rendezvous with Galina Kutuzova since the day she was recruited?"

"Yes."

"And how many times would that be?"

"I've lost count. Twenty-five? Thirty? We've been nursing her for over a year now."

"Did you always use the same car?"

"I didn't have any choice."

"Were you ever conscious of being followed?"

"No."

"Would you have known if someone had been on your tail?"

A slight narrowing of the eyes betrayed Norman's anger. "I like to think so," he grated.

"I was hoping you would say that."

"What . . .?"

Ashton smiled at him. "Thank you, Sergeant, you've been very helpful."

"I have?"

"You'd better believe it."

It was a few moments before Norman realised the interview was over. When the penny did drop, the frown lifted and the affable smile returned.

"I like him," Ashton said after the sergeant had left them. "Seems a good man."

"He is."

"Yes, well, he certainly makes it clear that there was no Soviet involvement in Whittle's murder."

"I don't believe what I'm hearing," Earley said incredulously.

"Semtex, tilt switch; it has all the hallmarks of the Provos."

"Are you saying they've got an active service unit in the Dresden area?"

"Is that so impossible?"

"Cross-border raids are what they go for in Europe and a safe haven in Holland is a long way from here. Something else you should bear in mind; a young woman answering to Galina's description was seen in the park with Bob Whittle shortly before he was killed. She lured him away from the car so that her friends could put a bomb under it."

"Is that your theory?"

"That's the way it looks to me."

"Then tell me why the Russians picked on Whittle and not Younger?"

"I can't even begin to guess," Earley admitted reluctantly.

"There you are then. The Whittle murder only begins to make sense if you accept the fact that the attack on Sergeant Norman was an unrelated incident. Okay, the Russians panicked and recalled Galina Kutuzova because they thought we would assume the GRU had done it. There would be no grounds for this supposition if it appeared she had failed to show up at the rendezvous. When they realised you knew she had met Whittle in Dresden, they hastily changed their cover story and announced she had gone absent without leave."

There was a long silence. As though compelled to do something, Earley took out a packet of John Player and lit another cigarette.

"So, Galina Kutuzova is back home in Leningrad with her divorced mother, Lydia, and the Provisional IRA is in the frame. Is that the proposition London would have us swallow, Mr Ashton?"

The Provos were favourites. If this theory met with resistance, London had authorised him to suggest that Whittle had been targeted by an Iraqi hit squad bent on extracting revenge for the catastrophic defeat in the Gulf. Ashton found both possibilities unconvincing and wasn't prepared to argue them with a hardened cynic like Earley.

"I've got an open mind," he said. "It's early days yet and there are other people I want to see."

"You'll be going to Detmold then?"

"What?"

"It's where the 3rd Carabineers are stationed. I assume you want to have a word with Simon Younger?"

The fourth-floor apartment on Leningrad's Nevsky Prospekt was close to the Griboyedov Canal and lay within reasonable walking distance of the General Staff Headquarters, the Hermitage, Winter Palace and the Admiralty on the south bank of the Neva. It was rented by Lydia Petrovskaya, divorced wife of air-force Colonel Sergei Vasilevich Kutuzov now residing in Star City, home of the Soviet cosmonaut community. Both of Lydia's parents were dead and few people of her marital status would have been allowed to retain a two-bedroom apartment for her sole use. But her father, Nikolai Yakulevich Petrovsky, had been head of the KGB's Fifth Chief Directorate and there were still a number of the general's influential friends alive who had not forgotten his daughter.

There were, however, some things influential friends could not have prevented even if they had been aware of what was about to happen. On Monday the twenty-seventh of May, some sixty hours after Whittle had been murdered, Lydia Petrovskaya had been placed under surveillance and her phone tapped. In the following six weeks, the listeners in the basement of the apartment house across the street monitored a total of twenty-seven innocuous phone calls, all of which originated within the Leningrad area.

The twenty-eighth was made on the ninth of July by a woman calling herself Vera Belinkova who claimed to have been a friend of Galina's at university and wanted to know her present whereabouts. The conversation lasted approximately five minutes; playing the recording back, the eavesdroppers thought that although Lydia Petrovskaya sounded guarded throughout, they could also detect a note of suppressed excitement in her voice. Even before the tape was sent for detailed analysis, they were fairly certain in their own minds that the incoming call had been patched through by satellite.

There had indeed been a Vera Belinkova among Galina's classmates at university; subsequently, she had been sent on a one-year post-graduation course in London where she had promptly defected.

CHAPTER 3

THE CHALLENGER Mark I rumbled past B Squadron office, its 1200 brake horsepower engine emitting a deep-throated snarl. A few yards farther on, there was a loud screeching noise from the tracks as the driver made a sharp left turn into the tank park. He then stopped, shifted into reverse and manoeuvred the 60-ton armoured fighting vehicle into its allotted place in the shed. Ashton waited for the driver to switch off the engine before he attempted to resume his conversation with Simon Younger.

"Are there any more to come?" he asked when peace of a kind had returned once more.

"No, that's the last of the squadron," Younger told him. "We shouldn't have any more interruptions."

Ashton hoped he was right. Fifteen Challengers had clanked by the office at two-minute intervals and so far, all he had managed to do was introduce himself and explain why he had come to the 3rd Carabineers barracks in Detmold.

"It's important I know exactly how you contrived to recruit Galina Kutuzova," Ashton said, resuming from where he had left off. "And I want to stress that whatever you do tell me will be in the strictest confidence. It won't go any further, you have my word on that, Simon."

"Why should I need it, Mr Ashton?"

Younger was neither so ignorant nor so naïve that he didn't know what Ashton was getting at but he spelt it out for him anyway.

"I think you had to get very close to Galina in order to hook her." Ashton paused, then said, "I also think you won't be completely frank with me if you suspect there is a chance that you might lose your positive vetting status because of some minor peccadillo."

"I get the picture," Younger told him calmly.

"I'm glad you do, Simon. I always make a point of being straight with people."

"Well, to be honest, it was Galina who initially made the running, though I can't think why."

Ashton could and he didn't have to try very hard. Simon Younger was the sort of good-looking, well-bred, well-heeled young man a lot of girls of her age would find irresistible. Even on a short acquaintance, it was apparent he had all the self-confidence in the world and a casual, laid-back attitude to life which, if contrived, certainly gave the impression of being natural.

"Let's not get introspective, Simon. Just tell me when, where and how you clicked."

"It happened one afternoon in April last year. I had gone across to the GRU compound in Potsdam to seek permission to observe some low-level battle group exercise Major General Ustenko, Commanding General of the 36th Mechanised Division, had set for his units, only to find that the liaison officer I usually dealt with was as pissed as a newt. So was the second-in-command of the GRU section who, according to Galina, had been helping her to celebrate her twenty-fifth birthday. They had all been drinking Russian champagne, but I gathered the other two had been pepping up their drinks with Armenian brandy. Anyway, Galina was the only one who was still reasonably sober and in a party mood. She insisted I had a glass of champagne and one thing led to another. You know how it is."

"Refresh my memory," Ashton said, poker-faced.

"Well, the office furniture had been moved back against the wall to leave a space and she put a cassette into an old-fashioned transistor and we started dancing. It was mostly sentimental stuff from way back in the seventies and pretty soon we were cheek to cheek."

"You didn't waste much time."

"Depends on how you look at it. We weren't complete strangers; I'd got into the habit of passing the time of day with her soon after she joined the GRU cell in September '89."

"You were attracted to her?"

"Wouldn't you be?" Younger pointed a thumb over his shoulder at the notice board behind the desk. "That's her over there."

Galina's photograph appeared amongst a montage of Soviet

22

armoured vehicles under the heading of "Know Your Enemy" which seemed a little passé to Ashton. The camera had captured Galina in profile at some official reception while she was talking to a senior East German officer who appeared to be hanging on her every word. Even without the jacket, the summer uniform was not exactly the height of fashion, but she had done something about that. The khaki shirt had been tailored to fit her figure and the dark blue skirt had been shortened until it barely covered her knees. Contrary to dress regulations, she was wearing low-heeled pumps instead of black, lace-up shoes.

"I can see what you mean, Simon," he said.

"Don't get the wrong idea, Mr Ashton. Until the birthday party, I'd only admired her from a distance. The Cold War might be over but the army wouldn't look kindly on any involvement with a Russian Intelligence officer and I wasn't anxious to lose my security clearance. Besides, she was supposed to be engaged to a guy called Eduard Tulbukin who was said to be going places in the Communist Party."

"So what are you saying? That the champagne broke the ice?"

"It definitely helped; Galina was pretty happy and she was certainly in a talkative mood. She really let her hair down; there wasn't anything bad enough she could say about the Communist Party and what a mess the country was in. She went on and on about how much better things were in the West."

"And all this came out while you were dancing cheek to cheek, did it, Simon?"

"The tape didn't last for ever. Matter of fact, I wish it had, I never met a girl who could ask so many personal questions. How much did the army pay me? What did my father do for a living? How much did he earn? How big was his house? Did my mother have to work? How long did we have to wait if we wanted to buy a refrigerator? How much did it cost? She was insatiably curious and had a passionate interest in consumer goods of every description. I remember thinking that even the smallest department store in the smallest town would be a veritable Aladdin's Cave to Galina. Then it occurred to me that she was a prime candidate for subversion . . ."

Younger had reported the incident the following morning and had recommended that he should be allowed to cultivate Galina

Kutuzova. The Head of Mission had been broadly in favour of the idea; Earley had been decidedly unenthusiastic. Having met him, Ashton thought his opposition was probably based on a suspicion that Younger's proposal was just a dodge to legalise an illicit love affair with the Russian girl.

"Fortunately, Colonel Dick eventually saw the light and I was given the go-ahead."

Ashton suppressed a smile. "Colonel Dick" was Richard Earley, and since the Head of Mission was a brigadier, it was hardly surprising that he had allowed himself to be converted.

"So how did Galina manage to persuade her superiors that fraternisation with the former enemy might be a good idea?" he asked.

"I furnished her with some very convincing arguments. You know the kind of thing – times have changed, the world has moved on, trust between East and West could only be fostered through closer liaison. Openness was a word I recall using a lot. As proof of good intent, I got permission to give her some classified information on future troop movements which seemed to do the trick. After the initial input, it wasn't long before we were getting even better stuff from Galina. At least, that's what the Defence Intelligence Staff at the Ministry of Defence told us."

"And when did she start charging you for it?"

"It must have been around the beginning of November last year," Younger said after thinking about it for a moment. "The payments were modest enough; I think the most I ever gave her was the equivalent of fifty quid. There were gifts of course – cosmetics, nylons, underwear . . ."

"She was getting two hundred off Whittle," Ashton said, interrupting him.

"How often?"

"Every time they met."

"Christ, what was she giving him – the keys to the Kremlin?"

"It would seem so," Ashton said and made a mental note to call on the Defence Intelligence Staff when he returned, to see for himself what they had received.

"The thing that puzzles me," Younger said, "is what Bob Whittle was doing in Dresden the night he was killed."

"Galina had arranged to meet him there."

"Really? We always used to meet in West Berlin."

"Whose idea was that?"

"Galina's. There was no nightlife in Potsdam and she was looking for a good time. Of course, we travelled separately to Berlin for the sake of appearances."

Ashton raised an eyebrow. "What else did you do for the sake of appearances?" he asked quietly.

"We used different RVs – the Europa Centre, the Komödie Theatre on the Kurfürstendamm, the Café Keeve. Galina never picked a rendezvous in East Berlin; that would have been too dull for her tastes."

"How often did you meet her, Simon?"

"About once a month, starting in May '90 until I passed her on to Bob Whittle at the beginning of February when I was due to leave the Arms Control Unit."

Ashton gazed at the photograph of Galina Kutuzova on the notice board. Although Sergeant Norman had told him that he had lost count of the exact number of times she had met her British counterparts, the NCO had thought it was somewhere between twenty-five and thirty. That meant Whittle had been seeing Galina at least three times a month and had paid her something like three to four thousand pounds. On the other hand, it was unlikely that she had received more than five hundred from Younger.

"Matter of fact, that last meeting we had was the one occasion we passed up Berlin in favour of Oranienburg." Younger smiled. "It was all a bit cloak and dagger and I had to borrow a vehicle with East German plates from the Mission House warrant officer."

"What about Sergeant Norman?"

"You mean my chaperone? Well, he was lurking in the background as usual. Colonel Dick wished him on me and I never managed to get rid of him. I think his mission in life was to make sure I didn't jump into bed with Galina."

"The GRU were probably watching her too," Ashton observed.

"I'd bet a month's pay on it. Galina had told them I was ripe for the old honey trap and they would want to satisfy themselves that she had scored."

The half-smile which had rarely left his mouth was fast becoming an irritant. Younger wanted him to believe that although he might have sailed close to the wind, he had managed to avoid compromising himself which was, Ashton felt, an insult to his intelligence.

"I know it's a tired old gimmick," Younger continued, "but the GRU are reluctant to abandon it. Times may have changed but their thinking hasn't."

"So how did you get round the problem?"

"We went through the motions," Younger told him coyly.

"Are you saying that you took her to your flat in Gartenstrasse?"

"How do you know where I lived?"

"Colonel Earley and I had a long talk about you before I left for Detmold this morning."

Potsdam was only a dozen miles from West Berlin. Unlike their Soviet opposite numbers at Bunde, personnel from the Arms Control Unit were able to commute to and from the office. After normal working hours, only the administrative staff, the duty officer and duty NCO stayed on at the Mission House, the rest went home to their quarters in Spandau. Most single men were accommodated in the officers' and sergeants' messes of Headquarters Berlin, but Younger was one of two bachelor officers who had been allowed to live out.

"We had to use a bit of psychology," Younger said eventually. "My flat was literally just round the corner from the barracks, so the Russians knew I wouldn't risk taking Galina there. They also reckoned I would be a bit leery if she suggested going to a certain hotel, so we did what most courting couples do on a spring evening and took a run out to the Grünewald in my car. It didn't take the GRU long to realise that if they were going to catch me in a delicate situation, they would have to settle for a long-range, infra-red shot under the stars."

Ashton couldn't believe what he was hearing. What Simon Younger had done was plain stupid and it was inconceivable that he had sought prior approval from his superiors. Nonetheless, he said, "Did you clear this with Colonel Earley?"

"Sort of."

It was the kind of evasive answer he was coming to expect from the young cavalry officer whenever he found himself in a tight corner, "What's that supposed to mean, Simon?"

"We discussed the sort of collateral Galina's case officer might be looking for before he felt confident enough to let her off the leash and what our response should be. After I'd said

26

my piece, I assumed I'd been given the green light to go ahead."

Ashton made no comment. At best, Younger was stretching the truth, at worst, he was lying in his teeth. Whatever his faults, Earley had both feet planted firmly on the ground and would never have agreed to such a harebrained scheme.

"Where was Sergeant Norman when you and Galina were canoodling in the woods?"

"I wouldn't call it canoodling exactly," Younger said, avoiding his gaze. "And I didn't give him the slip either, if that's what you're thinking. He knew where to find us."

"Actually, I was wondering if anyone had approached you since you've been here in Detmold?"

"Approached me?" Younger frowned. "We're talking about blackmail, are we?"

"We certainly are."

"No one's tried to twist my arm."

Ashton was inclined to believe him. It was doubtful if the 3rd Carabineers had a single Top Secret document or little else in the way of secret material. As the second-in-command of B Squadron, Younger was unlikely to have access to anything graded much higher than Confidential. The GRU would know this; if they did have their hooks into him, they would bide their time until he was in a sensitive staff appointment.

The Whittle case was something else. The whole pattern had changed after he had come on the scene. Rendezvous in West Berlin were out, provincial cities in the former German Democratic Republic were in. The financial inducements had soared and the contacts with Galina had become clandestine and secretive. The Russian girl might have scored with Younger; it would be stretching the imagination to breaking point to assume she had been equally successful with his successor. So many things didn't add up, it was difficult to find a common thread, and he had probably got all he was going to get from Younger except for one minor point of detail.

"That afternoon when Galina was celebrating her birthday," Ashton said. "Can you recall the names of the other two Russians who were present when you walked into the office?"

Younger nodded. "There was Alexei Leven, the second-in-command of the unit, and Yuri Rostovsky, the liaison officer I used to deal with."

"Good. I think that about covers everything."

"You'll stay to lunch of course?"

Ashton glanced at his wristwatch. He had caught the early morning flight to Hannover, rented a Volkswagen at the airport and driven the fifty odd miles to Detmold, arriving there shortly after 1100 hours. If he skipped lunch, he could make it to Düsseldorf in time to catch the late afternoon flight to Heathrow. With any luck, he would then get to Century House before the girls on the Armed Services Liaison Desk left the office.

"That's very kind of you, Simon," he said, "but there are things I have to do in London."

Younger said he quite understood, a complacent smile on his face; Ashton wondered if he would have been so completely unruffled had he known he intended to run a security check on him.

A former colonel in the United States Air Force, Lloyd D Osmonde was fifty-six, measured exactly six feet and tipped the scales at two hundred and twenty-five pounds, which meant he was at least two stone overweight, something his wife was for ever pointing out to him. Until 1969 when he had transferred to a desk job and said goodbye to a once athletic figure, he had had a fairly conventional military career, flying a total of two hundred and twenty-eight combat missions during two separate tours of duty in Vietnam. His way of life had changed for ever after the Republic F105 Thunderchief he was piloting had fallen victim to a battery of 37mm anti-aircraft guns while on a low-level bombing run to Hanoi. Osmonde had managed to eject but had damaged his spine in the process. The injury had then been aggravated when a crewman of a Jolly Green Giant helicopter had plucked him to safety as a North Vietnamese foot patrol closed in on his position.

Discharged from hospital six months later, Osmonde had been medically downgraded and declared unfit for further flying duties. The air force however could ill afford to lose the services of such a highly qualified and experienced officer. A number of fitness reports had commented on his suitability for employment as an air attaché; that, plus an aptitude for languages had led to a

28

series of diplomatic appointments and a gradual sideways move towards Intelligence. At the thirty-year point, he had retired from active duty and had been immediately taken on again in a civilian capacity by the Defense Intelligence Agency. For the last five years he had been stationed in Berlin.

An unashamed Anglophile, the youngest of his three daughters was married to an officer in the Royal Regiment of Fusiliers, currently part of the British garrison. The middle daughter lived in Houston with her architect husband, while the eldest was a realtor in Monterey where she was nicely placed to keep an occasional eye on the property he'd recently acquired in Carmel-by-the-sea. Next June he planned to retire for good, move to California and play some golf. This evening, however, he was sitting at a table on the sidewalk outside Da Gianni's on the Fasanenplatz waiting for his Ivan to show.

Privately, Osmonde thought he was getting too long in the tooth to be playing footsie with a captain in the GRU, but right from the first phone call five weeks ago, the Ivan had made it clear that he wasn't prepared to deal with anyone else. A voice on the line, a face he hadn't seen; two years ago, it would have taken more than a name he vaguely recognised and a couple of appetising samples to bring him to this RV even though he had chosen it himself. But, as everyone kept telling him, times had changed. Trouble was, these days you didn't know who the enemy was. However, this was West Berlin and nothing untoward ever happened in this particular neighbourhood. The Kurfürstendamm was only a little over five hundred yards up the road and the Fasanenstrasse which ran through the quiet square was undoubtedly the most fashionable address in the city. You only had to see the Ferraris parked near Annabelle's nightclub to know that.

Naturally, he felt a bit edgy, but who wouldn't in his position? The Ivan was going to make him famous. In twenty-two years as a military attaché and civilian employee of the Defense Intelligence Agency, all he had garnered were a few grains of wheat amongst a load of chaff. Now he was about to be given the whole damned granary, always provided the Ivan showed up.

Osmonde stole another glance at his wristwatch and really started worrying. The son of a bitch was already eighteen minutes late, the Italian restaurant was rapidly filling up and the waiters were casting predatory eyes on the empty spaces that were going begging at his table. There was no telling how much longer he would be left in splendid isolation and the Ivan had said time and again that there would be no meeting of minds if others were present. To forestall the waiters, he picked up the menu and studied it intently.

"Hello, Lloyd."

Osmonde looked up, recognised the face from the photograph he had been shown by the Brits and smiled. "Hi, Yuri," he said, "take a seat."

"Thanks." Yuri Rostovsky pulled out a chair from the table and sat down. "I am sorry to be late."

"That's okay. What kept you?"

"Signal failure on the U-Bahn."

"Yeah?" Osmonde passed the menu to him. "I'm having minestrone soup and then some ravioli. What do you want?"

The pistol shots sounded like firecrackers. A bullet punched into Osmonde's left shoulder, knocked him out of his chair and dumped him on the sidewalk. He could hear people screaming, tables overturning and the deep-throated snarl of a powerful motorbike. His whole arm felt as if it were on fire and there was this unpleasant sensation of weightlessness as though he was floating in space. Someone was telling him to hang on and he opened his eyes again to find himself looking up at Tony Zale. He wondered muzzily what the hell his assistant was doing there, then recalled that Zale had insisted on waiting for him and had been parked round the corner in Ludwigkirchstrasse.

"You're going to be okay, Lloyd."

It hurt him to talk but the question had to be asked. "How's Yuri?"

"An ambulance is on the way."

"Yuri . . .?"

"Should be here any minute."

"What about Yuri Rostovsky?"

"He's dead," Zale told him in a flat voice.

CHAPTER 4

FEW COMMUTERS travelling into and out of Waterloo had heard of Century House. Of those who had, the vast majority did not associate it with the concrete and glass structure on nearby Westminster Bridge Road. To them, it was simply another office block, despite the opaque windows on the top three floors and the television cameras, satellite dish aerials and radio antennae on the roof. The Director General, his deputy and the Directors of the Eastern Bloc, African, Asian, Pacific Basin, Middle East and Rest of the World Departments occupied the top floor. Of the Eastern Bloc countries, the Intelligence cells targeting the USSR, Poland, the former German Democratic Republic and Czechoslovakia were situated on the floor below. Ashton was the number two man on the Russian Desk and until a few months ago, had occupied the office next door but one to Victor Hazelwood, the Assistant Director of the department. That this was no longer the case was due to the fact that Hazelwood had been moved upstairs following the death of the Director.

Hazelwood had not yet had his new appointment confirmed for the simple reason that the whole organisation of his department was in a state of flux. Following the reunification of Germany, the GDR was already an anachronism and now that the Warsaw Pact had been formally wound up, Poland and Czechoslovakia scarcely posed a threat to the West. There was talk that the Hungarian, Romanian and Bulgarian cells should be amalgamated with a view to surrendering the overspill accommodation on the last of the high security floors to other departments. Cynics maintained that the previous Director's fatal coronary had been caused by the realisation that his once all-powerful empire was now a dinosaur facing imminent extinction.

No such doubts afflicted Victor Hazelwood who was much too

busy running his department while at the same time helping to formulate policy on the top floor. Almost continually in orbit, he left it to other people to worry about what the future might hold. Any other senior officer in his position would have vigorously pruned his extraneous commitments, but not Hazelwood. Yesterday evening, some ten minutes before Ashton arrived in a taxi from Heathrow, he had left for Petersfield to deliver a long-standing lecture to the training school. Today, however, it was a different story; having looked in the diary and seen the number of visitors Hazelwood was expecting, Ashton had made sure he was on hand to catch him the moment he walked into the office.

"You weren't long in Germany," Hazelwood said, waving him to a chair. "Hope you didn't run into any problems?"

"No, I kept a low profile and avoided Head of Station, Berlin."

It was a matter of office politics. Neil Franklin, the Head of Station, Berlin regarded East Germany as very much his territory and didn't take kindly to any trespassers. London had decided to bypass their man in Berlin because he had an uncanny knack of rubbing the military authorities up the wrong way and was the last person to put the Foreign Office view of the Whittle case to the army.

"Would you say you had a successful trip?" Hazelwood asked.

"Not really. No one I spoke to is willing to buy the IRA angle."

"It doesn't surprise me. I told the Foreign Office the army would never swallow it. They should have plumped for revenge attacks by Saddam Hussein."

"I don't think there are too many Iraqis in East Germany," Ashton said.

"But there are plenty of Turkish migrant workers and there must be some Islamic fundamentalists amongst them who identify with Saddam."

"Well, if there are, it's too late in the day to sell that one, Victor. I decided we had already discredited ourselves when we attempted to put the IRA in the frame, so I didn't push it. Besides, there are a number of factors completely at odds with that theory."

"Such as?"

"Like Galina Kutuzova's involvement and her subsequent disappearance. We don't have a shred of evidence to link her with the Iraqis."

But there was a lot of information concerning her wheeling and dealing that needed looking at with a very hard eye. In a few brief sentences, Ashton outlined what he'd learned from personnel of the Arms Control Unit whom he had interviewed and why he thought Younger could become a problem.

"What are you going to do about him?" Hazelwood asked.

"I've asked our people on the Liaison Desk to obtain his security file from the army – also Whittle's."

"Oh? Why are you interested in seeing his dossier?"

"Because he was paying the Russian girl four times as much as Younger did, and I want to be sure there is no kind of character defect on record which might lead us to think he could have been buying something other than information from her."

Hazelwood opened the ornately carved wooden box on his desk which he had bought on a trip to India, took out a Burma cheroot and inspected it closely. After sniffing it appreciatively, he then trimmed the end with a penknife. "Did you discuss your misgivings with the brigadier commanding the Arms Control Unit?" he asked.

Ashton shook his head. "No, they only arose after I'd interviewed Younger in Detmold. Of course, I could have gone to the nearest terminal and contacted him over the secure speech net but I thought it best to see the Defence Intelligence Staff first. I'd like to know if they reckon they were getting value for money."

"So would I." Hazelwood struck a match and lit the cheroot. "You'll keep me informed?"

"Then there's Galina Kutuzova," Ashton said, ignoring the hint to leave. "Her mother, Lydia, lives in Leningrad and is a curator at the Hermitage. Seems she divorced her husband about five years ago, shortly after the air force posted him to Star City which is where the cosmonauts are domiciled."

"Well?"

"It's pretty thin stuff, Victor. I'd like to see what other biographical details the Ministry of Defence have on Galina apart from her alleged engagement to some Communist Party official named Eduard Tulbukin. The Russians say she has gone AWOL and claim they have listed her as a deserter. I just can't help wondering if she ever mentioned anything about her fiancé to Whittle. I mean, if their relationship had cooled, it's possible she really has gone over the hill."

"And is hiding where?"

"Your guess is as good as mine." Ashton shrugged. "Some place in West Germany? The border is wide open these days. Could be she's gone even farther afield. The morning I left Berlin for Detmold, the brigadier in charge of the Arms Control Unit happened to mention that Galina was for ever pestering Whittle to get her a British passport. He said the request had been passed to the British Embassy in Bonn and thought the Foreign and Commonwealth Office were sitting on it."

"That wouldn't surprise me."

The acid tone was familiar to Ashton; Hazelwood was not one of the FCO's most ardent fans, an antipathy which was said to have originated at Oxford when his application to join the Diplomatic had been spurned. There had been nothing wrong with his academic record but even in those far-off days, he had been large and untidy. It was also entirely possible that the selection board had been far-sighted enough to recognise that Hazelwood was the sort of man who was likely to act first and ask for permission later. Such independence was admirable before the advent of cable and wireless when policy was made by Her Majesty's representative on the spot; it was regarded as a positive liability in the twentieth century when every decision was taken in London. Ashton got on well with him because in many ways they were two of a kind.

"Of course, knowing what the FCO did or did not do about the passport is largely irrelevant, isn't it, Peter?"

"It certainly won't help us find Galina," Ashton said.

"Do we want to?"

"Depends whether we are concerned to know who killed Whittle and why. We don't have to do anything. His death was a seven-day wonder and he is never going to become a cause célèbre. The holiday season has started and the interest isn't there for the murder to make headlines again."

"You've just talked yourself into a job," Hazelwood growled. "Go and find Galina for me."

34

"Right," said Ashton. The crisp directive didn't change anything, no fresh avenues were opened up and the Ministry of Defence was still the only place to start looking.

Tony Zale had been thirteen years old when the war in Vietnam had ended. Although he had been with the Defense Intelligence Agency since graduating from Cornell in 1985, he had never heard a shot fired in anger nor seen the damage that could be inflicted by a 9mm bullet when it struck flesh and bone. Yesterday evening his education had started when he'd found his boss lying on the sidewalk next to a man who'd had most of his head shot off and was leaking his brains on to the paving stones. He had thought Lloyd Osmonde had had it; his face had been deathly white, his hands were clammy to the touch, the whole of his left side had been soaked with blood and his heart had been palpitating. Nineteen hours later, Zale thought he still looked in bad shape.

The first ambulance on the scene had whisked Osmonde off to the Franziskan Clinic in Wichmannstrasse just off the Budapester and getting him transferred to the US Army's General Hospital had involved an undignified row with the German hospital staff. The duty surgeon had said he wouldn't be responsible for what happened to Herr Osmonde if he was moved and they had almost come to blows over it. But the Defense Intelligence Agency had standing operational procedures to cover such an emergency and it was clearly laid down that a wounded agent should be transferred to an American hospital as soon as possible and he had stuck to his guns. While they had waited for the US Army to send an ambulance, the hospital staff had given Osmonde urgent artificial resuscitation and had patched him up enough to withstand the short journey across town. Zale had then signed a certificate absolving them from all blame in the event that the patient died and the registrar had then reluctantly handed Osmonde over to his tender care. It was only after Osmonde had been wheeled into the operating theatre that Zale had got round to informing the next of kin.

Last night, Elaine Osmonde had been too shocked by what had happened to question him too closely; this afternoon, Lloyd was out of danger, she was calmer and her youngest daughter, Karen, was there with her British husband. Once they put their heads together, it wouldn't take them long to work out that he hadn't got in touch with anyone in the family until at least three hours after the shooting.

Zale could see them now conferring in the corridor outside the private room where Osmonde was recovering. They probably resented the fact that they had had to take second place to a comparative stranger, but it wasn't his fault. It was Osmonde who had asked to see him and had badgered the ward sister and house physician until they had finally agreed to phone the office. Trouble was, Osmonde kept falling asleep and he had yet to discover what was bothering him.

"Are you still there, Tony?"

Zale drew his chair closer to the bed in order to catch what Osmonde said. "Sure I am."

"Did you get it?"

"Get what?"

"The pack of cigarettes . . ."

"I don't think you should be smoking, Lloyd."

"Russian cigarettes," Osmonde said breathlessly. "Yuri was bringing me a special."

"Special?" Zale repeated blankly, then snapped his fingers as the penny dropped. "Meaning there was something else in the pack besides cigarettes – like microfilm?"

Osmonde smiled weakly. "Damn right," he whispered.

"No problem, I'll get them."

It had to be the most optimistic assurance Zale had ever given and he hadn't the faintest idea how he was going to fulfil his promise. Rostovsky's personal effects would now be in the hands of the Berlin Kriminalpolizei and it was going to take someone with a lot of clout to make them hand anything over, especially if they had already discovered the microfilm. He just wished Osmonde had seen fit to tell him what he'd had going with Rostovsky instead of being so damned secretive about it.

Ashton returned to Century House a few minutes after three o'clock that afternoon to find that the security files he had asked for had arrived by special delivery service from the army's vetting unit and were waiting for him on his desk. Whittle's dossier was the fatter of the two, which came as no surprise. All Intelligence Corps officers had to be positively vetted because of the nature of their work and he had been cleared before being commissioned from Sandhurst. He had already had one quinquennial review and prior to that, had been looked at every year until he had reached the age of twenty-one. It hadn't been necessary for Younger to have constant access to Top Secret material until he was posted to the Arms Control Unit and the initial clearance dated from January 1988. The first quinquennial was therefore still eighteen months away.

Throughout his career, every superior officer who had known Whittle had described him as loyal, hardworking, competent and reliable. He had enjoyed the occasional drink but had never been known to overindulge. He'd had no financial problems and had apparently followed a moderate life style. His hobbies were listed as bird watching and stamp collecting. No one had observed any homosexual tendencies. In 1987 when aged twenty-five, he had got engaged to a Lieutenant Avril Beckwith; approximately nineteen months later it had been broken off, seemingly by mutual agreement. It was the only aberration in an otherwise colourless life.

Younger, by comparison, was as different as chalk from cheese. He enjoyed a party, smoked twenty cigarettes a day, abhorred all drugs but drank in moderation. He had enough credit cards to paper a wall and ran a Porsche that had been bought with the help of a loan from a finance company. The retired police super-intendent from the vetting unit who had conducted the subject interview, had calculated that Younger had debts amounting to seven thousand eight hundred and sixty-one pounds plus a bank overdraft of nine hundred. No one had been too worried about his financial position, least of all his bank manager. Younger had expectations of inheriting half a million from a bachelor uncle as well as a pretty hefty sum from his parents. He was said to be loyal, quick-witted and cool under stress. One superior officer said he was as brave as a lion; no one had described him as hardworking.

It was universally agreed that he was liked and respected by the soldiers under his command who were prepared to follow him anywhere, something they had in common with an impressive number of young women. Three of his former girlfriends had been nominated as referees, not one of whom had had an unkind word to say about him. The only revelation that had made the army think twice before clearing him for PV was Younger's shamefaced

37

admission that, when a second lieutenant, he had had an affair with the wife of the second-in-command of his regiment. Whatever the norm in civilian life, the army still frowned on that sort of thing and it could have cost him his commission. Fortunately for Younger, the liaison had never come to light and it was evident that he had not been the first to bed the lady or the last. The second-in-command had left the army in 1984 and had subsequently divorced his wife on the grounds of her adultery with a stockbroker friend. In view of this development, it had been decided that Younger was not vulnerable to blackmail by a hostile Intelligence Service and he had therefore been cleared for constant access to Top Secret material.

Ashton opened the centre drawer of his desk, took out a sheet of A4 paper and wrote a brief minute to the officer in charge of the Armed Services Liaison Desk, then pinned it to the front cover of the security file. The dossier indicated that Younger had an eye for the girls and there were grounds for thinking he had been indiscreet with Galina Kutuzova which might leave him open to coercion. Much as he disliked doing it, the army ought to be alerted about his latest involvement. After all, Ashton told himself, what they then did with the information was their business and no concern of his, but it still didn't make him feel any better.

He put the file in the out-tray, then had second thoughts and transferred it to the pending basket. There was, Ashton decided, no point in dealing with the problem piecemeal; lifting the phone, he rang the Liaison Desk and asked them to find out if Lieutenant Avril Beckwith was still serving, and if so, where she was stationed. Failing that, he wanted the home address she had given the army on discharge. He had no sooner put the phone down than Hazelwood's secretary rang to ask if he could spare the Director a few minutes.

Despite having removed his jacket and draped it over the back of his chair, Hazelwood was still suffering from the heat, and no wonder. His corner office was all glass, the sun had been on it since early morning and the air conditioning was having one of its off days which meant the room was like a tropical plant house.

"How did you make out with the Ministry of Defence?" he asked before Ashton had even crossed the threshold.

"They were very helpful, showed me everything they had on Galina Kutuzova . . ."

"Good."

"They also let me see the material she had been providing. It looked to me as though the Arms Control Unit had been getting value for money . . ." Ashton dried up, suddenly aware that Hazelwood was only listening to him with half an ear. "Anything wrong?" he asked.

"Does the name Yuri Rostovsky mean anything to you?"

"Yes, he's with the GRU cell in Potsdam. He and the second-in-command of the unit were present when Younger made a pitch for Galina Kutuzova . . ."

"Rostovsky is no longer with us," Hazelwood said, cutting him short. "He was shot to death in the Fasanenplatz yesterday evening. There was an American with him, Lloyd D Osmonde, a former colonel in the USAF who works for the Defense Intelligence Agency. They were sitting at a table on the pavement outside some café when a gunman calmly walked up to them and opened fire. He put three bullets into Rostovsky's head at point-blank range, wounded Osmonde in the shoulder, hit one of the waiters in the ankle with a ricochet and generally upset a lot of people who were hoping to have a night out on the town. Anyway, a motorbike appeared on the scene and he jumped on to the pillion seat and got clean away. Our Head of Station in Berlin says the Kriminalpolizei reckon Rostovsky was trying to muscle in on the slot machine arcades owned by some of the Russian emigrés in the city and the local Mafia decided he had to go. They take the view that if it had been anything more sinister, the gunman would have killed Osmonde too instead of merely wounding him."

"But you don't go along with that theory?" Ashton suggested.

"Galina Kutuzova and Yuri Rostovsky were officers in the same GRU unit; one disappears, the other is murdered. That's too much of a coincidence; there has to be a connection."

"Well, only Galina can tell us what it is."

Hazelwood leaned back in his chair and gazed at him thoughtfully. "Would you like to develop the point you are trying to make, assuming there is one?"

"Galina told Whittle a good deal about herself and her family. She claimed that her maternal grandfather was a general in the KGB and that Eduard Tulbukin, an ambitious Communist Party official, had only proposed to her because he thought the family connection would help to further his career. The upshot is that she doesn't really give a toss for Tulbukin but keeps him dangling because it amuses her to do so. The only person Galina really cares about is her mother, Lydia, and I think she will have got in touch with her somehow."

"And what are you suggesting, Peter?"

"I think someone should go to Leningrad and have a word with her."

"And that someone is you?"

"Yes."

"It's out of the question . . ."

"I could go as a tourist on one of those week-long two-city breaks that travel agents organise. The KGB aren't going to look me up in the Diplomatic List and make a connection when there are thousands of Peter Ashtons in England. Besides, I've still got my old passport which says I'm a technical author."

"I don't know . . ." Hazelwood said doubtfully.

"Look, you can always change your mind. It will take me three weeks to get a visa . . ."

"I don't see how we are going to reimburse you . . ."

"Does that mean I can go?"

"You can have a week's leave whenever it suits you," Hazelwood told him. "What you do or where you go is not my concern. Do I make myself clear?"

Ashton grinned. "I don't see how I could possibly misunderstand."

CHAPTER 5

THE TRAVEL agency was roughly midway between Surbiton station and his flat in Victoria Road. The last time Ashton had booked a holiday with them was almost two years ago when he and Jill Sheridan had been going strong and they had decided to have a weekend break in Paris before she became Mrs Peter Ashton. It would have been the sort of marriage the SIS thoroughly approved of where "the little woman" having worked for the Service, knew what the life was all about. No scenes, no awkward questions when "hubby" came home late from the office or was sent off to the other side of the world at a moment's notice. Only Jill had happened to be one of the very few young women at Century House who were in the fast lane and she had suddenly realised that she wasn't yet ready to give up a promising career for a life of domesticity.

With the benefit of hindsight, Ashton supposed it was almost inevitable that Jill should have wanted to realise the full potential of her language qualifications. Her father had been, and still was, an executive with the Qatar General Petroleum Corporation and she had spent much of her childhood and adolescence in the Persian Gulf. Arabic had been her second tongue; Persian or Farsi was an additional language she had acquired at the School of Oriental and African Studies when a university student.

Jill was now in Bahrain masquerading as the personal assistant to the Second Secretary Consul while running the Intelligence operation in the United Arab Emirates. They had parted amicably enough to begin with but the flat was fast becoming a bone of contention. They had bought it at the peak of the inflationary spiral and had put it up for sale when the bottom had started to fall out of the property market with high interest rates. The flat was still on the books of the estate agent, yet even though

41

they had slashed the asking price to the bone, not one serious prospective buyer had been round to view the apartment. The problem was almost insuperable; Jill was no longer prepared to pay her share of the standing order to the building society and was even willing to lose some of her original deposit if it would get the property off their backs, and he couldn't afford the repayments on a second mortgage to buy her out. Ashton knew that most of her friends thought he was being selfish but, to him, it seemed that his ex-fiancée was the selfish one. Jill didn't have to pay a penny for her accommodation in Bahrain and was in receipt of a generous tax-free local overseas allowance; if he was forced to sell at a loss because she refused to wait for the market to pick up, it was bedsit land in Earls Court for him.

He pushed the door open, walked into the travel agency and found he had the place to himself. There were other signs that the recession was biting; two years ago, the phones hadn't stopped ringing, there had been four girls on the counter and a foreign exchange bureau. This morning, the phones were silent, the foreign exchange bureau had gone and there was only one girl on the counter. The lone survivor not only recognised him immediately but recalled his name without any prompting.

"Hello, Mr Ashton," she said cheerfully, "we haven't seen you in a long time. How can I help you?"

"I've got a week's leave coming to me, Vicky," Ashton told her after glancing at the dymo name tag on her blouse, "so I thought I would have a brief look at Russia. A colleague at work said I ought to go to Leningrad and Moscow. I think he said he went with Intourist?"

"Thomson also do a two-city break." She looked under the counter and brought out a couple of brochures for his inspection. "Leisure Travel do a short break as well but only to Moscow."

"I was told not to miss Leningrad."

"When were you thinking of going?"

"Soon as I can, but I hear it takes roughly three working weeks to get a visa out of the Russian Embassy."

"Your friend is right, Mr Ashton."

"He usually is." Ashton flipped through the Intourist brochure for the sake of appearances before plumping for Thomson. Despite glasnost, going with a Russian company would be tempting Providence bearing in mind the real purpose behind the holiday.

42

"How about this tour here, starting Friday the ninth of August, a month from now?" he asked and reversed the brochure so that Vicky could see the departure date.

"I'll see what I can do, but I don't hold out much hope at this late stage. I assume you want a double room?"

"Whatever is available," Ashton told her. "I'm on my own these days."

"Oh." She dropped her gaze, her face turning a delicate shade of pink. The countertop visual display unit was a welcome distraction and she tapped out the entry code she wanted on the keyboard. The information appeared on the VDU in a bilious combination of yellow and green letters. Another entry code got her the list of tour operators offering package holidays to the USSR. A third codeword put up Thomson's City Breaks, the fourth accessed the page for Moscow-Leningrad. "You're partially in luck, Mr Ashton. I can get you a booking if you don't mind sharing a room."

"Oh. What about the following week?"

"Nothing. I'm afraid the rest of August is booked solid. If you want a room to yourself, the earliest I can offer you is the tour departing on Friday the sixth of September."

There was, Ashton decided, something to be said in favour of sharing a room with a stranger. It could strengthen his cover, make him seem like the kind of tourist who was prepared to forgo a lot of privacy in order to see Russia. "I'll take it," he said.

Vicky lifted the phone, rang Thomson and made the booking, then prevailed upon him to buy excursions to Zagorsk, Pushkin and Pavlovsk, plus a seat at the Moscow State Circus. After paying the invoice with his credit card, Ashton walked to the station and used a Poly Photo booth to obtain three reasonable likenesses of himself for the visa. He then returned to the travel agency, completed the application form in triplicate on the spot, signed all three photographs along the edge and stuck them on to the visa applications in the spaces provided. While he was doing that, Vicky photographed the first six pages of his passport to send off to the Russian Embassy in Kensington Palace Gardens. The tickets, she informed him, would arrive in a fortnight, the visa would be delivered at Heathrow by a representative from Thomson.

The rush hour was long over by the time Ashton reached

the station and he had to wait a good twenty minutes for a stopping train. At Waterloo, he took the York Road exit and made his way on foot to Century House. The first post had already been sorted and placed on file. Amongst a lot of dross, there was a memo from Armed Services Liaison informing him that Lieutenant Avril Beckwith had been promoted to captain and seconded to the Territorial Army as a training officer with the Intelligence and Security Group (Volunteers). Subunits of the group were scattered throughout the length and breadth of the UK but she was with the command element located at the Duke of York's Headquarters on King's Road.

Ashton rang Liaison, thanked them for the information they'd provided and then asked the duty desk officer to set up a head to head interview with Avril Beckwith. Liaison phoned back shortly before lunch to say that arrangements had been made for him to see her that afternoon. A room would be set aside for his use at the barracks and the unit had been warned to expect a Mr Ashton from MI5 at four thirty.

The Polizeipräsidium, the central police station, was located on the Tempelhoferdamm. Although they hadn't put out the red carpet for him, Zale found himself being accorded VIP treatment when he arrived to see Heinrich Voigt, the officer in charge of the Rostovsky investigation. To get that kind of treatment from the Kriminalpolizei spoke volumes for the US Consul General whose diplomatic activity behind the scenes had opened doors which would otherwise have remained firmly closed. Unfortunately, the diplomat who could persuade Voigt to hand over any of the personal effects belonging to the deceased had yet to join the State Department. He was, however, prepared to show Zale what they had found on Rostovsky, but that was it.

"There is not a lot to see – a bunch of keys, a signet ring, a gold bracelet, one Biro, a spectacle case, a lighter and a cheap plastic wallet . . ." Voigt paused, then said, "which contains two thousand five hundred Deutschmarks."

"Something's missing," Zale said.

"But of course, his clothes are still with Forensic. The grey suit he was wearing was purchased from Kaufhaus des Westens department store in Tauenzienstrasse, so was the striped shirt . . ."

"No, I'm thinking about the Zippo lighter. A man doesn't carry one of those in his pocket unless he's a smoker. Didn't anyone find a pack of cigarettes on him?"

"Why not a pipe?" Voigt asked in a dangerously quiet voice.

"Yeah, why not?" Zale smiled, hoped he appeared a lot more relaxed on the outside than he was feeling on the inside. "It's just that most of the smokers I know are addicted to cigarettes," he added lamely.

"Like your friend Herr Osmonde?" Voigt suggested.

"Actually, he's trying to kick the habit."

"So why was Herr Osmonde waiting for his supplier outside Da Gianni's?"

"Supplier?" Zale didn't have to fake his anger; he could visualise Osmonde lying in hospital, a shadow of the man he had known, and it bubbled up like a geyser. "I'm obviously a little dense," he grated, "so I think you'd better spell it out for me."

"The dead man had two thousand five hundred Deutschmarks on him, money he had got from selling religious icons or video recorders or reefers . . ."

"Are we talking about marijuana?"

"Does that surprise you, Herr Zale? It shouldn't. You must know as well as I do that the Russians are into everything these days. It's all part of the new enterprise culture. Of course, it may not be what Gorbachev had in mind, but there are a growing number of ambitious entrepreneurs within the ranks of the Red Army. Captain Yuri Rostovsky had got a little too greedy and the Soviet Mafia here in Berlin decided he had to go."

"Who identified him?" Zale asked quietly.

"We did. There was a military identity card in his wallet. We contacted the Soviet military authorities and they confirmed he was one of theirs, said he was a quartermaster and had gone absent from the supply depot in Leipzig a month ago."

Zale didn't say anything. Rostovsky had been GRU and had been stationed in Potsdam. The Russians had been able to disguise his arm of service and unit location because the ID merely carried his photograph and recorded his name, patronymic and army serial number. He also had to give them credit for picking the right outfit for their cover story. No one was better placed to dabble in the black market than an officer in the Administrative and Quartermaster Corps who could order video recorders and other electrical goods from

45

South Korea for the troops and sell the bulk to German traders.

"The Russians are lying of course," Voigt continued. "Rostovsky belonged to a much more sensitive organisation."

"You know that for a fact, do you?"

"No, but I am aware that Herr Osmonde is employed by the American Defense Intelligence Agency and I don't believe he would be interested in buying marijuana, cocaine, heroin or any other kind of drug. I think our Russian friend was selling him military information."

"You do, huh?"

"What was in the pack of cigarettes, Herr Zale?"

"What cigarettes? You find a Zippo lighter on the body and I wondered out loud why he didn't have the makings." Zale sighed deeply, then said, "Don't let's make a big production out of a simple observation."

"Who do you think has the cigarettes now?"

"What is this?"

"Your whole purpose in coming here, Herr Zale, was to see if we had them. If by chance they had been in our possession, your consul would have returned to the fray and endeavoured to obtain the cigarettes through diplomatic channels. Since we obviously don't have them, you will have to look elsewhere."

"Don't be ridiculous." Zale knew he had handled the situation badly from the moment he'd inadvertently let the cat out of the bag. Voigt had picked up on it right off the bat and had had him on the run ever since. In the circumstances, all he could do was pour scorn on the suggestion.

"I don't think you people appreciate what has happened here in the last year or so," Voigt told him. "The Wall has come down, the political climate has changed and the Russians are going home. We no longer need your kind, especially when you are being deliberately obstructive."

"Me – obstructive?" Zale echoed in a hollow voice.

"I am investigating a murder and I have reason to believe that you are withholding information on the spurious grounds of national security. The time when you people could ride roughshod over a Kripo officer is long over. In fact, it would not be difficult to have the Berlin office of the Defense Intelligence Agency closed down provided I complained loudly enough about your lack of cooperation."

"Are you threatening me, Herr Voigt?"

"Let's say I am not prepared to see this city become another Chicago because you want to play war games."

Double glazing usually made for a quiet room but in the icy silence which grew between them, Zale could hear the traffic moving on the Tempelhoferdamm above the low hum from the air-conditioner. He was conscious of a distinct chill in the air but it would be nothing compared to the frosty reception he would receive in Washington if Voigt closed down the Berlin office.

"Rostovsky was a GRU officer . . ." he began.

"I already guessed that. What I want from you, Herr Zale, is how your colleague recruited him, the RVs they used and so on."

It was a tall order. Osmonde had played it close to his chest and had told him very little about the deal he had going with the Russian. What little he had gleaned didn't amount to very much and he would have to milk it for all he was worth.

"Rostovsky did the approaching, he telephoned my boss at the office and said he wanted to do business with him. As proof of his good intentions, Rostovsky said he had left a present at a drop in the Volkspark Jungfernheide, then told how he could find it. The second sweetener was delivered by a go-between. I think it was a setup so that Rostovsky would know who to look out for when they met for the first time outside Da Gianni's."

"Who was the go-between?"

"A girl called Tamara something or other. I don't know what she looks like because I wasn't there."

"But obviously Herr Osmonde could describe her?"

"Yeah, he was the only one who met the lady."

"Then I think you should talk to him and find out all you can about her." Voigt smiled fleetingly. "I believe it's in both our interests to find out who she is and where we can find her before someone else does."

May had been cold, wet and windy; when it hadn't been raining, June had been largely overcast. On those rare occasions when the sun had broken through, Avril Beckwith had evidently been on hand to soak it up. Ashton was no lecher but it was difficult to

47

ignore her long, tanned legs when she turned up for the interview in sneakers, ankle socks, brief white shorts and a track-suit top. Badminton, it seemed, was next on her agenda.

"The match was arranged before I learned you wanted to see me," Avril told him. "I hope you don't mind the get-up?"

"Of course not." Ashton smiled. "Did they tell you why I asked to see you?"

"I gather it has something to do with poor old Bob Whittle?"

"Yes. You see, I've read everything other people have said about him and he still remains a somewhat shadowy figure. I'm hoping you can flesh him out for me."

"Because we were once engaged?" Avril ventured.

"In a word – yes." Ashton cleared his throat. "Look, I don't want to sound heavy but what I am about to tell you is subject to the Official Secrets Acts. Okay?"

"I have signed on the dotted line, Mr Ashton."

"Yes. Nothing personal, but we both know some people have convenient memories when they see an opportunity to make a fast buck, and unfortunately I have to bear that in mind. Anyway, first of all, I want you to forget anything you may have read in the newspapers. The neo-Nazis didn't murder Bob Whittle, nor was it a case of mistaken identity as some journalists have suggested. At the time of his death he was running a Soviet informer who was still in place but has since disappeared. He inherited this Russian from another officer and almost immediately doubled the payments from the slush fund. Now, I don't think he was working a racket because the sums involved were not big enough to make the risk of discovery worthwhile, but I would like to be sure."

"Let me set your mind at rest," Avril said curtly. "Bob was scrupulously honest, almost painfully so. Whenever he claimed subsistence allowance, he always erred in favour of the Treasury. A good many officers would stretch the number of hours they were away from their normal place of duty in order to claim the higher rate, but not Bob, even if it only meant adding on another five minutes."

"You make him sound like a paragon of virtue," Ashton said gently.

"Well, it may sound hackneyed to cynics like you but he was loyal, thoroughly reliable, kind, generous . . ."

Although Avril wasn't telling him anything he hadn't already learned from reading Whittle's security file, Ashton chose not to interrupt her. Senior officers were not always infallible judges of character and it certainly wasn't a waste of time to have Whittle's assessment confirmed by someone who had been really close to him.

"Where did you meet Bob?" Ashton asked her when she paused for breath.

"At Ashford, the Intelligence Corps Depot."

As a newly commissioned subaltern, she had been posted there to look after the WRAC element. Most of the officers on the depot staff were married and lived out, which could have made for a pretty lonely existence during off-duty hours. Whittle had been one of the few bachelors living in mess and he had taken Avril under his wing. From being her self-appointed guide and mentor, he had become her fiancé and not very ardent lover.

"Bob was a military fanatic, Mr Ashton. The army came first and I was a long way back in second place."

"Is that why you broke off the engagement?"

"It was one of the reasons. I also discovered that Bob was a bore and suddenly I couldn't imagine spending the rest of my life with him. Does that sound awful to you?"

"No. Bird watching and stamp collecting are hardly riveting hobbies for those who don't share the enthusiasm."

"He did have other interests. Matter of fact, Bob was gathering material for a book he planned to write when he left the army."

"What sort of material?"

"Old Intelligence summaries that had been downgraded. He once told me he had amassed enough historical papers to fill a tea chest."

"I hope to God he wasn't carrying that lot around in his personal baggage," Ashton said grimly.

"Oh no. He gave the papers to his sister for safe keeping; they had inherited this house in Fulham from their parents."

Suddenly, Whittle was not the grey figure his security file had led him to believe. He had, in fact, been something of a thieving magpie with literary ambitions. Ashton wondered how much material he had entrusted to his sister's care while he had been serving with the Arms Control Unit.

* * *

49

Her name was Janina. She was twenty-one years old and came from Titu, a small town roughly forty miles northwest of Bucharest. Like thousands of her compatriots, she had travelled overland through Poland to reach the German frontier, lured there by stories of the fabulous standard of living waiting for her in the West. Near Frankfurt an der Oder she had joined up with a party of Russian and Bulgarian immigrants and had paid the equivalent of thirty pounds to a local guide who had led them to a spot where it was possible to ford the river. With only one man to each mile of frontier, evading the German border guards on the far bank had been child's play.

The illegals had split up soon after they had crossed the river. Most had headed for West Germany; Janina had been amongst the minority who had made their way to Berlin. She had arrived in the city with no papers, very little money and knowing only a smattering of German. Unable to register for employment, she had eventually got a job as a dishwasher in a sleazy restaurant on the fringe of the Kreuzberg district where all the Turkish guestworkers and their families lived. After enduring the sweaty embraces of her employer for well over a month, Janina had decided to capitalise on her physical attributes and had joined the sex trade. In a few short weeks she had progressed from being a sales assistant in a porno emporium opposite the Zoo Bahnhof to a call girl with an ever expanding clientèle. She had also moved from a room in a run-down tenement to a modest but comfortable two-bedroom flat overlooking the derelict Anhalter terminus which she shared with Tamara Chernenko.

Janina had not been near the flat in three days. One of her wealthier clients with a villa on the shores of the Wannsee had hired her for the evening to entertain his friends and she had stayed on because one of the house guests had got his kicks out of beating her up. In the process, she had collected a black eye, a split lip, sore ribs and a bruise the size of a grapefruit on her stomach. It had scared the hell out of mine host who, in addition to giving Janina an extra thousand to say nothing about it, had sent for his own physician to examine her. It had been the doctor who had recommended two days complete rest in bed during which time she had been waited on hand and foot.

Her stomach muscles were still very tender and every step on the way up to the flat on the third floor gave her a twinge of pain. She let herself in, called out to Tamara that she was back and walked into her bedroom. A hurricane could not have done more damage. The contents of every drawer had been tipped out on to the carpet, the duvet and bottom sheet had been stripped from the bed and the mattress slashed in a dozen places. The second bedroom was in a similar state but with one horrifying difference. Tamara was lying on the floor in her underwear, her eyes bulging, tongue protruding from a blackened face because the intruder had strangled her with a nylon stocking.

CHAPTER 6

VICTOR HAZELWOOD was wearing his other suit, a dark blue pinstripe which he had bought off the peg at a closing-down sale in Oxford Street. This morning he was in one of his tidier moods and had actually hung up his jacket instead of draping it round the office chairback. If he was hoping that the creases would fall out of their own accord, Ashton thought he was being more than a little optimistic.

"Had us packed in like sardines," Hazelwood said, following his gaze, "but that's the bloody Northern Line for you."

Hazelwood lived in Willow Walk midway between Hampstead Heath and the Underground station, a highly desirable neighbourhood with more than its fair share of politicians, actors, writers and intellectuals, all of whom seemed to be deeply concerned for the unemployed and professed to be horrified that their houses were worth upwards of half a million. Hazelwood was one of the fortunate residents who had moved into the area when it was still possible for a first-time buyer to afford a mortgage on a house that would be redeemable in his own lifetime. Apart from the large number of burglaries endemic to a place like Hampstead, the only other tribulation in his life was the vagaries of the Northern Line.

"This morning they turned us out at Camden Town," Hazelwood continued, "and we're standing there on the platform for a good twenty minutes before anyone thinks to tell us the smoke detectors at Goodge Street have triggered the fire alarm."

"What did you do?" Ashton asked out of politeness. "Take a cab?"

"You must be joking. How many taxis do you think are cruising round Camden Town looking for a fare in the morning rush hour? I caught a bus to Euston, made two changes on the Underground and walked the rest of the way from Waterloo which means I was fifty minutes late into the office with no chance of tackling the in-tray before the DG held his daily prayer session at ten thirty."

"You want me to come back when things are less hectic?"

"Things are never going to be less hectic," Hazelwood told him. "Just be as brief as you can."

Ashton did as he was bid, covering his session with Avril Beckwith on Friday evening in a few short sentences. That he didn't then leave immediately was entirely down to Hazelwood.

"Did Miss Beckwith actually see any of these classified documents she claims Whittle had been sending to his sister?"

"No, but Avril told me she was with him on one occasion when he had posted a largish parcel to her."

"Was that when he told her of his literary ambitions?"

Ashton shook his head. "No, it was some time before that."

"Could he have been having her on, Peter?"

"I don't think so. Whittle was a very serious fellow, definitely not given to childish pranks. One of his superior officers remarked that he lacked a sense of humour."

"Well, if you're right, it's up to the army to recover the documents."

"I think we should take an interest," Ashton said. "It's just possible he may have committed his impressions of Galina Kutuzova to paper. I'm not saying he would have gone as far as to name her because there was no necessity for him to do so. A few discreetly worded pen pictures is all he would need as a reminder."

Hazelwood sighed. "I don't know; finding his sister could be a time-consuming business."

"No, actually it was comparatively simple. Avril Beckwith told me Whittle and his sister had inherited this house in Fulham from their parents which seemed to indicate they were both deceased. So I got Armed Services Liaison to ring the army and find out who he had nominated as his next-of-kin and they came back with the information that the NOK was now his married sister, Mrs Sheila Wyman of 38 Burlington Avenue."

Hazelwood loosened his tie and undid the top button of his shirt to get at the prickly heat rash on his neck which was evidently bothering him. "Do we really want to get involved?"

he asked presently. "Wouldn't it be easier to alert the Ministry of Defence and let the army get on with the job of putting their house in order?"

"Well, it might make some people less inclined to rock the boat. I'm thinking of Richard Earley at the Arms Control Unit for one. It's not going to do him a power of good if Whittle had been collecting material that has supposedly been downgraded. A document could be knocked right down to Restricted and it would still be an offence to possess it or make a photocopy for your own private use. The army would say that Earley should have known what was going on and put a stop to it. All of this could help to bury the Whittle case, which is what the Foreign Office were hoping we would do for them. Not that there has been any media interest of late."

"Quite."

"Of course, if we are content to let sleeping dogs lie, I assume we'd forget all about Galina Kutuzova and what happened to Yuri Rostovsky."

"That's something I am not prepared to do." Hazelwood gave the prickly heat one last scratch, fastened the shirt button and adjusted his tie. "On the other hand, I don't think the police could obtain a search warrant on the strength of what Avril Beckwith told you."

"We don't need one," Ashton said.

"I hope you're not going to suggest we hire someone to burgle the Wymans?"

"Nothing so exotic. We simply tell them what we've heard."

"And if Mrs Wyman pretends she doesn't know what we are talking about?"

"I don't believe she will do that," Ashton told him. "I mean, what is she going to do with a load of confidential papers? Give them to the newspapers and start a witch-hunt that will only discredit her family? No, once Mrs Wyman realises that we don't intend to charge her with an offence under the Official Secrets Acts, she will be only too happy to hand over the documents."

"I hope you're right."

"Are you giving me a green light, Victor?"

"There are a lot of other interested parties – MI5, Special Branch, the army's Directorate of Security." Hazelwood paused,

54

then said, "Better have a word with Liaison and get their advice. I don't want us treading on a lot of tender corns."

It was Tony Zale's second visit to the Polizeipräsidium and his second encounter with Kommissar Heinrich Voigt in as many days. He sincerely hoped it would be his last. The description of Tamara which Osmonde had given him could fit almost half the young women in Berlin – light brown hair, brown eyes, round face, approximately five feet six, weight one twenty to one thirty pounds and very pretty. As he repeated the physical characteristics, he could tell from Voigt's expression that the Kripo officer thought he was being deliberately vague.

"I'm sorry it's not a more precise description," he said apologetically.

"I've known worse."

"We're not trying to be obstructive; Mr Osmonde is still very groggy and sometimes he doesn't make a lot of sense."

"It doesn't matter, Herr Zale." Voigt extracted several colour photographs from a large brown envelope and passed them across the desk for his inspection. "Her name was Tamara Chernenko. I'm quite satisfied she was the young woman Rostovsky used as a go-between."

So was Zale, yet the colour photographs of the dead woman so mesmerised him that he found it difficult to lay them aside. Osmonde had told him that the girl was very pretty, but in death she looked ugly. "Where did you find her?" he asked in a low voice.

"In a two-bedroom flat near the Anhalter station which she shared with another prostitute known as Janina. Although the pathologist hasn't completed the autopsy yet, he is prepared to say that death occurred between forty-eight and seventy-two hours before the body was found yesterday evening. This would tend to support the woman Janina's claim that she spent the previous three nights elsewhere. It would also indicate that Tamara was murdered the same night that Rostovsky was shot."

"Yeah."

"And it would seem there is a good chance the killer found what he was looking for."

Voigt began to deal a number of photographs across the desk, rather like a banker in a game of blackjack trying to get as close as possible to twenty-one. Sifting through them, Zale saw that every room in the flat had been turned over.

"Look at the bathroom," Voigt continued. "See how the toilet has been taken apart? I'm willing to bet that whatever the killer was looking for was hidden in the lavatory cistern. It's possible Rostovsky put it there without Tamara's knowledge."

"Why do you say that?"

"We showed Janina a photograph of Yuri Rostovsky that we took in the morgue. She thinks Tamara brought him back to the flat once, perhaps twice, but no more than that. In other words, they were not good friends."

"Do you know where she might have picked Rostovsky up?" Zale asked.

"Tamara used to work the bars on Tauentzienstrasse from the U-Bahn Ku'damm station eastwards as far as Wittenbergplatz. Naturally we're interviewing all the hookers who patrolled the same beat."

Zale went through the photographs again, picked out the one that showed the front door and studied it closely. There were no marks around the lock or the jamb to suggest it had been forced, which in turn led him to believe that Tamara had taken her killer back to the flat thinking she had scored. He also thought he knew what had prompted Rostovsky to use her as a go-between. The Russian Intelligence officer had been convinced he was being watched by the KGB; he had said so to Osmonde every time he'd phoned him. Tamara Chernenko had been his decoy to throw them off. Horny soldier hundreds of miles from home and family takes up with a good-looking hooker; it was the kind of liaison between the two oldest professions that had existed since time began and the KGB had probably bought it, at least to begin with. They had seen through the ruse the day he had sent Tamara to meet Lloyd Osmonde. Rostovsky could not have been the only one watching her that day; the KGB had been there and they too had made the connection.

"You are especially interested in that photograph?" Voigt asked.

Zale looked up. "Not particularly, I was thinking about something else."

"The killer tortured her. You can't tell that from the photographs, Herr Zale, because the body was in a fairly advanced state of decomposition when Janina discovered it. However, following a preliminary examination of the dead woman, the police pathologist concluded that she had been punched repeatedly in the stomach and kidneys. No doubt the killer had hoped she would be able to tell him where Rostovsky had hidden this mysterious package he intended to sell to you Americans. Unfortunately for Tamara, it appears he hadn't told her."

The way Zale saw it, the Russian Intelligence officer must have wrapped the package in a polythene bag and concealed it in the lavatory cistern for safe keeping until such time as he was ready to deliver it. It could have been done without Tamara's knowledge because she was unlikely to have stood there watching him urinate if he'd asked to use the toilet. And sure as hell, Zale couldn't think of one good reason why she would take it upon herself to look inside the cistern.

"What was in the package?" Voigt asked, as if reading his thoughts.

"I don't know. Rostovsky claimed he had proof that the Red Army was doing more than just cheating on the Force Reductions which Gorbachev had put his signature to. He hinted about a concealed order of battle which no satellite spy in the sky would be able to detect, but he didn't give Lloyd Osmonde any details over the phone."

"Well, whatever it was, someone was prepared to go to extreme lengths in order to recover the package."

"Yeah." Zale went through the photographs of the flat again. "I see they had an answering machine connected to the phone in the hall," he said.

"But of course. Janina had given up walking the streets in favour of advertising her services in various porno magazines, quoting her phone number so that regular clients could leave messages for her when she wasn't in."

Janina didn't bring the Johns back to the flat, she performed in hotel rooms and private houses. Zale thought that would explain why she had only seen Tamara with Yuri Rostovsky on a couple of occasions. It also occurred to him that the answering phone would have told the Russian whether or not anyone was at home.

"That bunch of keys you found among Rostovsky's effects," he said thoughtfully. "Have you tried them out on the flat, Herr Voigt?"

Sheila Wyman was thirty-two-years old, tall, thin, rather plain and wore her black hair scraped up on top of her head. She and her husband, Ralph, were both teachers at the local comprehensive and were keen supporters of Greenpeace, which they proudly proclaimed with several "Save the Whale" posters displayed in the windows of their downstairs front room. Ashton had been given the green light to see the Wymans because Head of Liaison had cleared it with the other interested parties – MI5, the Ministry of Defence and the army's Directorate of Security.

The MOD, having conferred with the army's Directorate of Security, had replied that they were not aware that any classified documents were missing and had also taken the view that they had no jurisdiction over civilians. MI5, having sought advice from their legal department and the Metropolitan Police Special Branch, who usually did most of the donkey work on their behalf, had intimated that the police would not be able to obtain a search warrant on the strength of the statement made by Captain Avril Beckwith. However, they had asked to be kept fully informed of any action taken by Century House which was the equivalent of inviting their rival service to grasp the shitty end of the stick.

The Wymans' occupations were recorded in Whittle's security file; after ringing the local education authority to check if they were still in the teaching profession, Ashton had then looked up their number in the directory and telephoned them at four thirty when he calculated they would be at home. He had spoken to Ralph Wyman and used Avril Beckwith's name as a means of introduction before asking when it might be convenient for him to have a word with them both about Bob Whittle. Somewhat to his surprise, the Wymans had said they would be quite happy to see him that same evening at seven. The false MOD pass for Mr Ashton did the rest and got him into the house with the minimum of fuss.

The photographs of Whittle in uniform which greeted Ashton when he walked into the small back room were a sign that brother and sister had been extremely close. They also warned him that he would have to watch his step.

"I never met your brother," he told Sheila Wyman, "but everyone I have spoken to who knew him thought very highly of him."

"That's nice to know," she murmured, "but it won't bring him back, will it?"

"No, it won't; no one can do that."

"And we still don't know who killed Bob and why."

"You mustn't think the German police and the military authorities have stopped looking for his killers," Ashton said gently. "That will never happen."

"I'm glad. But you didn't come here just to tell us that, did you, Mr Ashton?"

"No. As I told your husband on the phone, this has to do with something Avril Beckwith told me when I saw her on Friday evening."

"Oh yes? And what did that woman have to say about my brother?"

The hostility was there in her voice, in her choice of expression and in the way her eyes narrowed. Whittle may have told the case officer who had interviewed him that the engagement had been broken off by mutual agreement, but listening to the harsh criticism now directed at Avril Beckwith, it seemed she had succeeded in making him desperately unhappy, or so Sheila Wyman maintained. In the process, it appeared Avril had also earned the undying hatred of Whittle's sister which made Ashton's task much more difficult than he'd imagined. There was, he finally decided, no easy way of conveying what Avril Beckwith had told him other than repeating the allegation word for word.

"I haven't the faintest idea what she is talking about, Mr Ashton. One thing I do know; Bob never entertained any ambitions of becoming a writer."

Ashton caught the sideways glance Ralph Wyman gave his wife and knew different. "Perhaps he didn't tell you what was in the packages?" he said, offering them a way out.

"What packages?"

There were two ways of dealing with the impasse. He could either get heavy and threaten them with a search warrant or he could adopt a laissez-faire attitude towards the problem. He chose to take the softer line because he would be left with no room for manoeuvre if they called his bluff.

"Look, if you tell me Bob never entrusted any papers to you for safe keeping, I'll walk away and leave you in peace." Ashton smiled. "You can destroy them after I've gone and I won't be angry as long as you make a good job of it. Whatever you do, don't dump the papers on a rubbish tip where they are bound to be found. And if you're going to have a bonfire in the back garden, for God's sake make sure none of the papers get airborne on a gust of wind and are last seen floating above the rooftops of London. They'll only come to earth again and then I shall have to remember this conversation, and that will be very embarrassing for you as well as for me."

There was a long silence and it began to look as if they were going to ignore his veiled warning. Then Ralph Wyman, who hadn't said a word thus far, cleared his throat nervously.

"This house also belonged to Bob," he said hesitantly. "It was his home too – and he left some of his things here – stuff he didn't want to cart around with him – and naturally we respected his privacy – I mean, you don't look to see what he's packed away, do you?"

"Of course you don't," Ashton assured him.

"Well, supposing he had left some secret papers in the house which we didn't know about – how would it affect us?"

"It wouldn't, provided you voluntarily handed them over to the appropriate authority."

"Meaning you, Mr Ashton?"

"Yes. I'll give you a receipt for the documents and a statement absolving you and Mrs Wyman."

"I see." Wyman glanced at his wife and got a faint nod of approval. "Well, in that case, there are a couple of cardboard boxes in the attic which we haven't known what to do with since Bob was killed."

"Perhaps we had better take a look at them."

"I think so," Wyman said.

Ashton followed him upstairs. A do-it-yourself enthusiast, Wyman had installed a retractable ladder to the ceiling on the landing which could be lowered by remote control. Up above, floorboards had been laid in the loft to convert the roof space into a playroom for the most comprehensive model railway Ashton had ever seen.

"I'm a train buff," Wyman said, almost apologetically. "A pretty expensive hobby, I know, but it's my only vice."

60

The cardboard boxes measured some three feet by two and were approximately nine inches deep. Both of them were packed to the brim with Intelligence summaries, operational orders, contingency plans and geo-political assessments.

"What do you think, Mr Ashton?"

"I think I've got a lot of sorting to do," Ashton told him.

Although Janina had learned some German since she had arrived in Berlin, her vocabulary was somewhat limited and largely confined to the kind of conversation a call girl might be expected to have with a client. Experience had taught Heinrich Voigt that it was therefore advisable to have an interpreter present when interrogating her. Experience had also taught him that any question-and-answer session with the Romanian girl was likely to be a time-consuming business and before starting this one, he took the precaution of phoning his wife to warn her that he would be late home for dinner.

"Between eight and nine is my best guess, Liebchen," he told her, then put the phone down and faced the Romanian girl.

"So here we are again, Janina," he said. "You know my name and you remember Herr Antonescu, the interpreter, from last time. Is that not so?"

Janina looked to the interpreter, waited for him to translate, then nodded her head vigorously.

"Good. You will also recall that I showed you a photograph of a dead man and you told me you had seen him with Tamara on one or two occasions. Correct?"

On Friday evening he had had two dead Russians on his hands which could simply have been a coincidence. Even now, Voigt was not sure what had prompted him to show Rostovsky's photograph to Janina, but as it turned out, it had been the smartest thing he had done all day. Instead of having to run two separate investigations, he had established a link and could deploy his resources accordingly.

"She is not denying it," Antonescu told him presently.

"I should hope not." Voigt held up a key. "This was found on the dead man, Janina, and it opens the door to your apartment. How do you account for that?"

Antonescu didn't have to translate the question for her. The key made it obvious and Janina understood enough German to

61

fill in the rest. That she should claim that Tamara must have given it to him was no more than Voigt had expected. It seemed, however, that there were not enough bad words in her vocabulary to describe how angry she was with the dead girl for bringing her clients back to the flat after being warned not to do so.

"All right, all right." Voigt waved his hands to silence her. "That's enough. Now calm down and listen to this."

Voigt opened the centre drawer of his desk, took out a cassette and inserted it into a small Sony tape recorder, then depressed the play button. The voice belonged to a young woman who sounded both angry and not a little frightened.

"That message was left on your answering machine, Janina, and it was found by one of my detectives when he went to the flat this afternoon. In case you didn't recognise the language, the caller was speaking Russian and she informed Tamara that the message was intended for Yuri Rostovsky. What I want to know is, have you heard that voice before?"

It took Antonescu only half a minute to translate what he had said; thereafter, it seemed to Voigt that the Romanian had promoted himself to Kommissar and was now conducting the interrogation. The two-way exchange tried his patience to the limit but although sorely tempted to interrupt them, he had a hunch that Antonescu was on to something.

"Janina says this is the third time she has heard the voice."

"And?" Voigt could not believe that was all she had told the interpreter.

"The woman was not speaking Russian on the previous occasions."

"Did Janina recognise what it was?"

"Romanian is a Romance language with many archaic forms . . ."

Voigt closed his eyes, wondered why Antonescu could never answer a simple question without delivering a lecture.

"It also contains admixtures of Slavonic, Turkish, Magyar and French words. Janina recognised a few."

"What do you mean she recognised some of them?"

"She is saying the woman spoke French," Antonescu said, finally coming to the point.

Chapter 7

MI5 had laid claim to the documents the day after Ashton had recovered them from the Wymans. With the help of the MOD, it had then taken them almost three and a half weeks to catalogue the material and assess what damage, if any, had been done to the nation by the unauthorised disclosure of classified information. The various staff papers, contingency plans, Intelligence summaries and operation orders had been originated between October 1981 and January 1990; none had been graded higher than Secret, most were out of date and should have been destroyed long ago. Unfortunately, the most recent papers had been illegally photocopied and their security classification of Secret was still valid.

The inquiry had now entered the clean-up phase. The system of accounting for classified material was either defective or the rules had been disregarded; either way, the Ministry of Defence was responsible for putting its own house in order. MI5 were far more concerned to find out whether the material they had catalogued really was an accurate record of Whittle's private collection. It was, Ashton thought, a sly way of letting him know that they believed either he or the Wymans had retained certain papers. He could not of course answer for the Wymans, but in his case it happened to be true.

The officer chosen by Five to be the Grand Inquisitor was Clifford Peachey, one of the leading lights of K1. The men and women of this section were known as the Kremlin watchers because it was their task to ferret out the KGB and GRU officers in the Soviet Embassy, Trade Delegation and Consular Service. Peachey looked typecast for the job; he was a small man with sharp, pointed features that reminded Ashton of a rodent. He had dark hair flecked with grey which was cut short back and sides and

63

a neat toothbrush moustache which was not at all flattering. If his manner had matched his appearance, Ashton would have disliked him on sight. As it was, he was both friendly and a little shy. He also apologised for dragging Ashton to his office in Gower Street and wished they could have met somewhere nearer to Century House instead. He was, in fact, a past master at disarming people, a knack which made him a potentially dangerous adversary.

"First things first," he said. "Before we go any farther, I've been asked to express our appreciation for all you've done, Peter. And if the government hasn't already thanked you through the Cabinet Office, they jolly well ought to. There could have been some very red faces if any of the material you recovered had fallen into the wrong hands."

"Were the documents that sensitive?"

"You mean you didn't read them when you had the chance?" Peachey asked, feigning amazement.

"Didn't have the time," Ashton told him. "Of course, I listed them by the originator's reference number and date before I left the Wymans because I had to give them a receipt for the stuff. I then drove straight to Century House and handed the cardboard boxes to the night duty staff for safe keeping. The DG was briefed the next morning by my Director and they decided you people should be informed immediately. I never saw the papers again after that; all I know is that none of them carried a Top Secret security classification."

"I see." Peachey nodded sagely. "Well, of course their unauthorised disclosure would have caused a great deal of embarrassment all round but no lasting harm would have been done to the nation. Whittle was not selective; he took what he could, where he could. In January 1983 he was posted to Headquarters British Forces Falkland Islands. While there, he photocopied a Secret report on the behaviour of the local inhabitants towards the Argentinian occupation force. I would have said that that particular paper was the most embarrassing thing he could have purloined because certain members of the population didn't come out of it too well."

"Yes, I imagine that would have put the cat among the pigeons," Ashton said dryly.

Peachey took out a pipe and began to fill the bowl with Dunhill Standard Mixture from a tin he kept in the top right-hand drawer of his desk. The invitation, though unspoken, was self-evident to Ashton; having taken him into his confidence, Peachey now expected something in return.

"Are you at liberty to tell me what prompted you to seek out Captain Beckwith?" he asked after it had become equally self-evident that his subtle approach had fallen on stony ground.

"I don't see why not," Ashton said, and then proceeded to give the older man a sanitised version of the facts. "I went to see Military Intelligence at MOD the day after I returned from Germany," he continued. "They reckoned they were getting value for money, and I guess they were, but it seemed to me that inflation had influenced their opinion."

"Inflation?" Peachey repeated in a puzzled voice.

"The rouble used to be pegged at one to one with the pound, then it became six to one; now the official rate is forty-seven. There's a case for maintaining that Whittle was forced to raise the ante on the grounds that you only get what you pay for. You have his security file now so you know how highly he was regarded by his superior officers. I just thought it worthwhile talking to the one person who had been really close to him."

"And learned he wasn't quite the paragon of virtue everyone had said he was?"

"Right."

"So you then went hotfoot to see the Wymans."

"Hotfoot is not the word I would have used," Ashton said. "We waited seventy-two hours to give the MOD and you people a chance to get in first, but you both declined to get involved."

"You would have got a different reaction had we been told that Whittle was running a Soviet agent when he was murdered."

"I think that's something you should take up with your own DG."

There was no need for Ashton to labour the point. Once a week, the Directors General of the SIS, MI5 and the MOD's Intelligence Staff attended the meeting of the Joint Intelligence Committee which was chaired by the Cabinet Secretary. K, as the Head of MI5 was known, would have been present when the MOD representative announced that Whittle had been killed in Dresden and gave details of the incident.

"Was the name of the Soviet agent disclosed at the time?" Peachey asked.

"I wouldn't know. But if it's any help, it was Senior Lieutenant Galina Kutuzova of the GRU. Ever heard of her?"

"Can't say I have."

"Her parents are divorced; her father, Sergei Vasilevich Kutuzov, was an air force colonel but now has something to do with the cosmonaut programme and is said to be living in Star City."

"His name doesn't ring a bell either."

"How about Galina's fiancé? Eduard Tulbukin, a rising star in the Communist Party."

"In what area?"

According to the notes Whittle had made, Tulbukin was a middle-ranking official in the Foreign Ministry, but this was not recorded elsewhere and Peachey would know he must have retained certain papers if he disclosed it.

"That's something she omitted to tell Whittle," Ashton said, poker-faced.

"Pity."

"Yes. However, she was a little more forthcoming about her maternal grandfather – Nikolai Yakulevich Petrovsky."

Peachey raised his eyebrows. "We are talking about the KGB's Nikolai Petrovsky, are we? The man Yuri Andropov chose to head the Fifth Chief Directorate when it was created in 1969 to crush the dissidents?"

"We are indeed."

"A formidable if not evil man. He was seventy-seven when he died in 1988 and a lot of people heaved a sigh of relief."

"You sound as though you knew him personally," Ashton observed.

"I did in a way. In '62 I was attached to the British Services Security Organisation in Germany when the officer commanding the Russian infantry company which was then guarding Hess at Spandau walked into Wavell Barracks and asked for political asylum. He knew General Nikolai Petrovsky and his daughter Lydia Petrovskya rather well and hated them like poison. He had every reason to. Interested?"

"Very. I'd like to hear more."

Peachey tapped out his pipe and left it bowl downwards in the ashtray. "Well now," he said, "I'd like to hear what Whittle had to say about Galina Kutuzova."

"I'm not sure I follow you," Ashton said, playing for time.

"I went to see the Wymans too. From what they said, I got the impression that you hadn't listed all the papers you took away. I guessed they were probably some notes Whittle had made himself, so I gave them a receipt to cover his private papers. I must say they seemed very relieved."

"You're a pretty clever fellow, Mr Peachey."

"Thank you. The thing is, do we have a deal?"

"Yes."

"Good. I'm listening."

"It's not that I don't trust you," Ashton said, "but I think we should toss a coin to see who goes first."

Peachey blinked several times. There was a moment when he almost allowed his jaw to drop but he quickly recovered his composure and dug out a 10p piece. "If that's what you want," he said and flipped the coin into the air. "You call."

"Heads."

Peachey caught the 10p in the palm of his right hand and slapped it down on the back of his other wrist. His face registered mild disappointment when he lifted his hand and saw that Ashton had called it right. "You win," he conceded reluctantly.

"So tell me about Petrovsky."

"In 1937, Stalin purged the Red Army of those elements he considered were pro-German and therefore hostile towards him. Four out of the five marshals of the Soviet Union including Marshal Tukhachevsky, the Commander-in-Chief were liquidated. In scores of show trials up and down the country, seventy-five per cent of the officer corps down to the rank of major either went before the firing squads or ended up in one of the Gulags. My defector's father was a lieutenant colonel in the armoured corps and was one of the fifteen thousand who were executed. In those far-off days, Petrovsky was a junior officer in what eventually became known as the Armed Forces Directorate. He was the NKVD's spy in uniform and was the man who denounced the father of my defector."

Before the Wall came down and the old order collapsed, Lieutenant Colonel Richard Earley could have counted the number of times he had visited the GRU compound in Potsdam on the fingers of one hand; in the days when the Arms Control Unit had been known as BRIXMIS, liaison with a hostile Intelligence Service had not been within his remit. When he had met his opposite number, it had either been to register an official complaint or make small talk at some social function. Until the great thaw, the British had declined to attend any celebration commemorating the anniversary of the October Revolution and the Russians had habitually boycotted the Queen's Birthday.

It was different now; fraternisation was the in thing and both sides were bidding to outdo one another with invitations to see their military hardware. Certain items were of course still taboo; nuclear weapons were not on display and the Red Army was definitely not prepared to reveal the full extent of their chemical warfare capability. Some of the bonhomie struck Earley as a little forced and he personally found it nauseating at times, but he was as good as the next man at keeping a fixed smile on his face. Yet although the climate had changed for the better, this was only the second time he had visited the GRU unit since Whittle had been murdered all of eleven weeks ago.

An almost complete absence of familiar faces was the first thing Earley noticed when he entered the building. Rostovsky was dead and Galina Kutuzova was supposedly absent without leave, but although "trickle" postings would have accounted for a number of the new men, it was evident that the unit had been purged from top to bottom. The only survivor of the original team was the second-in-command of the unit, Alexei Leven, and he was now wearing two stars on each shoulder board instead of one.

"Congratulations," Earley said. "I see they have moved you up a rung to half-colonel."

For an army that was grossly over-officered with one commissioned rank for every seven enlisted men, Earley had often wondered why his opposite number, who also doubled as the second-in-command, should only have been a major.

"Thank you, Richard." Leven pointed to an upright ladderback and sank back into his own armchair. "But it was not entirely unexpected," he added. "I had been warned in advance that my name would appear in the June promotion list."

"Even so, it's no more than you deserve."

"I think so too." Modesty had never been part of Leven's make-up, and he was also inclined to take himself seriously.

68

"What's happened to everyone else?" Earley asked. "Have they been promoted too?"

"No. Our commanding officer, Colonel Vladimir Ilyich, complained of feeling unwell and was sent home for medical treatment after tests had shown he had a duodenal ulcer. The others were routine postings."

Earley didn't believe it. A duodenal ulcer could have been treated in the nearby military hospital and the Red Army's administrative staff would have made sure there was a degree of continuity in the GRU unit when rotating personnel.

"You must be carrying quite a load on your shoulders with all this upheaval, Alexei."

"I have been rather busy."

"And what happened to Yuri Rostovsky must have increased your difficulties."

"What do you mean?" Leven asked curtly.

"Well, I imagine you had to arrange the funeral and return his effects to the next-of-kin?"

"It was nothing. There are procedures for such eventualities."

"Was Yuri married?"

"He had a wife but in name only. She remained in Minsk with the children when he joined us." Leven shuffled some of the papers on his desk, transferring them from the "in" to "pending" tray. "However, I assume you didn't come here just to give me your advice on how to run my unit, did you, Richard?"

Earley barely managed a smile; the Russian was easily one of the rudest and most uncouth individuals he had ever met. He was a younger version of Nikita Khruschev but with a full head of hair and it would have given Earley a great deal of pleasure to tell Alexei exactly what he thought of him. Still endeavouring to appear friendly, he unlocked the government-issue briefcase, took out a copy of Exercise BROADSWORD and gave it to Leven.

"BROADSWORD is a 1(BR) Corps exercise which will run from Sunday the twenty-ninth of September to Friday the eleventh of October inclusive. Forces taking part are the 3rd and 4th Armoured Divisions and the manoeuvre area lies within the rectangle bounded by Minden, Celle, Luneberg and Delmenhorst. The manoeuvres will involve an assault crossing of the Weser and Aller rivers in the face of a nuclear threat. As you are no doubt aware, Colonel General Fedyanin, the previous commander of 6

Guards Tank Army, had accepted an invitation to attend. We very much hope his successor, Colonel General Vitali Lobanov will do likewise."

"I can not answer for the colonel general," Leven told him brusquely. "Doubtless, you will learn of his intentions through the usual channels in due course."

Earley didn't like the way he tossed the exercise instructions into the out-tray without even bothering to look at the heraldic device on the front cover. If that wasn't already insulting enough, the Russian then proceeded to ignore him and started to tackle the files awaiting his attention.

"Thank you for giving me so much of your time," Earley said icily and this time made no attempt to conceal his anger.

The outburst had no effect whatever on Leven who continued to act as though he wasn't there. Without another word, Earley got to his feet and stalked out of the building.

Galina Kutuzova had been on the take, and Yuri Rostovsky had evidently been hyperactive in the Black Market. Their combined activities were indicative of a complete breakdown of military discipline within the GRU cell and the commanding officer would have been sacked in anyone's army. Faced with a similar situation in a British Intelligence unit, Earley knew the MOD would get rid of anyone they suspected of being a rotten apple in the barrel. The Red Army had gone one better and purged the entire outfit with one notable exception. As the second-in-command, Leven should have known what was going on and done his best to put a stop to it. Earley could think of only one reason why he had survived. Leven was GRU in name only; he was the man who spied on the spies and belonged to the Armed Forces Directorate of the KGB.

Hazelwood dropped into the office ten minutes after Ashton had returned from Gower Street and while he was still chewing his way through a tasteless cheese roll which constituted a belated lunch. He was in shirtsleeves, had a slim file cover under his left arm and was smoking one of his favourite Burma cheroots.

"Don't let me interrupt you," he said brightly.

"Right. Be with you in a minute." Ashton swallowed the last of the cheese roll and washed it down with the remains of a cup

70

of coffee, then wiped his mouth on a paper napkin. "Sorry about that," he apologised, "but I missed my lunch hour."

"That's okay. I just wondered how you got on with Clifford Peachey?"

"We did a deal. He told me what he knew about the grandfather, I gave him a resumé of the notes Whittle had compiled on Galina Kutuzova and promised to send on a photocopy of the original."

"Was that wise?"

"I didn't have much choice," Ashton told him. "Peachey had been to see the Wymans and bluffed them into believing he knew they didn't have a receipt to cover all the documents I had removed from their house. I didn't see much point in denying it if he was prepared to give me something of value in return."

"And did he?"

"I think so."

"Good. Head of Station, Berlin has been earning his pay too." Hazelwood removed the file from under his arm and laid it on the desk. "Take a look at this fax."

The fax was classified Secret, consisted of four pages and had been given an Op Immediate precedence, which meant it had been transmitted ahead of routine and priority traffic. Through his contacts in the Kriminalpolizei, Neil Franklin had obtained details of Rostovsky's relationship with Tamara Chernenko, a known prostitute. He had also received a briefing from Kommissar Heinrich Voigt who was in charge of the dual murder investigation. The final paragraph of the fax contained a translation of a message that had been left for Tamara Chernenko on an answering machine approximately three days after she had been strangled.

"The caller was a woman," Hazelwood told him. "According to Neil Franklin, it was the third time she had rung the flat. On the two previous occasions, she left a message for Yuri Rostovsky in French."

"So why did she break the pattern, Victor? Why does she suddenly take Tamara Chernenko into her confidence?"

"Maybe she was in a panic. Franklin said her voice sounded nervous."

"Well, she was certainly taking a risk. I mean, it says here that Tamara was sharing the flat with another call girl. Ten to one, the only people who phoned them were punters wanting to hire their services. Now, unless Tamara had removed that cassette from the machine as soon as she had played it back, there is a strong possibility that the message would have been erased by other clients trying to make a date with her or this other girl, Janina."

"It's all rather academic, isn't it?" Hazelwood said dismissively. "Tamara never got the message."

"Look, the caller says that unless she hears from Yuri Rostovsky within the next forty-eight hours, she'll leave without him. So my question is, did she ring back two days later?"

"No." Hazelwood searched the desk for an ashtray, concluded Ashton didn't have one and flicked the ash from his cheroot into the metal wastebin. "Anyway, what exactly are you getting at?" he asked.

"The whole thrust of this message suggests the mystery woman had some kind of deal going with Rostovsky. If she didn't bother to phone back, it must mean that he knew where to reach her."

"I don't see where that gets us; it's more than three weeks since the message was left on the answering machine and there's no way we can pick up her trail without knowing who she is." Hazelwood smiled. "Maybe you would like to crack that one, Peter?"

"I'm supposed to be going on holiday tomorrow."

"Oh yes, so you are." Hazelwood flicked some more cigar ash into the wastebin, picked up the folder and tucked it back under his arm. "The Riviera, isn't it?"

"Right." If the acting Director wanted to pretend that he didn't know he was off to Leningrad and Moscow, Ashton wasn't about to disabuse him.

"When do we see you in the office again?"

"The nineteenth of August, a week from Monday next."

"Well, enjoy yourself but don't do anything I wouldn't do."

"Galina Kutuzova is a pretty bright girl, Victor. English isn't her only language; she is also fluent in French. Maybe Head of Station, Berlin should invite Simon Younger of the 3rd Carabineers to listen to the cassette? He's the only man who could recognise her voice if he heard it."

"Yuri Rostovsky and Galina Kutuzova?" Hazelwood said doubtfully.

"Why not? It could be he was her case officer. Can you think of a better cover?"

"Not offhand."

"Here's something else to mull over; the French also maintain a military presence in Berlin."

"So what?"

"Well, Galina was selling us information and we know the Yanks were listening to Rostovsky, so what was to stop them peddling the same stuff to our Gallic friends?" Ashton paused, then said, "It could be they were grateful enough to reward her with a passport."

CHAPTER 8

SOMEONE KICK-STARTED a motorcycle into life, then opened the throttle too soon and stalled the engine. Moments later, the rider got the two-stroke going again only to have it die on him once more when he revved up. It was not a case of third time lucky.

The noise finally got to Ashton and woke him up. He surfaced reluctantly, uncertain at first where he was, then the furniture began to take on a definite shape in the grey light of a northern dawn and he suddenly realised the motorbike was in the adjacent twin bed. The snorer was Stanley Inver, a sixty-six-year-old widower and jack of all trades who was also a repository of useless information. Ashton had been unaware of his existence on the British Airways flight to Moscow and had remained blissfully ignorant during the nineteen-mile coach ride from Sheremetyevo 2 International airport to the city centre. It was only when they were having an early dinner at the Ukraina Hotel on Kutuzovsky Prospekt before catching the Aeroflot flight to Leningrad that he had learned that Stanley Inver was to be his travelling companion.

Over dinner, he had also learned that Inver preferred the shortened version of his Christian name and was determined to be the life and soul of the party. Nothing was going to get him down, not the indifferent food, the grubby tablecloths and the haphazard service provided by surly waiters; Moscow and Leningrad were two cities he had always wanted to see and he was damn well going to enjoy every minute of the holiday. Furthermore, no mate of Stan Inver was going to suffer from hunger pangs. He had heard that things were difficult in Russia and had packed some iron rations in a small military haversack from World War Two. Ashton had wondered who Inver meant by his mate and discovered the honour had been bestowed on him when the older man had elected to sit next to him on the bus out to the airport and again on the TU 154 flight to Leningrad. He had talked nonstop throughout the journey and had kept it up all the time they had stood in line waiting for their room keys in the lobby of the Hotel Pulkovskaya. There was, in fact, no respite from Stanley Inver even when he was fast asleep.

Ashton vowed he wouldn't steal a glance at the wake-up alarm and immediately changed his mind. Three fifteen, and light enough to read a book even though the curtains were drawn. He closed his eyes, tried to concentrate all his thoughts on Lydia Petrovskaya, daughter of General Nikolai Yakulevich, mother of Galina Kutuzova, and the woman who had brought him all the way to Leningrad. A curator at the Hermitage museum with a flat on Nevsky Prospekt; it wasn't a lot to go on but unfortunately Whittle had been more interested in the daughter than in the mother. And Peachey hadn't been able to tell him much more. Sleep came to Ashton once more as he struggled to recall Lydia's age and other minutiae of her early life.

The high zinging noise of a mosquito woke him, or perhaps it was the resounding slap Inver landed on his forehead.

"Gotcha," he burbled triumphantly in a voice that was only marginally less intrusive than his usual tone.

"Congratulations," Ashton said, and rolled out of bed.

"I didn't wake you, did I, Pete? Only I usually get up at six."

"Is that what the time is now?"

"No, it's five minutes to seven. Had a good lie in for once."

"Mind if I use the bathroom first?"

"Be my guest," Inver told him and promptly lit a cigarette and started coughing just as promptly.

Ashton closed the bathroom door behind him, took a cold shower to freshen up, then shaved in lukewarm water that looked as if someone else had already washed in it. He opened a bottle of Perrier bought the night before in the hard currency bar, filled one of the glasses on the shelf above the washbasin and used the spring water as a dental mouthwash after brushing his teeth.

When he returned to the bedroom, Inver was reclining in the solitary armchair, his nose buried in a pocket edition of Baedeker's Guide to Leningrad. Even before he told him to listen to this, Ashton knew he was going to read great chunks of it aloud.

The only question in his mind was whether it would be a potted history of the city or the biographical details of some of its more notable personalities. He got the history lesson, starting in 1703 with Peter the Great's decision to build a window on the world in the boggy delta of the Neva, and managed to finish dressing as Inver began to tell him about the storming of the Winter Palace in October 1917.

"Where are you off to then?" Inver demanded as he moved towards the door.

"I'm going for a walk, Stan. I always take one before breakfast."

"I wish I'd known that; I would have come with you."

Ashton said he would bear that in mind tomorrow and got out before the older man could ask him to hang on a minute. He took the lift down to the ground floor, checked the tour itinerary for the day displayed on the notice board in the lobby, then went out into Moskovskiy Prospekt and turned left.

Ashton walked on past the vast war memorial to the defenders of Leningrad with its towering obelisk and twice life-size figures in bronze that had been erected in Victory Square on an island in the centre of the eight-lane avenue. Although it would have been difficult to use the phone in their room with Stanley around, the real stumbling block had been the absence of a local directory. No doubt the hotel switchboard operator would have been delighted to assist him, but she would automatically log all outgoing calls, and that was the last thing he wanted.

He crossed the road by the pedestrian lights and continued on towards the city centre. There were no big department stores on the avenue, only a string of dingy shops which looked as though the builders had only just moved out. The art of window dressing was nonexistent but with precious few goods available for sale, there was no need to entice a would-be buyer to step inside.

The bank of pay phones was about two hundred yards up the street from the hotel. Ashton ducked under the nearest perspex hood, pulled out the directory from the lower shelf and looked to see if Galina's mother was listed under her own family name or former married name. There was, he discovered, a Lydia Petrovskaya with an address on Nevsky Prospekt.

He stared at the phone, suddenly torn with indecision. If the KGB hadn't arrested Lydia Petrovskaya when Galina had gone

76

AWOL, they would certainly have put a tap on her line and might also have bugged the apartment while she was out at work. On the other hand, he could hardly walk into her office at the Hermitage without any forewarning.

Ashton lifted the receiver, found it was in working order and fed a five-kopek coin into the slot, then dialled the local code and subscriber's number. The woman who answered the phone had a brisk manner and a voice to match it. He asked if he was talking to Lydia Petrovskaya, then gave his real name and informed her that he was a technical author employed by British Aerospace.

"What has this to do with me?" she demanded, interrupting him.

"I'm coming to that," Ashton said. "It so happens that I occasionally contribute articles of general interest to the in-house journal and I've been asked to do one on the Hermitage. However, the editor is not interested in a rehash of the stuff you can find in any old guide book and is looking for something different. For instance, a lot of people in England would like to know what happened to the artefacts when the city was besieged for nine hundred days during the war."

"I think you are talking to the wrong person," Lydia Petrovskaya said curtly.

"You are one of the curators . . ."

"I'm aware of that."

"I sought advice from Intourist and your name was mentioned by Eduard Turkin – or was it Tulbukin? Anyway, I was advised that you might be able to help me."

"When will you be coming to the museum?"

To Ashton, she sounded calm and unruffled. Although there had been a momentary hesitation before she had replied, he thought that anybody who had just received a phone call from a perfect stranger would have behaved in a similar fashion. The important thing was that Tulbukin's name had triggered the response he'd hoped for.

"This afternoon at two o'clock," he said.

"I am not sure I shall be free then."

"Please try, I'm only in Leningrad for a couple of days."

"Very well, I'll see what I can do."

"So how do I find you?"

77

"That's easy," Lydia Petrovskaya told him. "Just ask for me at the ticket kiosk opposite the main entrance."

Tony Zale spotted a vacant space a few yards up the road from 16 Krahmerstrasse and reckoned there was just enough room for his car. On closer inspection, the slot was not as big as he had thought, but by dint of manoeuvring, he managed to squeeze his Audi 100 between a BMW and a Mercedes. Although car thefts were virtually unknown in this particular neighbourhood of the Lichterfelde District, Zale was a naturally cautious man who never left anything to chance. Despite central locking, he tried all four doors to make sure they were properly secured before he crossed the street and walked back to Number 16.

The house stood back from the road and was partially hidden from view by a group of fir trees. Additional privacy was provided by the Schlosspark in rear of the property which was one of the few private residences in Berlin to have survived the war intact. He had happy memories of dining there on several occasions with the Osmondes and it saddened him to think this would be the last time he would set foot inside the house. With the measured tread of a pallbearer at a funeral, he walked slowly past the Vauxhall Astra parked in the driveway and rang the doorbell.

It was answered by Karen, the Osmondes' youngest daughter and a former cheerleader at Ohio State who had been voted the most popular girl of her year and the one most likely to succeed. Zale had been Karen's most devoted admirer from the day he had first met her and he had never been able to figure out what she had seen in the Brit she had married.

"Tony," she said. "What a nice surprise. I was just thinking about you."

There was warmth in her smile and in her voice and he would have rolled over and died for her if she'd wanted him to. "You were?" Zale cleared his throat. "I'm not intruding, am I? Only when they told me you were packing up the house, I thought I'd drop by to see if you could use some help."

"You're not intruding, and Mom did most of the packing before she left for Frankfurt. It's good to see you, Tony, so come on in."

"Thanks." Zale stepped inside the hall. "How are your mom and dad? Have you heard from them since they went home?"

Ten days after he had been shot, Lloyd Osmonde had been transferred to the US Army's base hospital at Frankfurt where he had been detained for a further week before being flown back to the States.

"They're both fine," Karen assured him. "Dad's in the Veterans' Hospital in San Francisco but is expecting to be discharged any day now. The Defense Intelligence Agency is allowing him to retire ten months early. But I guess you already know that?"

"I had heard." Zale followed her into the living room, looked disconsolately at the wooden packing crates which, with one exception, had been nailed down and stacked in the centre of the room to await collection. "I'm retiring too," he added.

"You can't be serious."

"The people in Washington are. They've made it pretty clear that there is no future for me in the Agency."

"But that's not fair," Karen said angrily.

"Your dad and I had some bad luck, that's all. We were in the wrong place at the wrong time and were caught up in a wrong situation. It happens."

"What are they saying at the Pentagon? That Yuri Rostovsky was just a pimp and a racketeer?"

"Something like that. Anyway, they want me out of here. Not right away of course because that would look as if we were responding to pressure from the German authorities." Zale smiled ruefully. "I'm not exactly Heinrich Voigt's favourite American."

"I have something here that will make him change his mind." Karen walked over to the desk, picked up a notepad and gave it to him. "Mom rang last night to say Dad wanted you to have it."

"Yeah? What is it?"

"A record of every conversation he had with Yuri Rostovsky," Karen told him.

The official guide had been superfluous. Inver had brought his copy of Baedeker with him on the city tour and had bent Ashton's ear with a nonstop running commentary from the moment their coach had turned on to Nevsky Prospekt until they had stopped for lunch in the shadow of St Isaac's Cathedral. The Admiralty building, Palace Bridge, the Rostra Columns at Strelka Point on the Neva, the Peter and Paul Fortress, the Bronze Horseman, the

Winter Palace, the Field of Mars and the Smolny Convent; there hadn't been a single landmark Inver hadn't identified before the guide had drawn their attention to it.

Ashton had treated Inver to a liquid lunch at the Astoria Hotel in the hope that several large gins and the combination of a hot afternoon would slow him up. Unfortunately, Stanley was a beer drinker and could sup ale all day without it having the slightest effect on him. If anything, he was even more loquacious when they boarded the coach again for the short journey to Palace Square.

"One of the world's truly great squares," Inver informed him before they arrived there. "On one side you've got the Winter Palace, on the other is the bow-shaped General Staff Headquarters with a massive double arch linking the two wings of the building. The six hundred and fifty-ton, hundred and fifty-six-feet-high Alexander Column in the centre is a monument to the Russian victory over Napoleon."

"You mind if I have a look at your guide book, Stan?" Ashton said, interrupting him in full spate.

"No, go ahead."

The sights were listed in alphabetical order for easy reference. Unlike most entries, the one for the Hermitage ran to several pages, but it was the sketch map showing the lay-out of the ground floor rather than the accompanying text which interested Ashton. They would enter the museum from Palace Square whereas Lydia Petrovskaya's office was somewhere between the Jordan staircase and the ticket kiosk opposite the front entrance. Somehow he would have to lose the group without Inver making a three-act drama out of it, and that wasn't going to be easy. The official guide would be far too busy to notice his short absence and the other twenty-two members of the group were unlikely to be a problem. They had the measure of Stanley Inver and had collectively decided to give the two of them a very wide berth.

"We're here, Pete, my old son."

"So we are."

Ashton returned the guide book and followed him off the coach. One of the less endearing things about Inver was his habit of calling him Pete, but there were compensations. With Stanley constantly in attendance, no one else in the group was tempted to get friendly with him, which enabled him to remain a grey figure in the background. There were at least eight other groups waiting to enter the Hermitage and it was easy to get separated from the rest of the party. But not from Inver; the older man was like a sheep dog determined to round up the strays.

"I've got to find somewhere to take a leak," Ashton told him. "You go on with the others and I'll catch you up."

Ashton moved purposefully to his left, mingled with a group of German tourists, then walked on again to make his way in a clockwise direction towards the Jordan staircase. Approaching one of the attendants on duty near the ticket kiosk, he told her that he had an appointment to see Curator Lydia Petrovskaya at two o'clock and was directed to her office.

Galina Kutuzova had dark hair, high cheekbones, a sensual mouth and a straight Roman nose and in no way resembled her mother. Lydia Petrovskaya had light brown hair, eyes to match, a round face and a button nose. The room she shared with three male colleagues looked out on to the south embankment of the Neva opposite the Peter and Paul fortress. At a rough guess, Ashton thought it was about sixteen feet by twelve which meant there was just enough space for the desks and chairs plus an extra ladderback for visitors. Whatever the exact dimensions of the office, the close proximity of the other curators ruled out any question of a quiet tête-à-tête about her daughter.

"I'm Peter Ashton," he told her. "We spoke this morning."

"Ah, yes, you are the English journalist who wants to write about our museum."

"Well, that's only partly correct. What my editor is looking for is a story about what happened to the Hermitage during the Great Patriotic War."

Lydia Petrovskaya said that was quite understood and handed him some notes on the Hermitage in English that had been run off on an office duplicator and stapled together. She hoped he would find them useful, but if they were not exactly what he was after, perhaps he would like to come back and she would try the mayor's office to see what they had on the great siege of Leningrad. Ashton found himself retreating from the room as she steered him inexorably towards the door. As soon as they were outside in the corridor, she plucked the notes from his hand and still talking, flipped through the pages before returning them upside down. Written on the back of the penultimate page were the words "Gostinyj Dvor, Nevsky Prospekt 35."

"What time?" Ashton asked her in a low voice.

"Six o'clock. Wait for me in the right-hand lower gallery nearest the entrance."

Ashton nodded, shook hands with her for the benefit of the attendant on duty near the ticket kiosk, then walked away and used the ornate Jordan staircase to reach the first floor. Once there, he carefully folded the notes in four and tucked them into the hip pocket of his slacks before trying to find Stanley Inver and the rest of the group. After fruitlessly quartering the Winter Palace, he finally caught up with them at the exhibition of Dutch art from the seventeenth century in the New Hermitage Wing.

"Almost given you up for lost," Inver muttered out of the corner of his mouth. "Where've you been?"

"I had a run in with one of the cloakroom attendants."

"Typical," Inver snorted. "What happened to glasnost?"

"The lady was giving it a rest."

The tour party gradually moved back into the Winter Palace, taking in a collection of eighteenth century porcelain on the way. Even before they set foot on the second floor, several members of the party were beginning to look as if they were in a trance. A further ninety minutes spent on the French Impressionists and the ancient cultures of the East reduced even the indefatigable Inver to a comatose state. By the time the group left the Hermitage, Stanley was only too ready to go back to the hotel and could only shake his head in wonder when Ashton elected to stay in town, ostensibly to shop on Nevsky Prospekt.

With over an hour to kill before he was due to meet Lydia Petrovskaya, Ashton made his way to the metro station and caught a train to Gorkovskaya, the next stop up the line. From there, he walked to Peter the Great's cottage and then on to the Great Neva where the *Aurora* was moored. Built at the turn of the century, the coal-burning light cruiser had taken part in the Russo-Japanese War four years later but was chiefly noted for firing the blank shot which had signalled the storming of the Winter Palace on the twenty-fifth of October 1917. When Ashton eventually returned to Nevsky Prospekt, the evening rush hour was well under way.

The Gostinyj Dvor was Leningrad's equivalent of the GUM

store in Moscow. A neoclassical building with the main entrance on Nevsky Prospekt, it occupied a complete city block and although roughly quadrilateral in shape, no two sides were parallel. It was quite unlike any department store in the West. Food, clothes and household goods were sold from stalls like some jumble sale in a vast church hall.

Lydia Petrovskaya arrived a few minutes after six and greeted him as though they were close friends. Her daughter was a deserter and for all Gorbachev's talk of a more open society, Ashton couldn't see the KGB leaving her unmolested. But if she was being followed by the secret police, there were no outward signs of nervousness. According to Peachey's defector, she was a very cool, very tough number and having met her face to face, he could well believe it.

"I want to meet Galina," Ashton told her as they walked side by side towards the far end of the lower gallery. "I believe you know where she is."

"You are mistaken . . ."

"If you love your daughter, you'd better start trusting me because her life is in danger."

"What nonsense . . ."

"She was with an English officer called Whittle minutes before his car was blown to pieces by a bomb. She is lucky to be alive because whoever murdered him, meant to kill her too."

"I am not going to listen to any more of your lies . . ."

"She had another friend called Yuri Rostovsky," Ashton continued harshly. "He was shot to death outside a café in West Berlin. Now Galina is running scared because she was expecting him to join her."

"I know nothing."

"Galina told us you were devoted to each other and we are certain you have heard from her since she went absent without leave." It was a shot in the dark but a sharp intake of breath from Lydia Petrovskaya told him he had hit the target. "How long do you suppose she can last without money?"

"She has facilities."

"Where? In France?"

"Switzerland. My father opened an account for her in Zürich." Her mouth twisted in a sour grimace. "All the KGB senior officers have money in foreign banks. So do the politicians."

"Is Galina going to stay in Switzerland?"

Lydia shook her head. "No. My daughter's eyes are on the promised land."

"Where's that – America?"

"It isn't England." Lydia Petrovskaya walked a little slower, then stopped and turned to face him, suddenly tense. "You must go now, we'll talk again."

"When?"

"Tonight. I have friends in the Kalininski District. They have an apartment at Suvorov Street 136." She repeated the address, then told him how to get there and exactly where he was to wait for her. "You will come, won't you?" she asked, searching his face anxiously.

"Of course I will."

"Only it's very important."

"I'll be there, that's a promise."

"Good. Now shake hands and don't look back when you leave me."

Ashton obeyed her instructions to the letter and walked out into the street. The sky had clouded over while he had been in the store and there was a distant rumble of thunder in the air. He wondered if it was an omen.

The Russian champagne cost the equivalent of one pound a bottle from the bar on the third floor of the Hotel Polkovskaya. Ashton had bought two bottles, had helped Inver drink one and then left him half-cut to consume the other on his own while he went out for a breath of fresh air, or so he told Inver.

Although the rain had stopped while they were having dinner earlier in the evening, the sky had remained overcast, creating the impression that nightfall was approaching sooner than usual. Leaving the hotel, Ashton walked to the metro in Moskovskiy Prospekt, shelled out five kopeks for the fare, then rode the escalator down to the platform almost five hundred feet below. Even though it was only just nine o'clock, there were very few people about and the train was three parts empty when it pulled into the station. At the Technological Institute five stops farther on, he changed on to the Red Line and went on out to Komsomolskaya.

Suvorov Street, in the industrial northeast of the city, was a concrete jungle of soulless apartment blocks, uneven pavements and grass verges that had been allowed to grow knee-high. The winter frosts had eaten into the road leaving large zig-zag cracks in the asphalt, while close into the kerbside, the surface had actually begun to crumble away in places. The neighbourhood was a good two miles from the metro station and was served by a tram that ran every twenty minutes during off-peak hours.

There was nothing to distinguish 136 Suvorov Street from the other dreary apartment blocks, each of which looked as if the housing cooperative had simply modified some architect's plan of an army barracks for civilian use. In practice, this meant that every flat, other than those on the ground floor, had a small balcony. The areas between each apartment block had not been landscaped and no provision had been made for those residents who were fortunate enough to own a Lada saloon.

Ashton sat down on the park bench some two hundred yards from the tram stop where Lydia Petrovskaya had told him to wait while she persuaded her friends to entertain a complete stranger. He hadn't spotted a tail when she had met him at the Gostinyj Dvor earlier on and there were no obvious signs of a stake-out in the immediate neighbourhood. Galina Kutuzova had gone absent on Friday the twenty-fourth of May; eleven weeks later, it was conceivable that the KGB had relaxed their surveillance on her mother and were content merely to keep a wire tap on her phone. He also drew comfort from the fact that Lydia Petrovskaya was the daughter of the former boss of the Fifth Chief Directorate and was not exactly a greenhorn in these matters. If they had followed her from the apartment on Nevsky Prospekt, she would not show up at the rendezvous.

The two men appeared from nowhere. Ashton assumed they had come from the apartment block behind him but they hadn't made a sound as they approached the park bench where he was sitting, and he thought that was a mite ominous. They were in their late twenties or early thirties and looked capable of taking care of themselves while making a lot of trouble for other people. The taller of the two wore a leather jacket over a blue T-shirt with the bottom half of a paratrooper's combat suit. His companion had acquired a pair of Doc Martens, jeans and a check shirt.

"Give me a light," the taller man demanded.

It was not a good moment to pretend he didn't understand Russian. "Sorry, I don't smoke," Ashton said politely.

"I don't have a cigarette either, don't have the money to buy a packet."

"Neither do I."

The taller man half turned to face his friend. "We've got a real bright one here, Igor," he said and laughed harshly.

Ashton rose from the bench seat only to catch a vicious left hook to the jaw that virtually ended the fight there and then. As he started to go down, the smaller man grabbed his wrists and held them behind his back in a vicelike grip while his companion used him for a punchbag. The Russian hit him with everything he had, short arm jabs to the stomach, ribs and face. Finally a knee crunched into his abdomen and all the lights went out.

CHAPTER 9

ASHTON CAME to face down on the ground behind a clump of unruly bushes which screened him from the road. The plane trees above had afforded little or no protection from the cloudburst which had soaked him to the skin. His whole body from the waist up was one big ache and his left eye had closed to a narrow slit. His nose was swollen, both nostrils were blocked with congealed blood and the bottom lip was split. Slowly and very painfully he turned over and sat up. He raised his left arm to see what time it was and discovered the muggers had stolen his wristwatch. It was only then that he realised they had also stolen his shoes, showerproof summer anorak, Lacoste sports shirt and the leather wallet in his hip pocket which contained his credit card, Lloyds Premier Account card and three hundred US dollars in cash. They had even taken the wad of roubles out of his trouser pocket, leaving him only the small change which amounted to seventy-five kopeks in denominations of fives and tens.

He got to his feet like an old man with arthritis, a grinding ache in his groin where one of the bastards had kneed him. The bushes and plane trees were about thirty yards from the bench seat where he had been attacked and he assumed the muggers had dragged him into the copse when he was unconscious. Hidden from view, they had then stripped him to the waist and taken his wallet and Omega wristwatch. Obviously no one had witnessed the attack and Lydia Petrovskaya must have concluded that he had failed to show up at the rendezvous when she had been unable to find him. Now the shoe was metaphorically on the other foot. He didn't know the name of her friends or the number of their flat at 136 Suvorov Street so there was no way he could get in touch with her. His only hope was to find a pay phone, ring the Hotel Polkovskaya and get the switchboard to put him through to their room. He just hoped Stanley Inver was sober enough to hear the phone ringing.

Ashton left the copse and started to follow the tramlines, knowing they would eventually lead him to the metro. There were no other pedestrians about and it looked as though the whole neighbourhood had gone to bed. He was cold, wet through and angry with himself for getting caught by a sucker punch he should have seen coming a mile off. He was only marginally less angry about being robbed. Although his insurance company policy would cover the wristwatch, money and clothes that had been stolen, he hadn't brought any traveller's cheques with him and in taking the three hundred US dollars, they'd cleaned him out. It was, Ashton thought, a damned good thing that the hotel had retained his passport or he really would be in trouble.

He walked on in the rain, hugging himself to try and keep warm. Approximately ten minutes later, he heard a vehicle some distance behind him and instinctively moved back from the road into the shadow of the trees and saplings flanking the pavement. A relatively quiet engine told him he was looking at the headlights of a car; with the streetlights roughly a hundred yards apart, he also calculated that the driver was doing between fifteen and twenty miles an hour.

As he watched, the vehicle gradually came to a halt, roughly in line with the bench seat where he had waited for Lydia Petrovskaya. Two men got out and started to search the immediate area with their flashlights before working back towards the apartment block directly in the rear. They were too far away from his position and the nearest streetlight for him to see what they were wearing. But it didn't matter; KGB or militia, they were looking for him. What started out as a hunch became a conviction with the arrival of a second vehicle from the opposite direction. No car this time but a truck of some kind with six to eight men in it, if the noise they made jumping down on to the road was anything to go by.

To lie still in the hope that they would miss him was out of the question. The cover wasn't thick enough and the eight men were now advancing in line abreast like a row of beaters on a shoot. Besides, he didn't want some trigger-happy Russian blowing his head off a split second after tripping over him. Ashton moved out into the open and stood there waiting for them to close on him. Their flashlights danced and weaved across the ground like giant fireflies in the dark until at last one settled on his legs before moving swiftly upwards. The beam played on his face, dazzling his one good eye; then a voice from the darkness told him to put his hands up. It was pointless to pretend he didn't understand a word of Russian; even Stanley Inver whose vocabulary was limited to "da" and "nyet" would have got the message.

"Don't shoot," he shouted back in English and raised both arms head high.

They ran towards him from all directions, eager to make the arrest. A few lights appeared in the windows of the nearest apartment block and some of the more adventurous residents came out on to their balconies to see what was going on. Ashton played the idiot tourist and kept talking in English in the hope of compelling them to send for an interpreter which would give him more time to work something out. One of the militiamen cuffed his wrists behind him, then two others ran him over to the Zil truck and heaved him into the back of the vehicle like a sack of potatoes. The rest of the squad piled into the Zil after him, leaving the NCO in charge to raise the tailgate and lock it in position. The militiaman sitting next to Ashton grabbed a handful of his hair and twisted him round to face the cab so that he shouldn't see where he was being taken.

The battery sounded as though it was on its last legs but eventually the driver managed to coax the engine into life and get it firing on all six cylinders. The grating clunk announced he'd engaged first gear and they moved off, slowly gathering momentum, the propshaft whining in protest. Ashton started counting – one thousand, two thousand, three thousand, four thousand – the only way he could gauge the passage of time. According to this rough reckoning, they had been travelling for approximately fourteen minutes when the driver slowed right down, made a sharp left turn and bumped over cobblestones before coming to a halt. When he alighted from the truck, Ashton found himself in an enclosed courtyard. A few minutes later, he was in the windowless charge room facing the oxlike figure of the desk sergeant.

The room was painted a bilious shade of green and with the exception of a table, wooden armchair and collapsible bench, was as bare as a monk's cell. The bench was occupied by a girl with a black eye that matched her lacquered hair and the leather miniskirt she was wearing. Her eye injury also went some way to explaining her torn blouse.

"Is this the man?" the sergeant asked her.

The girl stood up, walked over to where Ashton was standing and looked him in the eye, then slapped his face as hard as she could. "That's the bastard," she screamed.

Ashton knew she was going to spit in his face and jerked his head out of the way, but was a shade too slow; the glob of sputum landed on the side of his neck and trickled down on to his chest.

"What the hell's going on?" he shouted. "I don't speak Russki. I am English. Je suis Anglais. Ich bin ein Engländer. Understand? I demand to see a doctor."

The sergeant hadn't understood a word; however, he didn't care for his tone and said so, loud and clear. Ashton didn't get to see a doctor; instead, the militia rushed him down to the basement and showed him the inside of a cell.

The handcuffs bit into his wrists cutting off the circulation. Long before the militiamen fetched him out of the cell, Ashton had lost all feeling in the thumbs and fingers of both hands. The numbness didn't extend to his limbs although the two guards seemed to think it did. Once outside the cell, they grabbed an arm apiece and ran him down to an interview room at the far end of the corridor.

The interview room was decorated in the same bilious green as upstairs, also lacked a window and was lit by a neon tube. The furniture consisted of a table and three chairs which was an improvement on the desk sergeant's inventory. Two men were waiting to interrogate him; both were in civilian clothes.

"I am Chief Investigator Chebrakin from the Prosecutor's Office," the elder one said in English, then pointed to his companion. "And this is Comrade Fomenko, the official interpreter who will assist me should the necessity arise. This interview is being recorded; typed copies will be produced in both languages and you will be given one of each for comparison."

"Terrific."

"The time now is 0145 hours on Sunday the eleventh of August."

"Thanks for telling me."

"And your name is?"

"Suppose we take the handcuffs off first?"

Chebrakin nodded, then spoke to the militiaman standing behind Ashton and curtly ordered him to remove the manacles. The tingling sensation began in his fingertips and rapidly spread to his wrists as the blood started flowing again.

"Your name please?" the chief investigator repeated.

"Ashton, Peter Ashton. I'm an English tourist staying at the Hotel Polkovskaya on Ploschad Pobedy."

"Well now, Mr Ashton, I have to tell you that you are accused of aggravated assault and attempted rape contrary to Sections . . ."

"Who's the plaintiff?" Ashton demanded, interrupting the chief investigator.

"The what?"

"The aggrieved party," Fomenko said, translating the question into Russian.

"Ah yes." Chebrakin turned to Ashton. "She is Elena Maisky of Tarasova Road 423, Gavan District, the young lady you met in the charge room."

"Young lady? You've got to be joking; she must have a record as long as your arm for soliciting. Or isn't that an offence under the Soviet Penal Code?"

"We are not concerned with that issue now. A taxi driver found Elena Maisky wandering along Suvorov Street in a distressed condition . . ."

Ashton held up his hands. "Look at them, Chief Investigator. The woman has a black eye – do you see any marks on my knuckles? Are they swollen?"

Chebrakin sighed. "We shall make much better progress, Mr Ashton, if you would stop interrupting and allow me to finish what I have to say. After I have summarised the evidence for the prosecution you may make a statement in your defence."

"I'm sorry," Ashton said. "Please continue, I won't say another word."

It was pointless to antagonise Chebrakin. There were no British Consulates in the USSR, the embassy in Moscow was four hundred miles away and it was no use expecting the tour representative to get him out of this mess. He was therefore on his own, and a hostile chief investigator from the Prosecutor's Office could only make things worse for him.

"The taxi driver brought Elena Maisky to this precinct station where she gave a description of the man who had attacked her and was also able to tell the duty officer exactly where the incident had occurred. A mobile patrol which happened to be near the area was alerted and a backup squad was also mobilised and despatched to Suvorov Street. Subsequently, you were arrested and brought here where you were then formally identified by Elena Maisky." Chebrakin took time out to light a pungent cigarette. "What do you have to say about that?" he asked presently.

"Plenty. The first time I saw Elena Maisky was when the militia brought me to this precinct. It's got to be a case of mistaken identity because I never laid a finger on her . . ."

"Laid a finger? What is that?"

"It means I didn't hit her," Ashton explained patiently. "I don't know who did but it's possible she was attacked by one of the two muggers who robbed me. I can hardly see out of my left eye, I've got a split lip, my nose is swollen, my ribs feel sore and my stomach is badly bruised. After they had beaten me senseless, they stole my shoes, the shirt off my back, an Omega wristwatch and a wallet containing three hundred American dollars. Are you saying all this happened after I had supposedly tried to rape Elena Maisky? Hell, if I had assaulted the girl, do you think I would have stayed in the neighbourhood?"

"What were you doing in Suvorov Street at 2200 hours, Mr Ashton? There's nothing in the Kalininski District to interest a tourist."

"I wondered when you were going to ask me that question."

"Then you should be able to answer it."

"I wanted to meet a typical Russian family . . ."

"You what?" Chebrakin said incredulously.

"I went out for a walk and I met this taxi driver on Moskovskiy Prospekt and we got talking about what life was like in Russia . . ."

"He spoke English, this driver?"

"Enough to get by on," Ashton said. "Anyway, he asked me if I would like to meet his family and I said yes please."

Chebrakin stubbed out his cigarette. "Does this man have a name?" he asked.

"Boris Yegorov. Of course I didn't ask to see his identity card, so he could have been lying. Come to think of it, he probably was. When we got to the apartment block on Suvorov Street where he said he lived, Boris asked me to wait outside while he warned his family they had a visitor. Soon after he disappeared inside the building, I was beaten up by two muggers and I never saw him again." Ashton frowned. "You don't suppose Boris set me up, do you?"

"Set you up?" Chebrakin repeated, looking blank.

"He thinks this Boris Yegorov may have been in league with the robbers," Fomenko explained helpfully.

"And I think our English friend has a very fertile imagination."

"Is this how you treat a guest in your country?" Take it easy, Ashton counselled himself, don't overdo it; you need to sound hurt and disappointed rather than angry. "All right, I admit I was naïve. Our guide warned us it wasn't safe to wander around Leningrad after dark, but I thought Tatiana was exaggerating. So okay, you can say what happened to me was my fault, but I've been here for well over three hours now and no one has examined my injuries or attempted to clean me up." He shook his head sorrowfully. "I don't think that's right," he said in an injured tone of voice.

"I will get a doctor to have a look at you."

"Thanks." Ashton looked up, his face assuming a hopeful expression. "Could you also telephone the Hotel Polkovskaya and let Stanley Inver know I'm okay? He's in Room 464 and will be wondering what has happened to me because I told him I was just going out for a breath of fresh air."

"Yes."

"And then there is Tatiana, our Russian guide, and Denise, the tour representative. I don't know their room numbers, but they ought to be told where I am."

"Is there anyone else you would like us to inform? The British Embassy in Moscow perhaps?"

"Not unless you think it's necessary."

Chebrakin nodded, then waved a hand towards the door. Ashton assumed the gesture was meant to convey something to the militiamen standing behind him and knew what it was the moment he felt a hand on his shoulder.

"Are you going to charge me?" he asked.

"That's up to the State Prosecutor."

The hand on Ashton's shoulder was joined by another which took hold of his arm and between them, the two men led him back to the cell. Shortly thereafter, a young intern from the Marx Engels Ophthalmic Hospital arrived to examine him.

The drunk had been put into the adjoining cell at 0340 hours or thereabouts. Ashton had been able to fix the time with some degree of accuracy because there was a small window just below the ceiling, at ground level, and with the summer solstice past its zenith, daybreak was now at 0330 and the prisoner next door had arrived approximately ten minutes after first light.

For the better part of an hour, the Russian had created bedlam, singing, cursing and shouting obscenities at the top of his voice. He had hammered on the door of his cell with his fists and had kicked it repeatedly while letting everyone within earshot know what he thought of Mikhail and Raisa Gorbachev, the Politburo and the whole fucking Communist Party of the Soviet Union. Fucking was a word he had used with monotonous regularity, as a verb, adjective, collective noun or punctuation mark. His antics had roused most of the other inmates in the cell block and had provoked a near riot.

The noise had finally disturbed the militiamen upstairs and retribution had followed swiftly. They had bounced the drunk off all four walls, clubbed him about the body and then put the boot in. Peace of a kind had returned after they had clumped out of the cell and left him moaning on the floor. A few minutes before he had dozed off, Ashton thought he heard the Russian throw up.

The sound of running water roused him briefly but he was too exhausted to pay much attention to the low murmur of voices in the corridor. He drifted back to sleep again and remembered nothing more until a gruff voice told him to get up. For a moment he almost forgot that he wasn't supposed to understand Russian. The turnkey, however, didn't notice anything and he remained in a squatting position until the Russian lost his temper, grabbed a fistful of hair and hauled him to his feet and then out into the corridor.

The door of the adjoining cell was wide open, the floor swimming in water. There was no bedboard, no urinal bucket and no sign of the drunk, only a strong smell of disinfectant. Suddenly, the low murmur of voices Ashton had heard earlier on began to have sinister implications. The militiaman answered his unspoken question with a thumbs down. "Dead drunk," he added and roared with laughter at his own witticism.

The man had either died from the injuries he had received when the guards had beaten him up or else he had drowned in his own vomit. Either way, he had snuffed it and disappeared without trace. It made Ashton realise just how vulnerable he was himself and sent a shiver down his spine.

Chief Investigator Chebrakin was waiting for him in the same interview room but this time it seemed he didn't need the services of an interpreter. He told the militiaman to leave them, then pointed to the chair positioned in front of the table and invited Ashton to sit down.

"I'd like you to describe the two men who attacked you," he said without any preamble.

Ashton wondered why the chief investigator hadn't asked him that four or five hours ago when he had first interrogated him, wondered too what had happened since then to arouse his interest.

Noticing his hesitation, Chebrakin said, "Don't tell me you can't remember what they looked like."

He wasn't far out. Ashton could remember what they had been wearing but not much else. He found himself struggling to convert their physical characteristics from feet, inches and pounds into metres, centimetres and kilos. One assailant shorter than the other, no visible distinguishing marks on either man, both in their late twenties or early thirties; the descriptions were vague enough to apply to half the male population of Leningrad.

"The shorter one was called Igor," Ashton concluded lamely.

"That could be helpful," Chebrakin said without a trace of irony. "Who knows? Perhaps this Igor has a criminal record."

"Well, I'd certainly recognise his face if I saw him again."

"Would you?"

Although Chebrakin left the room without saying another word, Ashton had every reason to believe the chief investigator intended to show him some mugshots of known criminals. He was therefore more than a little surprised when the Russian returned some minutes later with a pair of shoes and a complete change of clothing.

"That's right," Chebrakin told him, smiling, "they're yours."

"I don't understand . . ."

"Your friends brought them. They are waiting for you upstairs."

"You mean I'm free to go?"

"Yes. I have questioned Elena Maisky at length and she has admitted that you were not the man who struck her. She told me she was angry and frightened and ready to accuse the first man who was unfortunate enough to be paraded in front of her. She will of course be prosecuted for making a false accusation."

"I see."

"These things can not go unpunished." Chebrakin waited until he had finished dressing, then placed an official-looking form on the table and handed him a pen. "If you would please sign this," he said, looking embarrassed.

"What is it?" Ashton had read the heading at the top of the form and already knew what he was being asked to sign, but it was important to keep up the pretence that the Cyrillic alphabet was a closed book to him.

"It's a release form saying that you have been well treated while you were in custody."

"Why not? I've got a sense of humour too."

Ashton scrawled his signature across the foot of the page in the space provided and gave the fountain pen back to Chebrakin. In return, the Russian gave him a pair of sunglasses to hide his black eye.

"A little present to remember me by," he murmured awkwardly.

"Well, thank you," Ashton said, "though I am sure I shan't forget you, Chief Investigator."

A worried-looking Stanley Inver was waiting for him in the charge room upstairs, along with Denise, the tour representative. Both were relieved to see him, both had any number of questions they wanted to ask but they managed to contain themselves until they were safely on the way back to the hotel in a taxi. In satisfying their curiosity, Ashton stuck basically to the story he had given Chebrakin, but added a few embellishments.

"Didn't I tell you to watch your step?" Inver said when he'd finished.

"That you did, Stanley, and I should have listened to you. Still, it's not likely to happen again; they took every penny I had, so I'll not be wandering far."

"You don't have to hang around the hotel all the time. I've got a hundred in cash, half of it is yours."

"I can't let you do that, Stanley."

"Of course you can; we're mates, aren't we?"

"I guess we are," Ashton said humbly.

"Well, that's settled then. You can repay me when we're back in England. Of course, right now the best thing you can do is grab a few hours' shut-eye."

Ashton assured him it was one piece of advice he intended to follow. Once in bed, sleep came easily but it wasn't restful. In his dreams, he kept seeing Galina Kutuzova and her mother. They were always smiling and beckoning him on but each time he was on the point of catching up with them, they disappeared and all he could hear was their mocking laughter.

Chapter 10

A COMBINATION of factors roused Ashton – the sun playing on his face, the muggy atmosphere in the room, the hard bed. The combined clock and wake-up alarm built into the bedside table did the rest when it dawned on him that the hands were registering 1345 hours. Suddenly wide awake, he swung his feet out on to the floor and sat up on the edge of the bed. Propped against a tumbler was an envelope addressed to him; opening it, he found it contained fifty pounds, three hundred roubles and a note from Stanley Inver to say he had gone on a boat trip and would be back around five. The roubles, he discovered, were intended to tide him over until the foreign exchange bureau opened on Monday. His "mate", it seemed, had thought of everything.

Ashton walked stiffly into the bathroom. The face which confronted him in the mirror above the washbasin still looked as though it belonged on a Wanted poster. His nose, however, did not appear to be quite as swollen as it had been a few hours ago, but that was the only improvement he could see. He took a quick shower, shaved and got dressed, then removed the "Do not disturb" sign hanging on the door and went down to the snack bar on the third floor. Over a belated breakfast of cold ham and near white bread, he did a lot of thinking, mostly about Lydia Petrovskaya and just how much she had been responsible for what had happened last night.

It had been Lydia Petrovskaya who had asked him to meet her in Suvorov Street at nine thirty p.m. and had stressed just how important it was that he shouldn't let her down. His presence on that bench seat had been vital all right; if he had failed to show up at the rendezvous, the KGB would have concluded that she had double-crossed them and would have come knocking on her door. There was no longer any doubt in his mind that the two men who had attacked him had been working for the KGB. If it hadn't been for Elena Maisky, he would have gone on believing that he was merely one more statistic in Leningrad's rising crime rate.

A few years ago, the KGB would have arranged for him to meet with a fatal accident in the certain knowledge that their version of the truth would receive the full backing of the State. Today, things were different; today, they couldn't be sure how the authorities would react. So they had concocted what they had thought was a sophisticated plan to get him deported, only they had made the mistake of hiring the criminal fraternity to do the dirty work for them. Instead of blacking an eye and inflicting a few scratches on his face, the two muggers had gone into business on their own account and had picked him clean. The results of their handiwork had made a mockery of Elena Maisky's story and left her wallowing in the shit. And they had also reckoned without Chief Investigator Chebrakin, an honest policeman who could recognise a frame-up when he saw one and had declined to charge him with assault and attempted rape.

It was a likely explanation, but without supporting evidence, it would remain nothing more than a plausible theory. Any one of three people could substantiate it – Lydia Petrovskaya, chief investigator Chebrakin or Elena Maisky. The chief investigator was a nonstarter; whatever their nationality, men like Chebrakin were decidedly wary of civilians who they considered were poking their noses into police business. Even if she was no longer in custody, Elena Maisky would be too scared of the KGB to answer any of his questions.

That left Lydia Petrovskaya. He had always worked on the assumption that the KGB had tapped her phone shortly after her daughter, Galina Kutuzova, had gone over the hill. It seemed logical to assume that sometime after he had talked to Lydia early yesterday morning and before they had met at the Hermitage, she had been visited by the KGB. They had sanctioned their meeting, chosen the Gostinyj Dvor for a rendezvous and coached her in what to say. But they hadn't been able to control their puppet a hundred per cent of the time. Who was it who had told him that General Nikolai Yakulevich Petrovsky had opened a bank account in Zürich for his granddaughter, Galina Kutuzova? That was one item that hadn't been scripted by the KGB. And maybe the implication that Galina had her eyes on the States was another?

Ashton swallowed the rest of his coffee and pushed the cup and saucer aside. The lady was worth another visit. Of course, she would still be under surveillance, but after last night's fiasco, he couldn't see the KGB chancing their arm a second time within twenty-four hours. Although the roof might not have fallen in on them, the rafters weren't holding up too well. Everything pointed to a small clique of officers acting on their own initiative who had already been made aware that they couldn't rely on their superiors backing them to the hilt when things turned sour.

It was a good enough argument for Ashton to persuade himself to try his luck again. Leaving the snack bar, he rode the lift down to the ground floor. Another party of tourists had just arrived and were being checked into the hotel, but no one from his group was in the lobby. Those who weren't on the boat trip with Stanley Inver had gone to see the Catherine Palace at Pushkin and the one at Pavlosk set in thirteen hundred acres which Catherine the Great had presented to her son, Paul. It was one of the trips he had paid for when booking the holiday with the travel agents in Surbiton and had had to miss thanks to the militia.

The sky had clouded over, making for the kind of weather their Russian guide had assured them was typical of a summer's day in Leningrad. Between the hotel and the metro station in Moskovskiy Prospekt, no fewer than a dozen people turned to stare at him, evidently puzzled to know why he was wearing sunglasses.

The service on a Sunday was the same as a weekday, the trains running at three minute intervals. Nevsky Prospekt station on the Blue Line was opposite St Catherine's Church just up the road from the Gostinyj Dvor store. The red brick apartment building where Lydia Petrovskaya lived lay in the other direction next to the State-run Cooperative Bookshop across Griboyedov Canal.

The street door was made of oak and looked strong enough to resist a truck. There were no individual call buttons and apparently no means of announcing his presence. Ashton tried the door, found it wasn't locked and stepped into the hall. Before it had been converted into flats, the house had been built around the turn of the nineteenth century for a rich merchant and reflected a time when things were done on a grand scale. A spiral staircase, wide enough to take several people abreast, led him up to the fourth floor where Lydia Petrovskaya occupied one of the six apartments off the landing. He pressed the bell button; when that didn't produce any response, he thought perhaps it wasn't working and hammered on the door. A voice behind Ashton informed him that Lydia wasn't at home.

Ashton turned about and found himself confronted by a plump, middle-aged woman with a poor complexion and dyed red hair with grey roots.

"Would you know when she will be back?" he asked in fluent Russian.

"You are acquainted with Lydia Petrovskaya?"

"We have a mutual friend in Eduard Tulbukin – he's with the Foreign Ministry in Moscow. He suggested I should call on Lydia when I was in Leningrad."

"What is your name?" the woman asked.

"Ashton, Peter Ashton." He paused, then added, "I'm a journalist from England."

"You speak Russian very well."

"Thank you."

"Of course, I could tell you were a foreigner as soon as you spoke."

"Yes. Do you have any idea when Lydia Petrovskaya will be back?"

"Tonight? Tomorrow?" The woman shrugged her shoulders. "Who knows? The Hermitage is closed on Mondays and she has this dacha at Pushkin."

"Is that where she has gone?"

"I believe so."

Ashton smiled ruefully. "I should have called earlier," he said.

"You would still have missed her, she left yesterday evening."

"You mean last night?"

"No, it was soon after six."

Ashton thanked her for being so helpful and started down the staircase.

"Can I give Lydia Petrovskaya a message?" the woman asked, leaning over the banister.

"Just say I called and was sorry to have missed her."

What was it Lydia Petrovskaya had said to him when they had parted at the Gostinyj Dvor? – "Now shake hands and don't

101

look back when you leave me." Lydia hadn't been anywhere near Suvorov Street in the Kalininski District; she hadn't wanted him to look back because she was going to meet her KGB case officer to let him know the bait had been laid.

Ashton walked out into the street, turned left and went into the Cooperative Bookshop where he managed to obtain a street map of Leningrad. He had not changed his mind about Elena Maisky, but even a lousy witness like her was better than no witness at all. He looked up Tarasova Road in the index and saw that she lived near the docks.

Tarasova Road was like Suvorov Street but without the balconies. The neighbourhood also achieved the near impossible by being even more depressing. The concrete façade of the block of flats at Number 423 was streaked with grime and beginning to flake off in large scabs. The interior was no better; the skirting boards were coming adrift from the walls, much of the colourwash had rubbed off, the pattern of the composite tiles on the floor was no longer visible thanks to a mass of black scuff marks, and the solitary lift was out of order. The only thing which distinguished the tenement from some of the high-rise flats Ashton had seen in London was the absence of any graffiti.

There was no list of tenants displayed in the communal area on the ground floor and the open mail boxes had all been cleared. To find Elena Maisky he would have to knock on doors and ask the occupants if they knew her. A quick glance at the indicator above the lift, which showed there were twelve storeys, told him he could be faced with an uphill task in more ways than one.

But Ashton got lucky. A man on the sixth floor recognised her from his description and said he thought she lived on the floor above with those no-good drunken layabouts, the Nikolayev family. He climbed the two flights of stairs and checked out the flats in the four passageways leading off from the landing and eventually found the one occupied by the Nikolayevs. He removed his sunglasses and tucked them into his shirt pocket, then rapped on the door. A radio was blasting away somewhere in the apartment and he had a hard time making himself heard above the din.

The door was finally opened by a skimpily dressed Elena in a T-shirt and precious little else and whose dishevelled appearance suggested she had just crawled out of bed. Even though she was still half-asleep, she recognised him immediately and tried to slam the door in his face, only to find that he had a foot in the jamb. Before she could cry for help, Ashton hit the panel with his shoulder and sent her staggering back into the room. Arms flailing like windmills, she lost her balance and went down, hitting the concrete floor under the linoleum hard enough to bruise her rump. A stream of invective greeted him as he stepped inside and closed the door with his heel.

A curtain divided the room in half, separating the living quarters from the bedroom. To his left, there was a communicating door to the rest of the tiny flat. With no way of knowing how many Nikolayevs he could be facing, Ashton thought it was only prudent to isolate as many as he could. Moving round Elena, he removed the key on the inside of the communicating door, then swiftly closed and locked it.

The enraged bull who came charging through the curtains had a beer bottle in his right hand and a wild drunken look in his eyes. The last time Ashton had seen him he had been wearing a leather jacket over a blue T-shirt with the bottom half of a paratrooper's combat suit. This afternoon he was down to a pair of yellowing Aertex underpants that stopped short just above his kneecaps.

The fight was always going to be one-sided and something of a massacre; Ashton was stone cold sober, in a vengeful mood and ready for him. His reflexes were needle sharp and he had dabbled a bit in the martial arts. Timing it to perfection, he side-stepped out of the way, caught the enraged bull with a well-aimed kick which cut the legs from under the Russian and sent him head first into the wall. The beer bottle slipped from his grasp and shattered on the floor as he went down. He got up slowly, touched the abrasion on his forehead, then stared uncomprehendingly at the blood on his fingertips.

"I'd like my money back," Ashton told him calmly. "Also my wristwatch."

The Russian bellowed with rage and charged forward. As he did so, Elena scrambled to her feet and launched herself at Ashton. She would have been more successful had she saved her breath instead of mouthing obscenities. Forewarned was forearmed; Ashton spun round, grabbed one of Elena's outstretched arms and whirled her into the path of her angry boyfriend. The two Russians collided and went down in a heap, Elena underneath, flat on her back, the boyfriend on top, a knee in her stomach. He was still kneeling on a winded Elena when Ashton moved in and put an arm lock on him, bending the wrist of his right hand one way, the elbow in the opposite direction.

"I can break one and dislocate the other," Ashton told him in a loud voice. "All it will take is one little jerk."

He applied enough force to show the Russian what he meant, then danced him on tiptoe through the curtains into the poky bedroom. A double and a single bed were crammed into a space no more than nine feet by nine. The single bed was occupied by a thin, wizened little man who had been sick over the empty bottle of vodka on the floor and was still sleeping off the effects of what must have been an all-night binge. The intrusive radio was perched on a narrow wooden box squashed in between the beds. The sheets on the double bed which Elena obviously shared with her boyfriend looked as if they hadn't been changed in weeks.

Ashton said, "I'm only going to say this once more. Where's my money and my wristwatch?"

The Russian was in pain and didn't mind who knew it; whimpering like an injured child, he reached under the mattress and brought out the leather wallet and Omega wristwatch. The wallet didn't look quite as fat as it had been.

"How much have you spent?"

"A hundred and ten dollars," the Russian said defiantly. "I had to pay off some of my debts."

Ashton scooped up the Omega, slipped it into his left trouser pocket, then did the same with the wallet before releasing the Russian.

"Don't do anything stupid," he warned him.

But the Russian did. Ashton hadn't stepped back more than a couple of paces when he came at him, swinging a roundhouse left that had been telegraphed so far in advance it was almost laughable. Nothing could have been simpler to block, nothing could have been easier to execute than the forearm smash to the side of the jaw which dropped him in his tracks.

The drunk snored on. Dead to the world, neither the radio booming in his ear nor the people in the other room hammering on the communicating door could disturb him. Elena was sitting on the floor, hugging her stomach with both arms, her face the colour of paste.

"Don't bother to see me out," Ashton told her, then put on his sunglasses and left the flat.

He bumped into one of the neighbours on the landing who wanted to know what was going on and seemed quite satisfied when he told him it was just the Nikolayevs having a family quarrel. Some questions didn't have to be asked. The sight of Elena Maisky and her boyfriend together was all the confirmation he needed that what had happened last night had been a put-up job. Chief Investigator Chebrakin might be an honest cop but when the KGB told him to release Elena, there was nothing he could do about it. Feeling better, Ashton left the tenement, walked to the nearest station and rode the metro back to the hotel.

Inver returned from the boat trip a few minutes after five o'clock and spent the next half-hour telling Ashton what he'd missed. The only time he was lost for words occurred when Ashton returned the fifty pounds he had loaned him.

"What do you mean, you no longer need it? You had a run of luck on the fruit machines down in the lobby, Pete?"

Ashton shook his head. "The police returned my wallet." He held up his left arm. "Also my wristwatch," he added.

"Well, bugger me." Inver whistled. "That's a turn-up for the book and no mistake. How did you get to hear about it?"

"They rang the hotel and asked me to come down to the central police station."

"Well I never, there must be something to this perestroika lark after all. Wait a minute – what about your sports shirt and the other stuff?"

"Long gone," Ashton said cryptically. "The police reckon my shoes and shirt will have been sold several times over by now."

"Typical. Still, I expect you're insured?"

"Damn right."

"You got to give evidence against the blokes who robbed you?"

"Chief Investigator Chebrakin took an affidavit to save me appearing in court."

"Just as well, considering we're off to Moscow after an early lunch tomorrow." Inver unbuttoned his shirt and inspected the prickly heat rash on his chest. "Mind if I use the bathroom first?" he asked.

"Be my guest," Ashton told him.

The phone on the bedside table rang while Inver was still running the bathwater. Lifting the receiver, Ashton gave the room number only.

"Mr Ashton?" a voice said in more than passable English.

"Yes." He didn't have to ask who was calling but she told him anyway.

"It's Lydia Petrovskaya."

"I know, I recognised your voice. Why are you calling me?"

For a moment she was thrown out of her stride and didn't know what to say, but she quickly recovered her composure. "I've just learned what happened last night. Could we meet somewhere?"

"Have we got anything to talk about?"

"I think so."

"Then I'll take your word for it," Ashton told her. "Where do you suggest we meet? Your place?"

"No, that would not be fair – it's too far for you. Why don't I meet you at the Victory Monument?"

"When?"

"Ten, fifteen minutes time? I am at a public phone in Moskovskiy Prospekt."

"I'll be there."

Ashton waited for her to hang up, then slowly replaced the receiver. He thought there had been a noticeable improvement in Lydia's command of English since yesterday evening. True, the phraseology remained a little stilted but she was much more fluent, as if someone had rehearsed her. The only time she had sounded tense was when he had suggested they met at her flat. Lydia hadn't wanted that and had reacted sharply. The proposed rendezvous hadn't been somewhere chosen on the spur of the moment either. But the thing which bothered him most was the fact that at no time had he told Lydia Petrovskaya where he was staying in Leningrad.

A cautious inner voice urged him to give it a miss, another and more persuasive one pointed out that there were times when it was necessary to take a risk and that this was one of them. Ashton tapped on the bathroom door, told the yodelling Inver he was going for a quick stroll round the block and left.

There was a world of difference between taking a measured risk and being foolhardy. Before walking out into the street, he scanned the flat rooftops of the apartment houses on the opposite side of the avenue. When satisfied that a sniper wasn't lurking up there waiting to pick him off, he went through the swing door. Well tutored in fieldcraft, he kept within the shadows cast by the hotel for as long as possible as he made his way up to the intersection. While waiting for the lights to change at the pedestrian crossing, he made sure there was at least one Russian standing in front of him and was careful not to leave his back exposed.

Ashton approached the monument in Victory Square from Moskovskiy Prospekt and walked past the statues of a steel worker and Red Army man which shared the same plinth in front of the obelisk. Three flights of steps led him down into an open amphitheatre where he saw Lydia waiting for him near the entrance to the underground exhibition hall. As he drew nearer, she turned away and disappeared inside. He found her waiting for him halfway down the long flight of steps.

"It is better here," she murmured, then switched to Russian. "We must be very respectful and quiet."

"Yes, I understand," he said just as softly.

They descended into a vast room dimly lit by nine hundred electric candles, one for every day of the siege which had lasted from September 1941 to January 1944. A sense of awe was enhanced by a steady heartbeat punctuated by a few bars from Shostakovich's Leningrad Symphony. In '41, when the electricity supply had nearly failed, it had been this constant heartbeat on the radio which had told the besieged population that their city was still alive.

"I'm glad you came," Lydia whispered.

"How did you know where to find me?"

"I was with my friends in Suvorov Street when the militia took you away. I rang the precinct station but they wouldn't tell me anything at first. Eventually I was referred to Chief Investigator Chebrakin and he told me where you were staying."

Lydia had told the woman across the landing that she was spending the weekend at her dacha in Pushkin, but that could have simply been an excuse to satisfy the curiosity of a nosy neighbour.

"Do you believe me?" she asked.

"I'm here, aren't I?" he said.

"Yes."

"So what do you want from me?"

Lydia moved on past several exhibits of the siege to ensure that none of the attendants on duty in the hall could overhear their conversation. "Can you find Galina before the KGB catch up with her?"

"Can you tell me where to look for her?" he countered.

"Galina was always talking about America . . ."

"You implied as much the first time we met. Question is, how much money does she have in that Swiss bank account your father opened for her?"

"Nikolai Yakulevich gave me to understand that he had deposited a total of twenty-one thousand Swiss francs over the years."

At two francs fifty to the pound, Ashton calculated she had approximately eight thousand four hundred to play with, which itself was roughly the equivalent of fourteen and a half thousand US dollars. It would certainly get her to America and keep the wolf from the door for a few months, but it was hardly a fortune in Western terms.

"What about this Eduard Tulbukin? Could he have opened another account for her when they became engaged?"

"It's not impossible." Lydia placed a ten-rouble note in the collection box near the exit, then linked arms and led him out of the hall and up yet another flight of steps into the open forecourt. "Of course, if Eduard had done something of the kind, Galina is unlikely to have access to the account now that she is not going to marry him."

"If I am to find Galina, you will have to give me a lot more information about your daughter – her tastes, her moods, how she amuses herself, what her idea is of a fun time."

Lydia Petrovskaya talked nonstop about her daughter as they slowly walked on past the bronze figures of Leningrad's defenders – the aviator in goggles and leather coat, the sailor from the Baltic Fleet waving a PPSh sub-machine-gun above his head, the factory guards, the women who had dug the antitank ditches around the city. Only when they were right out in the open opposite the Hotel Polkovskaya did she stop and turn to face him.

"Chebrakin told me you had been attacked by two robbers," she said, changing the subject.

"You could say that," Ashton agreed.

"Did they hurt you badly?"

"They injured my pride and blacked an eye."

"And it was all my fault." Lydia Petrovskaya reached up and removed his sunglasses, then stepped back a pace. "It looks awful," she said, and moving forward, kissed him on both cheeks before returning his sunglasses. "Perhaps that will make it better."

"Perhaps it will."

She linked arms again, led him back to the amphitheatre and on up the opposing flight of steps. She embraced him warmly a second time when they parted company in Moskovskiy Prospekt, then walked away without so much as a backward glance.

On the roof of the Hotel Polkovskaya, the KGB photographer packed his camera and telephoto lens neatly away in a smart executive briefcase, well satisfied with the pictures he had taken of Ashton for the men in Moscow.

CHAPTER 11

MONDAY HAD been a six-hour train journey through mile after mile of birch forest which had got them into Moscow and the Kosmos Hotel on the northern outskirts in time for dinner. Tuesday had passed with a city tour which had taken in everything from St Basil's Cathedral to Moscow University with its view across the city from the Lenin Heights. Lunch at McDonald's had been followed by a visit to the Pushkin Museum and a stroll down the Arbat where Stanley Inver had bought enough matroshka dolls and lacquer boxes from the street traders to go into business on his own account. Today they had toured the Kremlin Armoury, Tolstoy's house and the Lady of Smolensk Convent.

For the best part of two days, Ashton had enjoyed an unwelcome notoriety with the rest of the group. As far as they were concerned, he was the man who had been mugged on the streets of Leningrad and almost without exception, they had wanted to know where it had happened and how he had been treated by the militia. Now at last their curiosity had been satiated and he had been allowed to merge quietly into the background again. With Stanley Inver determined to be his constant companion, this had not been particularly difficult. After alighting from the coach on Mira Prospekt, it was noticeable that the rest of the group gave them a very wide berth as they walked up the curving approach road to the Kosmos Hotel together.

Ashton showed his hotel pass to the militiaman on duty in the lobby, walked over to the bank of lifts beyond the gift shops with Inver and went up to their room on the nineteenth floor. The telephone rang barely ten minutes after they had collected the room key from the lady floor attendant.

Answering it, Inver listened to the caller with an increasingly puzzled expression on his face, then handed the phone to Ashton. "Some bloke for you," he said. "Didn't catch the name."

"I am Eduard Tulbukin," the caller told him. "Please excuse my English for not being good."

"You're doing all right," Ashton told him.

"Please?"

"Never mind. Why are you phoning me?"

"We have same friend – Lydia Petrovskaya. She write letter saying you are coming to Moscow, ask me to see you."

"Where are you now?"

"Here in hotel – downstairs," Tulbukin said.

"How am I going to recognise you?"

"Please?"

"Your clothes," Ashton said. "Tell me what you are wearing."

"Ah, I understand now. I have brown shoes, black trousers, white shirt and I am carrying purse on right shoulder. You are coming – yes?"

"In a few minutes – just wait by the desk. Okay?"

"Okay."

Ashton put the phone down, conscious that Inver was dying to know who the mystery caller had been. "A journalist from the Tass news agency," he told him. "Going to help me with an article I promised British Aerospace I would do for the in-house magazine."

"Going to be long?"

"Long enough for you to have a bath first, Stanley, if that's what you're getting at."

Eduard Tulbukin was about five feet eight inches tall and weighed around ten stone. An essentially neat looking man, he had black hair which was trained straight back without a parting and the sort of pencil-thin moustache that had been favoured by Hollywood movie stars in the late thirties. Ashton thought he was roughly his age, give or take a year or two. He also got the impression that the Russian had recognised him before he introduced himself.

The hotel lobby was like the concourse at Waterloo, a cavernous hall with lots of people coming and going and precious few seats for those who weren't on the move. The militiamen were there to deter the prostitutes but their presence seemed to make him nervous. A double Scotch-on-the-rocks in the hard currency bar on the mezzanine floor had a very calming effect on him.

"This is nice," Tulbukin said and sipped his whisky appreciatively.

"You said you had heard from Lydia Petrovskaya," Ashton reminded him.

"Heard?"

"She wrote you a letter."

"Ah, yes, now I am understanding again." Tulbukin unzipped the cheap plastic purse he was nursing on his lap and took out a crumpled envelope. "You can read Russian?" he asked slyly.

"I get by."

The Russian didn't appear to be wired for sound. His white shirt was a snug fit, the material thin enough to see the nipples on his chest, and there was no way the KGB could have planted even a microchip transmitter on his body above the waist without it being obvious. It could of course be concealed in the purse or taped to an ankle but he could hardly shake him down in public, just as he had been unable to search Lydia Petrovskaya.

"Lydia said you were much more fluent than you would have us believe," Tulbukin said in his native tongue.

The letter was everything the Russian had said it was but it could have been written by anyone. It was dated the eleventh of August and had presumably been posted early on Monday. That meant Lydia Petrovskaya had written it soon after meeting him at the monument in Victory Square. The internal and external postal services were notoriously inefficient and for a letter to be delivered to an address in Moscow within three days had to be something of a record.

"You did not answer me, Mr Ashton. I am perhaps speaking too quickly for you?"

"I wasn't listening. This handwriting isn't easy to decipher and I can only do one thing at a time."

"In America, they used to say the same thing about President Ford."

"Then I am in good company." Ashton put the letter back inside the envelope and returned it to the Russian. "Tell me something, Mr Tulbukin. Have the authorities been making life difficult for you?"

"Why would they do that?" Tulbukin countered.

"You used to be engaged to Galina Kutuzova and she has deserted her post."

"Lydia Petrovskaya says in her letter that you work for British Aerospace, yet you appear to know Galina. How can this be?"

"Bob Whittle was going to marry my sister."

"Whittle? I don't think I have heard the name."

"Don't give me that crap," Ashton snapped. "Whittle was an officer in our army; Galina was with him the night he was murdered in Dresden. If you didn't hear about it at the time, you would have got it from the KGB when they interviewed you."

"He was a spy, this man who would have become your brother-in-law?"

"He was a captain in the Royal Corps of Transport doing some kind of liaison job in Potsdam. I want to find out why he was killed and I'm pretty sure Galina Kutuzova can tell me. Now, are you going to answer my question or shall we drink up and go our separate ways?"

"You are a very impatient man, Mr Ashton."

"Yes, I know, it's got me where I am today."

Tulbukin nodded as if he quite understood. "There was a little trouble after Galina went absent," he admitted, "but not a lot. She broke off our engagement in January 1989 some four months before she was sent to Potsdam so they can hardly blame me for what happened two years later."

"Did you transfer any money into her Swiss bank account?"

Tulbukin threw back his head and laughed. "On my salary?" he spluttered.

"Is that why she sent you packing? Because you are poor?"

"Partly. There were other reasons. She was a very passionate young woman, very demanding. I could never satisfy her."

"We're talking about sex – right?"

"Yes." Tulbukin rattled the ice cubes in his empty glass. "It is all very embarrassing."

"I'm sure it is." Ashton relieved him of his empty glass, walked over to the bar and ordered another two large whiskies, then returned to their table. "Mud in your eye," he said and raised his tumbler.

"What?"

"It's an old English expression."

"Oh. Well, mud in yours."

"About Galina, are you saying that your ex-fiancée was something of a sexpot?"

Tulbukin was and a lot more besides. He had met Galina in his last year at the Smolny Institute when she had been a fresher and the way he told it, she had seduced him on their second date. General Nikolai Yakulevich Petrovsky had still been alive in those days and the head of the Fifth Chief Directorate had sent for Tulbukin when he was in Moscow being interviewed for an appointment in the Foreign Ministry. In what the general considered was diplomatic language, he had made it clear what would happen to him if ever he made his granddaughter unhappy. Conversely, provided he played his cards right, he could live the good life, by which the general had meant the latest hi-fi, TV set and video recorder to come out of Japan. But if Petrovsky had been corrupt, it seemed Galina had been all of that and more.

"She is totally unscrupulous and such a compulsive liar." Tulbukin finished his whisky and put the glass down on the table. "But oh so convincing; it was months before I learned that you couldn't believe a word she said. I'm glad we never married, Mr Ashton; she could have ruined me like she has her father. You should talk to him if you want to know what Galina is like."

"I don't have the time."

"He is stationed near Moscow with the 106th Guards Airborne Division . . ."

"I think you're wrong. Lydia Petrovskaya told me he was something to do with your cosmonaut programme and was living in Star City."

"That was before Galina disappeared. He has been removed from that post and is now in charge of the team of forward air controllers assigned to the Airborne Division. Of course, I am not a military man but it doesn't seem to me to be the sort of job you would give to a full colonel."

It didn't to Ashton either, but he wasn't going to say so. "I wouldn't know," he lied, "I've never been a soldier."

"Well, I can tell you Sergei Vasilevich doesn't think much of it."

"Who?"

"Sergei Vasilevich Kutuzov," Tulbukin said in a voice which suggested he was surprised Ashton should have asked. "We're still good friends and see each other quite often."

"Really?"

"It's very sad. When I first met him, Sergei Vasilevich was on his way to the top, couldn't fail to make lieutenant general according to his friends. Now he's on the slide and going downhill fast." Tulbukin shook his head. "And all because of Galina. Not that he will hear a word against her, you understand. Far from it; he is being driven out of his mind because no one will tell him what has happened to his daughter."

"What about Lydia Petrovskaya?"

"She claims she hasn't been told anything either." Tulbukin looked down at his empty glass. "But maybe you could give him some of the facts?"

"Me?"

"Yes. Wasn't this man Vittle about to marry your sister?"

"You mean Whittle."

"I am sorry. I got his name wrong. But yes, I do mean Whittle. Surely the British authorities must have told your sister what happened to him?"

Ashton knew what was coming even before the Russian suggested that if it could be arranged, a meeting with Kutuzov might also be to his advantage.

"I've already told you once," he said, "I don't have the time. Tomorrow is our last full day in Moscow before we go home on Friday and I'm off to Zagorsk in the morning with the rest of the tour party. Then we're going to the State Circus in the evening."

"You will enjoy every minute, Mr Ashton. It is a very spectacular show."

Tulbukin stood up, said what a pleasure it had been to meet him and shook hands. Ashton was equally complimentary as he walked him down to the lobby where they shook hands a second time before parting company.

The Russian had certainly done his best to discredit Galina Kutuzova. Trouble was, Ashton couldn't decide whether Tulbukin was simply the bitter, rejected lover or the hatchet man who had been told to do a demolition job on her character.

There was, Inver maintained, a limit to the number of icons a man could admire and he had already had his fill before they set off for Zagorsk. The paintings of Mother and Child all looked the same to him and he contended that when you had seen one, you had seen the lot. Perhaps not surprisingly, the monastery complex forty-six miles north of Moscow had proved altogether too much for him. The gold and sapphire onion domes had captivated him to begin with, but after tramping through the Cathedral of the Holy Trinity, the Cathedral of the Dormition, the Refectory and the Palace of the Metropolitans, he couldn't wait to get back on the coach.

"Too much bloody culture for the likes of me," he had confided to Ashton as they walked towards the car park outside the monastery walls. "Could feel myself coming all over faint more than once. Must have been the combination of the hot weather, the incense and all those candles burning away."

A mile out of Zagorsk, Inver fell asleep, his head leaning against the window, his mouth open. The occasional pothole in the highway roused him but only long enough to acquire a little extra space as he endeavoured to make himself more comfortable. After a time, Ashton gave up the unequal struggle and moved into the seat behind before he found himself sitting in the aisle.

The M9 Yaroslavl motorway became the Mira Prospekt, or Peace Avenue, as they crossed the Trans-Siberian railway and the Sputnik monument, which resembled a giant ski jump, appeared above the treetops. The coach driver made a left turn off the avenue, drove past several blocks of flats, then made two right turns in quick succession to park alongside the Kosmos Hotel.

"Wake up, Stanley," Ashton said and put a hand on his shoulder. "We're here."

"Wh-a-a-at?" Inver sat up yawning and looked about him. "Oh, I see what you mean."

Ashton got off the coach, waited for the older man to join him, then walked up the approach road to the hotel. Between the bottom of the slope and the top, they were accosted half-a-dozen times by nine- to twelve-year-olds wanting to sell them fur hats, T-shirts, tins of caviar and matroshka dolls. It happened in full view of the militiaman standing by the mail box outside the entrance but he wasn't interested in chasing off the street hawkers.

"Must be on their payroll," Inver observed sourly.

"Try saying it a little louder," Ashton told him. "I don't think he heard you."

The lobby was the usual melting pot of tourists from Eastern Europe with a bevy of air stewardesses from Japan Air Lines to make the gathering even more cosmopolitan. Entering the nearest lift, they found themselves sharing it with a group of Jordanians and two large, colourfully dressed ladies from one of the African states.

"Looks like the whole of UNO is staying here," Inver said after they had collected their room key.

"Must remind you of home, Stanley."

"Yeah, it's just like Oxford Street most days of the week. What time are we leaving for the circus?"

"Six thirty."

"Time for an hour's shut-eye before dinner then."

Inver had told him that he could sleep through anything after his experiences on the Anzio beachhead and it was no idle boast. Once he had set the wake-up alarm and got his head down, nothing disturbed him, not even the telephone which rang while Ashton was in the middle of packing. Answering it, he found himself talking to one of the girls on reception.

"Mr Ashton?"

"That's me," he said quietly, then heard the girl say that one of the security guards had detained an intruder who claimed to know him. "What's his name?" he asked.

"Tulbukin, Eduard Tulbukin."

"He's okay, I've met him."

"I think you should come down; the guard thinks he could be an impostor."

"Why don't I just describe him?"

The suggestion was rewarded with a sharp click as the girl hung up on him. Ashton put the phone down, glanced at Inver to make sure he was still asleep, then pocketed the key and left the room, closing the door quietly behind him.

He had expected to find Tulbukin by the reception counter; instead, he was standing in the middle of the lobby with a militiaman in tow who didn't seem all that interested in him. Communication was in sign language. As Ashton moved towards them, the militiaman pointed to Tulbukin and looked questioningly at him, then drifted away when he nodded.

"Thank you for rescuing me." Tulbukin gave him a nervous

smile and hurriedly wiped his face with a handkerchief. "The weather is very oppressive, don't you think?"

"I hadn't noticed. What are you doing here?"

"I came to see you. Sergei Vasilevich is waiting for us outside."

"I told you yesterday I haven't got time to see Kutuzov."

"Please, Mr Ashton." Tulbukin reached out, seized his left arm above the elbow and tried to lead him towards the swing doors in the entrance. "Please, you have to come with me. It won't take more than a few minutes."

Ashton thought there was a note of desperation in his voice which was reflected in the way his eyes kept darting about the lobby as if he was frightened of being seen with him. "What's this all about, Eduard?" he asked.

"We can't talk here, people are watching us."

"This had better be good." He followed the Russian out on to the pavement, then said, "All right, let's hear it."

Tulbukin walked on slowly down the slope towards the sidewalk on Mira Prospekt. "It's like this, Mr Ashton," he said in a low voice. "If you really want to find Galina, Colonel Kutuzov thinks he can point you in the right direction. Certain information has also come into his possession which he believes could explain why Galina ran away."

"And where is he now?"

"In the grounds of the exhibition centre on the other side of the avenue."

Ashton could see the exhibition centre, which glorified the economic achievements of the Soviet Union, from their bedroom. According to Inver's Baedeker, the eighty or more pavilions, exhibition halls, flower gardens, restaurants, cinema and shopping centre were spread over close on six hundred acres.

"Why doesn't Kutuzov want to show himself in the hotel?"

"Too risky. You saw what happened to me."

They were halfway down the slope when Ashton began to have an itchy feeling between the shoulder blades. He had felt it before on the streets of Belfast and again to a lesser extent in Leningrad a few days ago when Lydia Petrovskaya had met him at the monument in Victory Square. They were out in the open, there were precious few people about, apart from the usual hawkers, and Tulbukin was definitely edging away from him.

Ashton stepped on to the narrow pavement to his left and moved closer to the waist-high concrete wall. He wondered if he was being a touch paranoid but the feeling that something was terribly wrong persisted. Then Tulbukin lost his head and attempted to pull him towards the centre of the road and he suddenly knew there was a sniper on the roof of the hotel, twenty-nine storeys above him.

He broke free, placed both hands on the low concrete wall and vaulted over it. The grassy bank on the other side fell away steeply to the service road approximately twenty feet below. Landing awkwardly on the slope, Ashton succeeded in spraining his left wrist when he instinctively stretched out an arm to break his fall. The sky and earth changed places several times as he rolled over and over. On the way down to the bottom, he lost his sunglasses in the long grass.

He could hear screams and shouts coming from the road above which was an indication that the sniper had put somebody down. A 7.62mm Dragunov self-loading rifle chambered for the rimmed cartridge and fitted with a four power scope; that was the standard issue for a sniper in the Red Army and there was no reason to suppose the KGB was any different. The hidden marksman would have used special high-grade ammunition involving a flashless propellant and had undoubtedly attached a noise suppressor to the Dragunov because the one thing he hadn't heard was the gunshot itself.

Ashton re-entered the hotel via the service lobby on the lower ground floor where their bags had been delivered the evening they had arrived in Moscow. The doors could have been locked or a member of the hotel staff could have turned him away, but he was lucky. The service area was deserted and he didn't encounter anyone on the stairs to the main lobby above. The winning streak continued; not a single head among the crowd which had gathered in the hotel entrance turned in his direction as he made his way to the bank of lifts beyond the gift shops. And then, really to gild the lily, the key lady was absent from her desk when he alighted on the nineteenth floor.

Ashton walked down the corridor and let himself into the room. There was no sweeter sound to his ears than Inver in a deep sleep, grunting like a warthog. He checked his appearance in the full-length mirror in the small hallway and was relieved to see that he had removed the worst of the dust from his clothes when he'd quickly brushed himself down in the service lobby. There remained one other point of detail; opening the chest of drawers, he finished packing the suitcase which he had left on the bed, then walked over to the window.

A body was lying face down in the roadway, its feet pointing towards the hotel. Although someone had draped a jacket over the head and shoulders, Ashton knew by the clothes and position of the corpse that it was Tulbukin. Close by, a couple of militiamen and a male civilian were giving first aid to one of the twelve-year-old street hawkers who had also been hit, probably by the same bullet that had dropped Tulbukin then ricochetted after passing through his body. As he stood there at the window nursing his aching left wrist, an ambulance cut across the traffic on Mira Prospekt and turned into the elevated driveway, its siren still warbling.

"What's going on, Pete?"

Ashton glanced to his left, found Inver standing beside him. "Damned if I know. I heard a commotion while I was packing and got to the window in time to see the police sweeping everybody outside into the hotel and there were these two bodies lying in the road, one of them a child."

"A traffic accident?"

"I didn't hear a vehicle, Stanley."

"I never heard a thing from the moment I got my head down."

That Inver wasn't aware that he had left the room was only a small comfort. It was the receptionist who had phoned him when Tulbukin had arrived he had to worry about. There was also the militiaman who had seen them together in the lobby and the barman the night before. And the other streetwise kids who must have seen him vault over the wall a split second before the victim was gunned down. The list of witnesses seemed endless.

All through dinner, Ashton was on tenterhooks, expecting at any moment to be told that the police wanted to interview him, but nothing happened. He went to the circus, sat through the performance, came back to the hotel and watched TV. There was a report of the incident on the late night news but there was no photograph of Tulbukin and the news reader stated that the victim had not yet been identified.

At breakfast the next morning, the double shooting was still the number one topic of conversation with everyone trying to outdo everyone else with eyewitness accounts of what they had or hadn't seen. Somehow, Ashton managed to keep a smile on his mouth, somehow he managed to appear cool and relaxed.

The hours to check-out time crawled by and it didn't take long to wander through every gift shop in the hotel and pick up a new pair of sunglasses. He went for a walk in the grounds of the exhibition centre with Inver and wondered all the time whether the KGB would be crazy enough to take another crack at him. Because they were crazy, there was no doubt about that. Whatever it was they were hoping to cover up, common sense should have told them that murdering him would only stir up a hornet's nest which Mr Gorbachev wouldn't like one little bit.

There were, however, no further incidents. The tour group finally left for the airport at one thirty pm local time, spent the next two and a quarter hours going through customs and eventually got airborne at five o'clock, fifty minutes behind schedule. Ashton began to unwind once the captain announced they had left Soviet airspace.

The flight took a fraction under three hours which meant they landed at Heathrow at 1800 hours British Summer Time. All Ashton had to do then was file past Immigration, collect his suitcase, pass through customs and wait for the Cranford Airways minibus to pick him up so that he could collect his Vauxhall Cavalier from their car park. Two hours after touchdown, he let himself into the flat at Surbiton.

He phoned Victor Hazelwood at home, found himself talking to an answering machine and left a message to say that he was back. The letters which his cleaning lady had placed on the hall table were hardly uplifting; the brown envelopes contained bills, the airmail letter was from Jill Sheridan in Bahrain who wanted to know when he expected to sell their flat. It was not one of the best homecomings that Ashton could remember.

CHAPTER 12

ASHTON HAD caught the news headlines on Radio Two and knew that Gorbachev had been deposed before he left for the station. When he walked into Century House, he wasn't therefore surprised to learn that Hazelwood had called a conference of the whole Eastern Bloc for nine o'clock sharp. Although only the Russian Desk could make a useful contribution to the proceedings, Victor enjoyed performing before a full house and the Polish, Romanian, Hungarian and Czechoslovak Desks were going to be his audience. Few people could have looked happier than Hazelwood when he walked into the conference almost rubbing his hands with glee.

"I take it everyone has heard the news?" He paused long enough to see that no one was going to admit it if they hadn't, then said, "All right, I don't have to tell you we are back in business."

The liberals were out, the hardliners were back in power. After all the confusing signals that had been originating from the Kremlin, it was a comfortable feeling to know where you stood once more. Ashton doubted if Hazelwood had meant to give his audience that impression but his attitude, manner and choice of expression had certainly suggested it.

"First things first," Hazelwood continued. "The following signals have been received from Moscow Station."

The SIS cell in the embassy had fired off three cables between 0318 hours Greenwich Mean Time when the Tass news agency had announced that Vice President Gennady Yanayev had taken over as President because of Gorbachev's ill health, and 0615 when the British military attaché had reported that a column of BMP-2 armoured personnel carriers were moving towards central Moscow. The coup had started shortly after midnight on Sunday when many of the diplomatic staff and the SIS cell had either just returned from a weekend in the country or were still enjoying the hospitality of the embassy's dacha outside the capital. As a result, they had been pretty thin on the ground during the preparatory stage which was reflected in the brevity of the signals despatched to London.

"Besides Gennady Yanayev, I want detailed assessments of the following members of the coup." Hazelwood cleared his throat. "Defence Minister Marshal Dmitri Yazov, KGB Chairman Vladimir Kryuchkov, Interior Minister of the USSR Boris Pugo and Prime Minister of the Soviet Union Valentin Pavlov."

He also wanted all the information the Russian Desk had on Viktor Starodubtsev, the former chairman of the Farmers' Union who had become prominent since Gorbachev had moved him to the Arms Control Directorate in 1986. The armed forces were not overlooked, nor was the KGB; the coup was only going to succeed if they obeyed the orders handed down to them. All those present were tasked to provide specific answers to specific questions. Even the satellite Desks were required to anticipate the reaction of the Poles, Hungarians, Czechs and Romanians to events in Moscow. Only Ashton was left without a job to do.

"For more than a year we've been saying that Gorbachev is riding for a fall. Now it's happened and a lot of questions will be coming our way from Downing Street." Hazelwood looked round the assembled company. "So let's get on with it. Have those up-to-date assessments ready when we meet again at 1000 hours."

Twenty people got to their feet as one and started towards the door. As the only desk officer who was not under pressure, Ashton waited for the press to ease before he attempted to leave. As he tagged along at the back, Hazelwood signalled that he wanted to have a word with him.

"About the message you left on my answering machine," he said. "I didn't phone back because Alice and I spent the weekend at our cottage in Wiltshire and didn't return until late yesterday evening. I also thought that whatever you had to tell me would keep until this morning."

"And you were right, Victor."

"I'm not so sure. Who gave you the black eye?"

"A small-time crook in Leningrad who was working for the KGB."

"I think you had better give me the whole story, but keep it short and sweet."

Ashton did just that. In a few brief sentences, he told him what had happened after he had met Lydia Petrovskaya and how the sniper on the roof of the Kosmos Hotel had killed the wrong man.

"Are you saying this man Tulbukin was a decoy?"

"Yes, his job was to lead me out into the killing ground. It wasn't something he did willingly; in fact, he was scared stiff and if I had cottoned on to it a little sooner, he would still be alive today."

With the benefit of hindsight, Ashton could see certain other incidents in perspective. In Leningrad, the KGB had tried to establish a case for deporting him. When that ploy had failed, they had decided to pass the problem to Moscow. No attempt had been made on his life when he had met Lydia Petrovskaya at the monument in Victory Square because they had already shown their hand to Chebrakin and knew they would probably have to kill the chief investigator as well, which was one gamble they hadn't been prepared to take. Instead, they had settled for a portrait gallery of their intended victim; that was why Lydia Petrovskaya had led him out into the open and removed his sunglasses. Although a passport photo had been attached to all three copies of the visa application, it appeared this particular faction of the KGB had been reluctant to ask the border guards or the Second Chief Directorate for a copy.

"That's quite a story, Peter. I think maybe you'd better give me a full account of your activities in writing."

"On or off the record?"

"In longhand, single copy, no file number, no security classification, no date, no signature, and deliver it to me in person."

"I think I know what you want," Ashton told him dryly.

"Good. But what I need first of all is the Order of Battle for Moscow Military District. You've made some friends in the Intelligence Directorate of the MOD, so why don't you ask them how they rate the various divisional commanders?"

"Okay. It'll be interesting to see just how good an informant Galina Kutuzova really was."

"Right." Hazelwood snapped his fingers. "That reminds me.

Berlin acted on your suggestion. I marked their report up for your information."

"Thanks."

"A word of warning. Don't get side-tracked. Galina Kutuzova can wait, the brief on Moscow Military District takes priority."

"Whatever you say, Victor."

Ashton left the conference room, went downstairs to his office and rang his contact in the Intelligence Directorate. The call went unanswered. Borrowing a copy of the MOD telephone directory from the library, he rang every desk officer in the branch and still failed to raise anyone. Finally, he got the chief clerk and learned that all the officers were in conference. Hazelwood could therefore hardly accuse him of deliberately flouting the instructions he had been given.

No one had covered for him while he had been away and the report from Head of Station Berlin was near the bottom of the in-tray buried under a mountain of files. Ashton had no idea what it had cost the Service to get Simon Younger and Kriminalpolizei Kommissar Heinrich Voigt together in the same room, but whatever the final bill, it had been money well spent. The unknown woman who had phoned Janina's apartment and left a message on the answering machine which her flatmate Tamara Chernenko was supposed to convey to Yuri Rostovsky was no longer anonymous. Younger had only needed to hear the first sentence the caller had uttered to know that he was listening to Galina Kutuzova.

Armed with this information and additional material reluctantly supplied by the Arms Control Unit, Head of Station Berlin had then spent a long and very convivial evening with the Chef de Service de Reseignements during which the two Intelligence officers had done a certain amount of horse trading. In return for a great deal of classified source material, the Frenchman had admitted that Captain Yuri Rostovsky of the GRU had also been supplying them with information. One of the rewards the Russian had demanded and received was a French passport. It had been issued to Yvette Michel whose photograph bore more than a passing resemblance to Starshii Leitenant Galina Kutuzova.

Even though he had a window seat, Tony Zale didn't bother to sneak one final look at the countryside as the Pan Am 747 lifted off from Frankfurt. Although no one had actually tarred and feathered him, it was hard to shake the feeling that he had been run out of town. There had been no crowd of well-wishers to see him off at Berlin's Tegel Airport, only the security officer from the Defense Intelligence Agency and a plain-clothes officer from the Kriminalpolizei, both of whom had been there to make sure he boarded the shuttle. Much the same thing had happened at Frankfurt while he had been in transit waiting for the onward flight to JFK when a junior staff member from the embassy in Bonn had kept him company.

He waited for the No Smoking and Seat Belt signs to go out, then reached for the travel bag on the floor between his feet and took out the record which Osmonde had kept of every conversation he'd had with Yuri Rostovsky. Although Karen had said her father had wanted him to have the notepad, Zale knew that he should have handed it over to the Defense Intelligence Agency's chief of security in Berlin. When Lloyd Osmonde had spoken to his daughter, he had not been aware that the Pentagon had decided to fire his former assistant.

Osmonde had his own unique brand of shorthand which took some deciphering. Worse still, some of the entries didn't make a lot of sense to Zale. They weren't exactly a record of what he had said, more a series of jottings that were evidently intended to serve as a reminder. That was fine, but you had to know what was going on in his mind to understand what they meant. Until the Russian had arrived on the scene, Osmonde had never held anything back from him; unfortunately, the first time he had ever heard of Rostovsky was the night before the GRU captain had been shot to death outside Da Gianni's on the Fasanenplatz.

Karen had hoped the diary would help to square things with Heinrich Voigt but he hadn't bothered to show it to the Kommissar of Kriminalpolizei. Those entries he had been able to decipher would have told Voigt nothing about the men who had murdered Rostovsky and the prostitute Tamara Chernenko or even pointed him in the right direction. They did, however, tell Zale that Karen's father had not been exactly straight with him. Although the GRU officer had certainly rung him at the office, it had taken more than one phone call to persuade Osmonde that he wasn't dealing with a hoaxer. It was only after Rostovsky had called him at home that he had collected the present the Russian

126

had left in the Volkspark Jungfernheide. The notes he had made that evening had consisted merely of the first names of his wife, daughters and sons-in-law and one sentence which asked, "how did he know?" and was punctuated with several question and exclamation marks. If his interpretation was correct, it could only mean that the GRU had in their possession a very detailed card index on Colonel (Retired) Lloyd D Osmonde and his family.

Zale closed the notepad and tucked it back into the zipper bag. One day real soon, he would have to drop by Osmonde's house in Carmel-by-the-sea and ask him a few pointed questions.

The second meeting had been held at 1000 hours, a third scheduled for 1200 had been confined to the Russian Desk but had still dragged on all through lunch before breaking up three and a quarter hours later. The fourth one that day assembled at 1745 hours and rapidly became unproductive when a number of desk officers attempted to explain why their predictions had been negated by events. When the news had first broken, most people had assumed the coup would succeed on the grounds that the conspirators would not have launched the putsch unless they were sure they had the backing of the KGB and the Soviet Armed Forces.

It was not an improvident assumption. The Red Army formations in the Moscow Military District were among the best and, on paper, there was no reason to suppose the 106th Guards Airborne Division and the Tamanski Armoured Regiment would disobey the orders of Defence Minister Marshal Dmitri Yazov. And the initial reports had seemed to bear out that prognosis. By 1100 hours, troops in armoured personnel carriers had surrounded the offices of the Tass news agency, *Izvestia* and *Moscow News*. It was also a fact that the Baltic Fleet had blockaded Tallinn harbour in Estonia and had increased the number of patrol craft operating in the Gulf of Riga.

The experts had begun to revise their opinions around 1400 hours when it had become apparent that the KGB and the Red Army were not enforcing the state of emergency with their customary efficiency. There were no SIS agents on the streets of Moscow and Leningrad and the only source of information was the news reports coming out of the Soviet Union, but the evidence provided by TV cameramen was on the screens in front of their eyes and that had been enough to convince even the most hardened sceptic that the outcome of the coup was not going to be the foregone conclusion it had once seemed. Satellite surveillance was presenting a confused picture of tanks and mechanised units concentrating on the outskirts of the capital but little sign of military activity elsewhere. Signal Intelligence had so far intercepted very little traffic of a significant pattern. On the contrary, it was as if the command nets at every level were maintaining radio silence. The maintenance of secrecy up to H-hour was common practice in all armies but once action had been joined, command and control of any operation depended on effective radio communication.

But the Cabinet Office was looking for something more definite than informed comment from the Intelligence Services. The government wanted to know how they should respond to the coup and the only advice they were getting from the Foreign and Commonwealth Office was to wait and see. Hazelwood had called the fourth meeting in the hope that someone might give him a new slant which he could put to the Director General. What he had got so far was more of the same from a dozen voices.

"We haven't heard anything from you, Peter," he said, looking at Ashton. "You're not usually so reticent."

"Well, I don't have any new facts to offer. Same goes for the MOD Intelligence Staff across the river. All we have is a gut feeling, but if anyone feels like making a book, I'm willing to bet the coup has already failed."

"Convince me," Hazelwood told him.

"There is more to a successful coup than taking over the newspapers, TV and radio stations. You've got to grab the potential opposition and lock them up. That means scores, maybe hundreds of arresting officers simultaneously descending on addresses all over Moscow and every other major city in the USSR. But it hasn't happened, and you've got Boris Yeltsin calling for the release of Gorbachev. He still has access to the media and he has instructed all army, naval and air force units stationed within the borders of the Russian Socialist Federal Soviet Republic that they obey his orders and return to barracks. The KGB seem curiously inactive, the militia are not out on the streets in force and there has been no sign of their much vaunted black beret commandos. The army appears to be running the show but from what we have seen of them on television, they don't seem to know what they are doing in Moscow and are indecisive."

"That could change," Hazelwood said.

"Sure it could; the army could start getting tough, but the longer this stalemate persists, the less likely that becomes. Sixty per cent of those soldiers we're looking at are eighteen- to twenty-year-old conscripts; they are neither equipped nor trained to put down a riot. Okay – so right now there aren't all that many demonstrators outside the Russian Parliament building and elsewhere in the city, but their numbers will grow when people begin to realise that the troops are not attempting to break up and disperse the crowds. And what are the soldiers going to do when they eventually find themselves confronted by thousands of civilians? Are they going to run over them in their tanks or cut them down with machine-gun fire? Because those are the only two options they've got." Ashton shook his head. "Personally, I can't see them executing either one."

"Anyone want to take issue with Peter?" Hazelwood looked round the room, his jaw set pugnaciously as though ready to devour anyone who had the temerity to disagree. "No dissenting views? Right, that's it then – we'll advise the DG that the coup is going to fail and suggest the government backs Yeltsin."

Several faces round the table didn't look too happy with the advice which he would be putting forward in their name, but the room began to empty before they had a chance to water it down. Although Ashton was not one of the doubters, Hazelwood assumed he was when he remained behind after the others had left.

"Not having second thoughts, are we, Peter?" he asked.

"No."

"Good. I was beginning to wonder if I hadn't been a little too definite about Yeltsin. You see, I don't really believe that the Chairman of the KGB and the Defence Minister are a couple of prize idiots, but I do know that Mr Yeltsin is not exactly fond of Mr Gorbachev. I'm also aware that Mikhail Gorbachev is highly unpopular in his own country. So what if some intermediary approached Yeltsin before the coup and said, 'Look here, Mikhail has got to go, he's running the country into the ground' and Boris said, 'I quite agree with you but it's no use talking about it, you've got to do something.' Mightn't you think he was on your side? Couldn't that be the reason why the KGB didn't arrest him?"

"I wouldn't worry about it," Ashton told him. "If we advise the DG that we think the coup is going to fail, the Foreign Office will do the rest. Their noses would be decidedly out of joint if we were to do their job for them."

"Quite." Hazelwood looked at the notes he had jotted down on the top sheet of the wad of scrap paper the clerks had provided for everyone attending the conference, then said, "Better get the cleaners in here, Peter."

It was standard procedure. After every conference, the chief archivist of the branch and his team carried out a security check and automatically put the top three sheets of every pad through the shredder whether or not anyone had written on them.

"They're waiting in the corridor," Ashton told him.

"We'd better leave them to it then."

"Can you spare me a minute to discuss another matter?"

"I'm going back up to the top floor," Hazelwood said. "See if you can cover it before I reach the lifts."

"I want to put a trace out for Yvette Michel, better known as Galina Kutuzova."

"Come on, Peter, what's happened to your sense of priorities? The USSR may be on the verge of collapse and you want to go after some chit of a girl?"

"She's not just any girl, Victor. Her grandfather ran the Fifth Chief Directorate and there are a lot of people out there in the world who want Galina so bad that they are prepared to kill anyone who tries to get in touch with her."

"Okay, how do you propose to trace her? By using one of our friends in the Met to circulate her description through Interpol?"

"Why not? It's easy enough to make a case against her."

"How long has this girl been on the run now? Over twelve weeks?" They had reached the lifts and Hazelwood leaned forward and pressed the nearest call button. "You send a green tab request for information this late in the day to Interpol at Wiesbaden or any other national office and it will go straight to the bottom of the pile. It'll be a complete waste of time."

"I don't intend to involve the whole world, Victor, just Switzerland, Canada and the USA."

"Why only those three?"

"Galina had the equivalent of eight thousand four hundred

pounds in a Swiss bank account which General Petrovsky opened for her in Zürich. She would need that money because I doubt she had more than the six hundred Deutschmarks Whittle gave her shortly before she took off. I'm banking on Galina having used her French passport to get to Canada so that she can enter the States by the back door."

The up indicator light glowed red and the lift announced its arrival with a loud ping. Hazelwood stepped inside, turned about and pressed the stop button to hold the doors open.

"I suppose it's worth a try, Peter, but I don't think we will get a result."

"With your permission, I'd like to send a red notice."

"Isn't that the equivalent of an International Arrest Warrant?"

Ashton nodded. "I thought we could tell Interpol that Yvette Michel was wanted for questioning in connection with the murder of Robert Whittle."

"That should cause a flutter in the dovecote." Hazelwood pushed the up button. "Tell the Met to make it a priority request."

"I intended to," Ashton told him as the doors began to close.

CHAPTER 13

THE PISTOL aimed straight at her face seemed to have a barrel the size of a cannon. Like a rabbit hypnotised by the headlights of an oncoming vehicle, she stared at the huge cylinders on the revolver and watched the knuckle whiten as the killer slowly tightened his finger on the trigger. Then a cool hand ended the nightmare and brought Galina Kutuzova to the edge of wakefulness. It fell lightly on her exposed shoulder, then moved downward over the collarbone to cup her breast and gently tease the nipple to a stalk before undoing the pyjama jacket. Galina breathed deeply and occasionally sighed, the way she sometimes did when sleeping fitfully, but the pretence failed and the intrusive hand continued to abuse her. The husky voice murmuring in her ear made her feel even sicker.

"It's me – Danni. You've had a bad dream, angel, but I'm here now and everything is going to be okay."

Everything was not going to be okay. With hindsight, it was obvious that meeting Daniella Valli at the Hilton in Las Vegas was the one really bad piece of luck she had had since her Swissair flight had arrived in Montreal over five weeks ago. The investment broker from New York was on vacation with her latest girlfriend, Mary Beth Mallard, a blonde dental hygienist and former beauty queen from Scranton, Pennsylvania, who looked good in high heels but was not over-endowed with brains. The two Americans had joined her at the roulette table where she had been steadily losing more money than she could afford.

"You're not having much luck," Daniella had observed, then added, "Maybe we can bring you some."

With that, she had taken Galina's place at the table and played the percentage game, placing her chips to cover a square of four in each corner with the higher stakes going on odd and even

132

numbers, red and black. As soon as Daniella had established a winning streak, she had invited Galina to follow her play. No great fortunes had been made that night, but Galina had recouped her losses and had come out almost two hundred dollars ahead. More importantly, she had acquired a topnotch financial wizard who knew the money market from A to Z. But there was a price to be paid for all the advice she had received.

"Somebody must have been giving you a very bad time," Daniella murmured, "but I can change all that if you will let me."

Galina clenched her hands, angry because she had no choice in the matter. Daniella had guessed she was an illegal immigrant and to resist her sexual advances was a sure-fire way of collecting a deportation order. Death was waiting for her in Europe but it was pointless to ask for political asylum when there was an unsolved murder in Dresden and she had been the last person to have seen the victim alive. Once they learned where she was, the Germans would press for extradition and they would be supported by the British.

"From now on, I am going to take real good care of you, Yvette."

Daniella Valli was tall, slender, good-looking and superbly fit. An all-round athlete, she excelled at squash, golf and was just one step away from a black belt at judo. She despised all men yet aped them in every way and dominated her partner, Mary Beth, who appeared to worship the ground she walked on. The knowledge that she could beat the American girl senseless with one hand tied behind her back but had to lie there and allow Daniella to explore her body, infuriated Galina.

"You know what I'm thinking?" Daniella asked softly, then answered her own question. "I'm thinking we should set up house together."

"I'm not sure that would be a good idea," Galina muttered.

"Why not?"

"I can't cook . . ." It was the first excuse which came into her head and it sounded absurd, though it seemed to amuse the American.

"You're priceless," Daniella spluttered and yanked the pyjama bottoms down over Galina's hips, then turned her over on to her back.

"What about Mary Beth?"

"You can leave Ms Mallard to me, I'll get her clued in."

Mary Beth already was. Well before they had left Vegas and moved on to Phoenix, Arizona, the blonde girl had made Galina aware of her latent hostility. For all that Mary Beth wasn't too bright, there was nothing wrong with her eyesight and she had seen what was going on and had guessed her lover was getting ready to dump her. Any doubt on that score had been removed when Daniella had phoned the Red Lion La Posada Resort Hotel in Scottsdale and asked Reservations for a triple room. Last night, Mary Beth had made one last desperate attempt to hold on to her partner by making love with wild abandon. The grunts, the little cries of ecstasy, the endearments and the four-letter words had been entirely for Galina's benefit. Now it seemed Daniella was equally determined that her girlfriend should know that she had left her bed to make it with another woman.

Galina felt sick. The American had forced her tongue into her mouth and was moving up and down on her. Yuri Rostovsky had brought her to this with his careless talk of a better life which could be enjoyed by anyone who was prepared to take a chance. It was his loose mouth that had prompted Alexei Leven to call in the goons from Moscow. She had warned him time and again that their precious second-in-command was a KGB nark in the Armed Forces Directorate but he hadn't believed her until an acquaintance at Headquarters 6 Guards Tank Army had told him they were expecting a planeload of Moscow's finest to fly in on Tuesday the twenty-first of May. The day after their arrival, the deadbeat in charge of the GRU unit had informed them that the Chief of Army Intelligence had sent a team of staff officers in to carry out the biennial administrative inspection. After the announcement, Leven had been the only one who hadn't been walking around with a long face.

The inspection team had descended on the unit the day before she had been due to meet the English officer in Dresden. They had gone through all the usual motions of checking the files against the classified register, as well as the security arrangements for safeguarding cryptographic material. They had examined the documentation of every officer's record of service, and had satisfied themselves that the unit had the requisite number of personnel on strength who had attended a nuclear, biological and chemical warfare course and qualified as instructors. The team had in fact behaved as though they really were carrying out an administrative inspection, but that had simply been a ruse to allay suspicion. In her admittedly limited experience, no inspection went into a second day, yet she had spotted at least two members of the team when she had been waiting at the Hauptbahnhof in Dresden for Whittle to show up.

She had seen them again when she and the Englishman had been sitting in the car outside the exhibition hall near the Botanical Gardens. Whittle had just given her six hundred Deutschmarks in cash and three pairs of tights. There was also the little matter of the French passport in her handbag which would have been even more difficult to explain away had the goons from Moscow picked her up. But they hadn't; she had led the Englishman towards the zoo in the southwest corner of the Volkspark and then parted company with him at the lake, having noticed that the KGB narks were not following them. She had picked up a taxi outside the Freilichtheater and had been on her way to meet Yuri Rostovsky when the cab driver had run into another marauding crowd of neo-Nazis and been forced to make a detour through the Stubelalle.

Although they had arrived only minutes after the terrorist incident had occurred, two ambulances, a fire tender and several police cars were already on the scene. The Stubelalle had also been roped off at either end of the street. She was alive today because some instinct had prompted her to ask the driver to wait while she went forward to investigate. The bomb had reduced the car to a heap of scrap metal; a twisted number plate lying some thirty yards from the wreck told her it was the Trabant saloon Whittle had been driving.

She had walked back to the cab and had had to give the driver four hundred marks before he had agreed to take her to the old East German border at Eisenach, approximately one hundred and sixty miles from Dresden. It had been the start of her travels; from Eisenach she had gone on to Zürich and thence to Montreal courtesy of Swissair.

"Oh my, that's good, that's very good," Daniella said and chuckled throatily.

Galina opened her eyes. The American girl was still lying between her legs but had braced both arms to raise the upper half of her body. There was a sensuous smile on her lips and her face glistened with perspiration. Suddenly Daniella clenched her teeth and began to pump up and down until she achieved some kind of climax that left Galina feeling soiled and degraded.

"My God, that was wonderful," Daniella said and rolled off her. "How was it for you?"

"Terrific," Galina told her in a small voice.

It had been the most disgusting thing that had ever happened to her and it was imperative that she moved on before the Valli woman totally corrupted her. Mary Beth was another good reason for leaving as soon as possible; she must have heard them and a jealous, rejected lover made a dangerous enemy. She would need to cover her tracks again, but she was getting pretty adept at doing that. From Montreal, she had bussed her way to Windsor, Ontario where, in return for favours rendered, an obliging American salesman had told US Immigration officials she was his wife when he had taken her across the Detroit river. From Detroit, Galina had flown to Chicago and spent two nights in a Howard Johnson hotel near O'Hare Airport before moving on to San Francisco.

A week later, Galina had left California and made her way to Las Vegas, still without either a credit card or a chequebook. You couldn't get one without the other, and opening a bank account in the States was not the easiest thing in the world. Walk into a bank with ten thousand dollars in cash, and nine tellers out of ten would look at you with the utmost suspicion. She had gone to Vegas because she had heard bankers took a more relaxed view of things in Nevada where large amounts of cash regularly changed hands and people would readily believe that she had hit the jackpot. All Daniella had done was vouch for her when she had opened a checking account with Wells Fargo.

"A penny for them, Yvette."

"What?"

"What are you thinking about?"

"Oh, I was thinking how I would like a nice relaxing day by the pool."

"You've got it," Daniella said drowsily.

Galina lay there watching the early morning sunlight steal into the room, the possessive hand of an unwanted lover resting on her pubic hair. Although Mary Beth had been snoring intermittently, she could tell the dental hygienist and former beauty queen was wide awake.

Normally, the Eastern Bloc Directorate managed perfectly well with just one officer on duty during silent hours, at weekends and on public holidays. There was, however, nothing normal about a putsch in the USSR, which was why Hazelwood had decided that the Russian Desk should be fully manned round the clock. He had also decided to set up shop in the fall-out shelter in the basement which was designed to serve as an operations room during the transition to war phase. His critics in Century House maintained that he was simply using the crisis to justify the resources which were pumped into his Directorate year after year. They had a point; over seventy per cent of the funds allocated to the SIS went straight into the Eastern Bloc and until Gorbachev had started to dismantle the Soviet Armed Forces, no one had ever questioned whether it was cost effective.

Directorates like the Rest of the World still had to operate on a shoestring budget, even though nine years ago they had really earned their keep when Operation Corporate had been launched to recover the Falklands. Mid-East didn't have to justify their budget, at least not after Desert Storm. They could also take credit for having warned the government that Saddam Hussein was going to use the Iraqi army to settle his differences with Kuwait. Maybe that inspired piece of gazing into a crystal ball had not earned them a bigger slice of the cake but it had most certainly kept the cost accountants at bay and pointed them towards Hazelwood's empire instead.

The coup could not have arrived at a better time for Hazelwood; it was just unfortunate that the putsch was over almost before it began. The stalemate had persisted right up to Tuesday afternoon; thereafter, things had started to go Yeltsin's way with the President of Kazakhstan, the third largest republic, demanding to speak to Gorbachev and the Ukraine deciding that orders and decisions originated by the new hardline Kremlin were null and void. In the wake of these setbacks, Prime Minister Pavlov suddenly had a diplomatic illness; then three hours later, Estonia had declared independence.

The one time it had looked as if the Russian Desk had got it wrong occurred at 2230 hours when tanks had charged the barricades outside the Russian Parliament and three demonstrators had been killed. Then, as if to confirm there really was an iron fist inside the velvet glove, the Red Army had taken over every radio station and TV tower in Lithuania and Estonia. The show of strength hadn't lasted. Long before the official announcement from the Defence Ministry, the embassy in Moscow was getting reports that the tanks and armoured personnel carriers, which had been waiting on the Inner Ring motorway, were beginning to pull out of the city. At 1320, the troop movement had been confirmed by Moscow Radio; one hour later, it was announced that the leaders of the coup were flying to Sevastopol to meet Gorbachev at his villa in Foros where he and his family had been virtually under house arrest.

"The whole business was over before it really got started," Hazelwood said in a tone of voice that sounded faintly aggrieved.

"I wouldn't lose too much sleep over it," Ashton said. "Perhaps if the crisis had lasted a day or two longer it would have made us seem even more prophetic, but we got it right. That's something they can't take away from us."

"Quite." Hazelwood didn't sound convinced; he just stood there gazing round the deserted operations room apparently reluctant to leave even though he had dismissed all the watchkeepers.

"Cheer up, it's not the end of the world," Ashton told him.

"What?"

"There's still Galina Kutuzova."

"Really? After all that's happened, you don't think that perhaps we are going from the sublime to the ridiculous, do you?"

"Swissair came up with a trace. They keep a record of every flight manifest for sixty days on their computer and the print-out shows that a Mademoiselle Yvette Michel flew to Montreal from Zürich on Flight SR 160 departing 1155 hours Saturday the thirteenth of July."

"Where did you get this information?"

"From Interpol via our friend in the Met."

"I don't know," Hazelwood said, frowning. "It could be some other Yvette Michel."

"Right time, right place, right destination – that's just too much of a coincidence, Victor."

"Well, if it is, presumably the RCMP have been informed?"

138

"They have."

"Then there's nothing else we can do."

"I don't want to leave everything to Interpol and hope for the best. I've been talking to our friendly detective inspector in the Metropolitan Police who runs the UK (National) Office and what he had to say about Interpol and its success rate is pretty depressing. Do you know what the chances are of apprehending anyone even when the request carries a priority red tab? No better than fifty per cent, and then it's often months later before you get a result. I think we should stir things up a bit."

"How? By sending you over to Canada?" Hazelwood shook his head. "We would never get the finance people to sanction the expense on such flimsy evidence."

"They wouldn't have to – at least, not yet. What I would like to do first is give something to Lieutenant Colonel Alexei Leven, the second-in-command of the GRU unit in Potsdam, that will make his hair stand on end."

"Are you saying you want to meet him head to head?"

"How else am I going to see the fear in his eyes?"

"It's out of the question."

"Why? What have we got to lose, Victor? After what happened in Leningrad and Moscow, I'm not exactly the anonymous face in the crowd any more."

Hazelwood sighed. "I know I'm not going to like this," he said, "but I think you had better tell me what you hope to achieve by giving Alexei Leven the fright of his life?"

"I am going to make the Foreign and Commonwealth Office admit that everything in the garden isn't lovely. I'm tired of their pretence that Whittle was murdered by the Provos or was the victim of some mythical Iraqi hit squad or was the innocent bystander killed in some gangland dispute. I'm going to let Leven know that Galina Kutuzova is travelling under the name of Yvette Michel and has been traced to Montreal, then wait and see what he does with the information. I'm betting he will use the GRU communications network to pass it on to his superiors in Moscow."

"And presumably you expect the army to intercept the relevant transmission?"

Ashton nodded. In the British Army of the Rhine 13 Signal Regiment had no other role in life but to monitor the Soviet

139

military network in Eastern Europe, and with a squadron based in Berlin, they were nicely placed to eavesdrop on Potsdam. Their intercepts were, however, forwarded directly to Government Communications Headquarters in Cheltenham for analysis and Hazelwood would need to seek their assistance through official channels.

"What makes you think the Sig Int people will put their resources at our disposal, Peter?"

"Because they have agreed in principle to just that."

"Who have you been talking to?"

"Some old friends at Cheltenham. I did a three-year tour of duty at GCHQ from '84 to '87, remember? Anyway, several of them have moved upwards since those days and are in a position to help us. The upshot is that we've got the whole of the Berlin squadron for ninety-six hours from 0800 local time this coming Friday. Naturally, I'll need to liaise with the Signal squadron which is why we've already fixed a rendezvous for 1300 on Thursday."

"If you are planning on going to Berlin first thing tomorrow, how do you expect to get hold of traveller's cheques and D'marks before then?"

"I don't," Ashton told him. "I've got a Gold Card. It will buy a plane ticket, obtain money from a cashpoint and all the Deutschmarks I need from any German bank. All you've got to do, Victor, is make an official request to Cheltenham and the resources are ours."

"You have been busy."

"Yes, I have. When I organised the duty roster for the Ops room, I made sure I had time off during normal office hours to do what had to be done. All we were doing was looking at TV screens, getting our information second-hand from Cable News Network."

"You've really got a thing about Galina Kutuzova, haven't you?"

"I don't like being shot at," Ashton said grimly.

"I'll have to clear it with the DG."

"Well, I'm sure he will see the logic behind the operation. After all, the GRU cell at Potsdam is practically right on top of Headquarters 6 Guards Tank Army and we would be falling down on the job if we didn't try to find out how the Soviet forces are reacting to the failed putsch in Moscow."

A broad smile appeared on Hazelwood's face. "My thoughts exactly," he said, looking more cheerful.

"I'll tell you something else, Victor. If Leven does signal Moscow, even the Foreign Office will have to agree that Galina Kutuzova can scarcely be the small-time crook they would like us to believe she is."

That was only the beginning. Once they had the Foreign and Commonwealth Office on their side, it would be that much easier to get the State Department interested in finding the Russian girl, especially if they believed she was in their own back yard. By the time he had finished, Ashton hoped he would have a whole army looking for her.

CHAPTER 14

MARY BETH Mallard was reclining on a sunbed by the pool next to Daniella. She was wearing a bottle-green baseball cap on the back of her blonde head, a pair of Polaroids which hid the dark smudges under her eyes, and a two-piece latex swimsuit designed for maximum exposure of her cleavage and shapely legs. The swimsuit was bone dry and would remain so; the same could not be said for her throat. Mary Beth was on her third dry martini since brunch, which might have been okay if brunch had consisted of something more substantial than fresh orange juice and a green salad with Italian dressing. Although fairly high, she had not yet reached the stage of being loud with it. Her asides were, however, becoming more and more barbed and Galina knew she was getting ready to pick a fight with her. It was within Daniella's power to cool the situation whenever she wanted to, but it seemed she was enjoying herself too much to take on the role of peacemaker.

"Keep on the way you're going," Daniella said, "and you'll end up with a spare tyre in no time."

"You need to get your eyes tested," Mary Beth said and patted her stomach. "I'm in good shape, which is more than can be said for little Miss Freeloader here."

"Freeloader? What's eating you?"

"Nothing."

"So why the bitchy remark?"

"Bitchy? Hell, I was just making a pertinent observation." Mary Beth raised her sunglasses and glared at Galina. "I mean, what have you got in that purse of yours besides moths?"

"That's uncalled for," Daniella told her coolly. "Furthermore, it's untrue."

"Yeah? Well, I guess we both know how Yvette pays her dues."

Galina felt the colour rise in her face but somehow managed to steel herself not to trade insults with the former beauty queen. It had taken a lot of time, effort and guile to set up this opportunity to make a getaway and she wasn't about to let it slip through her fingers. When she got up and walked off, she didn't want Daniella running after her under the impression that she was leaving out of pique.

If it was possible to get Mary Beth alone, she might be able to put her straight, even win her over, but Daniella was having too much fun to leave them on their own together. Galina moved her chair nearer the sunshade and angled it to face the artificial waterfall cascading into the pool over massive rust-coloured boulders. By distancing herself slightly from the other two, she hoped to defuse the atmosphere. But the sniping continued. "You can leave Ms Mallard to me," Daniella had whispered, "I'll get her clued in." And in a roundabout way, she was doing just that. As the minutes dragged slowly by, Galina came to accept that things could only get worse, not better.

"A-agh." Galina winced as if in pain, gasped a second time and slowly got to her feet, one hand nursing her stomach.

"Are you okay?" Daniella asked her.

"I will be, as soon as I get to our room."

"I'll come with you."

"No," Galina said sharply. "No, that won't be necessary. It is just that time of the month. I'm going to change, fix myself up, and then I'll be back. Okay?"

"Sure, don't be long."

"I won't."

"Do you have a key to the room with you?" Daniella asked.

"In my handbag."

Galina walked away, leaving her towel behind as a sign she intended to return. The forecast was for a high of one hundred and six but not all the perspiration that ran down her face was due to the heat. Mouth dry with nervous tension, she hurried on past the clump of palm trees towards the gate and the path which led to their particular room in the bungalow-style complex on the left of the hotel proper.

How long would she have before Daniella began to wonder what was keeping her and was concerned enough to come looking? Ten minutes? Perhaps fifteen if she was lucky. Once out of sight of the pool, Galina kicked off her flipflops and dumped them behind the neat knee-high privet bordering the path, then started running in bare feet, only too aware that every second counted. To save time, she got the room key out before she reached the verandah steps.

A cool blast of air hit her as she opened the door and stepped into the narrow hall. Dumping her handbag on the nearest bed, Galina looked out a blouse and skirt and put them on over the two-piece swimsuit, then slipped on a pair of low heels. The alarm bells would start ringing with the hotel staff if any of them saw her carrying a suitcase; fortunately, Mary Beth possessed a large shoulder bag that was unlikely to excite anyone's suspicion. Big as it was, the bag could only hold a fraction of her wardrobe; after packing her toiletries, underwear, jeans and some T-shirts, there was just enough room left for an extra skirt and blouse.

A courtesy coach left the hotel for the airport on the hour and half-hour, but to catch it, she would have to walk past the swimming pool in full view of Daniella and Mary Beth. The Chevrolet Caprice Daniella had rented from Hertz? The keys were there for the taking on top of the chest of drawers. It was very tempting, but running out on her was not a crime, stealing the car most certainly would be. A cab to pick her up from the room then? Lifting the receiver, she punched the button for Reception and asked for the bell captain. As she waited for the hotel operator to put her through, Galina heard the door open and turned to face the hall.

"I see you've made a rapid recovery," Mary Beth said acidly.

Galina put the phone down. "I'm leaving."

"Yeah? What the hell are you doing with my tote bag, lady?"

"I was going to borrow it."

"Where I come from, we call it stealing . . ."

"I was going to leave my suitcase and fifty dollars as compensation." Galina opened her handbag and showed Mary Beth her billfold. "See, I have the money right here."

"And that's where it would have stayed . . ."

"Look, all I want to do is leave here as quickly as possible and with the minimum amount of hassle."

"Now I get it. You were hoping to sneak off, leaving us to pick up your hotel bill. Right?"

"Wrong. If you hadn't shown up when you did, I would have left more than enough money to cover my share."

"You're a goddamned liar," Mary Beth said angrily. "People like you belong in jail and I'm going to put you there."

"This is ridiculous, you should be glad to see the back of me. I'm not interested in Daniella and I never wanted to come between you two. Can't you understand that?"

"I understand a lot of things, like how you are a two-timing little bitch as well as a thief." Mary Beth moved towards the telephone on the low table. "That's why I'm going to call the police."

"Please, you're making a big mistake."

"Not as big as the one you've made."

There was, Galina realised, no reasoning with her. Mary Beth was so eaten up with jealousy, nothing she could say would make a jot of difference. She reached out, spun the American girl completely around, then grabbed hold of both shoulders and pulled her forward. With perfect timing, Galina waltzed through a reverse turn and threw Mary Beth over her outstretched left leg. It was a simple throw, executed with just enough force to deter rather than hurt her adversary.

"I can get a lot tougher if I have to," Galina warned her. "But that won't be necessary because you are going to be sensible and let me walk out of here. Right?"

"The hell I am."

"Then I'll have to lock you in the room and make sure you can't ring for help."

Turning her back on the blonde girl, Galina walked over to the low table and ripped the leads from the telephone. In the time it took her to do that, Mary Beth had armed herself with an ice pick. A combination of injured pride, humiliation and jealousy made her blind to all but an overriding desire for revenge.

Galina heard her coming, whirled about and reacted as she had been trained to do when confronted with someone intent on killing her. Throwing up her left arm to ward off the downward thrust of the ice pick, she struck for the throat, the fingers of her right hand rigid, the whole weight of her body behind the blow. She did not mean to kill Mary Beth but her fingers were like hardened steel, and when they smashed into the larynx destroying the vocal chords and the trachea, the blonde girl dropped dead at her feet.

145

For almost half a minute, Galina stood there unable to comprehend what had happened, then a subconscious voice urged her to get out before Daniella showed up, and the spell was broken. Grand auto theft was now a minor misdemeanour compared with homicide; grabbing the keys to the Chevrolet from the top of the chest of drawers, she tucked her handbag under one arm, picked up the drawstring tote bag containing her clothes and ran out of the room, slamming the door behind her.

The powder-blue Caprice was parked in the adjoining bay not twenty feet from their room; unlocking the doors, Galina tossed the shoulder bag on to the back seat and got in behind the wheel. After cranking the engine into life, she eased the gear shift into reverse, then released the handbrake and backed out on a right-hand lock. Compared with the Lada saloon she had used in East Germany, the Chevrolet seemed as big as a truck. She straightened up, put the automatic gearbox into drive and pushed down on the accelerator with a heavy foot. The engine responded with a deep-throated snarl and the rear tyres squealed in anguished protest. Thoroughly alarmed, Galina eased her foot on the gas pedal and almost stalled. She did not make the same mistake twice as she drove slowly past the swimming pool, mentally crossing her fingers that Daniella wouldn't see her before she turned on to the highway.

With no plan in mind other than to get out of Arizona before the alarm was raised, Galina headed towards Phoenix, turned left on Twenty-Fourth Street and followed the signs for Sky Harbor International Airport. She had exactly one thousand dollars in her purse.

Ashton found four items of junk mail, a postcard from a former colleague who was now living in Hong Kong, and a recorded delivery letter waiting for him on the doormat when he let himself into the flat. The fact that they hadn't been placed on the hall table told him the cleaning lady hadn't been near the place in the last four days.

There were also a couple of messages on the answering machine, which was something of a miracle because usually he forgot to put it on before leaving the flat, as had been the case when he'd gone to the Soviet Union. The first message was from the garage to remind him that his Vauxhall Cavalier was due for a ten thousand-mile service; the other was from the estate agent to say they had had an offer for the flat. It was a good deal lower than the asking price and he personally couldn't afford to accept the offer, but the decision wasn't his to take in isolation. He glanced at his wristwatch; Bahrain was two hours ahead of British Summer Time which meant it was almost nine p.m. over there. Not even Jill was likely to be still in the office at that hour, but Ashton supposed he could always ring her at home. Lifting the receiver, he punched out 010973 followed by 21448. The number rang out half a dozen times before a man with a somewhat plummy voice answered the phone and coolly informed him that Miss Sheridan was rather busy at the moment and could he take a message.

"Tell her I've had an offer for the flat," Ashton said tersely, "then let's see how busy she is."

The new man in Jill's life put the phone down with unnecessary force; then Ashton heard him call out to her and made a mental note of the "darling" bit. Jill, however, did not give him much time to ponder on its significance; the news that the estate agent had found a buyer for the property brought her hurrying to the phone.

"How much have we been offered?" she asked breathlessly.

"A hundred and five thousand."

"Take it, Peter."

"That's a hell of a drop considering we paid a hundred and twenty for the flat and took out a mortgage of eighty. We're going to lose fifteen grand and that doesn't take into account the fees for the solicitor and estate agent."

"So what? The property has been on the market long enough and we are not likely to get a better offer in the present climate."

"How would you know? You're three thousand miles away." Ashton took a deep breath, told himself that losing his temper would only make things worse and tried to follow his own advice. "Look," he said in a more reasonable voice, "let's think about this for a couple of days."

"There is nothing to think about," Jill told him abruptly.

"No? Well, maybe you can afford to write off eight or nine thousand quid, but I can't."

"That's too bad, Peter, because I'm going to instruct my bank

147

to cancel the standing order to the Halifax Building Society forthwith."

Jill did not give him a chance to come back at her; before he could say another word, she hung up, cutting him off. Replacing his phone with a good deal less force than Jill had, Ashton vented his anger on the recorded letter, ripping the envelope open with a thumb. Tucked inside was a banker's draft for six hundred and eighty-five pounds, the exact amount he had paid out for the trip to Leningrad and Moscow. "Well, thank you, Victor," he said aloud.

In a slightly better mood, Ashton fixed himself a whisky and soda, then took a shower. He was just reaching for the towel when the phone rang; dripping water, he went out into the hall to answer it. He hoped it was Jill calling him back to say that she had had second thoughts and was mildly disappointed to find himself talking to Victor Hazelwood.

"I've cleared it, Peter," he said tersely. "You can leave first thing tomorrow – that's official."

"Terrific. I'll call British Airways and make a reservation."

"That's already been taken care of. Pick up your ticket from the BA desk in Terminal One. Your flight departs at 0830."

"Right."

"Better tip your hat to our man on the spot as soon as you arrive; I wouldn't want to put his nose out of joint, especially as he's been told to provide whatever support you require."

Hazelwood wasn't allowing him much leeway. Berlin was an hour ahead of London and he would be pushed to make the RV with the representative from 13 Signal Regiment on time.

"I'll be very diplomatic," Ashton said and hung up.

There would, he decided, be no time to call the estate agent before he left for Germany and who could tell what might happen while he was away? With any luck, the prospective buyer might change his mind and withdraw the offer. Lifting the phone again, he rang the car hire service in the High Street and arranged for a minicab to pick him up at 0645 hours.

Detective 3rd Grade Lewis Dyce was thirty-seven and a widower. He lived on Peoria Avenue in Glendale with his two children, Gavin aged twelve and nine-year-old Tracy. His mother-in-law who had lost her husband in 1981, kept house for them.

While serving with the NYPD, Dyce had won four commendations for bravery and had really been going places when he had asked for a transfer to Phoenix. His wife, Julia, had been a chronic asthmatic and the doctors had advised him that the climate in Arizona would suit her better. So he'd had a word with the Bureau of Personnel and they had arranged everything. It had meant coming down to detective third grade, but Julia's health had come first and he had looked on the demotion as a small price to pay for that.

The change had certainly proved beneficial for Julia's asthma; it had just been one of life's bitter ironies that cervical cancer had claimed her barely three years after they had moved out west. Colleagues, as well as his superiors in the police department, reckoned that his wife's death had left him a burnt-out case and there were times when even he recognised that they weren't far wrong. Dyce had caught the Mallard killing because he had happened to be the only detective in the squad room when the call had come in and it had seemed a pretty open and shut case to the lieutenant.

A Blue and White had responded to the 911 call; by the time Dyce had reached the Red Lion La Posada Resort Hotel, the patrolman had summoned an ambulance, two other prowl cars and had taken a preliminary statement from Ms Daniella Valli who had identified the victim. It had looked an open and shut case to the lieutenant because the patrolman had learned that the killer had taken off in a powder-blue Chevrolet Caprice and the licence number of the stolen vehicle had already been passed to the State Police and Highway Patrol before Dyce had left for the resort hotel. The smart money was on the killer heading west on Interstate 10, then south on State Highway 85 to the Mexican border a little over a hundred and fifty miles away.

Dyce hadn't needed a medical examiner to tell him the cause of death; he had only to look at the marks on the dead woman's larynx to know the answer to that question. So he had left the scene-of-the-crime experts to it and returned to Civic Plaza with Ms Valli in tow.

"What I need to do now," he explained, "is get a more detailed statement from you to sort of tidy things up. We'll tape it first, then turn the thing over to an audiotypist who will get to work on a word processor. After that, we will ask you to read the finished copy and sign it. Okay?"

"Yes."

"Good. Now, can I get you a cup of coffee or something before we start?"

"No, thank you."

Dyce took out a pack of Marlborough. "Do you smoke?" he asked.

"I used to, but I gave it up."

"Would you mind if I did?"

"Not in the least."

He shook a cigarette from the pack, lit it and inhaled, then hit the record button. "For the record," he said, "can we have your name, date and place of birth, status, home address and occupation?"

"My name is Daniella Valli," she said calmly. "I was born on July twenty-sixth 1955 at Albany, New York. I'm single, my home address is 2291 George Street, Staten Island and I am an investment broker with Hanson, Baldwin and Geeker."

"And the deceased is?"

"Mary Beth Mallard. She was born on October sixth 1953 at Scranton, Pennsylvania. She was a dental hygienist and we lived together."

"She was your roommate?"

"Lover," Daniella said and raised her chin defiantly.

Dyce hadn't figured her for a lesbian. He supposed it was because he had found her attractive, well-groomed and refined. There was, in fact, nothing butch about her; she used make-up, eye shadow and he had particularly admired her copper bronze hair and the way she had it styled.

"Is there anyone we should inform?" he asked, breaking an awkward silence.

"Mary Beth's parents retired to Florida; they live somewhere in Bradenton, I don't know the address."

"No problem, we'll find them." Dyce stubbed out his cigarette. "Okay," he said, "let's talk about the suspect – Yvette Michel."

"You mean the murderer."

"We can't be sure of that."

"I am."

The venomous tone made her feelings about the missing woman

very clear. Yvette Michel had almost certainly killed her girlfriend and he supposed it was only natural that she should hate her, but all the same, he couldn't help wondering if it was really that simple.

"That's your privilege, Miss Valli . . ."

"Ms," she said, correcting him.

"Right. Now, as I understand it, you met Yvette Michel in Las Vegas?"

"She came and sat next to Mary Beth at the roulette table. After a while, they got talking and things sort of developed from there."

"Whose idea was it to come to Phoenix?"

"As I recall, Yvette said she had never seen the Grand Canyon and neither it seemed had Mary Beth. Of course, we had been going around as a threesome for at least a couple of days before this came up, and in the end I think it was me who suggested we should fly into Phoenix."

"And you arrived here when?"

"Monday noon. I rented a Chevrolet Caprice from the Hertz desk at the airport and we headed out of town on Interstate 17, then branched off to Sedona and stopped over at a motel on Oak Creek. Next day we went on to the Grand Canyon, stayed the night at the Howard Johnson Hotel and then drove straight back here. We arrived about six p.m. yesterday evening."

He thought Ms Valli had probably given him an accurate and truthful account of what had happened from the moment the three women had arrived at Sky Harbor International Airport because those particular facts could be verified. But when he had asked her earlier how they had met up with Yvette Michel, there had been a significant pause before she had laid it on Mary Beth. It therefore seemed to him that, for reasons known only to herself, Ms Valli wouldn't hesitate to lie in her teeth if she believed she could get away with it.

"And you spent today by the poolside?"

"Yeah, that was Yvette's idea. She hadn't been sleeping too well and was tired, even though we didn't get up this morning until it was time for brunch."

"Okay, you have had brunch and all three of you are at the poolside. Now what happened?"

"Well, Yvette was in a funny mood; she was sniping at Mary

151

Beth and I couldn't think why. Turned out her period was just starting; anyway, that's the excuse she gave when she left the pool to change into something more appropriate."

"What time was this?" Dyce asked quickly.

"I'm not sure. I didn't look at my wristwatch, but it must have been two thirty, maybe even three o'clock."

When it didn't matter, Ms Valli was very precise, when it did, she was vague. Delta, American and United were just three airlines which operated in and out of Phoenix and that half-hour difference could complicate things.

"Yvette told us she was coming back as soon as she had changed; when she failed to reappear, Mary Beth went looking for her. See, she had lost a couple of small pieces of costume jewellery when we were staying at the Howard Johnson Hotel. They weren't valuable and, in any case, Mary Beth couldn't prove Yvette had stolen them, but she no longer trusted her."

"Any idea what time it was when Mary Beth left the pool?"

Even as he asked the question, Dyce knew her answer would be unhelpful. By now, it didn't surprise him that Ms Valli was vague about her own movements. Amongst the trio she was obviously the dominant character and her long-standing girlfriend had got very uptight when she had taken a shine to the newcomer. He thought it likely that Daniella had enjoyed playing one off against the other, never dreaming her little games would have such a violent outcome. Her evidence wasn't to be trusted because she was distorting the facts in order to present herself in the best possible light. Nevertheless, he waited until she had finished telling him what had happened that afternoon before asking her to describe Yvette Michel.

"I don't think that is her real name," Daniella said. "And I can tell you she isn't an American citizen. One time she had her bag open and I caught sight of her passport, and it certainly hadn't been issued by our State Department. Something else you should know about Yvette; she's got a fat billfold and won't have to use a credit card to buy an airplane ticket."

Dyce lit another cigarette. A fat billfold also meant she didn't have to prove her identity and could travel under any name she cared to invent. And how many flights had departed from Sky Harbor International Airport since two p.m., the last time an independent witness had seen all three women together, and four thirty-seven when the 911 call had been logged? Fifteen? Twenty? Twenty-five? He could only hope not too many women had paid cash for their plane tickets. Stretching out his right hand, Dyce hit the stop button on the tape recorder.

"Tell you what we'll do," he said. "You give me a general description of Yvette Michel, then we will call in a Fotofit specialist and he'll help you to make up a face."

"That won't be necessary."

"Oh yeah? Why not?"

Daniella smiled. "Because I took several snapshots of her when we were up at the Grand Canyon."

CHAPTER 15

SIX WEEKS ago when Ashton had flown into Berlin, he had been met at Tegel Airport by a junior staff officer and taken straight to the Olympic stadium in a Ford Cortina. He had also been accommodated in the officers' mess. This time he was staying at the Excelsior Hotel on Hardenbergstrasse near the centre of town and had to find his own transport. Back in July, he had steered well clear of Head of Station, Berlin; on this occasion, he had been told to make his number with Franklin.

Neil Franklin was the twelfth Head of Station the SIS had had since the end of World War Two. He was also likely to be the last. When Berlin became the official capital and seat of government for a united Germany, the British Embassy would move house from Bonn and he would be out of a job. The SIS chief would then be locked into the embassy masquerading as a first secretary and about as inconspicuous as a Siamese cat in heat.

Like his predecessors, Franklin enjoyed a degree of anonymity that would almost certainly be denied to those who followed him. To the world at large, he was the owner of the English Bookshop on Budapesterstrasse opposite the Zoologischer Garten. Other business ventures which the SIS had used as a front in the past had included the offices of the British Council, a car body repair shop, a small travel agency and an extremely modest hotel in the Wittenau District. At the height of the Cold War in the fifties, these front offices had been necessary in the interests of secrecy; forty years on, the English Bookshop was an anachronism. The frontier had moved eastwards to the Oder-Neisse Line and Chancellor Kohl was not going to allow a foreign Intelligence Service carte blanche to operate on German soil in the way the SIS in Berlin had been accustomed to.

Five years was the normal tour of duty for a Head of Station.

Franklin had been appointed in 1986 and had been due to leave in November, but the destruction of the Wall had signalled the end of routine reliefs and he was now expected to remain in post until the British Embassy in Bonn transferred to Berlin.

He was fifty, the same age as Hazelwood, but that was about all they had in common. Franklin hailed from Newcastle-upon-Tyne, had a reputation for being abrasive and was very much a law unto himself. There was a long-standing antipathy between the two men, the cause of which was known only to the upper echelons of Century House. Matters had come to a head when Hazelwood had been made the acting Director of the Eastern Bloc Desk following the sudden death of the previous incumbent. Determined not to have anything to do with him, Franklin had sought and received permission to communicate directly with the DG. Ashton therefore received a less than friendly welcome when he made his acquaintance in the office above the bookshop and wondered what he had done to merit such a frigid reception. He found out soon enough.

"Putting things right, are we?" Franklin said after shaking hands perfunctorily.

"In what respect?"

"This isn't your first trip to the city; you flew in on Tuesday the ninth of July."

"It was a fleeting visit."

"I know, you departed the following morning on the shuttle to Hannover, having stayed the night in the officers' mess, Headquarters Berlin."

Franklin liked to project himself as a man who had his ear to the ground and knew exactly what was going on in his bailiwick, but in this instance it wasn't true. What irked him about the previous visit was the fact that he had only learned about it when London had suggested Simon Younger might be able to identify the mystery woman who had left a message on the answering machine for Yuri Rostovsky some time after the GRU officer had been murdered.

"I'm sorry we didn't meet the last time I was here, but I was doing an in and out job for the Foreign and Commonwealth Office and they told me to leave you well alone. In fact, they were adamant that there was to be no local SIS involvement."

"Why?" Franklin demanded truculently.

155

"The army looked as though it was going to rock the boat over the Whittle affair, so the FCO wanted us to convince them that it wasn't the Russians who had literally blown their man away. The information on the terrorist group who were thought to be responsible for the incident had to look as if it came from an Intelligence source outside Germany. The way people in London saw it, Headquarters Berlin would smell a rat if they learned I had been to see you."

With his abrasive manner and happy knack of rubbing the military authorities up the wrong way, it was also felt that Franklin was the last man to handle the assignment. But Ashton was not about to tell him that.

"But the army wouldn't buy it and now you're taking a different line?"

Ashton nodded. "We've every reason to believe Galina Kutuzova was the intended target. Naturally the KGB weren't too fussy about killing Whittle too if he was unlucky enough to get in the way."

"I see. Perhaps you can explain why the KGB should have waited until she went to Dresden before attempting to liquidate her?"

"We shan't know the answer to that question until we run Galina Kutuzova to ground."

"Well, if you do succeed in doing that, Ashton, don't expect any earth-shattering revelations. She was Rostovsky's partner and had a finger in every racket. In all probability, a rival firm decided to kill her as a warning to Rostovsky. That they failed to do so was of no consequence; they had served notice on Rostovsky to stay out of their territory and when he chose to ignore it, they went after him." Franklin leaned back in his chair, a derisive smile on his face. "Or is that too simple for you?" he inquired softly.

"No, we could even be thinking along the same lines. Of course, it depends on whether you regard trafficking in information as a racket and what you mean by a rival firm."

"We could go on like this all day. Clearly, you didn't come here simply out of politeness, so what is it you want from me?"

"I thought London had already told you. I need someone to watch my back in any tête-à-tête I may have with the Russians."

"I'm not running a private bodyguard service," Franklin told him.

"Are you turning me down?"

"Only if I find your demands are unreasonable. Contrary to what London might think, I don't have a private army at my disposal."

"I'm not planning to start a war. All I need is one local who knows his way around; he doesn't have to be an ace shot or a master at kung fu, karate or any of the other martial arts. Common sense, initiative and a cool head are the qualities I am looking for."

"Is that all?"

"With the exception of one final qualification. He should have enough clout with the Polizei to call on them for help, should I be lifted."

Franklin didn't actually hum and haw but his facial expressions suggested he had been landed with a baffling problem. "When do you want this paragon?" he asked eventually.

"I'd like to meet him before I phone our Russian friend this evening. Sometime around five o'clock would suit me. I leave the rendezvous to you."

There was another equally long pause while the Head of Station, Berlin apparently put his mind to solving a time and space conundrum. "You'd better meet him in Diener's Place on Seybelstrasse."

"How will I recognise him?"

"He's about five nine, weighs around a hundred and thirty-five pounds and has light brown hair. He lost the sight of his left eye in a fracas some years back and now wears a black patch . . ."

"Jesus," Ashton said with feeling.

"Name's Willie."

"Is that his surname or what?"

"It's all you're getting."

"Thanks a lot." Ashton stood up and started towards the door.

"One final point," Franklin said, stopping him before he reached it. "This is my parish and I expect to be kept informed of all your movements."

"Right."

"So where are you off to now?"

"I'm going to see a man about a radio."

"Who, where and what for?"

"That's all you're getting," Ashton told him.

By prior arrangement, the meeting with the Technical Officer Telecommunications from the Berlin-based squadron of 13 Signal Regiment took place at the junction of Badestrand Promenade and Wassernixenweg on the shores of the Wannsee. The TOT was a thirty-seven-year-old captain who had been commissioned from the ranks and had spent the whole of his service from the age of eighteen rotating between the Communications and Security Group (UK), 9, 13 and 14 Signal Regiments. Eavesdropping on the Soviet Armed Forces had been his bread and butter ever since he had put on a uniform; there was therefore very little he didn't know about the art of electronic warfare.

He also knew how to blend in with the background and turned up at the rendezvous in sports clothes driving an '87 model Audi 100. The pert brunette in shorts and suntop he had brought along with him was the troop officer commanding the WRAC element of the squadron.

"Camouflage," he informed Ashton with a completely straight face. "Take a good look at the lakeside and you'll see what I mean."

It was a typical August day with hardly a cloud in the sky and the temperature somewhere in the mid-eighties. Every child of school age in Berlin appeared to be on the beach, so it seemed was a high proportion of those good-looking secretaries whose best work was done out of office hours.

"Two blokes on their own wouldn't look right," he added in case Ashton hadn't grasped the allusion.

"I take it you two don't have any secrets from one another?"

"You don't have to worry about Lorna," the TOT assured him. "She's been cleared for Signal Intelligence and constant access to Top Secret, and you can't get any higher than that."

You could, but Ashton didn't see any point in making an issue of it. Lorna had the requisite clearance for what he proposed to say to her companion.

"Have you been told what this is all about?" he asked.

"We had a confirmatory signal from the MOD last night, not to mention GCHQ."

"So can it be done?"

The TOT satisfied himself that no stranger could overhear him, then said, "If this guy you are interested in tries to get a message to Leningrad or Moscow by radio relay or over a teleprinter circuit, we'll intercept and break it. Scramblers don't bother us and it doesn't matter what cipher he uses either."

"Suppose he pre-records the message and squirts it through in a one-minute blast?"

"You'd be surprised how many frequencies we can monitor simultaneously. The one thing which could throw us would be a major change of frequency by your boy at the very last minute before he transmitted. If he went way outside the range we were covering, we might not lock on to him again in time to intercept the squirt."

"But the receiving station would have to know about the switch in advance?"

"Too right."

"I think our friend will want to hide his message amongst all the other classified transmissions. To do that, he will have to stick to the planned schedules for the day." Ashton paused, then said, "It's not only us he has to worry about; in these uncertain times he'll have one eye looking over his shoulder."

"That's okay then. But we would still be in trouble if the material was sent by hand of courier. And I don't have to tell you that we can't intercept an international call made from a pay phone somewhere in Eastern Europe."

"There's no way you can plug every loophole," Ashton said, and left it at that.

He didn't have the resources to mount a surveillance operation on Alexei Leven and, in any event, the sceptics in London and Washington would hardly sit up and take notice simply because the Russian had been seen to use a pay phone. They wouldn't be convinced that the KGB were determined to eliminate Galina Kutuzova unless there was hard evidence to support the contention. And only a transmission from Potsdam which had been intercepted, recorded and decoded was likely to satisfy the doubters.

"You've got every available intercept station in the squadron," the TOT informed him. "Deployment starts at 1600 this afternoon and will be completed by 1800, twelve hours before the operation starts."

"So what are the chances of using some of the stations ahead of schedule?"

"You're pushing your luck, aren't you?"

"You never get anything without asking," Ashton said.

"I suppose we could put a couple of stations on to the GRU channel this evening."

"Let's do it then." Ashton smiled. "Now all I need is the dialling code to break into the Soviet telecom grid."

"For their main exchange it's 98 116 04273. After that, you add the number for the unit switchboard. I take it you already know the one for the GRU?"

"Yes, I got it from the Arms Control Unit via the MOD."

The TOT made him repeat the ten digit dialling code until it was firmly implanted in his memory, then asked if there was anything else they needed to discuss.

"No, I think we've covered everything," Ashton said.

"Good. We'll go our separate ways then."

The TOT turned about and made his way down to the beach, the attractive WRAC officer at his side. When Ashton last saw them, they were holding hands like any other courting couple.

The split-level house set amongst the pine trees on Beach Drive enjoyed a breathtaking view of the ocean and was less than a quarter of a mile from the shopping precinct in the centre of Carmel. Zale had no idea what Lloyd Osmonde had paid for the property, but whatever the retirement home of his dreams had cost him, it had to be worth every penny. The worrying thing was that he didn't look well enough to entertain visitors and certainly wouldn't be going anywhere near a golf course in the foreseeable future.

Elaine had warned him that her husband was still convalescing when he had telephoned her yesterday evening from Monterey, but he hadn't realised just how poorly Lloyd was until they met face to face. He was pale and drawn, his eyes were dull and he had lost a lot of weight which made him look much older than fifty-six. Six weeks after the shooting outside Da Gianni's, the former air force colonel still had not recovered the full use of his left arm. He spent most days on the patio soaking up the sun; occasionally he went for a walk on the beach, but it seemed he tired easily and the uphill drag back to the house took it out of him.

"I shouldn't have come," Zale said after Elaine had left them alone together on the patio.

"Hey, I'm glad you did," Osmonde told him. "Our eldest daughter in Monterey drops by once a week, but apart from the family, we don't get too many visitors. So I don't want you running off the minute you get here. Okay?"

"You're the boss. How did you manage to talk your way out of the Veterans' Hospital so soon?"

"With difficulty." Osmonde smiled. "Now it's my turn to ask you a question. What's in that envelope you've got there?"

"Your personal record of every conversation you had with Yuri Rostovsky. Karen gave it to me when I called round to your old house on Krahmerstrasse. She said you wanted me to have it."

"I thought you might find it useful."

"Thanks. Trouble is, some of the passages are in a code I can't recognise."

"It's a private one." Osmonde reached for the pair of binoculars on the low table beside his deck chair and, using one hand, focused them on a white shrimp boat fishing close inshore. "Have you been fired, Tony?" he asked softly.

"I'm not sure; I think the jury is still out."

After leaving Berlin under a cloud, he had reported to the Defense Intelligence Agency in Washington expecting to be informed that his services were no longer required. Instead, he had been quizzed about the events leading up to the shooting and had then been told he could take a week's vacation provided he kept in touch with the Agency.

"According to Washington, our friend Yuri Rostovsky was also doing business with the French." Zale scratched a heat spot on his neck. "Seems they were so grateful they gave him a passport for his girlfriend who is now walking around as Yvette Michel. The Brits claim her real name is Galina Kutuzova."

"The Starshii Leitenant with the GRU cell in Potsdam who went AWOL?"

"The very same. They figure she was with their man Whittle in Dresden the night he was murdered."

"Can the Brits prove it?"

"They claim one of their sergeants saw her get in the car Whittle was driving. They also say they know she was in cahoots with Rostovsky."

"Interesting," Osmonde drawled and lowered his binoculars. "What do our people make of all this?"

"Opinion is divided. One faction maintains that Rostovsky was iced by a rival mob because he was getting too greedy; the opposing school of thought believes he was a genuine double agent. That's why I was hoping you would tell me what you had going with Yuri?"

"The biggest Intelligence coup since the end of World War Two, or so he tried to convince me with a couple of free samples. And I have to admit the one I found in the Volkspark Jungfernheide appeared to indicate he had access to Top Secret Exclusive. Hell, I had just graduated from high school and you hadn't even been born when the East Berliners took to the streets and rioted in June '53. But back in those days, the Joint Chiefs of Staff figured we were on the brink of World War Three. So did the Russians. The document Yuri gave me was part of an operational directive for the seizure of West Berlin on Codeword Orange. I figured there were three possibilities. The extract was a fake, or it had formed part of a feasibility study which had been presented for consideration at one of those seminars for senior officers which the Soviets are always holding – or it was the genuine article."

"Where is this document now?"

Osmonde raised the field glasses again, seemingly fascinated by the shrimp boat. "I burned it," he said quietly.

"You did what?"

"The document was thirty-eight-years old, Tony. If I had shown it to our Chief of Staff, he would only have said that Rostovsky was leading me around by the nose, same as he did when I showed him the snapshots."

"You're losing me," Zale complained. "There is no mention of any snapshots in this diary of yours."

"They were the first sweeteners. One showed Stalin with some young, hard-nosed official and a cute looking little girl who couldn't have been more than eight- or nine-years old. The other snapshot must have been taken at least fifteen years later – same girl, only now she is a young woman and she is standing outside a dacha somewhere with Yuri Vladimirovich Andropov who was then the number two man to Semichastry, the chairman of the KGB from 1961 to 1967. Her father is with her, so is her fiancé, a young lieutenant in the Soviet Air Force. The young woman was identified as Lydia Petrovskaya, mother of Galina Kutuzova. I think Rostovsky was trying to tell me that he had important connections."

"But our Berlin office refused to believe it?"

"Yeah. That's why I hung on to the snapshots and started keeping that secret diary you are holding."

"Do you have any idea what sort of material Yuri was planning to deliver?"

"No. We hadn't even gotten around to discussing a price. Of course he said it had to be worth at least a million dollars, but that was just sales talk."

Osmonde finally tired of looking at the shrimp boat and laid the binoculars aside, then reached for a cigarette from the pack of Marlborough on the low table. "The last time he phoned me, Rostovsky just said the General Staff had an ace up their sleeve and it was something we would never see, never hear and never find. Then he laughed and said that was why the clique in Moscow had replaced Colonel General Fedyanin, Commander of 6 Guards Tank Army with Lobanov."

"The former chief of the Spetsnaz?"

"That's the bastard."

"It still doesn't make a lot of sense . . ."

"Yeah, well, you are the one who will have to solve the puzzle, Tony, because I'm out of the Service." Osmonde removed the cigarette from his lips and broke it in two. "And in case you haven't already noticed, I've got a bad heart condition."

Black one-way glass in the windows ensured that Diener's Place on Seybelstrasse was in perpetual gloom. The most notable feature of the nightclub was the bar which the management claimed was only marginally smaller than the one in Raffles Hotel in Singapore. The similarity ended there; none of the staff knew how to fix a gin sling and the clientèle knew better than to ask for one. The beer cost ten marks for a third of a litre and no one was allowed to sit over a drink for more than ten minutes. Whether empty or not, a burly waiter automatically replaced the glass and added a further ten to the existing tab. Everyone who came in off the street was at least thirty marks the poorer before they left, a sum which more than covered the cost of the in-house entertainment. This consisted of a lewd girlie cabaret repeated at two-hour intervals from seven p.m. onwards and a nonstop selection of porno movies shown on four small video screens positioned high up on the wall behind the bar.

When Ashton arrived at Diener's a few minutes after five, the staff outnumbered the clientèle by two to one. Among the half-dozen men watching the porno movies, Willie was instantly recognisable by his black eyepatch. He was wearing a dark green sports shirt, a pair of buff-coloured linen slacks with knife-edge creases, white socks and grey loafers, a combination which, in any event, would have made him somewhat conspicuous.

"Hello, Willie," Ashton said in German. "How's business?"

"Not bad, not bad at all."

A beer appeared in front of Ashton before he had time to perch himself on one of the bar stools. Up on the small screen, a couple of vacuous blondes were performing with five men whose faces were never seen on camera. The writhing tangle of bodies was accompanied by grunts, sighs of ecstasy and a great deal of panting. It was difficult to imagine a more unedifying or boring spectacle.

"I hear you are looking for a set of wheels," Willie said eventually, his one good eye still riveted on the screen.

"And I was told you might have something for me."

"How does a year-old Porsche 944 grab you?"

"Depends what you want for it," Ashton told him, keeping up the pretence.

"Eight thousand less than you'll have to pay for a similar model elsewhere."

"Sounds a bargain. When can I see it?"

"Now's as good a time as any. Where I've left it is only a five-minute walk from here."

Willie slipped off the barstool and made his way to the exit, leaving Ashton to pick up both tabs. When he caught up with the German in the foyer, a doorman built like a house expressed a hope that they had enjoyed what Diener's had to offer and urged them both to come again.

"Where do you want to go now?" Willie asked him as they moved off down the road.

"The nearest pay phone."

"Your best bet is Adenauerplatz just off the Kurfürstendamm."

"Is that an educated guess?"

"Local knowledge. Would you like to improve it?"

"What have you been told?"

"Very little other than that my head will roll if anything happens to you. Herr Franklin was not very forthcoming."

"He didn't have too much to say about you either." Ashton cleared his throat. "Are you really blind in that eye?" he asked.

"Yes. Does it bother you?"

"The black patch tends to make you very conspicuous."

"Well, naturally people zero in on it but the plus thing is they don't remember too much else about me. They also tend not to see me as a threat and that could be to your advantage. After all, who is going to take me for a guard dog?"

"I suppose that's one way of looking at it," Ashton said with unconscious irony.

"Listen, if it will make you any happier, I've got a very lifelike glass eye at home I can wear."

"I wouldn't hear of it."

"Whatever pleases you."

"Would you mind if I asked you another personal question?"

"Depends what it is," Willie said affably.

"How did you lose the sight of your left eye?"

"A drug pusher gouged it out with his thumb and the surgeons couldn't put it back again."

"Christ."

"I believe in getting even," Willie told him, "so I threw him downstairs and he happened to break his neck. It was done in the heat of the moment, but a number of people tried to prove otherwise. The pusher was a college kid and well connected – plenty of money in the family and lots of influence to go with it. Anyway, they made sure I was taken off the streets."

"You were a police officer?"

"Detective sergeant. Didn't Herr Franklin tell you?"

"No."

"Funny, I thought he would have done. The reason I'm useful is that I still have some friends in the Kripo, contemporaries who think I was given a raw deal and feel bad enough about it to do me the odd favour."

Willie improved on acquaintance and was no longer the faintly absurd figure Ashton had originally taken him for. He could also understand why Franklin had picked the German to look after him.

"I don't expect anything to happen tonight," he said, taking Willie into his confidence, "but how do I get in touch with you in a hurry when something does break?"

The German reached for the wallet in his hip pocket and took out a business card. On it was printed – Blitz Taxis, Theodor-Heussplatz. Telephone 335 5855 56.

"Is this your own company?" Ashton asked.

"You ring the number and ask for Willie. Day or night, the despatcher will know where to reach me, Herr Peter."

Willie and Peter: no surnames, no personal details, that was how it was going to be. Ashton walked on in silence towards Adenauerplatz thinking it was better that way.

The only pay phones in the square were the three-sided variety which were not exactly the last word in privacy. Ashton found a skeleton kiosk that was vacant, lifted the receiver and feeding the meter with coins, punched out the secret code which would hook him into the Soviet military network, and more importantly, the GRU cell in Potsdam. With Willie standing guard outside, he was confident that no one would overhear his conversation; when the military operator answered, he demanded to speak to Podpolkovnik Alexei Leven in fluent Russian. A belligerent manner had the desired effect and ensured he was put straight through to the newly appointed commanding officer.

"I have something to sell, Colonel," he told Leven. "It concerns a black sheep who left the flock."

"I don't know what you are talking about."

"The black sheep is Galina Kutuzova, and don't tell me you have never heard of her."

"Who are you?"

"My name is Peter. I am an Englishman. A lot of files cross my desk and I want a nice nest egg for when they retire me."

"Go peddle your stuff to someone else, Mr Englishman. We're not interested . . ."

"I'll give you a couple of free samples to whet your appetite, Colonel," Ashton said, talking him down. "Item one – on Sunday, August eleventh an SIS officer called Ashton met Lydia Petrovskaya in Leningrad. Item two – Starshii Leitenant Kutuzova possesses a French passport in the name of Yvette

Michel. I can tell you what else the SIS have on her and where she went after leaving Dresden, but it will cost you."

"I'm not interested," Leven repeated, but his voice lacked conviction.

"Look, I've got just another twenty-four hours in Berlin. I'll call you again at one o'clock tomorrow; if you still don't want to do business, that's okay by me. You are not the only buyer in the market place."

There were a number of ways of bringing psychological pressure to bear on a man. Ashton chose the simple approach and slammed the phone down before the Russian had a chance to say another word.

Chapter 16

ASHTON LEFT the English Bookshop on Budapesterstrasse and walked back to the Excelsior Hotel. A Head of Station was the equivalent of an Assistant Director and few people were more conscious of their status than Neil Franklin. He had therefore not been best pleased to find himself cast in the role of a glorified messenger boy for a junior officer even though it had been unavoidable. No one in the Signal Intelligence world was going to contact Ashton at the Excelsior Hotel to let him know what, if anything, had happened last night; they were only prepared to divulge the information over a secure link, which had meant using the cipher protected line in Franklin's office. Ashton thought the atmosphere would have been slightly less electric if Hazelwood had been more forthcoming with the Head of Station, but it seemed Franklin had merely been given a shopping list and kept largely in the dark.

Security had been better than good. Franklin hadn't known who he was talking to, neither had the TOT from the Berlin squadron of 13 Signal Regiment who had left a message with him. Quite meaningless to a third party, the message informed Ashton in veiled language that Leven had been as quiet as the grave. He hadn't used the teleprinter circuit, the radio telephone or a high-speed transmitter to get in touch with his superiors. Clearly, it was going to take more than one brief conversation to alarm the Russian.

Ashton collected the Volkswagen Golf from the hotel car park and headed north on Hardenbergstrasse, then went on round Ernst Reuterplatz into Marchstrasse. A hundred yards short of the Landwehrkanal, he pulled off the road and parked the VW in the grounds of the Berlin Institute of Technology. With the faculty and student body down for the long vac, he thought it unlikely that anyone on the administrative staff would challenge his right to be there. Locking the car, he made his way on foot to the pay phone he'd spotted back down the road.

Five past one: he punched out the code which enabled him to break into the Red Army's telecommunication network and raise the switchboard operator at the GRU cell in Potsdam. This time, the military operator wanted to know who was calling and there was a significant delay before he was put through to Leven. The gambit was obvious and ultimately unproductive because it would take for ever to trace the call no matter how many signalmen were assigned to the task.

"I don't like to be kept waiting," Ashton said angrily in Russian, "especially when it hasn't been easy for me to slip away from my colleagues during the lunch hour."

"You're lucky I didn't hang up on you, Mr Englishman . . ."

"If you don't want to do business with me, just say so here and now."

"I don't like your attitude," Leven said testily.

"I don't care for yours either, but who said we had to be friends to talk about a numbered account?"

"I'm not interested in fairy tales . . ."

"I wouldn't call the hundred thousand Swiss francs that General Nikolai Yakulevich Petrovsky salted away for his granddaughter a fairy tale. Now, wouldn't you like to know the name of that obliging bank in Zürich?"

Ashton waited expectantly for some kind of reaction from the Russian. He had deliberately inflated the amount Lydia Petrovskaya had said her father had placed on deposit in order to capture his interest, but the longer the silence continued, the more it began to look as though Leven suspected a trap.

"I assume you are not interested then?"

"Did I say that?" Leven asked sharply.

"Well, not in so many words . . ."

"You shouldn't jump to conclusions, Mr Englishman."

"I'm sorry . . ."

"I was about to suggest that we should discuss the matter over a drink like gentlemen."

"I'd like that," Ashton told him.

"Can you get away this evening?"

"I could tell my colleagues I wanted to bring something back from Berlin for my girlfriend."

"Good. Suppose we meet at the Gasthof Reinbecker in Hennickendorf . . ."

"Where's that?"

"It's a small village roughly sixty kilometres southwest of Berlin."

"Forget it." Ashton contrived to sound both alarmed and impatient. "I would have to rent a car and I'd be away too long. My colleagues would miss me. If we are going to meet, it has to be somewhere inside the city . . ."

"Take the U-Bahn out to Tierpark," Leven said, impatiently interrupting him. "Leave the station, cross the main road and wait for me in the Café Rosa on the edge of the park. Bring a small bunch of white roses for your girlfriend."

"Right."

"Be there at seven," Leven said before hanging up on him.

Ashton slowly replaced the phone. It was one thing to meet Lydia Petrovskaya in Leningrad while he was still an unknown face, quite another to hobnob with an officer from what was still a hostile Intelligence Service after he had been compromised. Because who could doubt he had been identified after Moscow when they had shot and killed Eduard Tulbukin by mistake? The GRU had probably recorded his conversation with Leven and if they subsequently photographed the two of them together, it was going to look very bad for him. Indeed, even Hazelwood might find it hard to believe he had not been turned.

But he was working on the hypothesis that, even if he wasn't pitted against a small isolated faction, both the GRU and the KGB were now so demoralised that they were incapable of taking advantage of the situation. If nothing else, it was a comforting thought to hang on to. Reaching for his wallet, Ashton took out the business card Willie had given him and rang the number printed in the bottom right hand corner. Blitz Taxis, it seemed, were equally swift to answer the phone.

"My name is Peter," he told the woman who took the call. "May I speak to Willie, please? It's important."

"He is having lunch."

"Any idea when he will be back?"

"He won't be in this afternoon, Herr Peter. If you wish to see him, he is eating at Bertholt's in Pommernallee. Do you know where that is?"

"'Fraid not."

"It's just off Theodor-Heussplatz," the woman said and hung up before he had a chance to thank her.

Bertholt's was a back street Frühstückskneipe. From three o'clock in the morning until late at night, the café served a breakfast consisting of ham, liver sausage, salami, cheese and pickled herring with rye bread and pumpernickel. For those diners who fancied something lighter, the waiters recommended two four-minute boiled eggs, shelled and served in a glass with a choice of tea, coffee, hot chocolate or draught beer.

When Ashton arrived at the café, there were ten other diners including Willie who was sitting alone at a small round table at the back of the room near the kitchen. Engrossed in reading a newspaper while he was eating, Willie appeared unaware of his presence until Ashton sat down at his table and told the hovering waiter that he would have a cup of coffee.

"You have to order breakfast as well," Willie told him without looking up from his copy of *Der Tagesspiegel*.

"I'm not very hungry."

"Have the boiled eggs then."

Somewhat reluctantly, Ashton followed his suggestion, then made small talk until his order arrived and the waiter left them in peace. "The meeting's on for tonight," he said, abruptly changing the subject.

"Where and when?"

"Seven o'clock at a place called the Café Rosa near the entrance to the Tierpark. I'm supposed to use the U-Bahn to get there."

"It's a long way out from the centre," Willie said thoughtfully.

Ashton nodded. "Trouble is, we are probably going on from there. I've been told to bring a bunch of white roses and that's going to look pretty odd unless a young woman meets me in the café."

"And her job is to take you on to the real meeting place."

"That's the way I see it. I doubt we will go there on foot either."

"Best thing I can do is get there ahead of you and park a car in the neighbourhood."

"Better bring a girl along with you, don't you think?" Ashton said. "Someone is going to smell a rat if they see two men sitting alone at separate tables."

Like all the good homicide officers Dyce had worked for, Lieutenant Max Graber was a natural born sceptic. Unfortunately, he carried it to extremes. He didn't theorise, didn't follow hunches, he worked from facts which could be verified and would hold up in court when some smart-assed attorney tried to demolish the case for the prosecution. This often pedantic approach was a dictum he constantly impressed on the squad and was one Dyce tried to keep in mind when he walked into Graber's office to update him on the Mallard case. But it wasn't easy when Forensic had matched the prints on the ice pick to the deceased's and there were grounds for thinking Yvette Michel had acted in self-defence.

"Now hold it right there, Lew," Graber said and leaned forward, both elbows on the desk. His eyes were deep-set and hooded so that he frequently looked half-asleep, but they were wide open now and almost popping, the way they always did when he was excited. "How do we know it wasn't the other way around?" he demanded. "Why couldn't Mary Beth Mallard have picked up the ice pick to defend herself against a vicious attack?"

"Because the autopsy doesn't support it," Dyce told him. "Apart from the fatal blow to the larynx, all the pathologist could find was a small bruise on the right shin as if the deceased had accidentally bumped into a solid object, like a piece of heavy furniture."

"In other words, you're saying the evidence points to the deceased being the aggressor?"

"Yeah, I believe she attacked the Michel girl."

Graber lit a cigarette. "Can you show a motive?" he asked.

"I've got a statement from Ms Daniella Valli admitting that she and Mary Beth Mallard were lovers." Dyce pushed the case file across the desk. "Now take a look at the snapshots in the Cellophane envelope attached to the inside cover, then tell me how you think the deceased felt about the twosome suddenly becoming a threesome."

The snapshots had been taken at Oak Creek and the Grand Canyon. Although all sixteen exposures were from the same reel, the three women had used the camera in turn to photograph one another.

"Look at the expression on Mary Beth's face, Max, and check out how she has distanced herself from Yvette Michel. But that's nothing to the spite she revealed when she had the camera and managed accidentally on purpose to decapitate Daniella and Yvette when they were standing together. It's obvious she was eaten up with jealousy."

"Maybe."

"Aw, come on," Dyce protested, "the deceased was nudging thirty-eight and beginning to put on weight. The new chick in Daniella Valli's life has to be at least twelve years younger and she has a better figure. Mallard was very possessive where Ms Valli was concerned; you can see that by the way she is hanging on to her lover's arm. She is glaring at the camera, warning Yvette Michel to back off."

Graber pulled an ashtray towards him and stubbed out his cigarette. "You've got an imagination, Lew," he said. "Much as I appreciate it, I'd sooner you stuck to the facts."

"The facts are that the deceased had been drinking on what was virtually an empty stomach."

"How much had she had?"

"Enough to put her well over the limit, and booze can make some people aggressive."

"Did Ms Valli tell you that?"

Dyce shook his head. "It was just an observation."

"Let's not have too many of them, Lew. What else should I know?"

"The Chevrolet Caprice has been found in a parking lot in rear of the State Capitol building."

"That's cool," Graber said dryly.

It had taken the city's finest the better part of two days to run the stolen vehicle to ground, probably because no one had thought Yvette Michel would have had the nerve to abandon it in a parking area reserved for government employees. Dyce thought it significant that she had taken time out to do that; in her shoes, most of the criminals he knew would have dumped the Chevrolet at the airport.

"Are we looking for the taxi driver who took her to Sky Harbor Airport?" Graber asked.

"Yeah, I personally gave the cab company two enlargements of her photograph to go on their notice board. The despatchers will make sure every driver sees them and I've got a patrolman checking out the independents."

After the reel had been developed, Dyce had got the lab technician to cut one of the negatives in two in order to remove Mary Beth from the frame before it was enlarged. From this initial blow-up, the police photographer had gone on to produce an enlargement of Yvette Michel's head and shoulders which Dyce had then sent to the various airline desks at Sky Harbor International Airport.

From earlier inquiries, he already knew that between two and five p.m. on the afternoon of the murder, only one person had bought a plane ticket for cash. According to one of the girls on the United Airlines desk, the person in question was a Carolyn Jacobs who had booked herself on to the New Orleans flight exactly fifteen minutes before departure. One look at the enlargement had been enough for her to confirm that Carolyn Jacobs and Yvette Michel were the same person. In the circumstances, the cab driver who had taken her to the airport was not an essential witness, but Graber liked to have things sewn up tight.

"You've done a damn good job, Lew," Graber told him. "Now it's just a question of waiting for the New Orleans Police Department to trace her."

"I know someone who's not content to do that. Ms Valli is itching to return to New York."

"She can itch all she likes . . ."

"We don't really need her, Max. At least not until we have Michel and a date has been fixed for the trial. We have traced Mary Beth's parents in Bradenton, Florida, and they are flying in to identify their daughter and claim her body. I think Daniella would like to leave before they arrive."

"Serve her right if she had to face them." Graber pondered on it for a few moments, then threw up his hands as if surrendering. "What the hell, let her go."

Dyce thanked him, returned to the squad room and got himself a cup of coffee from the vending machine out in the corridor. Daniella had told him that she believed Yvette Michel was an alias; she had also claimed to have seen a passport which had not been issued by the State Department. Although neither allegation had a material effect on the conduct of the investigation, he couldn't help wondering if

Graber would have been quite so accommodating had he known about them.

Ashton left the Volkswagen Golf on the wasteland that had once been the site of the notorious Gestapo Headquarters in Prinz Albrechtstrasse and walked to the U-Bahn station in the nearby Potsdamerplatz. From there he took the Pankow Line as far as Alexanderplatz where he caught a train to Tierpark. An hour and five minutes after setting off from the Excelsior Hotel, he walked into the Café Rosa clutching the bunch of white roses he had bought from the florist that afternoon.

The Café Rosa was a hangover from the days of the German Democratic Republic, a drab edifice decorated in chocolate brown and dull cream paint. Net curtains hung halfway down the windows to prevent those on the outside looking in; further cover was provided by the potted ferns and mother-in-law's tongue perched on the shelves above the radiators. The brown and white tiles which had been laid in a diamond-shaped pattern on the floor scarcely improved the décor, neither did the furniture. The tables and hoop-back chairs looked as if they belonged in a museum housing memorabilia of the thirties, as did the lampshades suspended from the panelled ceiling. The lights were on to combat the lowering sky of an approaching thunderstorm, but out of eight 60-watt bulbs, three were blown.

Even supposing the Café Rosa had been a popular haunt in the past, it was evident from the lack of patronage that it could not begin to compete with the attractions in West Berlin now the Wall was down. Consequently, it wasn't difficult to spot Willie among the dozen or so couples who were there. Unlike the first time they had met, he was soberly dressed in a dark grey suit that was shiny with age. To make himself less conspicuous, or as a sop to Ashton, he had also abandoned the black patch in favour of a glass eye. The pale brunette with him looked equally drab in a navy raincoat which she had unbuttoned to reveal a nondescript print dress.

Ashton found a vacant table for two, told a bored waitress that he was expecting a friend to join him and ordered a cup of coffee to be going on with. Seven o'clock came and went with no sign of the guide he had assumed Leven would send to collect him. An elderly couple, a large woman with an equally fat dachshund and

175

a studious-looking man in his late thirties left the café before the storm broke; three girls accompanied by two youths came in to shelter from the rain. The woman in dark glasses, headscarf and buff-coloured trenchcoat appeared at his table as he was finishing the cup of lukewarm coffee.

"For me?" she asked in German and immediately picked up the bunch of roses.

"You're late," Ashton growled, a nervous edge to his voice like a man under stress.

"Then what are we waiting for?"

She moved away before Ashton could get to his feet. Leaving fifty pfennigs under the saucer as a tip, he hurried after Leven's emissary and caught up with her in the entrance as she opened the door. Outside, the rain was teeming down. First Leningrad, now Berlin; bad weather seemed to follow him wherever he went. He hoped it wasn't an omen.

"Don't worry, Mr Englishman," she told him contemptuously, "you won't get too wet; my car is across the street."

It was a primrose-coloured Lada Riva, the licence-built Fiat 124 that had been adapted to withstand motoring conditions in the Soviet Union. An '87 model, it was showing signs of wear and tear; there were dents in both fenders and the offside front wing had been crumpled in some minor accident, then crudely restored to something like its original shape.

The guide fancied herself as a Grand Prix driver; revving the engine until it was almost screaming, she slammed the gear stick into first and let out the clutch while Ashton was still trying to fasten the seat belt. She crashed up through the box, got into top in just over a hundred yards, then slammed on the brakes. Grating into reverse, she backed into a side road and came out again to make a right turn on the highway and double back past the Café Rosa. An Audi travelling without lights passed them going in the opposite direction.

They went under a railway bridge, flashed past a sign which told Ashton they were entering the Karlshorst District and continued on through the outer suburb. Instead of apartment blocks, there was now a ribbon development of single houses each with its own garden. The streetlights gradually got farther and farther apart, then suddenly the last housing estate was behind them and they were out in open country. There was very little traffic heading into town; worse still, he couldn't see any headlights in the wing mirror which might have indicated that the faithful Willie was sitting on their tail.

"That's it," Ashton shouted. "Pull over, I'm not going any farther."

"What do you mean? I don't understand . . ."

"You want me to repeat it in Russian? I told your Colonel Leven I'd meet him in Berlin, not the back of beyond."

"We haven't left the city . . ."

"Oh yeah? Well now, you listen to me, Natasha, or whatever your name is. You either tell me how much farther we are going or we turn back right now."

Fear with just the right amount of bluster. It was how he imagined she would expect a man who was about to sell classified information to a foreign power might behave.

"Five minutes," she said. "We'll be there in five minutes, and my name is not Natasha."

"It'll do for me," Ashton told her.

The rain was slashing down and the single wiper that was still working could barely cope, but even though the visibility was lousy, she still kept her foot hard down on the accelerator. Forking right into a minor road, they passed under three rail bridges in rapid succession and headed straight into a thick wood.

"Where are we?"

"The Berliner Stadtforst," the woman told him and signalled their presence by repeatedly dipping the main beams.

"Is this where I meet Colonel Leven?"

"You'll know soon enough."

Ashton had learned from experience that the one thing every Intelligence Service had in common was a mania for total secrecy even when dealing with inconsequential matters. "I wonder where I've heard that one before," he said acidly.

Up ahead, a light flashed among the trees on the left of the track. Responding to the signal, she reduced speed and changed down into third before rolling to a halt. The Mercedes was parked in a clearing abutting the forest ride.

"This is where you leave me, Mr Englishman."

Ashton undid the seat belt, opened the door and got out. As he moved towards the Mercedes, "Natasha" selected first gear with a loud clunk and drove off down the track.

Three men in civilian clothes were waiting for him by the Mercedes. Leven he recognised but the other two had not featured in the rogues gallery which BRIXMIS had maintained in the days before it had become the Arms Control Unit North West Europe. He did not, however, make the mistake of letting the Russian know he had seen his face before.

"Good evening, Mr Peter."

"I recognise your voice," Ashton told him. "You're Colonel Leven, aren't you?"

"Would you come with me please?"

The Russian did not shake hands with him. Instead he turned on his heel and walked to the back of the Mercedes. Ashton heard him open the boot and his heart started beating that little bit faster. The fir trees around the clearing looked as dark and foreboding as the sky above and he thought of the Katyn Forest and recalled from books read long ago how the NKVD had shot thousands of Polish officers through the head after they had been taken prisoner. This time, there was no need to pretend he was alarmed.

"What's going on?" Ashton demanded, his voice full of anxiety.

"I want you to get in the trunk," Leven told him quietly.

"You are going to kill me."

"Of course we aren't."

"I'm being kidnapped – is that it?"

"Calm down, Mr Englishman, we are not going to hurt you. We are taking you to a safe house and naturally we don't want you to know where it is. Surely a man with your background can understand that?"

"Maybe."

Leven sighed. "Look, you contacted us. We did not come to you asking if you had any information for sale. If you have changed your mind since this morning, you are free to walk away. But do something before we all get soaking wet."

Ashton thought it over. If they were going to kill him, they could do it here and now in the depths of the forest. "I'll trust you," he said and climbed into the trunk.

Leven slammed the lid down and turned the key in the lock, entombing him. Lying there in the dark and curled up in the foetus position, he heard all three men get into the limousine. Moments

178

later, the engine throbbed into life and the car moved forward, bumping over the uneven ground until it reached the forest ride where the driver turned right. Shortly after that, Ashton became totally disorientated.

CHAPTER 17

THE ENGINE purred like a contented cat, its noise level so muted that Ashton found it no help at all when trying to estimate how fast the driver was going. However, the hiss made by the tyres on the wet surface of the road suggested he rarely went above thirty to thirty-five miles an hour even on the straight. The theory that the Russian seemed to be observing a speed limit was given added weight by the number of times they had stopped and started since leaving the forest. In his own mind, he was pretty sure they were still somewhere within the Berlin area; he just wished there was more traffic about to confirm his theory.

The Mercedes slowed right down and he felt a slight nudge as the automatic drive went into a lower gear. The driver made a sharp left turn and presently he heard the distinctive crunch of a gravel or cinder path. A few seconds later, the Russian braked to a halt and switched off the engine. Ashton peered at his Omega; according to the luminous figures, it had taken them exactly twenty-one minutes to reach the safe house.

Three doors opened and closed in rapid succession, but only one man moved round to the back of the car. The key made a funny grating noise when it was inserted in the lock, then the lid sprang open and he was breathing fresh air again. Sometime during the journey the rain had stopped, but there was still some thunder in the air. Limbs stiff and cramped from being imprisoned in a confined space, Ashton slowly climbed out of the boot and stood there flexing his aching muscles under the watchful eye of one of the heavies Leven had brought with him.

The safe house stood back from the road at the end of a cinder lane. It was enclosed on three sides by a narrow belt of trees and there was no other dwelling place in the immediate vicinity that Ashton could see. Beyond the trees there were open fields in both directions, but he drew comfort from the lights of Berlin which were clearly visible in the distance.

"We go now," the Russian said and prodded him in the back.

Like most German farms, the house was tacked on to the side of a huge barn, but the agricultural machinery had gone and the pigsty just within the entrance had fallen into disrepair. There were other signs of neglect; most of the loft above the rear half of the barn had collapsed and there were puddles of water lying on the floor where the rain had come through the roof. The damage obviously hadn't been done overnight which led Ashton to believe that, at some time in the distant past, the farm had been incorporated in a local training area for Soviet units stationed on the periphery of East Berlin.

Leven and the other heavy were waiting for him in what had once been the family parlour. All that remained of the original furniture were a large kitchen table, a dilapidated easy chair with a missing castor and two high-back kitchen stools. An army blanket had been pinned over the window and the only light in the room came from a kerosene pressure lamp.

"I don't know what you think you're playing at," Ashton said indignantly, "but it took me over an hour to get to the Café Rosa and now you and that half-witted woman have wasted at least another forty-five minutes. How do you think I am going to explain my absence?"

"I don't think you will be missed," Leven told him calmly.

"Oh? How would you know?"

"What's your name, Mr Englishman?"

"I've already told you on the telephone – it's Peter."

"Peter what?"

"That's all I'm prepared to disclose."

The taller of the two heavies stepped in front of Ashton and slapped his face, first across one cheek, then the other. It was an insulting gesture which was intended to humiliate rather than hurt him. The second heavy was more purposeful; grabbing hold of Ashton's jacket from behind, he pulled it off his shoulders to trap both arms, making it that much easier for his companion to remove the wallet from the inside pocket and hand it to Leven.

"You're going to be disappointed," Ashton told him. "You won't find anything in my wallet other than a hundred and fifty Deutschmarks. My credit cards are with my passport and traveller's cheques in the hotel safe."

"How very professional of you, Mr Peter."

"Well, I didn't want you to think you were dealing with a blockhead."

"I see. Exactly where are you employed?"

"Century House of course."

"You are a senior desk officer perhaps?"

Ashton smiled. "Nothing so exalted. I'm an administrative assistant – one of the clerical grades."

"An office boy," Leven said contemptuously.

"You ought to know better than that, if you're worth your promotion. I'm a paper keeper, I get to see all the classified stuff that comes into the Russian Desk. I not only log it in, I'm also the custodian. That's how I got to know your name. Century House gets a copy of everything the Arms Control Unit North West Europe sends to the MOD. I even know when you were made up to half-colonel; it happened after Galina Kutuzova went AWOL and Captain Yuri Rostovsky got himself shot. They sacked your former commanding officer, Vladimir Ilyich, for incompetence."

"I'm impressed."

"So you should be."

"I meant by your command of Russian. It's very good," Leven smiled, then added, "for a clerk."

"I spent two years learning the language and I passed the Civil Service First Class Interpreter's exam. They were going to send me to Moscow on accelerated promotion to chief archivist until some clever dick in Security remembered I'd worked in Central Registry before going on the long language course. So naturally they cancelled the posting."

"Why?" Leven asked.

"Because everything coming into Century House goes through Central Registry before it's booked out to the appropriate Desk. Same applies to outgoing mail which means that it's the bloody post office for the whole SIS. Security was worried that I might shoot my mouth off in Moscow because I'm a guy with a reputation for having a photographic memory. That's how I got shunted off as a paper keeper to the Russian Desk instead of going overseas."

"There has to be more to it than that."

Ashton looked down at the floor, shifted his weight from one foot to the other. He had to make Leven believe he was a very ambitious clerk with an outsize chip on his shoulder because he had been passed over for promotion. Such a man would portray himself in the best possible light and would be reluctant to disclose any character defects.

"The stupid bastards reckoned I'd got an eye for the girls and might get my leg over some shapely Muscovite."

"Why did they think so badly of you?"

Ashton shrugged. "Search me," he said in a surly voice.

"They must have had a reason."

"Well, they didn't, take it from me."

Leven stared him down. "I think you are a liar, Mr Peter Englishman."

"Who are you to call me a liar?"

"Listen to me. If we are going to do business, there can be no secrets between us. You understand what I'm saying?"

"Yes."

"Well then?"

Ashton cleared his throat. "One of the women in the typing pool filed a complaint against me, said I'd touched her up. It was supposed to have happened at the office Christmas party. Well, you know what those affairs are like . . ." Ashton shook his head. "No, of course you wouldn't . . ." He smiled briefly. "Well, normally everyone's in a good mood and ready to let their hair down, especially if the drink is flowing like water. The girls usually doll themselves up to the nines, and this Mrs Julia Silvers turned up in a nifty little black number which was at least one size too small for her. After the top brass had made their customary brief appearance, one of the blokes put a tape on and most people started dancing. So there I am having a quiet drink in the corner when this Julia Silvers accidentally bumps into me while she's jigging around in time to the music with a drink in her hand. She looks over her shoulder, gives me a great big smile and says sorry; then before I know it, she does it again and this time she's wiggling her bottom. Well, I can take a hint as well as the next man, so I gave her a friendly pat and believe me she liked it until she noticed that the old hag in charge of the typing pool was watching her. The first day we worked after the Christmas break she made an official complaint to cover herself. Luckily, I had plenty of friends who were prepared to swear I'd never laid a finger on her."

"But you didn't get away with it."

"No, in the end that bloody party cost me my posting to Moscow."

"And selling information to us is your way of getting even, is it?"

Ashton was tempted to say yes, but the Russian was no fool and would never believe that a man would sell his country short purely out of spite. That could only be a part of it.

"I need the money. Until a few weeks ago, I was living with this woman and we were buying a flat on a hefty mortgage. Now we've split up, the bottom has fallen out of the property market, interest rates are sky high and I'm strapped for cash. Can you think of a better reason for trying to make a little extra on the side?"

The Russian believed him; Ashton could tell it from the expression on his face. The best cover stories were always the ones closest to the truth and he had simply exaggerated his own situation.

"How long do you think you'll need our financial support?" Leven asked.

"For the foreseeable future."

"Then I will have to know a great deal more about you. There are things we need to arrange – convenient drops, RVs, cut-outs and so on. You will also have to meet your controller in London."

"No one is going to see my face over there," Ashton told him firmly. "I'll give you a number which your friends in Kensington Palace Gardens can ring the first and third Tuesday of every month at seven p.m. and we will make whatever arrangements are necessary there and then."

"Obviously it's a public call box."

"So what? All you have to do is dial 399–9210." Ashton repeated the number slowly and watched him write it down with a sense of elation. "One other thing," he added. "I select the information, not you people. That way I can minimise the risk to myself."

"It sounds a very one-sided arrangement."

"Don't worry, I always give value for money."

"Prove it," Leven snapped. "Tell me how you were able to raise our switchboard from a civilian pay phone?"

184

"Ah, well, that's a trade secret I'm not prepared to divulge."

Leven slapped the kitchen table. Before Ashton could protect himself, the nearest heavy thrust a hand into his crotch, grabbed him by the testicles and crushed them in a vicelike grip. His bowels felt as if they were about to drop out on to the floor and the whole room started to revolve. The pain was agonising and he cried out. Then a grey mist descended in front of his eyes, his legs buckled under him and he would have gone down if the two heavies hadn't caught his arms in time and carefully lowered him on to a chair.

"Jesus," he gasped. "Jesus Christ."

The bile rose in his throat and he thought he was going to be sick. One of the heavies thrust a mug of water into his hand and he sipped it gratefully, taking as long as he could over the drink to give himself time to work out how he could fool Leven.

"Now, do I get an answer or do you want more of the same?"

Ashton raised his head. "What did you want to do that for?" he complained bitterly.

"I'm waiting."

"Galina Kutuzova told a British officer called Younger what code he should use to break into your telecom grid, and there was a copy of his report on our file. I memorised it when I knew I was coming to Berlin."

There was a certain amount of truth in the story. Six months ago, GCHQ had stumbled on to the code while monitoring the radio relay telecommunications of 6 Guards Tank Army. Since then, however, they had developed a more sophisticated and less vulnerable method of entry utilising one of the Telstar satellites.

"Well, don't stop there, Mr Englishman. What are the magic numbers?"

Ashton saw no harm in telling him. The TOT of the Berlin Signal Squadron had only disclosed the code to him because they no longer had any use for it.

"There are ten digits – 98 116 04273. That gets you into the main exchange; thereafter, you simply add the number of the unit switchboard. I don't suppose I have to tell you who gave us the number of the GRU cell in Potsdam?"

"You are referring to Starshii Leitenant Galina Kutuzova."

185

"She's the lady with the Swiss bank account and the French passport."

"What else do the SIS know about her?"

"We think she closed her account with the Union Bank of Zürich shortly before she flew to Montreal on Saturday the thirteenth of July. We're using the Metropolitan Police to trace Galina through Interpol. Matter of fact, they have put out an international arrest warrant for her. You want to be kept informed?"

"Moscow has indicated an interest in knowing her whereabouts."

"It'll cost you."

"I didn't imagine you would do it for nothing." Leven reached inside his jacket, took out an envelope and placed it inside Ashton's wallet before returning it to him. "Two hundred pounds," he said. "Consider it a down payment."

"I was hoping for more."

"You will have to earn it."

One of the heavies helped Ashton to his feet and led him out to the Mercedes. He had travelled to the safe house in the boot and it was evident they weren't about to change the arrangement. Still feeling groggy, he climbed in and curled up. When the lid closed, sealing him in, the confined space wasn't any less claustrophobic the second time around.

There was no subterfuge on the return journey. Instead of the twenty-one minutes it had taken them to reach the safe house, they made it back to the same forest clearing in a fraction over nine minutes. The fact that "Natasha" was waiting to take him on in the Lada saloon did not fill Ashton with joy. Although he tried to explain that he wasn't in a hurry, she still insisted on driving like a lunatic in search of an accident. She did, however, choose a different route and hugged the River Spree and Rummelsburgersee before dropping him off at Magdalenenstrasse, three stops up the line from the U-Bahn station at Tierpark.

No one had attempted to break into the VW Golf while he had been away, which Ashton thought was just as well because he would have had a hard time explaining to the rental agency why the car had been left in Prinz Albrechtstrasse. He did a tour of West Berlin, continually doubling back on his tracks to see if anyone was following him before he returned to the Excelsior Hotel. If anyone noticed that his suit was rumpled and damp

186

when he collected his room key and valuables from the safety deposit box, they were too polite to mention it.

He called Blitz Taxis from his hotel room and asked the despatcher on duty if she could put him in touch with Willie and was given a number in the Charlottenburg District. He rang it before changing and again at half-hourly intervals following a late supper, but there was no answer.

The accident was easily the worst the traffic cop had seen since he had joined the force in 1976. It had happened on a deserted stretch of the Am Tierpark Throughway in poor visibility and atrocious weather conditions. There had been no eyewitnesses, or at least none had come forward and as far as he could tell, it seemed that no other vehicle had been involved. There were grounds for thinking the driver had been going far too fast with the result that the Audi saloon had started aquaplaning on the wet surface and he had lost control of the vehicle.

The pale blue Audi had skidded across the Throughway on to the wrong side of the road and collided with a streetlight some twenty-five metres from the railway bridge. There was no disputing that because the structure was now leaning at a drunken angle and the large dent approximately one metre from the base was smeared with cellulose from the car. The impact had flattened the offside of the saloon from headlight to rear mudwing and flipped the car over on to the roof. With virtually no loss of momentum, the vehicle had then smashed into the abutment supporting the railway bridge and rolled back into the road, coming to rest on its nearside.

The accident had been reported at 1923 hours by a motorcyclist coming up on Hermann Dunckerstrasse from the direction of the horse-trotting racetrack in Karlshorst. The traffic cop had arrived at 1926 hours and had been joined one minute later by an ambulance from the District Hospital, which fortuitously was less than three kilometres from the scene of the accident. Shortly thereafter, further police assistance had materialised in the shape of four patrolmen, a sergeant and an inspector. By the time the fire brigade reported, hazard warning lights were in position and the traffic cop had found himself on point duty.

The Audi had been compressed to about half its normal size, as if the chassis had been inserted between blades of a giant

187

crusher and slowly squashed. The driver had been trapped in his seat which had come adrift from the guide-rails and was canted across the transmission tunnel so that he had ended up pillowing his head in the lap of the woman sitting beside him. Considering the gap between the roof and the floor had been no more than fifty centimetres, he couldn't understand how the man had survived the crash.

It had taken the firemen almost an hour to cut the driver out of the wreckage. To a comparative layman like the traffic cop, his injuries had looked ghastly, but the paramedics had openly said that he had got off remarkably lightly. It was unlikely the driver would have agreed with their verdict had he been conscious. He looked as if he had been scalped; there had been a flap of skin hanging from the forehead, there had been an empty socket where the left eye should have been and a sizeable chunk of hair had appeared to be missing. His left leg had been in a hell of a mess with the foot at ninety degrees to the shin and the kneecap neatly sheared off as if someone had used a guillotine on it. If that hadn't been bad enough, the left arm had been broken in two places and the elbow dislocated.

But at least the driver had still been alive when they had whisked him away in the ambulance, which was more than could be said for his passenger. She had been decapitated when the car had rolled over and her head had burst through the roof. He had watched the firemen collect the remains and place them in a body bag and had very nearly been sick on the spot. The traffic cop knew that for the rest of his life he would have nightmares about a headless corpse in a bloodstained navy raincoat.

Although a handbag had been found inside the car, the contents had failed to disclose the identity of the dead woman. Similarly, the driver had not been carrying an ID card in his wallet.

The clock radio woke Ashton at seven thirty with a low buzzing noise which preceded an English language newscast from Rhine Army's British Forces Broadcasting Service Cologne. Wide awake within seconds, he rolled out of bed and switched off both the alarm and the radio before ringing Willie's contact number in the Charlottenburg District. Unable to get an answer, he rang Blitz Taxis again, but no one there had seen or heard from him since yesterday lunchtime.

He rang room service, ordered a continental breakfast, took a quick bath before shaving and dressing in slacks, thin roll-neck sweater and a sports jacket. Willie had been present at the rendezvous last night when "Natasha" had picked him up and he thought he'd seen the German again going the wrong way in an Audi saloon when they had been heading towards the Berliner Stadtforst. There had been no further sightings and he had assumed that Willie had simply fallen down on the job. Now he wasn't so sure and was beginning to wonder if something had happened to him.

Breakfast arrived with a complimentary copy of the *Berliner Morgenpost*. Recent events in Moscow were still making the headlines and there was speculation that Raisa Gorbachev had suffered more than a minor heart attack when the family had been under house arrest in the Crimea. Elsewhere, there was a report that the European Community was thinking of sending a peace-keeping force to Yugoslavia.

At eight thirty, Ashton left the hotel and made his way on foot to the English Bookshop in Budapesterstrasse. It being a Saturday morning, Franklin wasn't in the office. Holding the fort in his absence was a locally employed woman called Helga von Schinkel, a formidable lady in her mid-sixties who had served every SIS Head of Station since the end of World War Two when she had been poached from AMGOT, the Allied Military Government Occupied Territories. The SIS had taken her on as a shorthand typist even though her qualifications for the post had been nonexistent. She had never been to secretarial college, had been incapable of typing more than eight words a minute with her two index fingers and had used a combination of longhand and guesswork when taking dictation.

On the other hand, she had been fluent in English, French and Italian. Furthermore, her political credentials had been beyond reproach; in 1944, when a nineteen-year-old university student, Helga von Schinkel had been a courier for the Bendlerstrasse conspirators. Arrested after the failure of the July Bomb Plot, she had appeared before the People's Court in January 1945 charged with high treason and had been found guilty. Sentenced to death by Judge Roland Freisler, she had been taken to the Lehrterstrasse prison to await execution and had still been there three months later when the Russians had stormed the city.

In the days when she had worked for AMGOT, no one had been better qualified than Helga von Schinkel to root out the diehard Nazi element within the ranks of the reconstituted civil service. In the early fifties, no one had been better equipped to point the SIS in the right direction when it had been decided to organise a German resistance movement to counter any possible Soviet aggression. Under the impression that the Allies were simply continuing the denazification process, it had been some considerable time before she had realised she had been helping the British to recruit former members of the Waffen SS.

The discovery had led to a crisis of confidence, with Helga tendering her resignation. She had been persuaded to withdraw it on the understanding that henceforth she would only be employed on administrative duties. In practice, this had meant that she had run the front office, the latest one being the English Bookshop. Ashton had met her for the first time yesterday morning.

"I need to use the private office," he told her and walked straight in before she had a chance to object.

The cryptographic coding on the secure telephone was changed daily at 0900 hours. With exactly ten minutes to go before the current one expired, he rang the Berlin squadron of 13 Signal Regiment, spoke to the TOT and learned that Leven was still maintaining electronic silence. Replacing the phone, Ashton called Helga von Schinkel into the office and informed her it was vital he saw Herr Franklin soonest.

"But this is Saturday," she protested. "And it's almost nine o'clock."

"Is there a problem?" he asked.

It seemed there was. At nine o'clock every Saturday morning, Neil Franklin was to be found on the first tee of the Wannsee golf club come hail, come shine. And apparently it was more than Helga's life was worth to interfere with this time-honoured ritual.

"This is one Saturday when his plans are going to be disrupted," Ashton told her. "Now please ring the club secretary, the professional, or whoever you have to and say there has been a death in the family and he's to ring this number."

"A death?" she echoed in a hollow voice.

"It's just a figure of speech," he said tersely. "But Willie is missing and I think he could be in serious trouble."

CHAPTER 18

NEIL FRANKLIN was not in the best of moods when he arrived at the bookshop. His grim expression put Ashton in mind of a proud owner of a brand new car who'd woken up the following morning to find that his pride and joy had been vandalised during the night. The moment he walked through the door, Helga von Schinkel, who knew him almost as well as Mrs Franklin, recognised the danger signals and decided she had some personal business to attend to.

Franklin had been aggressive on the phone when he had rung the office from the Wannsee golf club and his temper hadn't improved on the journey into town. The only form of greeting Ashton got was a demand to know what the hell was going on.

"Willie's missing."

"What do you mean – he's missing?"

"Precisely that," Ashton said quietly. "Willie was supposed to watch my back while I was head to head with the Russians. He was at the RV yesterday evening and I'm pretty sure I saw him in an Audi saloon when we moved on, but then he disappeared. No one at Blitz Taxis has heard from him and I can't get an answer from the contact number in Charlottenburg."

"Shit." Franklin opened the top right-hand drawer of his desk, took out a city map of Berlin and unfolded it. "Show me where this RV was and where you went from there," he said curtly.

Ashton pinpointed the location of the Café Rosa, then traced the route they had taken to the Stadt Forst. He also indicated roughly where he had last seen the Audi saloon.

"What colour?" Franklin asked.

"Pale blue. Willie had a girl in tow, a brunette, sallow complexion, nothing much to look at. She was wearing a navy raincoat over a cheap print dress. Any idea who she might be?"

"No."

"Pity. If we knew who the lady was, we could look her up in the telephone directory and give her a ring. It's possible she might have saved us a lot of trouble."

"Us?" Franklin snorted in disgust. "You mean me, don't you?"

"Well, that's true enough. I doubt Kommissar Heinrich Voigt would do any favours for a complete stranger."

"I'd rather he didn't have to do any for me."

Ashton could understand his reluctance to involve Voigt, but the traffic police were likely to ask just as many awkward questions and it wasn't really practical to phone every hospital in the Karlshorst and Friedrichsberg Districts. "I don't see we have much alternative," he said.

"No, you wouldn't. I assume your antics yesterday evening were connected with Galina Kutuzova?"

"I didn't have any other reason for seeing Leven."

"That's what I was afraid of. When the hell are you bloody people in London going to accept that she is just a poxy little tramp who was up to her eyeballs in the Black Market like her boyfriend, Yuri Rostovsky? The only remarkable thing about Galina Kutuzova is that she was lucky enough to survive the attempt on her life and had the good sense to run. Whittle got caught in the crossfire because the people who wanted to put her out of business didn't care who else got killed in the process."

Ashton had heard it all before. It was the cosy explanation favoured by people like Franklin who didn't want to look too deeply in case they discovered that everything in the garden wasn't as lovely as they had thought it was.

"What about Willie?" he asked. "Are we quietly going to forget all about him?"

"Don't be so bloody impertinent. If anything has happened to him, just remember who was responsible for getting him into trouble in the first place."

Franklin moved the secure phone aside, picked up the one supplied by the Bundespost and tried Voigt's home number first before eventually catching him at the Polizeipräsidium. In a few sentences, he then proceeded to do a hatchet job on Willie. The way Franklin told it, the German was a sleazy little businessman who scratched a living buying misappropriated government stores from equally crooked officers and enlisted men in the Red Army's Quartermaster Corps which he subsequently sold at vastly inflated prices. Lately, he had been doing a number with one of the sales assistants at the bookshop.

The lies got bigger and better. Having asked the girl out to dinner, Willie had failed to turn up. He hadn't answered his phone all night and there had been no sign of him when she had called round to his flat this morning. Furthermore, it seemed none of the neighbours had seen him since early on Friday, and she had this absurd idea that he was lying unconscious in hospital. It sounded plausible, even believable, and Franklin did the good employer concerned for the wellbeing of an employee bit with conviction. But the Kripo officer knew who he was dealing with and Ashton could guess how he had reacted before Franklin put the phone down.

"He didn't believe a word I told him. As good as said so."

"Is Voigt going to help?"

"He'll make some inquiries."

Franklin left his desk to open the combination wall safe, took out the crypto tape for the day and ran it through the cipher on the secure telephone. Feeding the used tape into the secret waste destructor, he then activated the shredder and accounted for the document in the Signals Classified Register.

"I wouldn't close the safe just yet," Ashton told him. "At least not until you have put this envelope away and given me a receipt for it."

"What's in it?"

"Two hundred pounds, money Colonel Leven gave me as a down payment for information received. You'd better count it."

"You've met with him?"

Ashton nodded. "Last night at a safe house somewhere not too far from the Berliner Stadtforst. They made sure I wouldn't know the precise location."

"They?" Franklin repeated with heavy emphasis.

"Leven had a couple of heavies with him."

"You can bet there was a fourth man, a photographer who took a picture of you accepting this envelope from Leven."

"I'm sure there was, that's why I want a signature for the money."

Franklin examined the envelope, turning it over to look at the flap. "Soviet Army issue," he said. "Grey, poor quality, flimsy and very little adhesive. Leven didn't even bother to seal it down."

"He expected me to count the money."

"So what did he get for his two hundred?"

"He thinks I'm a greedy little paper keeper for the Russian Desk who wants to supplement his income. I told Leven that the SIS had discovered that Galina Kutuzova had a numbered account with the Union Bank of Zürich. I also said they knew she had flown to Montreal on Swissair flight SR160. I asked him if he wanted to be kept informed of future developments and he jumped at the offer."

"And what was the object of this one-way exchange of information?"

"The idea was to panic Leven into communicating with his superiors in Moscow."

"Which 13 Signal Regiment would intercept?"

"Yes."

"And have they?"

"Not so far."

"Really, you do surprise me." Franklin was reverting to type, dripping acid like a leaky battery. "Did Hazelwood run this bizarre scheme past the Director General?" he asked venomously.

"I'm only a desk officer," Ashton said. "Why don't you ask him?"

"I can imagine the sort of answer I'd get."

Franklin intended to exercise his right of direct access to the DG. Furthermore, he would go out of his way to make life as difficult as possible for Hazelwood. The undoubted pleasure that would give him was reflected in the smile which he made no attempt to conceal from Ashton.

"About the two hundred . . .?"

Franklin opened the envelope, extracted the wad of ten pound notes and counted them, then wrote out a receipt. "How much good do you think this will do you?" he asked. "It won't impress MI5; they will say you were trying to cover yourself. You show me two hundred – how do I know Leven didn't give you a cool thousand?"

"Because both the KGB and the GRU are notoriously mean."

"Well, I'm glad I am not in your shoes."

Franklin didn't know the half of it; there was the little matter of his trip to Leningrad and Moscow. If Hazelwood decided to keep his head down, how was he going to prove he had cleared it with his superiors? The fact was the KGB had the means to destroy him.

"When do you propose to leave Berlin?"

"Tuesday afternoon at the latest." Ashton picked up the receipt and slipped it into his wallet. "GCHQ gave us their Berlin Signal Squadron for ninety-six hours; after that, they revert to their normal tasks."

"Tuesday can't come soon enough for me, Ashton."

There was a lot more to come but the phone started ringing and Franklin had to break off to answer it. The exchange which followed was largely one-sided and clearly disagreeable, though he did remember to thank Voigt before hanging up.

"That's it," he said grimly. "I want you to go straight back to your hotel, pack your bags and check out. Berlin is my bailiwick and you are not staying in it a minute longer. I don't care if you can't get a seat on a plane, or if all the trains are going in the wrong direction. You've outstayed your welcome and you are leaving today if you have to steal a car, ride a bike or walk."

"I get the picture," Ashton said angrily. "Now tell me what's happened to Willie?"

Franklin blinked at him, completely taken aback. "He was smashed up in a traffic accident. The police say he will pull through but the girl with him wasn't so lucky. She's dead."

"I'm sorry . . ."

"So you damn well should be. The traffic police don't know how the accident occurred because the doctors won't allow them to question him until this afternoon at the earliest. Which is another reason why I want you a long way from here before they do."

"I'll be gone inside the hour. Okay?"

"Yes. Just don't run away with the idea that I am going to save your hide." Franklin paused, then said, "Matter of fact, I would start looking for another job if I were you."

Whittle's successor was the third officer Sergeant Norman had been paired off with since he had joined the Arms Control Unit. As his tour of duty had now been extended to June '92, there was likely to be a fourth because this studious-looking major in the Royal Electrical and Mechanical Engineers was strictly a stop-gap replacement. By the time they had established any kind of working relationship, Major Geoffrey Beadle would be packing his bags and moving on to greener pastures. He was a boffin, an Associate Member of the Institute of Mechanical Engineers and a graduate of the Technical Staff College, Shrivenham. He knew everything there was to know about the internal combustion engine and damn all about real soldiering.

Everyone who mattered agreed that Beadle was wasted in his present appointment. In fact, his next posting had already been decided upon by the Military Secretary's Branch who had selected him for a second-grade staff appointment at the Armoured Fighting Vehicle Research Establishment, Chobham. Beadle was filling in time with the Arms Control Unit because there was a shortage of Russian linguists in the army and at some stage in his career, he had wanted to become a military attaché and had been sent on a long language course run by the Royal Army Education Corps. The assistant military attaché post in Moscow had fallen through, but the language qualification was recorded on his computerised Record of Service and had appeared on the visual display unit when the appropriate staff branch had been looking for someone to replace Whittle.

In the long term, the Arms Control Unit would be getting a young captain in the Royal Artillery, but he was the last in a long chain and five other officers had to move into various slots before he would be free to join them. Meanwhile, they had Beadle. Most people in his position would have been content to jog along, doing no more than they had to, but the major was keen, too bloody keen for Sergeant Norman's liking. They were spending most of Saturday in the marshalling yards at Wittenberg, fifty miles southwest of Berlin, because he had volunteered to witness the departure of yet another Soviet mechanised formation from East Germany, and where the major went, so did Sergeant Norman, which had pleased Mrs Norman no end.

No one to help with the weekly shopping, no one to keep the kids amused while she had her hair done and he had promised to take them to the zoo. "I bet you put Major Beadle up to it," she'd said, as though he had planned the whole thing. Well, he had news for Angie; unless these damned trains got away on time, she needn't bother about fixing a cold supper for the baby-sitter he'd laid on because they wouldn't be going to any dinner dance.

Norman walked on down the track past flat after flat, each one loaded with an elderly 14 ton BMP-1 Armoured Personnel Carrier. The newspaper and TV reporters were always calling them tanks because the turret housed a 73mm smooth bore cannon and there was a coaxially mounted launch rail for a SAGGER antitank missile. But there was an eight strong infantry section seated back to back in the hull behind the turret, each man facing a rifle port.

Thirty flats to each train, three trains to lift the armoured personnel carriers of one mechanised infantry regiment. Two trains ready to go, one still loading, and a right mess they were making of it. He had seen a British brigade load twice as many vehicles in half the time, and some of these BMPs weren't properly secured either. You were supposed to chock both tracks in front of the leading bogie wheels and behind the two rear ones. The wooden triangular-shaped blocks were then nailed down to the flat to prevent forward and lateral movement. Finally, the hull was anchored to the railway wagon fore and aft by steel hawsers or heavy duty chains. But this particular train was likely to shed some of its load on the first sharp curve.

"Is good, no?"

Norman turned round and found himself face to face with an absurdly young-looking senior sergeant in dress uniform. His cap badge, a five point star surrounded by two oak leaf branches and the magenta-coloured shoulder boards denoted he was in the mechanised infantry.

"We going home."

"Me too, I hope," Norman said.

"You take picture of me," the Russian said in broken English and pointed to the camera Norman carried on a thin leather strap round his neck.

"Sure, why not?"

Before he knew what was happening, the sergeant was joined by four other NCOs, all of whom wanted to be in the photograph. With the aid of his limited Russian vocabulary and a certain amount of sign language, Norman managed to group them together between the tracks with the freight train on their right.

"Okay," he said, "now let's have a great big smile."

Norman pressed the button, waited for the film to wind on automatically, then took a second shot. He was about to go for a third when the group suddenly broke up and scattered like chaff before the wind. He did not have to look very far to discover what had caused the stampede. Glancing over his shoulder, Norman recognised the athletic figure of Colonel General Vitali Ilyich Lobanov, Commander-in-Chief 6 Guards Tank Army.

Ever since he had relieved his predecessor, the Colonel General had gone out of his way to court publicity. He had organised a series of farewell parades and had spent more time on reviewing stands than he had on manoeuvres. He had been photographed handing over the keys of a barracks that had just been vacated, had posed for the TV cameras in front of an imposing array of Multiple Rocket Systems which were being returned to the USSR for destruction and had given a series of exclusive interviews to Western journalists. As a result of overexposure, his activities were no longer considered newsworthy and consequently, few representatives of the media had turned up at Wittenberg to record this latest junket.

The Colonel General did not look at all happy and appeared to be berating the unfortunate regimental commander; then it dawned on Norman that the stocky officer on the receiving end of the diatribe was Alexei Leven. He wondered what the GRU man from Potsdam was doing there and rapidly came to the conclusion that that was a question best answered by the high-priced help. Visual sightings were all very well, but Earley would want to see the evidence for himself. Raising the camera again, Norman finished off the reel of film.

The sign outside Jean-Paul's Club on Bourbon Street boasted it had the best modern jazz band and the best-looking girls in New Orleans. The four-man combo on drums, guitars and electronic keyboard could be heard half a block away, but it wasn't possible to judge whether there was any truth in the other half of the claim without stepping inside. There was a cover charge for doing so and the drinks didn't come cheap either, but there were few complaints since it was a male orientated establishment and the waitresses aimed to please. They wore high heels, fishnet stockings and little else. Not surprisingly, they were frequently groped; not surprisingly, those who weren't hard-boiled enough couldn't take it and there was a correspondingly high turnover of staff.

Two days after she had arrived in New Orleans, Galina Kutuzova had walked into Jean-Paul's and asked for a job. The Carolyn Jacobs who had arrived on the United Airlines flight from Phoenix had dark glossy hair, the Colette Lefarge who had been taken on by the club's owner was a redhead. The new hairstyle and yet another alias were not the only things Galina had acquired in the forty-eight hours that had elapsed since she had fled from the Red Lion La Posada Resort Hotel in Scottsdale. To change her appearance, she had replaced her existing wardrobe and ditched the stolen tote bag in favour of a suitcase. These necessary expenses together with the plane ticket, cab fares and two nights at a small hotel in the Garden District had made a significant hole in the thousand dollars she had started out with in her purse. Although there were about ten thousand dollars with Wells Fargo, Galina believed she couldn't draw on the account or move it to another bank without alerting the police. The remaining traveller's cheques which she had purchased from the Union Bank of Zürich were of no use to her either because they could only be cashed by Yvette Michel. To survive, she had had to find a job and an employer who wouldn't ask for a reference or question her too closely. That kind of job wasn't advertised in the newspapers under Situations Vacant; that kind of employer didn't recruit staff from a reputable agency. Both were, however, to be found in the French Quarter.

The pay at Jean-Paul's Club was a hundred and sixty a week, less twenty for the room she rented overlooking the small walled garden at the back. The hours were long, from six in the evening to four in the morning with just one rest day a week, but if she was nice to the customers, a girl could pick up almost as much again in tips. She could of course triple her income provided she was willing to be extra nice, but you needed to have a room somewhere on Esplanade Avenue where all the hookers hung out because Jean-Paul didn't allow any of his girls to turn a trick on the premises.

The girl who had taken Galina under her wing and put her wise was a Creole named Leonora who seemed to have some kind of private understanding with Jean-Paul regarding the number of hours she worked. Not for Leonora the six to four routine. She came and went as she pleased. She also had the run of the self-contained apartment overlooking Bourbon Street and spent most afternoons sitting out on the balustrade. "Just promoting the club, honey," she had said in her thick Southern accent.

Although they had little in common and had only met a couple of days ago, Leonora seemed to want her friendship and had got into the habit of dropping into her room to make girl talk. Galina could hear her now, gently tapping on the door, and called out to her to come on in, then realised Leonora couldn't. Still half-asleep, she crawled out of bed, staggered across the room and unlocked the door.

"What time is it?" she asked, bleary-eyed.

"Twenty minutes after ten a.m."

"The middle of the night. What are you doing up this early?"

"I haven't been to bed yet, honey." Leonora closed the door behind her. "At least, not to sleep," she added with a throaty chuckle.

"Where have you been?"

"Esplanade Avenue. Where else?"

"Oh." Galina shuffled back to the bed and sank down. Esplanade Avenue was the Red Light district; she had learned that much in the short time she had been in New Orleans.

"You look as if you've had a pretty active night too," Leonora observed. "I hope he treated you right."

"What?"

"The blond stallion who was giving you the eye before I left the club. Don't tell me you didn't notice him? He was real smitten, asked me your name, where you came from . . ."

Suddenly, Galina was wide awake, her pulse racing from the surge of adrenalin that came with fear. "Did he say who he was?" she asked in a muted voice.

"Mike. Well, we know him as Mike. Comes from somewhere up in Mississippi – Natchez, I think."

"He's been here before?"

"Lots of times, he's on the payroll."

"I don't understand . . ."

"He's a cop, honey." Leonora opened her handbag, took out a pack of cigarettes and lit one. "Vice squad," she said, blowing a smoke ring towards the ceiling. "You don't want to get busted, you make sure he's happy."

CHAPTER 19

THE HOUSE which Hazelwood owned in Willow Walk near Hampstead Heath had been built in 1900 when things were done on a grand scale. Beneath the slate roof there had been six large bedrooms, two bathrooms, a study, library, games room, parlour, dining room, drawing room, conservatory, kitchen and scullery. The walls were Mendip stone and some eighteen inches thick. Outwardly, little had changed since those days, except for the Virginia creeper which had gradually increased its stranglehold on the mortar. Internally, it was a different story. Over the years, various builders and interior decorators had converted the property into three maisonettes, artfully subdividing the original bedrooms so that each residence had a minimum of three. However, they had been unable to do anything about the huge sashcord windows which defied double glazing, and it was still necessary to use a step ladder to remove any cobwebs from the ceiling.

Ashton paid off the cab outside the maisonette known as Willow Dene, walked round to the front door, which was on the left side of the house, and rang the bell. There were two reasons why he wasn't kept waiting on the doorstep; he had phoned Victor from Heathrow and the Hazelwoods were hosting a dinner party at seven thirty for eight. With only fifteen minutes in hand before their guests were due to arrive, Victor was eager to give him a drink, listen to what he had to say and get him out of the house in double quick time.

"So what's the problem?" he asked while adding a splash of soda water to Ashton's whisky.

"I've been kicked out of Berlin. Franklin's got the dead needle because we didn't tell him what was going on and I have lost one of his helpers, a guy called Willie."

"What do you mean, you lost him?"

"He was smashed up in a traffic accident; the girl who was with him was killed. We don't have the details yet but chances are it was deliberate."

Hazelwood walked over to the desk facing the study window, opened the cigar box and helped himself to one of his favourite Burma cheroots. With almost loving care, he trimmed the end, pierced the leaf with a matchstick and lit it. "You'd better tell me the worst," he said with the air of a martyr.

It was the second time Ashton had been invited to relate what had happened when he had met Leven and repeating the bald facts didn't make them any more palatable. If anything, his own situation sounded even grimmer.

"What made you give Franklin the two hundred?"

"It would have looked bad if I hadn't. I had to tell him Willie was missing; think what a meal MI5 would make of it if I had said nothing about the money Leven had given me."

"It didn't stop Franklin implying that you had held on to the lion's share."

"The allegation won't stand up," Ashton said. "Everyone knows the KGB are a parsimonious lot, same goes for their little brother the GRU."

"Still doesn't look good. In fact, if they did photograph you in Leningrad with Lydia Petrovskaya they could do us all a lot of harm."

"They could certainly hurt me, Victor, but you mustn't get drawn into this because it will damage the whole Department if you do. Officially, you don't know I've been to the USSR and it's better we keep it that way."

"But I knew you were going to play footsie with Leven."

"It's deniable," Ashton said tersely. "The thing is, you have got to pre-empt the situation with the DG before Franklin gets to him."

"Maybe it won't come to anything, maybe they won't connect the two incidents. After all, you said yourself that what happened in Moscow and Leningrad could only have been the work of a dissident faction, otherwise you would never have survived."

"I'm beginning to think I was perhaps a little too sanguine, Victor. There are about two million men and women in the KGB including the border guards and pen pushers;

if only half of one per cent are hardliners, that's still ten thousand."

"What are you saying?"

"You can't afford to leave anything to chance," Ashton said. "I don't know what you told the DG before I left for Berlin, but this would be a good time to acquaint him with all the facts before Neil Franklin gets in with his version."

Hazelwood turned his back on him to window gaze at the evening sky as if seeking some sort of inspiration from a 747 inbound for Heathrow. In the next-door garden, a neighbour was trying to start his lawnmower.

"I can never understand that man," Hazelwood mused. "Why he has to wait until this time in the evening to cut the grass is beyond me. I suppose it takes all sorts . . ."

"Quite."

"I presume our friends in 13 Signal Regiment have nothing for us?"

"I'm afraid you're right," Ashton said grimly.

"Well, you never know, something may turn up before Tuesday. The fact is, I can't talk to C, he's out of town."

C was the traditional name for the head of the SIS in honour of Commander Manfield George Smith-Cumming RN, the man who had founded the original foreign section of the Secret Service Bureau in 1909. The current DG lived in South Audley Street and owned a cottage at Burford in the Cotswolds. Both were protected residencies with secure communications. If Hazelwood couldn't reach him, it meant the DG was staying with friends who didn't have the same facilities. And he wouldn't have done that without first clearing it with the Cabinet Secretary and nominating a senior officer who would be readily available in the event of an emergency.

"Might it not be an idea to have a word with the Deputy DG?" Ashton suggested.

Hazelwood turned away from the window with a muttered expletive. It really wasn't his evening and his face showed it. Apart from the bad news Ashton had brought him, an ember from the cheroot had burnt a neat round hole in his shirt front. Before he could express his feelings adequately, the next-door neighbour finally managed to start his lawnmower and the melodic chimes announced the arrival of the first dinner guest. He stuck his head out into the hall, called to Alice and was promptly told by his wife to answer the door.

"You'd better wait here," Hazelwood growled. "I won't be a minute."

He was never going to be that. When the first guest arrived, the remainder were never far behind, and no hostess, least of all Alice, was prepared to cope with the sudden influx on her own. By the time Hazelwood reappeared, the rhubarb of noise from the drawing room suggested that most of the guests were on their second drink and were unlikely to miss him.

"Have you got your car with you?" he asked.

Ashton shook his head. "I came straight here from the airport by taxi."

"Okay, the best thing you can do is ring for a minicab; you'll find the number in my desk diary. I'm sorry I've got to leave you to it but you can see how things are."

"You don't have to apologise to me, Victor. I'm only too glad I found you at home."

"Yes, well, don't you go losing any sleep over Franklin."

"Does that mean you are going to brief the Deputy DG?"

"That would be a bad tactical move, Peter. It would create the impression that we knew we had made a balls-up and were anxious to cover ourselves. I'm going to let Franklin have the first word and when C sends for me, I'll politely imply that Head of Station, Berlin is panicking unnecessarily and must be losing his grip." Hazelwood stopped by the door and looked back. "Don't worry," he said. "Believe me, everything is going to be all right."

Ashton hoped his confidence wasn't misplaced, but there was little he could do about it even if it was. Opening the desk diary, he looked up the number of the minicab firm and arranged for a car to take him to Waterloo Station.

When he walked into the flat a little over an hour later, there was a pile of junk mail waiting for him from local firms anxious to drum up trade in what were undeniably hard times. It wasn't only the retailers who were feeling the pinch; there was, in fact, another message from the estate agent on the answering machine urging him to accept the offer they had received for the flat.

*   *   *

Franklin lived on the corner of Grunerweg and Alsenstrasse in the Wannsee District, which put him within walking distance of the golf club. It was only the third or fourth time that Voigt had been to the Englishman's home and on this particular night it was anything but a social occasion. He had in truth invited himself and had refused to be put off when Franklin had burbled something about having tickets for a concert by the Radio Symphony Orchestra at the Philharmonie.

Voigt turned into the garage drive and pulled up behind a dark blue Mercedes. The light over the front porch came on and Franklin was there at the door to meet him before he could get out of the car. For a man who was still hoping to catch the second half of the concert, Voigt thought the Englishman was dressed in remarkably casual attire. For a man whose evening had supposedly been ruined, he was singularly cheerful, which in the circumstances had to be out of character. Before Franklin had arrived in Berlin, his predecessor had warned him that he had a reputation for being prickly and difficult. Voigt had never encountered this side of his character, probably because he had not seen as much of him as he had the previous Head of Station.

No one, however, could have made him feel more welcome than Franklin did. He had gone there determined to have it out with the Englishman; instead, he found himself nursing a very large malt whisky and apologising for having messed up his evening.

"Think nothing of it, Heinrich," Franklin told him airily. "One of Ella's friends from the golf club was only too happy to go to the concert with her. Matter of fact, I wasn't sorry to give it a miss, never did care much for Bartok. Now, what's all this about Willie?"

"How long has he worked for British Intelligence?"

"Willie? Work for me?" Franklin snorted as though he found it hard to contain his mirth. "What on earth gave you that idea?" he spluttered.

"Because you were concerned to find out what had happened to him."

"Only on behalf of one of my sales assistants."

Voigt swallowed the rest of his whisky and set the glass down on the occasional table next to his armchair. "Yes, of course. And what is the name of this young lady?"

"Fräulein Gretel Jungclaus, and I am afraid I lied to you about her being one of my employees. Actually, she is an acquaintance of Fräulein Helga von Schinkel's, but if I had told you that at the time, I don't think you would have looked into it."

The whole story was one big preposterous lie but Voigt knew the von Schinkel woman would support it to the hilt. With her length of service to the Crown, she was practically British by adoption. Franklin had had plenty of time to brief her since this morning and there obviously was a Gretel Jungclaus because whatever else he might be, the Englishman wasn't stupid and would never make up a name. Furthermore, this Gretel Jungclaus would swear black was white that Willie was her boyfriend, and he was smart enough to catch on. He would also be suitably embarrassed that Gretel now knew that he'd been with another girl that evening.

"Willie Baumgart used to work for your predecessor."

"Really?" Franklin poured him another whisky. "He didn't introduce us, perhaps because he had been told by London that I always recruit my own team wherever I go. I don't like anyone's leftovers. Of course, Fräulein Helga von Schinkel knew of him; it was she who told me that Baumgart had a finger in every racket. I'm surprised you haven't made his acquaintance, Heinrich."

"I may just do that," Voigt told him grimly. "The traffic police are not satisfied with his statement."

"The doctors have allowed them to question him then?"

"Earlier this evening. Baumgart said he was heading towards Karlshorst on the Am Tierpark Throughway and was about to overtake a truck when he lost control of the car as it started to aquaplane on the wet surface. He careened across the road, side-swiped a streetlight and flipped over. The vehicle then rammed into the abutment of a railway bridge, rolled over again and came to rest on the nearside. There were no witnesses."

"What about the truck driver?"

"Baumgart reckons the vehicle was throwing up so much spray in its wake that the driver couldn't have seen him in his wing mirror."

"Why do I get the impression that you don't believe Baumgart?"

"Because the damage to the Audi is inconsistent. That truck driver deliberately nudged him off the road."

"Can you prove that?"

Voigt thought the Englishman sounded completely indifferent and was merely inquiring out of politeness. "Not yet," he snapped.

"So what do you propose to do, Heinrich?"

"The traffic police will charge him with reckless driving."

"That's a bit hard, isn't it? You told me his left arm had been broken in two places and his leg is in a hell of a mess, never mind the fact that he has almost been scalped. Seems to me he's suffered enough already."

The English and their sense of fair play – so hypocritical. Willie Baumgart had gone out on a limb for this man and he chose to repay his misplaced sense of loyalty by quietly abandoning him. Voigt wondered why he should be surprised when it was the way the British Secret Intelligence Service invariably behaved in such circumstances.

"He was speeding," Voigt said angrily. "By his own admission, he was doing well over ninety kilometres an hour in poor visibility and appalling weather conditions. As a result of his recklessness, a young woman is dead. What would you have us do? Pat him on the head and tell him not to do it again?"

"Yes, I was forgetting the young lady. What was her name?"

"Lisolette Quirnheim."

"One of his numerous girlfriends, I presume?" Franklin shook his head and looked regretful. "I suppose Helga will have to be told?"

After twenty years with the Kripo, Voigt had encountered more than his fair share of cold-blooded and callous individuals, but this Englishman was in a class of his own. Baumgart had been running an errand for him and there was no way he would have involved an outsider; Franklin had known the girl all right, yet her death had left him completely unmoved. But if Voigt despised anyone, it was himself for sitting there drinking Franklin's whisky as if they were the best of friends.

"Did Baumgart say what he was doing in Karlshorst, Heinrich?"

"He was just riding around, trying to straighten things out with his latest girlfriend. At least that's the reason he gave, so you are safe enough, my friend."

"I can't think what you mean," Franklin said stiffly.

"The Cold War is over and there is no need to continue with your ridiculous games. You are a guest in my country and the time is long since past when you could meddle in our internal affairs and get away with it."

"You are referring to the Rostovsky case, are you? Well, let me remind you it was Captain Younger who identified Galina Kutuzova's voice on the tape your people found in Tamara Chernenko's flat."

"What are you trying to do – make me feel ungrateful?"

Franklin shook his head. "I was merely trying to point out how we usually help one another. For instance, it may interest you to know that Galina Kutuzova is travelling on a French passport. Matter of fact, Scotland Yard have traced her to Montreal."

"When did you hear this?"

"Oh, some time ago. I'm surprised the Police President of Dresden didn't pass the information on to you. Of course, he may have been looking at the Whittle case in isolation and not appreciated its wider implications."

Voigt couldn't understand how it could have happened. He had called on Franklin with the express intention of roasting the Englishman alive; instead, he found himself expressing his gratitude for the few crumbs of information that had been thrown his way.

Still in a mental daze, he shook hands with Franklin on the doorstep, then got into his BMW and backed out of the drive. He drove home very carefully, one eye on the lookout for a prowl car, conscious that thanks to Franklin's hospitality, he was definitely over the limit.

It was possible to lead a very hectic social life in Berlin, and while Earley enjoyed a party as much as the next man, there was a family rule that no invitations were accepted during the Easter, summer and Christmas holidays when their two boys were home from boarding school. Friends and neighbours were still invited round for drinks, or a barbecue, weather permitting, but mostly the time was spent strictly en famille. Saturday nights they either went to the cinema, watched TV or hired a video from the Army Kinematographic Corporation. That particular evening, they were watching *Star Trek IV, the Final Frontier* and were thirty-odd minutes into it when someone rang the doorbell. With the exception of Earley, the unwelcome intrusion was greeted with a loud groan; since science fiction did not appeal to him, he was only too happy to see who it was. Of all the possible callers, Sergeant Norman was the last person he had expected to find on the doorstep.

"Hello, Sergeant," he said. "What brings you here?"

"I'm not intruding, am I, sir?"

"Good God, no." Earley showed him into the study, then fetched a couple of beers from the fridge in the kitchen. "Nothing wrong, is there?" he asked.

"I'm in the doghouse," Norman told him. "Major Beadle and I were late getting back from Wittenberg which meant we had to give the dinner dance at Garrison Headquarters a miss."

"Sorry to hear that."

"Angie will get over it soon enough."

Angie was a twenty-five-year-old brunette from Oldham and one of the new breed of army wives. She had been to Liverpool Polytechnic, was a computer buff and had given up a promising career to marry Sergeant Norman. Bingo, Beetle Drives and other activities favoured by the Wives' Club were a complete turn-off for her. She was not interested in earning pin money as a check-out girl at the Navy, Army and Air Force Institute supermarket. She wanted a job that was satisfying and would stretch her mind and if the army couldn't find some gainful way to employ her, they were going to lose one very good sergeant.

"So how did things go at Wittenberg?" Earley asked.

"That's why I came to see you. Your old friend, Lieutenant Colonel Alexei Leven turned up."

"Did his name appear in the public relations hand-out?"

"No. He wasn't one of the star attractions but he was there all right. He was having a heart to heart talk with Colonel General Lobanov and they didn't look at all happy."

"Are you sure it was Leven you saw?"

"I'm absolutely positive. Anyway, you will be able to see for yourself as soon as I've developed the reel of film."

Earley rubbed his chin. "Did the general have his aide with him?"

"Yes. There were a number of staff officers there too, but they were sort of hanging back while he was conferring with Leven."

"Conferring?"

"Well, Leven did most of the talking to begin with, but then the general held forth as though he was laying down the law, and our favourite GRU man was nodding away, doing his yes sir, no sir, three bags full routine. About ten or fifteen minutes later, they parted company and the staff homed in on the colonel general. The speech-making began and eventually the trains got away a good hour and a half behind schedule."

Earley wasn't sure what to make of it. As the C-in-C of 6 Guards Tank Army, Lobanov could send for who he liked, when he liked, but from what Sergeant Norman had told him, it looked as though the GRU man had sought out the general, and that was certainly unusual. Junior officers, and that included lieutenant colonels, did not go out of their way to corner a four-star general unless they had a very good reason. Maybe it was all a bit tenuous but something was definitely going on and it would do no harm to fire off a signal to the MOD acquainting the Intelligence Staff with the facts, such as they were.

"I'd give a lot to know what Leven is up to, Sergeant."

"So would I, sir."

"Major Beadle hasn't met him, has he?"

"Not yet."

"We'll have to put that right," Earley said cheerfully. "Monday is a Bank Holiday but first thing on Tuesday I want you to run the major over to Potsdam and I'll ring the unit to let Leven know you are on the way."

"Do you think he will agree to see Major Beadle at such short notice?"

"I don't much care if he doesn't. What I want you to do, Sergeant, is have a good look round, get the feel of the unit. What morale is like. Has there been another upheaval? Have any more faces disappeared and so on? You get the idea?"

"Yes, sir." Norman smiled and got to his feet. "It's going to be quite like old times," he said, "when we had a proper job to do."

"Yes, well, that will certainly make a change." Earley walked him to the front door. "Incidentally," he said, "when do you expect to have those photographs ready?"

"I'm going to work on them tonight."

"Won't Angie have something to say about that?"

"Plenty," said Norman, "but I like living dangerously."

CHAPTER 20

THE SURVEILLANCE operation mounted against the GRU by the Berlin squadron of 13 Signal Regiment was terminated at 0700 hours local time on Tuesday the twenty-seventh of August. Berlin was one hour ahead of London; at eight fifteen, a quarter of an hour after the stand down, Ashton rang GCHQ Cheltenham, asked for the army liaison officer, then went through the drill for switching to secure speech.

"This is Ashton," he told the liaison officer. "What have you intercepted from the rival firm in Potsdam?"

"Nothing – they're hibernating."

"That's up to yesterday – right? I mean you wouldn't have received the log for the last twenty-four hours yet, would you?"

"I'm sorry to disappoint you, but we have, and the answer is still the same. They've not been talking to anyone."

"Are you saying there has been no kind of traffic whatsoever?" Ashton was conscious of sounding desperate and realised what sort of impression he had created when the liaison officer patiently explained that that was indeed the case.

"Listen, they couldn't even have sent a letter without our knowing it unless they wrote it in longhand. I shouldn't be telling you this but when they provided their clerks with electronic typewriters, they forgot to have them protected. Every key emits a different signal which we have the means to capture on tape. We then translate these individual notes into computer language, run it through one of our machines and, Bob's your uncle, out comes the letter. One of these days, the GRU are going to wake up to the fact that we are reading their classified letters before they are even signed, let alone despatched. But until they do, we are having a whale of a time."

"Maybe they have caught on?" Ashton suggested. "Perhaps that is why they have gone off the air?"

"No, they are just frightened, like you and I would be if we were in their shoes. They don't know where their loyalties should lie or who to look to for orders. Yeltsin has abolished the Communist Party in the Russian Soviet Federal Socialist Republic, Gorbachev could find himself out on his ear at any moment, the Soviet Union is fragmenting and every breakaway republic wants its own army and air force. I tell you, the officers and enlisted men stationed in East Germany don't know whose army they're in."

The liaison officer wasn't indulging in idle speculation. Government Communications Headquarters Cheltenham didn't have to rely on the army for its signal intelligence; GCHQ had its own civilian-manned intercept stations at Skipton near Harrogate and Wick up in Scotland. They had been monitoring the signals traffic originating from the Defence Ministry in Moscow to all internal military districts as well as Soviet army formations stationed outside the borders of the USSR. Every communication they had intercepted had reflected the growing confusion in the Kremlin as Defence Ministers and Commanders-in-Chief were appointed, only to be sacked and replaced a few days later.

"You picked a bad time to eavesdrop on the GRU in Potsdam. Everyone is keeping their heads down. Still, better luck next time, eh?"

"I doubt there will be a second time," Ashton told him. "But thanks for your help anyway."

He put the phone down and tried to concentrate on mundane things like opening his safe and going through the files which had been languishing in the pending tray since the day before he'd left for Berlin. But he couldn't remember the damned combination and had to go cap in hand to the Department Security Officer and ask to see the copy which he held in a sealed envelope against just such an emergency. When he did get his safe open, most of the files in the pending tray which were marked up for his information, didn't register with him and he might as well have initialled the individual folios blind. Always present at the back of his mind was the thought that in meeting Leven he had taken one hell of a risk and had put himself in jeopardy for absolutely no return.

Ashton kept waiting for Hazelwood to send for him and the more time that went by without a summons, the more tense he became. Halfway through the morning, he left the office to get a cup of coffee from the vending machine near the lifts and was horrified to find on his return that he had walked out leaving both the door and the safe wide open. It was a stupid thing to do, the kind of fundamental breach of security that people committed when they allowed themselves to be distracted. He was still thanking his lucky stars that the duty security officer of the day hadn't been walking the floor at the time when Hazelwood's PA buzzed him to say his presence was required on the top floor.

Hazelwood looked grim and worried too, like a man with a four-figure overdraft who had bet his shirt on a horse only to see it come in last. If his week had started badly, Ashton couldn't imagine how it was going to end for him. The curt way he was told to close the door so that they could have a little privacy was, he thought, a foretaste of what lay in store.

"Franklin got in first," Hazelwood said tersely. "Bastard must have rung the DG's house in South Audley Street all day until he finally caught him late yesterday evening when he returned from the country. Didn't give C the whole story of course, just wanted to advise him that a full report was on the way in the diplomatic bag, then proceeded to put down the rat poison for you and me. Made himself the hero of the hour while he was at it."

"What exactly did he say, Victor?"

"I gather Franklin made a big production of the traffic accident, said he had had to smooth a few ruffled feathers in the police department before taking steps to ensure Willie's version of the incident held up. Seems he sent Fräulein Helga von Schinkel and a young woman round to the hospital to coach him."

But Franklin hadn't stopped there. He had also let it be known that, in his opinion, the SIS should have kept Leven at arm's length. Getting close to the GRU officer had been a big mistake which might well have unfortunate repercussions.

"That's his way of saying that you allowed yourself to be compromised," Hazelwood growled.

"He practically told me so to my face. He said it was a bizarre operation and wondered if we had cleared it with the DG."

"I know. The temptation to repeat it was too much for him."

Ashton could see what had happened. Victor had not been entirely open with the DG when he had persuaded him to sanction

213

the operation and had had to do some fast talking after Franklin had taken it upon himself to enlighten him. His grim expression earlier on suggested he had not been entirely successful.

"I take it 13 Signal Regiment didn't come through for us?"

"I would have been pounding on your door if they had, Victor."

There was a lengthy and awkward silence while Hazelwood took a cheroot from the box on his desk and examined it with a puzzled frown as if he had never seen one before.

"C wanted me to rein you in," he said presently.

"Oh yes? What did he mean by that?"

"I was invited to restrict your access to classified material." Hazelwood cleared his throat. "You weren't to see anything above Confidential."

"I might as well turn in my official pass here and now. We haven't got anything graded lower than Secret in the whole bloody department."

"I talked him out of it."

"You did?" Ashton smiled. "Well, that's terrific. I owe you one, Victor."

"You'll have to watch your step, Peter. From now on, a lot of people will have their beady eyes on you. Don't give them any cause for alarm. Make sure all your personal affairs are in order. You understand what I am saying?"

"I'm way ahead of you," Ashton told him.

"I was told to give you an official warning; the rest of our conversation didn't take place."

"Right."

"One final point," Hazelwood said as he started towards the door. "Get rid of any souvenirs you might have bought in Leningrad and Moscow."

It was the first time Alexei Leven had been to Moscow since June 1988, and he found the experience unnerving. The impressions he had formed from watching the newscasts on the West German networks had in no way prepared him for the reality. It was one thing to watch the mob demolishing the statue of Feliks Dzerzhinsky outside the KGB Headquarters on TV, quite another to be in the capital and feel the underlying tension.

The old order had collapsed, the new one was still evolving, and yesterday's ally could be tomorrow's enemy. He had not felt safe from the moment his plane had touched down at Sheremetyevo 2, the international airport serving Moscow. Early on Monday morning, Colonel General Lobanov had given him two letters, one addressed to Marshal Yevgeni Shaposhnikov, the newly appointed Defence Minister, the other to Pavel Trilisser, Deputy Head of the KGB's First Chief Directorate. The first letter assured the Defence Minister that there were no political revisionists serving within the ranks of 6 Guards Tank Army; the second, and more important one, was a letter of introduction. Without the first, he would have had no justification for flying to Moscow; without the second, he would have felt a lot safer.

He had spent Monday night in the guest wing of the GRU Headquarters building in Znamensky Street, two blocks from the last stop on the Kirovsko-Frunzenskaya Metro Line. First thing this morning he had called at the Defence Ministry, delivered the letter addressed to Marshal Shaposhnikov to one of his aides and had been granted a five-minute interview with the great man himself. For someone who was carrying a highly incriminating letter on his person, the interview had come as a singularly unpleasant surprise. Even now, a good half-hour after arriving at the complex housing the First Chief Directorate at Yasenevo on the Moscow peripheral road, he still felt on edge.

Leven also felt conspicuous sitting there on a bench outside Pavel Trilisser's office in his army uniform. People wouldn't have stared at him quite so much had he been able to wear civilian clothes, but officially he was in Moscow to represent Colonel General Lobanov and the Defence Minister would have thought it odd if he hadn't appeared in uniform. All the same, it was very disconcerting to find oneself an object of curiosity, and he wanted to let everyone know that he was KGB too, but that would be both stupid and dangerous. Glasnost and perestroika, Gorbachev and Yeltsin; all that heady combination had spawned was chaos, distrust and treachery.

A clerk emerged from Trilisser's office and walked towards the registry at the opposite end of the corridor. Leven had lost count of how many people had been to see the Deputy Head of the First Chief Directorate since he had been sitting there on the bench, but the number was certainly in double figures. He wondered if there had been something in the introductory letter from the army commander which had put Trilisser off, or perhaps he believed the infrared photographs of the mysterious Englishman known as Peter were fakes? He was sure of one thing. If he didn't get to see Trilisser very shortly, he was going to miss his Aeroflot flight to Berlin and would be forced to stay over.

The clerk returned from the registry carrying a medium-size brown envelope, entered the Deputy Chief's office, only to reappear moments later to retrace his steps. The minutes ticked slowly by; then the PA in the adjoining room stuck her head out into the corridor to announce that Pavel Trilisser was ready to see him now.

Pavel Trilisser was a tall, lean, ascetic-looking man in his early fifties. He had startlingly blue eyes that burned with the intensity of an oxyacetylene torch and a manner that had all the warmth of an iceberg. Leven feared and disliked him on sight.

"What are you doing in uniform, Comrade Colonel?" he asked with evident disdain.

"With respect, Comrade General, I had to wear it to avoid arousing suspicion at GRU Headquarters and when I went to the Defence Ministry." Leven licked his lips. "I admit it makes me somewhat conspicuous in these surroundings."

"It's lucky for you my office is not in Dzerzhinsky Square."

Leven had news for the KGB general; if Pavel Trilisser had been in either the Second or Eighth Chief Directorates instead of the Foreign Intelligence Department, he wouldn't have gone anywhere near the rococo-style building that had once housed the All Russian Insurance Company in the days of the Czar. The people there had taken leave of their senses and were running what amounted to a guided tour for every foreign journalist who wanted to do a story on the KGB.

"Well now, Alexei Leven, this letter from your army commander informs me that you have obtained some valuable information from an English traitor known to you as Peter?"

"That's correct. He claimed he was a clerical assistant employed at . . ."

Trilisser raised a hand, silencing him in mid-sentence. "Would this be your mysterious Englishman?" he asked and gave him a batch of prints.

Leven examined them one by one. The pictures had been taken at long range with a telephoto lens and in some cases the negatives had subsequently been enlarged. The composition was the same in every photograph and featured a man and a woman in conversation with a very impressive war memorial in the background. The pictures had clearly been taken somewhere in the Soviet Union, but he couldn't identify the location, nor did he recognise the woman. Initially, the man had been wearing a pair of sunglasses which obscured the upper part of his face, but in later exposures the woman had removed the polaroids and was holding them in her left hand.

"That's him," Leven said.

"Then you will be interested to hear that his full name is Peter Ashton. According to his passport, he is a technical author and he told Lydia Petrovskaya, the woman in the photographs, that he is employed by British Aerospace. However, there is also a Peter Ashton in the British Diplomatic List."

"He told me he was a paper keeper at Century House."

"He is a little more than that." A bleak smile made a brief appearance on Trilisser's mouth. "The man you have been dealing with is a middle-ranking officer in the British Secret Intelligence Service. Now, what exactly did he tell you?"

"He said the SIS were looking for Galina Kutuzova and had traced her to Montreal through Interpol."

"Why should Ashton believe we would be interested to learn of the whereabouts of a deserter?"

It suddenly dawned on Leven that the Englishman had tricked him into admitting that Moscow had indicated just such an interest. But it was more than his life was worth to disclose this to Pavel Trilisser.

"Ashton didn't say, and I thought it safer not to ask. At the time I had every reason to believe I was dealing with a disgruntled clerk who was in financial difficulties. I didn't want him to get the impression that we were willing to pay a lot of money for the information he was prepared to give us."

"You did well, Alexei Leven."

"Thank you." The best lies were always the ones which contained an element of truth.

"How many deserters were 6 Guards Tank Army showing on their last strength return? Twenty? Thirty? Fifty? More than a hundred?"

"Forty-one," Leven said promptly.

"So why should we be worried about one among so many?"

"Because Fedyanin, the previous commander of 6 Guards Tank Army, had an eye for a pretty woman and took a fancy to Galina Kutuzova. What is bad from our point of view is that he was indiscreet where she was concerned, in more ways than one. In short, she has heard of TRIPWIRE and knows something of what it entails. She could certainly hurt us."

"I doubt it. Fedyanin was involved in the recent coup and is now under arrest."

Leven wondered what he was supposed to read between the lines in that assertion. Had the former paratroop general really been involved in the attempt to depose Gorbachev or was this a cover story the KGB intended to use should Galina Kutuzova surface from cover and attempt to sell her story to the highest bidder? Or had Pavel Trilisser changed sides? The possibility that he was talking to the enemy made his blood run cold. Whatever the explanation, silence was his only means of defence.

"A question for you," Trilisser said. "Now that we know who Ashton really is, do you believe his story?"

"He could be discontented about something."

"But on balance, it's unlikely. Agreed?"

"Yes."

"So what is he up to?"

"I've no idea."

"Come now, you are an intelligent man, you must have some opinion."

Leven desperately wanted to give the KGB general an answer that would satisfy him because there was no way of ducking the question.

"I think the British Secret Service is determined to exploit the situation created by Galina Kutuzova and Yuri Rostovsky. To this end, Ashton is attempting to undermine further the morale of my unit and render it ineffective."

"You could be on to something."

It seemed he had struck exactly the right note and had got himself out of a tight corner. Still feeling his way, he asked Pavel Trilisser what message he should give Colonel General Lobanov on his return.

"Tell him to carry on. You may also add that we will do whatever is necessary to contain the situation."

It was a politician's answer, so full of ambiguity it could be taken to mean almost anything. When Trilisser spoke of containing the situation, Leven hadn't the faintest idea whether he was referring to the one Ashton was attempting to create or the latent threat Galina Kutuzova would continue to pose until she was dead. To seek clarification was, however, the last thing he had in mind. There was a plane leaving for Berlin at 1625 hours and he wouldn't feel safe until he was on it.

Galina left Jean-Paul's Club, turned right on Bourbon and walked towards Esplanade Avenue as far as the intersection with Orleans Street where she made another right turn. Although there had been no sign of the blond stallion from the vice squad on Sunday night, the reprieve had been short-lived. Twenty-four hours later, he had turned up again like a bad penny, this time with a tall, mouse-haired girl in tow whose muscular biceps suggested she was a fitness fanatic. The fact that Leonora had told her she hadn't seen the girl before was of little comfort to Galina; on more than one occasion she had caught both of them looking at her and had found their scrutiny unnerving.

When a police officer began to show that much interest in you, it was time to move on. The three hundred and twenty-one dollars in her purse wasn't going to take her very far, but she still had a further nine hundred in traveller's cheques. Cashing them meant taking a risk but nothing like as big a one as she had previously supposed. Although the police in Phoenix would have circulated her description, she thought it unlikely that every bank in the neighbouring states had been asked to keep a lookout for Yvette Michel.

Galina went on past the Bourbon Orleans Hotel, jinked into St Peter Street and cut through Jackson Square to Decatur where she turned left. The Gulf Coast Investment and Trustee Savings Bank was on the corner of North Peter and the French Market. She went through the revolving door, tagged on to the queue which snaked through an S-bend to the tellers. With only two of the five windows open, the line moved slowly so that it was a good fifteen minutes before she was served. The teller asked Galina how much she wanted, checked her passport and made a note of the serial number on the front cover, then waited patiently while she signed all the cheques before giving her the nine hundred in a combination of twenties and fifties. Galina counted the money, put the bills away in her handbag with the passport and walked out of the bank straight into the arms of the blond stallion and the fitness fanatic.

They were fast, very fast. Before she knew what was happening, they rushed her into an alley round the corner from the Gulf Coast Investment and Trustee Savings Bank and stood her up facing the wall, arms and legs spread while the muscular policewoman searched her. Galina supposed that either Leonora must have told them she was going to the bank or else they had followed her from Jean-Paul's. Either way, she cursed herself for not spotting them. She was still castigating herself for being so stupid when the Amazon announced she was clean and the blond stallion cuffed one wrist to the other behind her back.

"A lot of people have been looking all over hell and half a Georgia for you, gull," he said in a thick Southern accent.

"Who are you?" Galina demanded, playing for time.

"I am a po-leece officer," he drawled, "and you are Yvette Michel and we are arresting you for the murder of Mary Beth Mallard at the Red Lion La Posada Resort Hotel in Scottsdale, Arizona, on Wednesday, August twenty-first 1991. You have the right to . . ."

"I am not Yvette Michel," she said, interrupting him. "My name is Galina Kutuzova. I am a Russian citizen and a senior lieutenant in the GRU."

"Of course you are, honey. And for the record, I'm Brigadier General P.G.T. Beauregard."

Before submitting them for Treasury approval, estimates for the next financial year were discussed and finalised by a committee chaired by the Director General of the SIS on the first Monday in October. In a break with tradition, this meeting had been brought forward to Tuesday the twenty-seventh of August and widened to include the future structure of the Service because the government was looking for a peace dividend from the Foreign Office as well as from the armed forces. The meeting had lasted almost seven hours with only a thirty-minute break for lunch, so that it was after six before Ashton was able to catch Hazelwood in his office.

"I hope this is going to be brief," he said wearily.

"As bad as that, was it?"

"The Rest of the World Department is to be merged with the Pacific Basin and our establishment is to be cut by forty per cent. It is hoped that most of the reductions can be achieved through normal wastage but there are bound to be some compulsory redundancies in all grades."

"When is all this going to happen?"

"The merger is to be completed by the end of the current financial year; we've got twelve months' grace. There is a rumour going the rounds that the next Director is likely to be an outsider. Seems the government wants someone to implement the cuts who won't be diverted from the task by misplaced feelings of loyalty to our people." Hazelwood scowled. "You're not going to give me any more bad news, are you?"

Ashton shook his head. "I rang the MOD this afternoon to ask what they had received from the Arms Control Unit lately. Apparently, the 189th Mechanised Infantry Regiment were backloading their armoured personnel carriers from Wittenberg on Saturday and who should turn up at the farewell ceremony but Alexei Leven. He was seen in earnest conversation with the army commander."

"So?"

"Well, he wasn't down on the programme to be there. This morning, Earley tried to arrange for one of his officers to meet Leven and was informed that no one had seen him since late on Sunday."

"On Friday night you tell him that we have traced Galina Kutuzova to Montreal; 13 Signal Regiment doesn't pick anything up because the following morning he decides to go and see Colonel General Lobanov in person." Hazelwood got to his feet, walked over to the safe and checked to make sure it was locked before leaving the office. "I'd like to believe it," he said. "But where's the proof?"

"I'm working on it," Ashton told him. "The MOD has agreed to ask their Arms Control Unit if they can find out where he has gone."

"Good." Hazelwood started towards the door. "Don't think me rude," he said, "but I've got a home to go to and I've had enough for one day."

So had Ashton, though how much longer he could hold on to his home in Victoria Road was becoming problematical. He accompanied Hazelwood to the bank of lifts, then got off at the floor below to clear his desk and lock up before walking to Waterloo Station.

If a day started on a sour note, it usually ended on one. As he made his way through the crowded concourse at Waterloo, an anonymous voice on the public address system told him that the six twenty-five semifast to Woking had been cancelled because of staff shortages. Consequently, he had to wait for the stopping train to Guildford via London Road, and it was gone seven thirty when he finally got home after detouring to pick up chow mein from the Chinese takeaway in the High Street.

Ashton never did get around to eating it. Although there was no sign of a break-in, he knew someone had been inside the flat after the daily cleaning woman had left. The evidence that there had been an intruder was there before his eyes when he checked the bookcase-cum-writing desk, but it took him well over an hour to spot it. The latest statement from Access was in the left-hand pigeon hole where he had put it but the windowpane in the envelope was now facing the wrong way. Whoever had taken it out would have found only one entry on the statement. Dated the twelfth of July in the sum of six hundred and eighty-five pounds, it had been raised by the Getaway Travel Agency.

CHAPTER 21

THE BARGAIN of the month was a fortnight in a 3-star hotel in Lanzarote in the Canaries for a hundred and forty-nine pounds. Other tempting offers included ten days in Rhodes for a hundred and sixty and a week on Corfu for a mere seventy-eight pounds. It was the height of the holiday season and something had to be done to boost the flagging tourist trade in the middle of a worldwide economic recession, but it appeared the inducements were not having quite the effect the promoters had obviously hoped for. When Ashton had booked the Leningrad and Moscow Two-City Break, there had only been one girl on the counter and he'd had the place to himself. This time, Vicky was dealing with a retired couple who couldn't make up their minds where they wanted to go and were in no mood to be pressured – but that was the only difference.

"I'll be with you in a minute, Mr Ashton," she said a trifle optimistically.

"That's okay," he told her, "I'm not in a hurry."

Ashton wandered over to the display racks and picked out the Swiss Ski brochure for 1991/1992 from the winter sports section. The resorts were listed on pages six to forty-nine; those for the Bernese Oberland appeared towards the back of the publication. Grindelwald was the last place he wanted to be reminded of but somehow the promotion fell open at that particular page and he found himself confronted with a photograph of the Hotel Regina, and the memories came flooding back. He and Jill had spent ten days there at the end of March 1988 to celebrate their engagement. Their room had been at the front of the hotel overlooking the mountain railway to the Kleine Scheidegg and the cable car to Fiest.

The south-facing rooms offered the best view but they had

already been taken before Ashton had even thought of booking the holiday. Not that it mattered; as Jill had repeatedly assured him after they had arrived at the Regina, she hadn't come to Grindelwald to sit out on a balcony gazing at the Eiger. And she hadn't been kidding; as soon as it had been light enough to see, they had gone on up to the Kleine Scheidegg and had stayed out on the slopes until they had been in danger of missing the last train back to the village.

They had spent the first three days on the red pistes, after which by mutual agreement, Ashton had relegated himself to the blue or so-called easy pistes, while Jill had skied the black. It had been the first of many things which Jill had shown she could do better than he. It had probably also been the first time she had begun to wonder if he was really the man for her.

"That's sorted them out," Vicky said behind him. "Now, what can I do for you, Mr Ashton?"

He turned about, uncertain how to broach the subject despite rehearsing the opening line over and over again in his mind.

"It's about the payment I made on my credit card," he said hesitantly.

"I can guess how you must have felt about that." Vicky smiled. "And I would have done exactly the same in your position. Nobody likes to pay twice, especially when some of the digits have been reversed. That extra eight hundred and sixty-odd pounds must have given you a nasty shock."

Vicky had told him what he wanted to know and he hadn't had to give her a cock and bull story to get it either. He could also see how the snoopers had tricked her into revealing the information they wanted by pretending there had been two payments to the Getaway Travel Agency on his statement.

"You had a phone call about it then?"

"Yes, Access called me yesterday afternoon. Apparently, you have a namesake who also has a Gold Card and the girl quoted two different sums at me and wanted to know what they were for."

And surprise, surprise, Vicky had only been able to tell her about the smaller one for six hundred and eighty-five pounds. Someone had broken into the flat, someone had looked at the latest statement from Access; the one remaining doubt in his mind now was whether the bogus inquiry had been made by MI5 or the watchdogs of his own Intelligence Service.

"I'm glad you managed to straighten her out," he said ironically.

"So am I. Are you planning a winter holiday in Switzerland, Mr Ashton?"

"I'm thinking about it, Vicky. Mind if I take this brochure with me?"

Of course she didn't, and Swiss Ski wasn't the only company in the field. Ingham, Thomson, Kuoni and Thomas Cook; she plucked their brochures from the rack and pressed them on him in the hope that he would return once he found a package deal which suited his pocket. There was nothing wrong with her sales technique, but Ashton stood to lose a minimum of eight thousand pounds on his share of the flat, and an expensive holiday was the last thing he needed. The brochures therefore ended up in the first litter bin he came across on the way to the estate agent.

He still felt it was a mistake to let the property go for a hundred and five when they had paid a hundred and twenty for it, but he didn't have any choice. Jill might threaten to cancel her standing order to the Building Society but whether she would carry it out was another matter. The decisive factor for him had been the answering machine. Any message left on a Dialatron remained on the tape until the next one was recorded over it. The intruder who had broken into the flat would have hit the play button and learned of the offer that had been made for the property, and he didn't want the Security Service prying into his financial affairs if it could be avoided.

When he and Jill had bought the flat, the conveyancing had been handled by the very discreet firm of solicitors retained by the SIS who had charged them less than the going rate. Despite the extra cost, he thought it best this time around to use someone on the outside, even if it meant picking a name out of the yellow pages. The estate agent, however, had a better idea and suggested that it would save both time and money if he left it all to the legal department of the Building Society whose logo just happened to appear above the entrance. It was, Ashton thought, the same sort of cosy arrangement that existed at Century House with the difference that everyone was going to see the colour of their money a whole lot quicker.

From the estate agent, he made his way to Surbiton station and managed to catch a semifast to Waterloo with two minutes to spare. The sudden spurt didn't alter the fact that the mid-morning coffee break had already come and gone by the time he walked into the office. By the time he got to see Victor Hazelwood, the acting Director of the Eastern Bloc was already on his third Burma cheroot.

"You look down in the mouth," he observed. "What's happened? Have they put the bank rate up again?"

"They know I've been to Leningrad and Moscow."

Hazelwood blinked, stubbed out his cheroot in the ashtray, then calmly asked him if he would care to enlarge on that somewhat stark announcement. In a few sentences, Ashton told him why he suspected an intruder had been through the contents of his writing desk and how a hunch had become an established fact after he had talked to Vicky at the travel agency.

"They were quick off the mark, Victor. While you were telling me to watch my step, the watchdogs were already inside the flat, searching every nook and cranny."

"How can you possibly know that?"

"Because the girl who claimed she was with Access rang the travel agency early yesterday afternoon. Now, until they learned I had contacted Alexei Leven, neither MI5 nor our own security people had any reason to take a good hard look at me."

"You told me what had happened in Berlin on Saturday evening," Hazelwood said thoughtfully.

"And Franklin knew before you did. But he wouldn't have started the ball rolling without consulting the DG and "C" was out of town until Monday evening. Furthermore, I didn't leave the flat until we all returned to work after the Bank Holiday which means yesterday was the first opportunity they had to do an in-and-out job."

"What exactly are you hinting at, Peter?"

"Something else you should bear in mind," Ashton said, ignoring the question. "They had inside information. My cleaning lady comes in three times a week – Mondays, Wednesdays and Fridays. She doesn't make up the time if a public holiday happens to fall on one of those days. Now, how do you suppose they knew that?"

It took some time for Hazelwood to draw the appropriate conclusion and even then he wasn't sure he'd got the right answer. "From your personal security file?" he suggested in a voice full of doubt.

Ashton nodded. The security file was detailed enough to provide a writer with most of the material needed for an in-depth biography. Superior officers' assessments, reports from nominated referees and university tutors, psychological profiles and two highly personal subject interviews which had covered every aspect of his private life. There was also an update interview that had been conducted when Victor Hazelwood had submitted a Change of Circumstance Report after learning that he and Jill had split up. The Intelligence officer from the vetting unit who had conducted it had wanted to know what effect the breakdown of the relationship had had on his financial position.

"I don't have to tell you how nosy our vetting people can be, Victor. When Jill decided that marriage was not for her, I had to produce the latest statement I'd received from the bank as well as a complete list of all financial commitments. They wanted to know what we were going to do about the flat, the joint mortgage and who would be responsible for the gas, electricity and phone bills if we didn't sell up. Credit cards, hire-purchase agreements; you name it, they went into it. The IO even recorded how many hours a week I had a cleaning lady in to look after the place and what were her terms and conditions of employment. But it never ends there, does it, Victor? Once the vetting people get the impression that you could be in financial difficulties, they do a follow-up job on you at six- or twelve-monthly intervals when they go over the same old ground again and again. I had my last visitation from them on the twenty-seventh of June. That's how MI5 and our own security people knew when it was safe to go into the flat."

"Are you implying that I put the security people on to you?" Hazelwood demanded angrily.

"The thought never entered my mind. Hell, you were the one who gave me a banker's draft for six hundred and eighty-five pounds, Victor."

Hazelwood reared back in the chair as if he had been struck, the colour draining from his face to leave him ashen. If the intruder had found the latest Gold Card statement from Access, it was highly unlikely that Ashton's paying-in book would have been overlooked and a banker's draft could be traced back to the source.

"It's all right, Victor, you can stop worrying." Ashton patted the breast pocket of his jacket. "I haven't had a chance to bank your draft yet. I'm still carrying it around in my wallet."

"Thank God for small mercies."

"You want it back?"

There was a momentary hesitation before Hazelwood shook his head. "No, you hang on to the draft, just don't pay it in until we get this business sorted out with the DG."

"Sure."

Hazelwood wouldn't be able to sort anything out with the Director General because it was good old "C" who had called in the watchdogs. The great man only had a couple more years to do in the hot seat and no one in later years was going to accuse him of failing to take remedial action after certain facts had been brought to his notice. The DG had wanted to restrict his access to confidential material; when Hazelwood had opposed him, he had gone one better.

"I want you to keep your head down," Hazelwood continued. "You know the old saying – out of sight, out of mind."

"Are you telling me to stay away from the office?" Ashton said.

"Don't get all obtuse with me, you know very well what I mean. I want you to get on with your ordinary desk work and avoid drawing attention to yourself while I sort things out. All right?"

"Up to a point. See, I gave Leven the number of a pay phone in Surbiton and told him his colleagues in Kensington Palace Gardens were to ring 399–9210 at seven p.m. on the first and third Tuesday of every month. Now am I going to wait for that call in six days time or will you get someone else to do it?"

"I don't know," Hazelwood admitted. "Let me think about it."

"Then there's Galina Kutuzova."

"I knew we would get around to her eventually."

"Because everyone was buying what she had to sell; us directly from the source, the French and the Americans through Rostovsky, her middleman. She's the fountainhead."

"So you keep telling me."

"We should be liaising with the US Defense Intelligence Agency," Ashton told him. "We should be comparing notes with that retired air force colonel of theirs – Lloyd Osmonde."

"He's back in the States, out of hospital and pensioned off."

"He would have had an assistant, wouldn't he?"

"Tony Zale, and he has been recalled to Washington."

"America is not on the far side of the moon, Victor, and we've got people in Washington."

"And they are not under my control. If I want to use them, I have to go through the DG or his deputy." Hazelwood reached for the box on his desk and took out yet another Burma cheroot. "And they in turn will have to consult the Foreign and Commonwealth Office, which could be tricky because officially peace has broken out and they don't want us turning over any stones. It appears the US State Department is of much the same mind because I hear they prevailed upon the Defense Intelligence Agency to recall Zale."

"So we're going to give up?"

"I didn't say that." Hazelwood struck a match and held it to the cheroot. "It's a question of picking the right moment to tackle the DG," he said between puffs, "and having something that will make him sit up and take notice."

Ashton wondered how much more was needed to convince the sceptics. Whittle, Rostovsky, Tamara Chernenko, Tulbukin and Willie's girlfriend, Lisolette Quirnheim; four murders and one probable, but it seemed there was a steadfast refusal by some people to see the connection.

"We can get photographs of Leven in conversation with Colonel General Vitali Ilyich Lobanov. Suppose we had information that he flew to Moscow soon after meeting the commander of 6 Guards Tank Army? Would that strengthen your hand, Victor?"

"It certainly would. Unfortunately, the DG would not be receptive if he knew the information had come from you, but I'm sure you can overcome that small problem."

"I know I can," Ashton said.

Once a week, the Joint Intelligence Committee met under the chairmanship of the Cabinet Secretary. It was attended by the Directors of MI5, the SIS, GCHQ Cheltenham and the Defence Intelligence Staff. As Ashton saw it, there was nothing like using a vice admiral as a mouthpiece.

It was the first time Detective 3rd Grade Lewis Dyce had been to New Orleans and he had known before leaving Phoenix that he wasn't going to see an awful lot of the city. The New Orleans

Police Department had phoned late yesterday afternoon to say that they had picked up Yvette Michel, and Graber had calculated that he would be able to collect their prisoner and be back in Phoenix before noon on Wednesday. So he had spent last night in a motel near the airport and all he had seen of New Orleans was the Superdome, City Hall, Police Headquarters and Airline Highway from both directions.

Things might have been different had the officers of the NOPD been a little less efficient, but they had been ready and waiting for him when he had walked into Police Headquarters downtown. All he'd had to do was sign on the dotted line and they had turned the whole caboodle over to him – Yvette Michel, her clothes and possessions and three copies of the statement she had made to the arresting officers. They had also provided a Blue-and-White to convey them to the International Airport and had fixed it so that he and Yvette Michel had boarded the 737 ahead of everyone else.

Dyce had never known such a cooperative police department, and he figured their attitude had a lot to do with the French passport they had tucked into the Manila envelope he was nursing on his lap. Those good ole Southern boys could recognise a hot potato when they saw one and they had off-loaded it just as soon as they could.

"You are making a big mistake, Mr Dyce."

"So you keep telling me," he growled.

"I am not who you think I am. My real name is Galina Kutuzova and I am Starshii Leitenant Glavnoye Razvedyvatelnoye Upravleniye. You might know it better as the GRU."

Dyce glanced about him. They were in the last row on the starboard side of the plane. The girl was on the inside by the window. The seats in front of them were unoccupied, yet although there was not the slightest chance that anyone could hear what they were saying, he still kept his voice low.

"This passport I'm holding says different," he told her quietly, "so does the register at the Red Lion La Posada Resort Hotel. As far as I'm concerned, you are Yvette Michel and you are wanted for the murder of Mary Beth Mallard on . . ."

"It was self-defence," she said, and tossed her head. "Mallard attacked me with a knife."

She had told the same story to the arresting officers, and in great detail. It was all there in the statement she had made after being informed of her rights under the Miranda-Escobedo ruling, and which she had signed twice, once as Yvette Michel and again as Galina Kutuzova. He didn't think the alias would render the statement inadmissible because the same signature appeared in the French passport, but there was one apparent omission which bothered him.

"Did the New Orleans police say anything about you being allowed to make a phone call, Yvette?"

"My name is Galina."

"Okay, I'll call you Galina if that'll make you happy. Now, please answer the question."

"I don't remember."

Dyce tapped the envelope on his lap. "Was an attorney present when you made this statement?" he asked.

"A what?"

"A lawyer."

"No."

The statement was inadmissible, fit only for the office shredder. Fortunately, the case didn't hang on a confession; with Daniella Valli and the girl from the United Airlines desk as witnesses, there was enough circumstantial evidence to get a conviction.

"I didn't mean to kill her."

"I wish I had a dollar for every time I've heard that one."

"Well, it happens to be true. She tried to wrestle me on to the floor but I threw Mary Beth off and told her not to be stupid. I tried to make her understand that I wasn't interested in Daniella but she refused to believe it and came at me again with an ice pick when my back was turned. We do a lot of unarmed combat training in the Soviet Army and I instinctively reacted the way I had been taught. I parried the knife with the left arm and aimed for her throat. I didn't have to think, it was automatic . . ."

Dyce let her ramble on, knowing that what she was telling him was as close to the truth as they were ever likely to get. Ms Mallard had left enough of her prints on the ice pick to show that she had been holding it like a dagger and the goddamned thing had ended up on the floor right by her body. This Yvette Michel, or whatever she liked to call herself, was one very attractive young woman and the more men there were on the jury, the better her chances became. Hell, even without a

231

good lawyer contesting every point, the district attorney would have a hard time convicting her of manslaughter. The trial was not, however, the only thing he had to worry about; there was an even bigger foul-up factor lurking in the background.

"Tell me something," he said. "Did you tell the New Orleans police about all this training you'd done in the Soviet Army?"

"Of course."

"And what was their reaction?"

"You want their exact words? They told me to cut the crap."

Dyce knew what he had been handed and it wasn't a commendation. The French passport wasn't the only reason those good ole Southern boys had been glad to see the back of Yvette Michel aka Galina Kutuzova. He glanced at his wristwatch. Phoenix was a little over two hours from New Orleans and they would be landing at Sky Harbor International Airport in another forty minutes. It was time he put things on a correct footing and made sure a lawyer was present when he questioned the girl because, as sure as eggs were eggs, he would have to get a statement from her that would stand up in court.

Dyce reached for the Cellnet phone clipped to the seat back to his left, inserted a credit card and punched out Graber's number.

"What are you doing?" Galina asked him.

"Phoning the office."

"You can do that from up here?"

"Yeah, no problem."

"That's incredible."

"Not really," he said, "it's just one more example of American know-how exploited by Japanese technology."

Ashton let himself into the flat. There were no letters waiting for him on the hall table but the cleaning lady had left a note on the tray to say that she had sent a pair of sheets, two pillowcases and the contents of the linen basket to the laundry. It was her way of letting him know that she had been there in case he didn't notice that she had given the kitchen and sitting room a good dusting.

He lifted the receiver on the phone and tapped out 010973 followed by 21448, the subscriber's number in Bahrain. This time, it was Jill and not the man with the plummy voice who took the call.

"Hi," he said, "it's me. I just thought I'd let you know that I've seen the estate agent and accepted the offer of a hundred and five thousand."

"Thank you, Peter. I know it can't have been easy for you."

"I also said we would use the Building Society's solicitors which should speed things up a bit."

"That was very sensible of you." There was a longish pause and he had a mental image of Jill standing there by the telephone, her forehead creased in a puzzled frown which always happened when she wasn't sure what to say next. "What will you do now?" she asked eventually.

"Find somewhere else to live. I've got plenty of time; it'll take a minimum of six weeks to exchange contracts and that's assuming our buyer isn't stuck in a chain. If all else fails, I may be able to rent a place in Dolphin Square from the firm."

"Look, I didn't mean what I said about cancelling my banker's order to the Halifax."

"Sure."

"I was being bitchy."

"Hey," he said, "there's no need to apologise. I was being pretty selfish, thinking only of myself."

"Why are you being so nice to me?"

"Because I still like you."

"Nothing's changed, Peter."

"I know that, but it doesn't hurt to say it."

He waited for Jill to hang up, then slowly put the phone down. He wondered what the eavesdroppers would make of the conversation, wondered too how many other bugs the intruder had planted elsewhere in the flat.

CHAPTER 22

THE CONFERENCE was held in Max Graber's office with the district attorney in the chair and the lieutenant of detectives relegated to a wooden upright next to Dyce. What had once appeared to be an open and shut case was becoming more and more complicated by the minute. Before Dyce had left for New Orleans, Assistant District Attorney Samuelson had been calling the play, now the DA himself had taken charge, which only went to show how much the situation had changed in less than twenty-four hours.

They had the woman who had killed Mary Beth Mallard all right, but they weren't at all sure about her name and nationality. The French passport issued to Yvette Michel stated that she had been born in Lille on April sixteenth 1965 and was a dactylographe by occupation.

"What the hell is a dactylographe?" the DA asked. "Does that mean she can take dictation?"

"No, she's just a typist," Dyce informed him. "The French for stenographer is sténographe."

"You speak the language, Detective?"

"Uh huh. It's the answer I got when I asked the same question."

"What about this passport – is it a fake, or what?"

"Looks like the genuine article to me," Graber said. "What do you think, Lew?"

"I don't think the passport can have been in her possession too long," Dyce said carefully. "It's in mint condition and was issued by the French Consulate in Berlin."

"So what are you saying?" The DA leaned forward, elbows on Graber's desk, his hands clasped with the index fingers pressed together and levelled at Dyce. "That she stole it from someone else?"

"No, that's her photograph on page three all right and it doesn't look as though it has been substituted for another."

"So you'd say the passport is genuine too?" the DA said, pressing him for an affirmative answer.

"Yeah. I just don't happen to think her name is Yvette Michel, that's all."

"Because she can speak Russian and claims to be a senior lieutenant in the GRU?"

There were other reasons. Everything Galina had told him about herself rang true to Dyce. As an officer in the GRU, she undoubtedly had had access to valuable information which other Intelligence agencies would have coveted, and the unit she had been serving with in Potsdam had been close enough to Berlin for her to deal with representatives of the French garrison. The date stamp inside the passport indicated that it had been issued on November twenty-fifth 1989, but in no way did the document look almost two years old. He didn't know why the French should have back-dated the passport but its pristine condition was definitely the reason why he believed they had given it to her as a part reward for services rendered.

"What has she been doing in the States – spying?"

"Your guess is as good as mine. All I know for sure is that she killed Mary Beth Mallard."

Dyce didn't bother to conceal his anger. The DA had been getting at him from the moment he had been called into Graber's office as if he personally was responsible for turning a simple case of murder into a political minefield. Fact was, he'd had the sonofabitch in the biggest possible way and there was a limit to the amount of shit he was prepared to take from him.

"Well, that's my considered opinion too," the DA told him, "but I'm the one who will be presenting the case for the prosecution in court and I don't want to see her walk away on a technicality. I'm satisfied this passport is not a forgery and that's why I am going to make sure the French Embassy in Washington is informed that we are holding one of their nationals on a murder charge."

"What if she is a Russian?" Dyce asked.

"I'm not worried. The way things are in Moscow, Gorbachev's got better things to do than worry about some chit of a girl. Take it from me, Detective, while the begging bowl is out, we won't be getting any complaints from Moscow."

"Are we going to advise the FBI people here in town?" Graber asked.

"I don't see why, Max. After all, we've got no proof that she is a Russian Intelligence officer. Furthermore, the New Orleans Police Department didn't see fit to inform their local FBI office after she had told the arresting officers that she had deserted from the GRU in Potsdam."

Dyce concealed a smile with a hand. It was noticeable that whenever the DA addressed Graber it was always by his first name, whereas he was simply Detective. Of course, you couldn't get any lower than Detective 3rd Grade and the DA had always had a proper regard for the pecking order.

"If we drop this on the FBI now, Max, the New Orleans Police Department won't thank us for landing them in it."

Dyce had news for the DA. The only reason why the New Orleans police had kept the FBI in the dark was a heartfelt desire to get shot of Galina Kutuzova just as soon as they could.

"I'll talk to the Justice Department, Max, and ask them how we should inform the French."

"Right." Graber nodded sagely as if between them they had solved a ticklish problem. "Now, how about this Yvette Michel?" he continued. "Do you want Lew here to see if he can get a statement from her, or what?"

"Ullander is with her now, isn't he?"

"He's advising the lady of her rights."

"Yup." The DA pursed his lips, the first of a series of facial contortions connected with his thought process which finally enabled him to reach a decision. "I think we had better review this case and see what we've got," he said.

Dyce could understand his reluctance. John Wendell Ullander was bad news, especially with an election year looming on the horizon. He made no secret of his political ambitions and while he had not attacked the district attorney directly, it was pretty obvious which particular public office in his field was up for grabs in '92. It was said by his enemies that Ullander won most of his cases outside the courtroom; what no one disputed was the skilful way he made use of the media. It had been his unwelcome intervention that had prompted the DA to remove Assistant District Attorney Samuelson and take charge of the case himself.

* * *

Ullander lit a cigarette. The girl seated across the table from him had blue eyes, neat ears and high cheekbones with a good nose and jaw to complement an inviting mouth. The rest of her wasn't bad either – firm bust, slim hips and legs that could do a lot for a hosiery manufacturer. Definitely photogenic, but he didn't like the way she had dyed her dark hair to an unnatural auburn in an effort to change her appearance.

"Well now," he said, "what do you want me to call you? Yvette Michel, Galina Kutuzova, Colette Lefarge, the name you used at Jean-Paul's, or Carolyn Jacobs, the girl who flew United Airlines to New Orleans?"

"My name is Galina Kutuzova and I was a senior lieutenant . . ."

"Yeah, yeah, I've read the statement you gave the arresting officers. Tell you what, I'll call you Galina, and you can call me J.W. like everyone else does. Okay?"

"Yes."

"Fine. Now let me tell you something else about myself. I'm an attorney and a darned good one, which means I make a lot of bucks . . ."

"I have very little money."

"Don't give it another thought, Galina. I didn't take your case for the money."

It was the potential coverage by the media that had attracted him. "Jealousy amongst lesbian threesome results in violent death" – he had begun to compose the headlines in his mind as soon as he heard about the murder from his source in the Public Relations Department at Police Headquarters. The source cost him five hundred a month and was worth every penny, especially now that the Russian angle was going to run and run.

"What is going to happen to me, Mr Ullander?" she asked.

"J.W." he said, correcting her. "Well, first thing the police will do is put you in a line-up to see if the girl who was on the United Airlines desk the day you bought a plane ticket to New Orleans can pick you out. It's one thing to recognise someone in a photograph but the DA will want to be sure she won't slip up in court. They will probably want some of the hotel staff to identify you, too. But unless they run into problems, I doubt they will drag the Valli woman all the way down here from New York before the trial, which means we'll be able to make all the running."

"Running?"

"With the newspapers; reporters will be falling over themselves to interview you."

"They will be allowed to see me in jail?"

"You won't be in jail," Ullander told her. "After they've charged you, they have to bring you before a judge to set a date for the trial. Naturally, the DA will want to keep you behind bars, but I will object and the judge will set bail. Could be as low as ten thousand or twenty-five at the top, depending on who's presiding."

"I don't have that kind of money, J.W."

"It's not a problem, I'll have a bail bondsman see to it." Whatever surety the bail bondsman needed, he would supply and gladly because what he stood to gain from the media exposure would be worth his weight in gold. There were, however, certain matters which needed to be aired before he committed himself irrevocably. "Are you gay?" he asked her bluntly.

Two spots of colour appeared on her cheeks and her eyes narrowed in anger. "No," she hissed.

Ullander believed her, no one was that good an actress. "I'm sorry to put you through all this," he said, "but that's an example of the sort of hostile questions some reporters are likely to throw at you and you've got to be ready for them, especially during a live interview on the air."

"On the air? You mean I will be talking on the radio?"

"Damn right. We are going to win this case before it ever comes to court. You know how many radio stations there are in Arizona? One hundred and twenty; hell, there are sixteen right here in Phoenix serving one point five million people. Now, as for TV – we are talking network ABC, CBS, NBC, CNN . . ."

"I can't do it."

"'Course you can."

"You don't understand, J.W. – the authorities will deport me."

"No, they won't. First comes the trial, then we claim asylum." Ullander eyed her thoughtfully. "Once we've established your credentials," he added.

"You don't believe I am Russian?"

"Did I say I didn't? Listen, if I had any doubts on that score, I'd call the language faculty at Arizona State and have one of their instructors come over and talk to you. The university is less than nine miles away and it wouldn't take him any time to get here."

Ullander smiled as he spoke; it made him seem warm, friendly, a man you could trust. The smile was going to win him a lot of votes one day and the time he spent practising it in front of a mirror was not wasted. Right now, it had a soothing effect on Galina.

"I think we were talking at cross purposes," he said. "What I meant by credentials is your background – family, education, career. That's not a problem, is it?"

"No."

"Well then, suppose you tell me about yourself?"

Galina Kutuzova didn't need a second invitation, and unlike most of the people Ullander had represented, she didn't once repeat herself. She was also very fluent, in fact so fluent that he was convinced that someone else at some other time in some other place must have asked her the same question. He closed his mind to the possibility and listened instead to the sensational list of family friends – Stalin, Beria, Malenkov, Bulganin, Shelepin, Andropov, Fedorchuk – men her grandfather had been on first-name terms with, the "uncles" whom her mother had known when she was a child, or in some cases as a young woman. Then there were the senior army officers Galina had known; most of the names didn't strike a chord, but one or two sounded familiar.

"I bet you know a thing or two about those guys," he said when she paused for breath. "Juicy titbits a gossip columnist would give his eyeteeth for."

"There were several it was best to avoid after they had been drinking," she said.

Ullander used his vote-winning smile again. "You know something, you're sitting on a fortune. Write a book about your experiences and publishers will be standing in line to offer you a six-, maybe seven-figure advance." He allowed the prospect of untold wealth to dangle in front of her for a few more moments, then went for the jugular. "Provided you can furnish the necessary corroborative evidence."

"Such as?"

"Letters, documents, photographs – that sort of thing."

"Oh, I'm sorry, I forgot to bring them with me."

"Being sarcastic with me won't help you at all."

239

"Look, I deserted from my unit in Germany because I had been denounced for passing information to a foreign power and was under investigation. I got out while the going was still good and didn't wait to pack even a change of underwear."

The granddaughter of a KGB chief betraying her country's secrets? It didn't sound remotely credible. "Which foreign power?" Ullander asked.

"Great Britain. But I was also dealing with the French and the Americans through a colleague."

"So there were two of you selling information?"

"I've just said so, haven't I?" Galina snapped.

"Well, I can certainly understand why you didn't waste any time. What did you do for money if you had to leave in such a hurry?"

"My grandfather had opened a Swiss bank account in my name; I had enough on me to get to Zürich."

"Okay. What's the name of this colleague?"

"Yuri Rostovsky. But he's dead; the KGB murdered him."

"Yeah?" Ullander found it hard to conceal his scepticism. "Where and when did this happen?"

"In Berlin on the tenth of July. They also wounded the American colonel who was with him. I read about it three days later in the international edition of the *Herald Tribune*. There was a small paragraph at the foot of page two."

He had begun to think Galina Kutuzova was a phoney; now at last she had given him something which could be verified. "Would you happen to know the name of the colonel?" he asked.

"Osmonde – Lloyd D Osmonde, United States Air Force, but he is no longer a serving officer. He was employed in a civilian capacity by your Defense Intelligence Agency."

Ullander made a note of Osmonde's particulars on his scratch pad, then looked up. "Anything else you can tell me about him?"

"He is married; his wife's name is Elaine, and they have three daughters. The youngest, Karen, is married to a British army officer stationed in Berlin."

It was getting better every minute. Ullander nodded encouragement while his ballpoint raced across the scratch pad.

"Yuri gave him two snapshots of my mother," Galina continued in a flat voice. "One showed her as a little girl with Stalin, the other was taken much later with Yuri Vladimirovich Andropov shortly before she married my father." Galina frowned. "That's all I can tell you about Colonel Osmonde," she said.

"It's enough." Ullander slipped the scratch pad into his briefcase and snapped the locks. "I'm going to tell the DA we are ready, but first I'm going to call my office." He would get his secretary to phone the Defense Intelligence Agency in Washington and check out Lloyd D Osmonde. That was the great thing about the Freedom of Information Act – people like the former colonel in the USAF could no longer hide themselves behind a veil of secrecy. "Don't look so worried, Galina," he said. "Believe me, we've got this thing licked."

Ashton stacked the "in", "pending" and "out" trays on top of one another before placing them on the top shelf, then closed the safe and spun the combination dial, having first checked to make sure the locking bars were engaged. It had been one of those days when he'd had to look for work so that every minute had seemed like five and the hours had crawled by. The only interesting phone call he had received all day had come from the detective inspector in charge of the UK Interpol bureau at Scotland Yard.

In response to the red tab request, Royal Canadian Mounted Police Headquarters Ottawa had asked the immigration authorities at Montreal to check the landing card which Yvette Michel had completed on arrival on the thirteenth of July. In the box headed "Reason for Visit", she had written "Visiting relatives in Quebec Province" and had then given a false address in Joliette where she was supposed to be staying. Beyond that, they had run into a brick wall.

Naturally, City and Provincial Forces had been notified, but Canada was a vast country and the DI had told him that getting a lead on her now would be more a matter of luck than good police work. On a positive note, the RCMP trace showed that Galina Kutuzova had been determined to cover her tracks; conversely, the information was unlikely to persuade anyone who had already prejudged the Whittle affair to think again.

The second phone call of any consequence came through as Ashton was looking round the office to make sure nothing had been left out that should have been put away. Returning to the desk, he discovered the caller was from Defence Intelligence at the MOD and learned that Lieutenant Colonel Alexei Leven had returned to his unit in Potsdam late on Tuesday afternoon. According to the driver who had collected him from the airport, he had been to Moscow.

"How do you rate this information?" Ashton asked.

"It came from Sergeant Norman. He says it's amazing what a bottle of whisky and a little hard currency will buy you these days. He hasn't given us a bum steer yet, so we'd have to grade the report as probably true."

"The next meeting of the Joint Intelligence Committee is on Tuesday. Correct?"

"Ten hundred, same as always."

"Can you get your Director to raise this incident at the meeting?"

"I can ask our Chief of Staff to put it on the agenda, but there's no guarantee he will accept it."

"It's important. If he's reluctant to include the report, get him to ring me."

"Right."

"One last thing," Ashton said. "Make sure your Admiral produces the photographs Sergeant Norman took of Leven in conversation with Colonel General Lobanov."

The phone started ringing soon after they had sat down to a pot roast. Neither of them made a move to answer it in the hope that if they stuck it out for a couple of minutes, the caller would conclude they were not at home and would hang up. The ruse worked most times, but every now and again someone would ring them who refused to believe they weren't in. This evening was one of those rare occasions.

Osmonde smiled wryly at Elaine across the table and put his napkin on a side plate. "I guess there's no fooling this one," he said.

"Perhaps it's Karen?" Elaine suggested.

"I don't think so, it's two in the morning over there in Berlin."

"One of the other girls then?"

"There's only one way to find out." He left the table, walked through the archway into the sitting room, picked up the phone and said, "Hello."

"Colonel Osmonde?"

The caller had a slightly nasal voice and an accent he couldn't place.

"Yes. Who am I talking to?"

"I'm John Ullander, but most people call me J.W."

"You're not trying to sell me something, are you?" he asked.

Ullander laughed. "Hell no, but I would be very grateful if you would give me a few minutes of your time."

"Is it important?" Osmonde wanted to tell him they were just about to have dinner and would he mind calling back in half an hour, but he never got the chance.

"The Defense Intelligence Agency in Washington put me on to you," Ullander said quickly. "I'm an attorney and I'm hoping you can assist me. I believe you are acquainted with a Miss Galina Kutuzova?"

Elaine was making signals, urging him to hang up before the pot roast started to congeal, but Ullander had captured his attention now and he shook his head regretfully. "I've heard of her," Osmonde admitted cautiously.

"Yeah? How about Galina's mother, Lydia Petrovskaya?"

"Her too."

"My information is that a third party who is now deceased, gave you some snapshots of the lady. Is that correct?"

"Yes. Listen, what's going on? Why are you so interested in Lydia Petrovskaya?"

"I've been retained by her daughter, Galina."

Osmonde deliberately turned his back on a very angry Elaine who was glaring at him. "You mean she's actually over here in the States?" he said incredulously.

"How else would I have met her?"

"Is Galina in trouble?"

"Put it this way," said Ullander. "A number of people are not of a friendly disposition where she is concerned."

"The State Department ..." Osmonde began. Behind him, Elaine kicked the swing door open and stormed into the kitchen, heels clacking on the pine floor.

"You've got it," Ullander told him. "That's why I'd like to borrow those snapshots. It's our contention that she is a genuine political refugee and those photographs will go a long way towards establishing the claim."

"I'm afraid I no longer have them."

Two serving dishes went into the oven with a loud clatter, then the kitchen door swung back on its hinges with a thump as Elaine returned to the dining alcove.

"Did I hear you say the snapshots were no longer in your possession?"

"That's right. I gave them to Tony Zale when he was here six days ago."

"Is he also with the Defense Intelligence Agency?"

"He used to be my assistant, but his future is now a little uncertain."

"Why? Is he thinking of quitting the Agency?"

"It's possible," Osmonde said guardedly.

"Uh huh. Can you tell me how to get in touch with him?"

"Hold on." Osmonde reached for the flip-top personal directory next to the telephone and opened it at the letter Z. "You can try his parents in New York at 212–555–6438. They might know where he is."

"Thanks."

"You're welcome," Osmonde said, then asked out of curiosity where Ullander was calling from and was answered with a continuous burr as the lawyer hung up on him.

CHAPTER 23

DYCE RECKONED Paradise Valley was an appropriate name for the neighbourhood, but it was difficult to view it other than with a jaundiced eye at five o'clock in the morning with the sun just beginning to rise above the horizon. However, no realtor who chose to describe 1622 Lincoln Drive as a highly desirable residence could be accused of poetic licence. It was approximately nine miles from Sky Harbor International Airport and a round dozen from the McDowell Building in downtown Phoenix where J.W. Ullander's law practice was located. The sprawling ranch-style house with its lush green lawn in the midst of an arid desert was an accurate indication of just how successful an attorney he was.

The desert had not been entirely banished; pride of place in the yard was given to a saguaro cactus which would eventually grow to a height of fifty feet and live for up to two hundred years. Right now, it was less than a third of its full height and had yet to acquire its first arm, but very few houses on Lincoln Drive had one and Dyce was prepared to bet that this was the reason why J.W. Ullander had bought the plot. The cactus and the paloverde trees with their yellow flowers were part of the natural habitat; the million-year-old boulders and the petrified conifer had obviously been imported at great expense.

This was the fourth night in a row he had been parked outside 1622 Lincoln Drive and he wondered how much longer the DA intended to involve the police department in what amounted to a personal vendetta. Ullander had made a monkey out of him at the arraignment last Friday; the trial date had been set for November twenty-first, bail had been set at thirty-five hundred and Yvette Michel had walked. That was the bottom line, though the DA was never going to admit it. Ostensibly, they were keeping an eye on the place because the Ullanders had taken her in as a house guest, and it was essential to know exactly where Yvette Michel was in case the State Department began to take an interest and the whole thing went political. It was, Dyce thought, a pretty feeble reason especially as the French had shown precious little interest in Yvette Michel thus far. For his own part, he couldn't help wondering how much longer it would be before the lawyer filed a complaint alleging police harassment. The only thing he was certain about was that it wouldn't happen today because, at the moment, Ullander evidently had other irons in the fire. Late yesterday afternoon, he had taken off for Washington and Dyce was damn sure he hadn't gone to the nation's capital for the benefit of his health.

He glanced down at the clock in the dash again and was disappointed to see less than ten minutes had elapsed since the last time he had looked. Officially, he was supposed to stick around until 0600 hours but the department didn't have the manpower cover to do more than run a night watch on Lincoln Drive. Furthermore, this particular shift had left him with a splitting headache, hot and cold shivers and a throat that felt as if it was about to close up at any minute. Not too many people went down with flu this early in September, but there were always exceptions and he was obviously going to be one of them. In the circumstances, Dyce couldn't see what difference it would make if he left three quarters of an hour before the appointed time. Cranking the engine into life, he shifted into gear and pointed the Dodge in the direction of Glendale. He hadn't the faintest idea why Ullander had gone to Washington but he did hope the lawyer was doing his level best to make life as uncomfortable as possible for the district attorney.

The Joint Intelligence Committee assembled at the usual time of 1000 hours only to disperse thirty-eight minutes later, which was something of a record. Well before the Intelligence chiefs had met in the Cabinet Office, Ashton had rung the MOD to check that the head of the Defence Intelligence Staff still intended to draw the attention of the other committee members to the latest Intelligence reports on Alexei Leven. Specifically, he had wanted to make sure their Admiral produced the photographs of the GRU man in conversation with Colonel General Lobanov, and had been asked how many more times they had to tell him that everything had been fixed and would he please stop worrying. Even so, he had been on tenterhooks all morning until Hazelwood rang shortly before noon to enquire if he could spare him a few minutes. The boom was lowered with three little words as soon as he walked into Victor's office.

"It didn't work," Hazelwood told him abruptly.

"What happened exactly?" Ashton asked as calmly as he could.

"The Admiral told the meeting that Leven had flown to Moscow thirty-six hours after seeing the commander of 6 Guards Tank Army and produced the snapshots taken by Sergeant Norman. Everyone round the table said how very interesting and they moved on to the next item on the agenda."

Ashton supposed Leven's activities would hardly be of special interest to the Directors General of MI5 and GCHQ Cheltenham, but he couldn't understand why their own DG should have been so dismissive. "Why didn't C enlighten them?" he demanded. "Christ, even the Admiral didn't appreciate the significance of the information he was imparting, but our man knew."

"No, that's not correct. The DG is aware of your interpretation, Peter, but he doesn't agree with it. If you think about it, there's no proof that Leven acted the way he did because of Galina Kutuzova."

"Is that what he told you?"

"Not in so many words," Hazelwood admitted.

"No, he doesn't want to commit himself, does he, Victor? I mean, when was the last time you attended a meeting and heard him offer an opinion that hadn't already been voiced by at least three other people round the table?"

"Keep your voice down."

"What for? Because the DG might hear me?" Ashton smiled grimly. "I think there's a fat chance of that. He only hears what he wants to hear."

"Don't push your luck, Peter."

"I want to see him."

"No, you don't."

"You want to tell me why?"

"Because one of the pieces in your jigsaw doesn't fit." Hazelwood picked up the stub end of the Burma cheroot he had left in the ashtray on the desk and relit it. "I still happen to think your interpretation is correct," he continued, "but how do you explain the thirty-six-hour delay between the time Leven saw the general and when he departed for Moscow?"

"I don't know. Maybe he couldn't get a seat on a plane before then?"

"Are you saying he didn't have the necessary priority?"

"What are you inviting me to do, Victor? Shoot myself in the foot? Why has the DG got to be so pedantic? I'm not recommending the Polaris fleet should be placed on Red Alert; all I want is for us and the US Intelligence agencies to trade whatever information we have on Galina Kutuzova."

"Hasn't it occurred to you that the DG could have put the same jigsaw together and got an entirely different picture? Wouldn't that explain why he didn't say anything when the Admiral produced those snapshots?"

The implication suddenly hit Ashton like a bullet. "My God, he thinks Leven went to see the general because I'd offered to sell him classified information." And Lobanov had told the GRU man to go away and prepare a written evaluation for submission to the First Chief Directorate of the KGB, a task which had taken him the better part of thirty-six hours. "I gave Leven the number of a public phone box in Surbiton," Ashton said slowly.

"Yes."

"And today is the first Tuesday in September."

"Don't worry, somebody will be there to take the call, if there is one," Hazelwood said, taking a final puff on the cheroot before stubbing it out.

Somebody. Ashton recalled Franklin's words as he wrote out a receipt for two hundred pounds. "What good do you think this will do you?" he'd asked. "It won't impress MI5; they'll say you were trying to cover yourself." It seemed the DG shared his opinion.

Although Ullander had stayed the night in the de luxe Embassy Row Hotel on Massachusetts Avenue North West, on Zale's insistence they met for a working breakfast at the far more modest Claremont on Fourteenth and R Streets where he happened to be living temporarily. Cornell '85, government service, Italian extraction, rising thirty and still single; Ullander had known that much about Zale before he had spoken to him on the phone a couple of times. After hearing his voice, the picture in his mind had been complete; dark, olive-skinned, lean face, neat appearance, slim, five eight, a hundred and forty pounds. Meeting him in the flesh, it turned out Zale was a couple of inches taller and twenty pounds heavier than Ullander had imagined. He also had short blond hair, blue eyes, a round face and looked decidedly Swedish.

He was undoubtedly honest and incorruptible; a man who passed up a freebie because he didn't want to be beholden to anyone and bought his suits off the peg in a chain store could hardly be anything else. Zale had something he wanted; persuading him to part with it was clearly going to be a problem. Money would not be the irresistible inducement it would be for some people. A more subtle approach was needed – like being frank and open with him.

"I'm going to level with you," Ullander said and attacked his pancakes with a fork. "Any deal between us won't be even-handed. Matter of fact, I know you can do far more for me than I can for you."

"So Lloyd told me."

"He phoned you right after I had spoken to him?"

"He left a message asking me to call him back."

Ullander had figured as much. He must have rung the New York number half a dozen times before he got to talk with the one member of the Zale family who mattered to him. And Tony Zale had been mighty evasive when finally he had managed to catch him. Returning to Washington first thing in the morning, didn't know whether he would be staying or where he would be living if he did. The excuses he had made to avoid meeting him face to face would have filled a book. He had given Zale his home and office numbers and extracted a promise that he would call him the minute he was settled.

That had been last Thursday. When, yesterday morning, he still hadn't heard from him, Ullander had put his staff on to it. Once the Defense Intelligence Agency had confirmed that he was still in their employ, they had then rung practically every hotel and realtor in Washington before running him to ground at the Claremont. Consequently, this working breakfast represented a considerable investment of time and money.

"As things stand at the moment," Ullander told him between

mouthfuls, "the real truth about this case is never going to come out. Don't get me wrong, I'm not complaining. If nowhere else, the trial will make the headlines in my own back yard and that's all the publicity I need. But no one outside the State of Arizona will ever hear of Galina Kutuzova and I believe the American people have a right to know why Washington is so hot to discredit the lady and suppress her story at the same time."

"But you can change all that?"

"Galina tells a pretty sensational story. If only half of it is true, I can make her a household name."

"So what's stopping you?"

"You're an intelligent man, Mr Zale. I think you already know the answer." Ullander washed down the last of the pancakes with a mouthful of coffee, then wiped his mouth on a napkin. "But I'll tell you anyway. Unless I can produce some evidence to support her story, the media will simply dismiss Galina Kutuzova as a crank. In other words, I need those snapshots Colonel Osmonde gave you."

"Yeah, I know you do. Lloyd told me on Thursday night when I called him back."

"Well then, do I get them?"

"I'm thinking about it."

Ullander lit a cigarette while he considered what sort of argument would most appeal to the younger man. No one who worked for the government expected to make a fortune. Maybe Zale hadn't joined the Defense Intelligence Agency out of a sense of patriotic duty, but some of the ethos must have rubbed off on him.

"Galina says the Soviet Army is cheating on the Arms Reductions Agreement, and there must be something in the allegation because the KGB tried to kill her."

"I'm familiar with the claim," Zale told him.

"Well, don't you think her story should be investigated rather than suppressed?"

"Of course I do."

Ullander stubbed out his cigarette. He was getting nowhere fast and judging by the way Zale kept stealing glances at his wristwatch, he would be making noises about going into the office any minute now.

"Let me ask you a question, Tony. What do you plan to do with those snapshots?"

"I'm still chipping away on the inside. When the right moment comes, I'll show them to the Director of the Agency."

"When is that likely to be?"

"It's impossible to say. I've been transferred to another department and . . ."

"The right moment will never come," Ullander said, interrupting him. "They've put you out to pasture in Computer Records where you haven't got anyone's ear."

"How would you know?"

"Let's stop fencing with one another. You want me to keep my nose out of this in case I make things worse for you. But I'm not going to drag your name into it because I figure you are in enough trouble already without me adding to your problems."

"You wouldn't have to mention my name; the people at State are plenty capable of putting two and two together."

Ullander shook his head. "Not the way Galina will tell it. She will say that Yuri Rostovsky was murdered before he could deliver the information. That way, they've got nothing to beef about. Right?"

"I suppose so."

"Look, Lloyd Osmonde got shot in the line of duty, but the Defense Intelligence Agency doesn't seem to care about that and they will break you in two the moment you open your mouth. Can't you see, I'm the only one who can vindicate the both of you?"

The question went unanswered for what seemed like for ever, then Zale slowly reached inside his jacket and took out a small envelope. "Just remember I didn't give you this," he said.

Twelve minutes to seven: Ashton stared at the clock on the mantelpiece in his living room and wondered if anyone really was waiting in the call box up the road from the Getaway Travel Agency. No matter what the DG might have told Victor, he doubted if there was a stand-in. The man would have to say more than hello, he would have to identify himself, and that would be it. The KGB didn't go in for half-measures; if Leven had had a cameraman in place to film their meeting at the deserted farmhouse, it was a racing certainty he also had his voice on tape. The moment they compared his voice print with the recording of the conversation with the stand-in, they would know their contact man had been talking to an impostor.

251

So why hadn't the DG allowed him to take the call? They could have set up a phone tap, or bugged the call box, or taped a throat mike and transmitter to his body and heard every word. He had sanctioned none of the options because each one entailed a degree of risk and he was in his last year in office and he preferred to play it safe. Although the DG obviously suspected he was a double agent, he wanted to avoid a headline-grabbing scandal at all costs. It was the reason why he had favoured a policy of isolation rather than investigation, ignorance instead of enlightenment.

But how did he prove that? The Security Service had bugged his phone and there was no way of removing the device without alerting them. He could dial the number of the call box in the High Street at seven o'clock. If someone answered the phone, he was wrong; if there was no reply, he was right. Unfortunately, the eavesdroppers would twig he had been checking up on them. While the digits on a Dialatron did not emit an individual tone, the fact that he had only pressed seven buttons would tell them he had tried to call a number in the London area and it wouldn't take them long to draw the appropriate conclusion. To fool them, he would have to punch out immediately another seven digit number and pretend he'd just tapped it out incorrectly and nearly got the wrong subscriber.

The phone rang, shattering his concentration and making him flinch. Ashton went out into the hall, lifted the receiver and said hello.

"Hi, it's me," Jill said.

"Well, well," he said inadequately.

"Surprised?"

"You could say that."

"I'm not interrupting anything, am I?"

It was three minutes to seven and he had to make that call on the dot or he would never know whether or not the DG had lied to Victor. "No, of course you aren't," Ashton told her.

"I'm really phoning about the flat . . ."

"It's going to take a minimum of six weeks to exchange contracts."

"I know, you told me so the last time we spoke."

"Well then?"

"Well, I wouldn't like you to think I'm in a hurry, Peter."

"I'm not with you," he said, genuinely puzzled.

"I may not be staying out here much longer. The locals don't like dealing with a woman and there is an opening in London. It won't be a demotion if I took it."

For locals read Arabs. He could imagine the heads of Intelligence around the Persian Gulf would be loath to treat a mere woman as an equal and obviously Jill had been forced to operate more and more through her front man, the second secretary consul. He could imagine how that would piss her off. In her shoes, he would be pissed off too.

"When is this transfer likely to happen, if it does?" he asked.

"A couple of months from now . . ." A hesitant pause, and then, "I'll need a roof over my head until I can find a place to live."

"Sure."

"That's why I'm not in a hurry to complete."

"It's no problem; the mortgage is in both our names, so your signature has to be on the contract too, and you know what the post is like."

"Thank you, Peter."

"It's my pleasure."

"Nothing's changed."

"I know that," he said and waited for Jill to hang up first before he put the phone down.

Four minutes after seven; he lifted the receiver again and punched out 399–9210. The tumblers clicked and then the number started ringing. No one answered the call, but he was late and there was no telling what had happened at 1900 hours.

The statue of Feliks Edmundovich Dzerzhinsky might have been removed from its plinth on the traffic island fronting the old All Russia Insurance Company building in Moscow but the KGB continued to exist and function pretty much as it had always done. This was particularly true of the First Chief Directorate located at Yasenevo on the ring road which was responsible for all Foreign Intelligence operations.

Although the centre enjoyed worldwide satellite communications, in the matter of Galina Kutuzova, Deputy Head Pavel Trilisser chose to contact the KGB Residents serving in the embassies in Ottawa and Washington by more traditional methods dating back to the nineteenth century. The same applied to the KGB colonel attached to the permanent Soviet delegation to the United Nations Organisation in New York.

Trilisser's decision to use the diplomatic bag did not reflect a lack of faith in the integrity of Soviet cryptography. It was, in fact, prompted by a desire to restrict the number of people with a need to know to the absolute bare minimum. Whatever the security classification, signals for despatch were always prepared in triplicate. One copy of the clear text was retained by the originator, the other two were sent by hand of messenger to the signals centre where they were seen by the supervisor in charge and the duty cipher operator who had to encode the message before it was transmitted. The second copy of the clear text was retained by the signals centre in case part of the encoded message was received in a corrupted form. Immediately after despatch, the third copy was returned to the originator, date-stamped and signed by the supervisor. A minimum of four administrative and communications personnel at Yasenevo who were unconnected with the operation would therefore be aware of the KGB's interest in Galina Kutuzova. Add to this the diplomatic wireless operators, cipher custodians, archivists and filing clerks at the two embassies and the UNO delegation and the total number of outsiders was increased by a further twelve. By writing a personal letter to each Resident, Trilisser eliminated all the middlemen and thereby minimised the risk of an internal leak.

It was of course impossible to establish the political reliability of individual Residents in the aftermath of the failed coup d'état. In writing to them, Pavel Trilisser had therefore been careful not to implicate himself. His instructions to the Residents had been couched in terms sufficiently explicit to leave them in no doubt as to what they were required to do. At the same time, he had ensured they had no reason whatever to query their orders with the newly appointed Chairman of the KGB. The Englishman had told Alexei Leven that the SIS had traced Galina Kutuzova to Montreal; he had seen fit to alert Washington and New York in the belief that she was unlikely to have remained in Canada for very long.

Like his counterparts in New York and Ottawa, the KGB Resident in Washington had received his instructions in the diplomatic bag on Thursday the twenty-ninth of August, forty-eight hours after Alexei Leven had visited the First Chief Directorate at Yasenevo. Because the envelope had been addressed "Personal For", the letter from Pavel Trilisser had been delivered direct to him unopened. Although graded Secret, the enclosure carried the standard exclusion clause of "For Your Eyes Only" which ensured it was not recorded in the classified register.

The content had not, however, caused the Resident to wonder if the Deputy Head of the Foreign Intelligence Directorate had been one of the disaffected officers behind the attempted coup. In these troubled times, he thought it was only natural that Moscow should be worried about the political harm someone like Starshii Leitenant Galina Kutuzova could do to the programme of democratisation which was now taking place in Russia. It was self-evident that anyone who had deserted from the GRU and was implicated in the murder of a fellow officer would say and do almost anything to obtain political asylum. Moreover, it had seemed to him that Comrade General Pavel Trilisser's instructions were entirely reasonable. The embassy's KGB staff were already in the habit of reading all US newspapers and periodicals with a circulation exceeding half a million; the additional requirement to monitor every TV newscast put out by the major networks had merely entailed the installation of a few extra television sets and video recorders.

Normally, the Resident only saw the video of any news item featuring the USSR. On this particular occasion however he happened to be present when the early evening CBS newscast was in the process of being recorded. The familiar State Department building on C Street caught his eye, then the camera panned to a tall, loose-limbed man in the foreground. The Resident noted that he was wearing a black-and-white check pattern sports jacket over a dark blue shirt with button-down collar and black pants. There was an ornate leather belt around his waist with some kind of silver medallion for a buckle. He was in his early forties, good-looking and smiled a lot.

"John Wendell Ullander," the news reporter said off screen, "is an attorney in Phoenix, Arizona. Not the most popular lawyer in town with the district attorney, he is about to win himself no friends in the State Department either. And why? Because he is determined to obtain political asylum for his client, former senior Intelligence officer Galina Kutuzova of the Glavnoe

Razvedyvatelnoe Upravlenie, better known to most of us as the GRU . . ."

Years of training helped the Resident to conceal his innermost thoughts. Seemingly unaffected by the news, he sat there calmly smoking a cigarette while Ullander, or J.W. as he preferred to be known, portrayed Galina Kutuzova as a latter-day heroine who would probably be murdered by hardline Communists should she be deported.

"Anyone who believes that nonsense," he announced for the benefit of his subordinates, "will believe anything."

Still keeping up normal appearances, the Resident left the embassy on 16th Street at the usual time and drove to his rented house on Georgetown's N Street, a little over two miles away. As far as he was aware, the FBI had not identified him as the KGB Resident, but the District of Columbia had more agents per square mile than anywhere else on earth and it was never safe to assume anything. He was, however, quite certain that no one had followed him home from the embassy, and was equally positive that no one was tailing him an hour later when he and his wife, Ludmilla, drove into town, ostensibly to see a movie.

Three quarters of the way through *Billy Bathgate*, he left the theatre by a side exit and flagged down a passing cab. From a phone booth in the concourse of Union Station on Massachusetts Avenue North East, he dialled 0107 095 19153, the number Pavel Trilisser had put in his letter. Moscow was eight and a half hours ahead of Washington which meant it was four thirty in the morning over there, but the phone rang only twice before a woman answered it.

CHAPTER 24

THE ALARM was shrill, intrusive and persistent. Still three parts asleep, Ashton reached out, groped for the clock on the bedside table and depressed the button to shut it off. As usual, he promised himself another five minutes in bed but the damned clock kept on ringing even after he had swept it on to the floor. Reluctantly he opened both eyes, expecting to find that the sun was up and encountered the grey light of dawn instead. Leaning over the edge, he picked up the clock and stared in disbelief at the luminous face. Eighteen minutes to four. Only the birds were awake at that hour, except you couldn't hear them because of the noise the telephone was making. He kicked the duvet off, staggered out into the hall and lifted the receiver. Someone with a horribly cheerful voice identified himself as Wyvern, then rang off.

Ashton broke the connection his end and dialled the number of the duty officer at Century House. "I hope you didn't get the wrong subscriber just now," he said when Wyvern answered.

"Who's calling?"

"Jesus." He closed his eyes. "It's me, Pyxis."

"You're in breach of security, Pyxis."

"It's the middle of the night," Ashton snarled. "Now tell me what you want or I'll drop the phone on you."

"Pack a bag, bring your passport with you and come on in."

"What – right now?"

"If it's not too inconvenient," Wyvern said acidly, and hung up on him for the second time in as many minutes.

It took Ashton roughly three quarters of an hour to shower, shave, change, pack a suitcase and write a note to his cleaning lady while breakfasting off two slices of wholemeal toast and a glass of orange juice. The first train up to town was the 0451 and using the car hire firm in the High Street was not going to earn him any Brownie points. Although every postman in Lambeth knew where the SIS was located, anyone in the Service who rolled up to Century House in a taxi was automatically logged for a breach of security.

Leaving the flat, he walked round to the courtyard behind the building where his Vauxhall Cavalier was parked in its usual slot between the Mini Metro belonging to the schoolteacher on the ground floor and the 1960 Austin Healey that had been lovingly restored by a somewhat precious hair stylist who occupied the apartment across the landing from him. Ashton inspected the boot carefully, then unlocked it and took out the "peeper", a stave some four feet long with a mirror slotted into the tip at an angle of five degrees. He pushed the mirror under the car and walked round the vehicle, checking the underside to make sure nothing had been attached to the chassis. He didn't think anyone had followed him home from the office, but at least one active service unit of the IRA was thought to be operating in the London area and it was foolish to take any unnecessary risk.

The check completed, he drove off down the road and made his way across Surbiton to pick up the A3 trunk road into town. At that hour of the morning, traffic heading into London was comparatively light and he made good time. Just beyond the Oval cricket ground, he turned off the A3 into the quieter Kennington Road where the only vehicles he overtook before reaching the office were a milk float, two buses moving in tandem and a Corporation refuse truck. Parking on the forecourt of Century House was restricted to heads of departments, but the Assistant Director, Rest of the World, was on holiday in the south of France and he had no hesitation in claiming his allotted space. The only other vehicle on the forecourt was the dark blue Rover 800 belonging to Victor Hazelwood.

Ashton walked across the forecourt, showed his identity card to the security guard on duty in the foyer and was informed that Mr Hazelwood wanted to see him right away. Outside, the sun was now shining brightly, inside the building every light in every office was on and was likely to remain so long after the small army of cleaners from the contract firm arrived at six. Only one of the four lifts wasn't immediately available; choosing the nearest one, Ashton went on up to the top floor to find Hazelwood on the phone to the DG when he walked into his office. Cupping a hand over the mouthpiece, Victor passed a signal across the desk and invited him to read it, then resumed his conversation.

Galina Kutuzova: the name would have leapt at him even if it hadn't been spelt out in block capitals throughout the signal. His eyes automatically went to the date/time group in the top left-hand corner of the flimsy. 040045Z September 91 – the signal had therefore been despatched at a quarter to one in the morning Greenwich Mean Time on Wednesday the fourth of September. It had been originated by the embassy in Washington; allowing for the fact that Eastern Standard Time was five and a half hours behind GMT, the information concerning Galina had been gleaned from the seven o'clock CBS newscast yesterday evening. In his elation, the text barely registered with him. The Russian girl had been found where he had always said they should look for her; that was the only thing that mattered for the moment.

"I bet that's made your day," Hazelwood observed as he replaced the phone.

"Damn right it has." Ashton smiled. "Thanks, Victor."

"What for? I haven't done anything."

"You must have asked our people in Washington to keep their ears and eyes open."

Hazelwood shook his head. "I'd like to take the credit but it was a pure fluke. The most junior member of the SIS cell happened to catch the newscast, decided that London should know that a Russian Intelligence officer had surfaced in the United States and took it upon himself to fire off a signal. Had he sought the advice of his superiors, they might well have dismissed the news item as a publicity stunt by her lawyer and we would still be relying on Interpol to find Yvette Michel."

"Do you want me to ask our friend at Scotland Yard to cancel the red tab request?"

"Wouldn't do any good. Kommissar Voigt knows we traced Galina Kutuzova to Montreal. Franklin was so damned anxious to make amends, he gave him the whole story. I doubt if anyone at the German Embassy in Washington has appreciated the significance of that particular news item, but we can't afford to take a chance on that. Things will be tricky enough with the US Immigration authorities as it is without Bonn applying for her extradition. Since Franklin created the problem, he can bloody well solve it. He will have to talk to Voigt and persuade him to hold off until you have had a chance to question Galina."

"Me?"

"You know more about her than anyone else in this building."

"Maybe, but what does the DG have to say about it?"

"I told him he shouldn't allow his judgement to be clouded by what the Head of Station Berlin may have said about you."

"Does he know I've been to Leningrad and Moscow?"

"I didn't see any point in raising the issue; as far as he is concerned, you're going out there as an observer."

In other words, the DG was prepared to let him go because he had been assured that when Galina Kutuzova was interrogated, it would be the Americans who asked all the questions. And he could accept their record of the proceedings because he had no reason to suppose they had an ulterior motive for disseminating false information.

"What it is to be trusted," Ashton said bitterly.

"You've got my support. What more do you want?"

"Nothing," he said after barely a moment's reflection.

"Well then, suppose you go away and get yourself on a flight while I talk to the people in Washington."

"Right." Ashton read the signal again and looked up frowning. "There's something here that doesn't fit," he said.

"Like what?"

"J.W. Ullander. If he's a lawyer in Phoenix, what is he doing representing Galina Kutuzova? I mean, is it likely that she ran foul of the Immigration authorities in Arizona?"

"I wouldn't know," Hazelwood said.

"It says here that both the State Department and the Secretary of the Interior deny all knowledge of Galina Kutuzova, which must mean they've never heard of Yvette Michel either."

"Just what are you getting at, Peter?"

"I don't believe the fact that she is an illegal immigrant is the real issue here. I have a feeling Galina committed some other offence in Arizona which led to her arrest."

He could only hazard several guesses why there had been no mention of it in the signal from Washington. It could be that the SIS man on the spot had only caught the tail end of the interview and had missed it. Or perhaps Ullander had deliberately withheld the information from the CBS interviewer and then again, maybe it had been edited out.

"Tell you what," Hazelwood said thoughtfully. "While you're at it, why don't you enquire about flights to Phoenix?"

Ullander knew something was wrong the moment he left the TV and newspaper reporters on the drive and let himself into the house. He hadn't lived with Lois for sixteen years without acquiring a sixth sense for trouble and consequently he had received forewarning of the hostile reception that awaited him as he stepped across the threshold. Confirmation that the sullen, brooding atmosphere was not a figment of his imagination came with a terse "In here" from the direction of the kitchen when he called out to her. No terms of endearment like honey, darling or even J.W.; just two peremptory words delivered in a voice crackling with static. Leaving his bag out in the hall, he went on through the house and entered the largest kitchen on Lincoln Drive.

Lois was perched on one of the high stools at the breakfast bar, a cup of coffee in front of her, a cigarette burning between the fingers of her left hand. She was wearing a cut-off T-shirt that just about covered her belly button and a pair of apple-green shorts. Thirty-seven years old, a natural honey blonde, her once sylphlike figure was now some twelve to fourteen pounds heavier and it showed in the telltale bulge around her waist.

"I want that bitch out of here," she told him before he had a chance to say anything.

"Who are we talking about?"

"How many bitches do you know?"

"A few at the country club," he said jocularly and instantly regretted the levity.

Lois stubbed out her cigarette, then rounded on him, her face contorted with fury. "Goddamn it, you know very well who I mean, you stupid asshole."

"Hey, come on," he said feebly, "tell me what's bothering you."

"Galina Kutuzova, that's who. The bitch treats this place like a hotel and seems to think Garcia and Conchita are her personal servants. The way she treats them, we'll be lucky if they're still here this time next week."

Garcia was the Filipino houseboy, Conchita the Spanish-speaking maid from Acqua Zarca across the border in Mexico. Both lived in and would be hard to replace.

"And another thing, what's mine is apparently hers. Know what I caught her doing this morning?"

"I couldn't even hazard a guess." Ullander moved over to the kitchen window and stood there looking out at the Olympic-size swimming pool beyond the patio. Galina was lying on a sunbed in the shadow cast by the filtration plant at the deep end. The black latex swimsuit she was wearing looked familiar.

"She was sitting at my dressing table, using my lotions, my nail varnish, eye shadow and lipstick. The only damned thing that woman has done since she came here is sit around on her fanny, looking beautiful. I'm telling you, I want her out of my house right now while the kids are still at school."

He would have been happy to oblige Lois, but there was the little matter of the TV and newspapermen who were camped outside the house waiting not too patiently for him to make some kind of statement. They were expecting to see Galina too, though she wouldn't be giving any interviews.

"Dammit, J.W., are you listening to me?"

"Heard every word you said, honey."

"So what have you got to say?"

"I'm thinking where I can put her."

"What's wrong with a hotel in town?" Lois demanded belligerently.

"This girl is going to make us a fortune so I want to keep her under wraps until terms have been agreed. I don't want her doing something for nothing."

The cabin he owned in Oak Creek between Sedona and Munds Park? That was far enough off the beaten track to guarantee a little privacy. Furthermore, it was only a hundred and twenty miles from Phoenix, which meant that Galina would be readily available whenever he needed to produce her. The place was comfortably furnished and ready for immediate occupation, but who was going to keep an eye on Galina while she was up there? Not their houseboy, Garcia; she would twist him round her little finger. His secretary then? Janice wouldn't stand for any old buck from the Russian girl. She was also a divorcée, had no boyfriend at the moment and lived alone. No ties to

262

hold her back and she would do anything for him if he asked her nicely.

"The cabin," he said. "I'll drive Galina up there tonight. Okay?"

"No, it's not okay. I want her out of the house before the school bus comes by."

"Listen, I do that and all those reporters out there are going to follow me all the way up to Sedona and everything I'm working for goes down the tube."

"You think I care?"

"Well, not right now maybe." Ullander stole a glance at his wristwatch. Five minutes before two, and he had told the newsmen he would hold a press conference at two fifteen after he'd had a chance to shower and change. The way things were, he would have to give the shower a miss. "Let's talk about it some more while I change, huh?" He reached out, took hold of Lois firmly by the wrist and led her into their bedroom. "What we have got to do is put our heads together and figure out how we can get rid of those reporters."

"Don't expect me to come up with any bright ideas."

Still surly, still sulking. He turned Lois towards him, put a finger under her chin and raised it. "Did you miss me while I was away in Washington?" he asked.

"Not especially."

The pink tongue moistening her lips told him different. "Well, I surely missed you," he said and kissed her hard.

Lois put both arms around his neck and moved against him, a gentle sashaying from side to side that was exciting. "Is this what you call putting our heads together?" she murmured.

"Not exactly." Ullander steered his wife towards the bed. "More like this," he said and unbuttoned her shorts.

The shit was about to hit the fan and he was standing right in the way. Dyce supposed he might have guessed that when he'd answered the phone and Max Graber had been truly apologetic about dragging him into the office from his sickbed, allegedly to deal with some minor problem. The truth was you didn't think too clearly when you were bunged up with flu and the penny hadn't dropped until he walked into Graber's office and saw Assistant

District Attorney Samuelson perched on the windowsill, a morose expression on his face.

"Hello, Bernie," he croaked, "you back on the case?"

"We have a problem," Samuelson told him. "With J.W. Ullander. The man's determined to turn the Michel trial into a three-ring circus."

"How?"

Graber snorted in disgust. "Hell, Lew, didn't you catch the late night news?"

Dyce took out a tin of lozenges and popped one into his mouth. The pastille didn't do a lot for his throat but the taste was not unpleasant. "I was sick in bed. Remember?"

"CBS interviewed him in Washington earlier in the evening," Samuelson explained, "and he obviously warned every TV station in Arizona to catch it because a hell of a lot showed the interview on their local newscasts. Result is, every newspaperman for miles around is camping out on his porch hoping for an interview. And the TV and radio station which doesn't give him prime time is likely to run out of sponsors. I tell you, the way things are shaping up, J.W. will win this case before it ever comes to court."

Dyce looked from Samuelson to Graber and back again. "So what do you expect me to do about it?" he asked in a hoarse croak.

"We've got to put our heads together and work out how we can stop him trashing our case. By the time he's finished, we won't be able to find a jury that doesn't see Galina Kutuzova as a heroine and martyr."

"Show them she isn't little Miss Innocent, plant the idea that maybe she wasn't acting in self-defence."

"Well, gee, we'd just love to do that, Lew," Graber said with studied mockery, "but you mind telling us what we are going to use for ammunition?"

"Try looking in the case file. Lift something from that inadmissible statement she gave the NOPD when the arresting officers played fast and loose with Miranda." Dyce went over to the water cooler, filled a paper cup and drank it all to give his throat some relief. "Fasten on to the paragraph where she tells them how the GRU trained her in all the martial arts," he continued, his voice a shade less harsh than before. "Make them see that when she struck Mary Beth

Mallard in the throat, it was the old killer instinct in her coming out."

"It could work," Samuelson said, hope in his voice.

"Yeah, well don't tell the DA first, otherwise he'll want to hog the limelight again." Dyce crumpled the empty cup and tossed it into the waste bin. "Is that it, Max?" he asked Graber. "Because if it is, I'd like to go home and crawl back into the sack."

"'Fraid I can't let you do that," Graber told him. "At least not until you've seen this Mr Zale from Washington who's due here any minute now."

The Spetsnaz team despatched by Pavel Trilisser consisted of two men and a woman. All three were aged between thirty and thirty-two and were single, well-motivated, highly trained, superbly fit and politically reliable. In the context of the mission for which they had been selected, politically reliable meant they had not been contaminated by glasnost, perestroika or Yeltsin's concept of a Russian Federation, Commonwealth or whatever happened to be the flavour of the week. Well-motivated was simply another way of saying that they were intensely proud of being members of the élite Spetsnaz force to whose commanders they gave their unquestioning and unconditional loyalty.

Although none of them had participated in a lethal operation before, they were not raw and inexperienced. In the autumn of 1985 they had slipped into the United Kingdom to observe BRAVE DEFENDER at first hand. Ironically enough, this nationwide exercise involving units of the Regular and Territorial armies, the police and civil authorities had been designed to test Britain's defences against Spetsnaz operations.

The female member of the team had boarded a cross-channel ferry at Zeebrugge, entered the country on a Canadian passport and had then spent a month with the Greenham Common women who were camped outside the Cruise Missile base in Berkshire. Although she had taken part in several CND demonstrations, she had been careful to stay on the fringe. Consequently, the police had never had any cause to arrest her for a breach of the peace. It was also significant that none of her fellow protesters had suspected she was a Russian.

The two men had come ashore at Liverpool with other crew members of a Latvian freighter. No visa was required and with something in excess of forty thousand Russian seamen taking shore leave every year, they had known in advance that it was impossible for the British to keep track of every visitor. It had also been a fact that during Exercise BRAVE DEFENDER, the number of Eastern Bloc cargo ships and fishing vessels off the British coast had almost doubled from the usual seasonal average of forty, making the risk of detection even more remote.

Once ashore, they had separated, the team leader journeying north into Scotland to observe the security measures in force at the Polaris submarine base at Holy Loch before doubling back to North Yorkshire to assess whether it was feasible to take out the early warning radar station at Fylingdales with a Spetsnaz company. Meanwhile, his companion had checked out the number of soldiers assigned to guard such vulnerable points as the Atomic Weapons Research Establishment at Aldermaston and the Air Traffic Control Centre, West Drayton. Their activities in Great Britain had been of an entirely passive nature and therefore bore no relation to the mission they had now been given. What they had gained from BRAVE DEFENDER was confidence in their ability to escape detection in an alien environment. They had also learned to be completely self-sufficient after they had been inserted.

The team had been placed on stand-by forty-eight hours after Galina Kutuzova had deserted her post and had been held at varying degrees of readiness ever since. From a maximum of eight hours notice to move, they had come down to forty-five minutes following information that the target had been traced to Montreal. The time spent in waiting for something to happen had not been wasted; after studying material supplied by the army and her ex-fiancé, Eduard Tulbukin, they knew Galina Kutuzova better than their own families and could recognise her from any angle, day or night. They had also used the time on stand-by to absorb their new identities furnished by the First Chief Directorate.

Unlike the BRAVE DEFENDER reconnaissance, the team leader was now paired off with the woman. Travelling on separate Irish passports as Eric and Helen Teale, they had both allegedly been born in Cork within eight months of one another. Eric Teale was an insurance broker while his wife, Helen, described herself as a freelance journalist. The third member of the team had become William Stanford, a salesman from Sidcup in Kent. All three had some practical experience of the occupations shown in their passports.

Their final briefing had been held one hour after the KGB Resident in the Washington Embassy had phoned the contact number Pavel Trilisser had given him. Although the available information on J.W. Ullander was a little thin, the Deputy Head of the Foreign Intelligence Department was confident his team would find the lawyer without too much difficulty. And once they latched on to him, Pavel Trilisser was equally certain he would lead them to Galina Kutuzova. Each member of the team had been given five thousand American dollars in cash and advised that no assistance would be provided by any of the "illegals" currently operating in the United States. In addition, they had been warned not to contact either the Washington Embassy or the Soviet delegation at the United Nations.

Eric and Helen Teale had boarded the Lufthansa flight to Frankfurt departing Moscow's Sheremetyevo 2 Airport at 0750 hours local time to connect with American Airlines to JFK New York. Stanford, who had been routed to San Francisco via Rome, had left ninety minutes earlier. They planned to rendezvous in the concourse of Sky Harbor International Airport Phoenix at 0900 hours Thursday, September the fifth. The only lethal weapon they had among them was the cutthroat razor belonging to Eric Teale.

The faint pinging noise didn't sound like an alarm clock to Ashton, so he decided to ignore it and steal a few extra minutes in bed. Then a hand on his shoulder shook him gently and he surfaced reluctantly, uncertain where he was until he looked up and saw the No Smoking and Seat Belt signs.

"Please fasten your seat belt," the air stewardess told him and then moved on before he could ask her where they were.

Still muzzy with sleep, he wondered why she had a different uniform from the one worn by the girl who had served dinner; different accent, different sort of plane too. He extracted the inflight magazine from the pocket on the back of the seat in front of him. "Come Fly The Friendly Skies" it said and invited him to go United Airlines.

The tumblers in his mind began to click a little faster. Hazelwood had told him Washington was out and he had flown British Airways to Chicago O'Hare to connect with a flight to Phoenix because that was where Galina Kutuzova was out on bail facing a murder charge. Was it still Wednesday? Had to be; he had picked up seven hours flying west and Tony Zale would be waiting for him at the Holiday Inn. Wide awake now, he glanced to his right and saw the lights of the city below as the pilot banked to make the final approach into Sky Harbor.

CHAPTER 25

THERE WAS, both men agreed, nothing like a good, single malt whisky to break the ice. Ashton had bought the litre bottle of Old Fettercairn in the Duty Free shop at Heathrow in the confident expectation that unless the American was teetotal, he would find the smooth, smoky taste to his liking, no matter what his own favourite tipple might be. Fortunately, in spite of his youthful appearance, Tony Zale was not an abstainer and he particularly liked the warm afterglow and sense of wellbeing that had come after the very first swallow.

They had met in the hotel bar, though not by prior arrangement. Ashton had enquired if there was a Mr Tony Zale from Washington staying at the Holiday Inn when he had registered and it had transpired that the American had asked the desk clerk to inform him when a Mr Ashton from London, England checked in. One Bloody Mary, one John Collins, much small talk and a lot of salted peanuts later, they had adjourned to Ashton's room, collected a bucket of ice cubes from the machine down the corridor and broken the seal on the Old Fettercairn.

"I was a mite surprised to be given this assignment," Zale confided.

"So was I," Ashton told him. "Why were you out of favour?"

"I got thrown out of Berlin. The Kripo chief complained I was hampering his investigation – at least, that was the official reason."

"And the unofficial one?"

"I think the State Department people had made up their minds that Yuri Rostovsky was a crook and were determined that no one was going to prove them wrong."

"Our Foreign Office feels the same way about Galina Kutuzova."

"So what are you doing in Phoenix, if that's not a silly question?"

"Whatever information we get from her, they will use me to discredit it." Ashton refilled their glasses, then added a few cubes of ice from the bucket. "I'm what they call contaminated," he continued. "You see, I tried to make Alexei Leven show his hand and to do that, I had to approach him. I was the disaffected clerk who was strapped for cash and had something to sell. I guess I was pretty convincing, in fact too convincing for some of our high-ranking people."

"And they think you've been turned," Zale said in a flat voice.

"They did at one time, only now they're not so sure. I'm not Persil white you understand, just a less unpleasant shade of grey. If I return to London with anything sensational, these same people are going to infer I'm anxious to prove my loyalty."

"They transferred me to computer records when I returned from Berlin."

"Is that the equivalent of being in the doghouse?"

"It means you're going nowhere fast." Zale raised his glass, stared at the amber-coloured liquor. "Maybe Washington is trying to tell Ullander something by sending me out here?"

Ashton thought he was right. A defector of Galina Kutuzova's status would normally be debriefed by high-ranking Intelligence officers. By giving the job to a middle-grade civil servant like Zale, Washington was serving notice on the lawyer that they didn't attach too much credence to his client's story. News of such a put-down would travel fast, and if Ullander was hoping to sell her yet unwritten memoirs to a publisher back East, he could stop fantasising about a million-dollar advance.

"Ullander is already playing hard to get," Zale said. "First thing I did when I arrived in Phoenix was call his office. All I got was one of his staffers who told me J.W. was out of town and couldn't be reached. Same went for his secretary."

"Whereabouts is Galina?"

"Good question. Ullander has got her under wraps somewhere. According to the police, she was staying at his house on Lincoln Drive, but she isn't there now. And before you ask, his wife, Lois, won't come to the phone. I must have rung his home number half-a-dozen times this evening and never got farther than the Filipino houseboy."

"Can't you force him to produce Kutuzova?"

"I'm not empowered to do that. The people in Washington have opted for the soft-shoe approach."

"What about the police?"

"They are not interested in tracing her for our benefit."

Zale had been to see Dyce, the detective in charge of the Mallard case and had also met Assistant District Attorney Samuelson. In a nutshell, it seemed the DA's office were merely interested in doing a character assassination on Galina Kutuzova, while the police department would only get heated if she failed to appear on November the twenty-first, the day the trial began. And that appeared to be unlikely, given that Ullander had a number of very good reasons to ensure she was present in court. Most of these didn't register with Ashton; it was still Wednesday, but with the time zone difference, more than twenty-five hours had elapsed since the telephone call from Century House had dragged him out of bed, and he found it difficult to concentrate on what Zale was saying.

"Listen, Tony," he said, interrupting him. "First thing tomorrow we'll get word to Ullander that I would like to see him."

"Yeah? No disrespect, but I doubt your name is going to cut much ice with him."

"I never thought it would. On the other hand, if we tempt him with the right kind of bait, he'll stop acting like a recluse."

"What sort of bait are we talking about?"

"When CBS interviewed him, Ullander claimed that Galina's life would be in danger if she were deported, but he didn't say why or offer any evidence to support the allegation. That omission can only mean she hasn't told him what happened in Dresden the evening a captain in our Intelligence Corps was blown up by a bomb which was intended for her."

He would also tell the lawyer about her relationship with Simon Younger and where and how often they had met in West Berlin. Although technically the information was still classified, disclosing it to an unauthorised person was not going to bring the nation to its knees. It wasn't, however, the only piece of bait he would use to hook him.

"We'll also tell Ullander I'm with the British Secret Intelligence

271

Service, which happens to be true, and am in charge of the Russian Desk, which happens to be a whopping big lie. Only he won't be able to prove it because we don't have such a thing as a Freedom of Information Act. He can phone who he likes from the embassy in Washington to the Cabinet Office in London and the most anyone will tell him is that my name appears amongst the executive grade officers in the Foreign and Commonwealth Office Staff List. I think there is a pretty good chance Ullander will conclude the Brits are deliberately trying to mislead him and will accept my version of the truth."

"I guess it could work," Zale said thoughtfully.

"I hope so. We'll know for sure one way or the other tomorrow."

"Right. I'll meet you for breakfast at seven."

"Make it an hour later. I've got a lot of sleep to catch up on," Ashton said and gently shepherded him out of the room.

Ashton closed the door behind the American and stripped off. No bed had ever looked so inviting and he was dead to the world moments after climbing into it.

The arrivals hall at Sky Harbor International Airport was a lot more crowded at nine o'clock in the morning than Eric Teale had been led to expect. However, it did not bother him; the precise rendezvous had been set before they had left Moscow and the Hertz desk was a good fixed point. He looked up at the flight information board, saw that the shuttle from San Francisco had landed on time and moved to the appointed spot where Bill Stanford couldn't fail to see him when he came through the gate. Eric Teale, Helen Teale and Bill Stanford; they had not used their Russian names since the twenty-sixth of May when they had been placed on standby. They would not become Anatoli Ovechkin, Irina Gouzenkova and Nikolai Sokolov again until they had completed their mission and returned to base. When on active service, you were what your legend said you were; it was the only way to survive within the enemy camp.

He spotted Stanford among the passengers moving towards the exit before the latter noticed him. The salesman from Sidcup in Kent was wearing a none-too-smart two-piece pale grey pinstripe which had collected a fair number of creases since leaving Moscow.

Easing his way through the crowd of onlookers, he intercepted Stanford and greeted him warmly.

"Good to see you, Bill," he said and pumped his hand. "How was the flight?"

"Pretty good. Helen not with you?"

"She's back at the hotel, making some phone calls." Teale relieved him of the airline holdall he was carrying over one shoulder and then walked on past the Hertz desk towards the side exit. "Car's out this way," he said.

The rented Dodge Spirit was slotted between a look-alike Honda Accord and the much larger Buick Roadmaster on the first floor of the adjoining multistorey parking lot. Opening the trunk, Teale dumped the holdall inside, waited for Stanford to do the same with the Revelation suitcase he was carrying, then closed the lid and unlocked the car doors. A copy of *The Republic* was lying on the dashboard.

"Better take a look at it, Bill," he said.

Galina Kutuzova had made the front page. The photograph showed her standing next to a tall, loose-limbed man with an engaging smile whose name Stanford learned was John Wendell Ullander. The caption below said the photo had been taken outside the lawyer's house on Lincoln Drive which appeared to him only marginally smaller than a palace. The treacherous whore Kutuzova was wearing a short skirt that barely covered her crotch.

"I don't see how we are going to deal with her when she is staying with this man," Stanford said.

"Helen is working on that problem now." Teale left the airport, picked up Thirty-fourth Street, then headed east on Indian School Road. "We're staying at the Paloverde in Scottsdale," he continued. "I am going to drop you at a motel about a mile up the road from where we are. When you check in, tell the desk clerk you want to rent a car and ask him where you can get the best deal."

"Right."

"Soon as you are mobile, head back into Phoenix and buy yourself a pump-action shotgun. If the salesman should ask, you can say you are going after mountain lion. I don't know whether you need a licence for that but you can always give the impression your friends have taken one out."

"You don't have to dot every i and cross every t," Stanford told him.

"The shotgun isn't vital," Teale continued unperturbed. "If the salesman starts quoting regulations at you, just back off and walk away."

They didn't need a shotgun to deal with Galina Kutuzova. It was merely an insurance in case the lawyer had provided her with an armed bodyguard. All being well, he, or Bill, or Helen would kill the whore swiftly and silently with their bare hands in one of a dozen ways they had all learned from the close-quarter-combat instructors at the Spetsnaz training school.

"What are you going to be doing while I'm out shopping?" Stanford asked.

"Buying a couple of shovels from a hardware store."

"To dig a grave?"

"What else?" Teale smiled lopsidedly. "You don't think we are going to leave her out in the desert under a pile of rocks, do you?"

The McDowell Building on Central Avenue faced the Phoenix Art Museum and Public Library with the State Fair grounds in the rear. The offices of Ullander, Power, Ironwood and Riker occupied most of the sixth floor, which was hardly surprising considering the size of the law firm. In addition to the four partners, there were eighteen associates, four personal assistants/secretaries, one office supervisor, a switchboard operator, one receptionist, seven shorthand typists and a varying number of students from the university's law faculty.

Zale had phoned the office from the Holiday Inn shortly after eight thirty to ask when it would be convenient to see Mr Ullander and had been unable to get an answer from any of the staff. He had then tried to contact the lawyer at home but had only succeeded in raising the Filipino houseboy again who had told him "lady not at home" and whose understanding of English had progressively diminished with each successive question. In the end, they had gone to the McDowell Building, determined to wait there all day if necessary.

Ullander had finally arrived at nine twenty and had promised he wouldn't keep them waiting more than another few minutes.

An hour and ten minutes later, the girl on the reception desk invited them to go on in.

Ashton supposed it was only fitting that the senior partner should have an office reflecting his status, but Ullander clearly believed in flaunting it. The room was almost twice the size of a tennis court, had oak-panelled walls and an oak floor which was partially hidden by the largest Persian carpet Ashton had ever seen. There was a desk with a marble top, two leather armchairs for visitors that looked as if they belonged in the smoking room of an exclusive club and a more functional executive model. The oak refectory table and seven matching upright chairs suggested that the lower right-hand section of the room was used as a conference area. Two Impressionist landscapes, one by Utrillo, the other by a painter Ashton didn't recognise, reinforced an already obvious message that here was an attorney who didn't come cheap. The mounted heads of deer, moose and a couple of mountain lions proclaimed the machismo of a hunter who ranged far and wide. This exaggerated display of manliness was not however likely to win him many votes from the ecologists amongst the electorate.

"Are you in the same line of business as Tony here?" Ullander asked after Zale had introduced him.

"I'm with the SIS at Century House," Ashton told him and was rewarded with a blank look of incomprehension. "The equivalent of the CIA, Langley," and added, "only smaller."

"Right. So what can I do for you gentlemen?"

"We'd like to see Galina Kutuzova," Zale said.

"You're not alone; that girl is news, everyone wants to interview her – TV, radio, newspapers. Matter of fact, fitting you in will be quite a problem."

"Are you telling me we shall have to stand in line and wait our turn?"

Ullander beamed. "You got it in one, Tony," he said, thoroughly pleased with himself.

"I think you should move us to the head of the queue," Ashton said quietly. "It could be to your advantage."

The smile vanished as quickly as it had appeared. "Are you threatening me?" Ullander demanded in an ominous tone.

"No, of course he isn't," Zale said hastily.

"I don't hear your British friend saying it."

"Maybe I should start again . . ." Ashton began.

"Just as long as it doesn't take too long," Ullander said, looking pointedly at his watch.

"You and Galina Kutuzova had a pretty good press in the *Gazette* yesterday evening and in *The Republic* today, but the DA has started to smear your client . . ."

"I read the same piece on page four, and it didn't bother me."

"It should, because it's only a foretaste of what is to come. You surely don't need me to tell you that a lot of people in Washington are determined to destroy her credibility. Why else would Tony have given you those photographs of Galina and her mother, Lydia Petrovskaya, if it wasn't true?"

"You're not telling me anything new. I know why they put a muzzle on Mr Zale."

"Well, don't underestimate the amount of dirt they have on her. She's no angel, Mr Ullander, and she certainly isn't a heroine."

"Seems to me you want to bury her too."

Ashton shook his head. "No, you're quite wrong. I've got too much of my own future invested in her to want that."

"You going to get to the point?"

"Galina told you the Soviet Army is cheating on the Arms Reduction Agreement. We want to debrief her and get the whole story because, so far, she hasn't given you too many examples. Correct?"

"You sound like a man who is about to make a proposition."

Ashton smiled. "I think you should invite someone to listen to this."

Ullander ignored the suggestion. "Just make your pitch," he said.

"I tell you what I know about Galina Kutuzova, you tell us where we can find her."

"How about a sample of what you have to offer?"

Ashton was happy to oblige. He knew Zale thought he was sticking his neck out but with the right kind of presentation, even the most mundane fact could be made to seem like a state secret.

"Did she tell you about that evening in Dresden when they tried to kill her and got one of ours instead?"

The look of interest on the lawyer's face which he was slow to kill said it all. From the time Younger had first recruited her, Galina

276

had always been economical with the amount of information she chose to divulge and clearly she had told Ullander no more than she'd had to. In his eagerness to promote her, the interviews he had given to the press and on TV had swallowed up everything he had learned about the Russian girl. And without fresh material to whet their appetites, the media would rapidly lose interest, if they hadn't already done so. Maybe the reason why he had left them to cool their heels for over an hour was because he had been on the phone trying to drum up further interviews for his client?

"When did this happen, Mr Ashton?"

"Friday the twenty-fourth of May."

"You mind if we get this on record?"

"I'll allow you to tape it," Ashton told him, "provided you tell us where Galina is."

"You've just got yourself a deal," Ullander said.

Teale had purchased the border spade from a garden centre, the shovel from a hardware store in Glendale's shopping mall. While both implements had sharp blades, their wooden shafts were much longer than the helve of the entrenching tool favoured by the Spetsnaz. The entrenching tool could be thrown like a dagger and in the right hands could kill a man at twenty paces. On the other hand, although the border spade and the shovel were potentially lethal, they could only be used effectively at close quarters.

Teale glanced into the rear-view mirror, saw the nearest vehicle was at least a hundred yards back and moved across into the nearside lane, then tripped the indicator to show that he was turning right into the driveway of the Paloverde Hotel. He swept through the gates, went on past the front entrance and slotted the Dodge into the first vacant space he came to in the parking area on the west side of the hotel. He locked the car, checked the trunk to make sure it was also secure and then made his way to the coffee shop in the lobby where he had arranged to meet Helen. Finding no sign of her, he left by the side entrance and walked round to the swimming pool in rear of the hotel.

Helen was sitting at a table near the steps at the shallow end of the pool. Apart from the teenager in a bikini who was sunbathing on a Lilo and the fat man fast asleep in a deck chair, she had the place pretty much to herself.

"I thought we had arranged to meet in the coffee shop?" Teale said in a low voice.

"If you had arrived on time, that's where you would have found me." Helen leaned forward to stub out her cigarette in an ashtray. "But after waiting there an hour, I began to feel conspicuous."

"I can understand that."

It was the nearest thing to an apology she was likely to get from Teale and it was pointless to hope for something more fulsome. Without waiting to be asked, she told him what she had learned about J.W. Ullander from the newspapers, his office and yellow pages. It didn't amount to an awful lot.

"He has a personal secretary called Janice Xavier. According to the girl I spoke to at Ullander, Power, Ironwood and Riker, she suddenly went on vacation yesterday afternoon."

"So what conclusion do you draw from that?" Teale asked.

"I think she is wet-nursing the whore somewhere not too far from Phoenix. The photographs of Kutuzova which appeared in the *Gazette* yesterday evening and in this morning's *The Republic* were taken outside Ullander's house on Lincoln Drive and the one thing both newspapers agree on is that she is no longer staying with him."

"What are you getting at?"

"I think Ullander drove her to wherever she is hiding. I asked the girl at the law firm when he would be in the office and she told me he had arrived an hour ago and was in conference. This was a few minutes after eleven. That's why I don't think Kutuzova can be too far from here."

Teale did not question her assumption, nor did he ask for a line by line account of the story she had pitched to the girl at the law firm. There was no need to; Irina Gouzenkova knew what she was about. She was a highly trained Spetsnaz soldier, not some greenhorn fresh out of the training school.

"I suppose we could follow the lawyer around in the hope that he will eventually lead us to her, but that could take days, and time isn't on our side."

"I have another suggestion. Janice Xavier is in the phone book and I have made a note of her address. I could show my press card to her neighbours, tell them I am doing a human interest story on her employer and ask if they know how I can get in touch with her. I can tell more or less the same story to Ullander's neighbours on

278

Lincoln Drive. If he should have a second house, they might know where it is. I reckon I could be back here in four to five hours at the most."

Teale considered her suggestion, weighed the risks involved and decided they were acceptable. Reaching into his pocket, he took out the keys to the Dodge Spirit and passed them across the table. "Better get on with it then," he said quietly.

CHAPTER 26

THEY LEFT Phoenix heading north on Interstate 17, a divided multi-lane highway that ran almost arrow straight to New River and Rock Springs and then on towards Cordes Junction. Zale drove, right hand on the wheel, left elbow on the door-mounted armrest, his foot on the accelerator keeping the speedo needle dead on the fifty-mile-an-hour restriction as they motored through what he called Apache and Navajo country. A cloudless, sapphire-blue sky, giant saguaro cacti, scrub, the towering red rock buttes rising from the desert floor and the mesa, the high steep-sided plateaux; the scenery could not have been more familiar had Ashton been born and bred in Arizona instead of acquiring it second-hand from seeing countless Westerns in his formative years. And what could sound more familiar than the place names on the Arizona road map he was holding – Fort Apache, Jake's Corner, Dutch Woman Butte, Star Valley, Tonto Village, Kohls Ranch, Bloody Basin?

"I think you succeeded in worrying J.W." Zale took his eyes off the road momentarily to glance sideways at him. "Were you serious about the KGB catching his interview on the CBS newscast?"

"I wasn't making small talk," Ashton told him. "If it was seen by one of our guys in Washington, it's only reasonable to assume someone in the Soviet Embassy on Sixteenth Street was watching the same newscast."

"I'd go along with that."

"Mind you, whether the Russians follow it up is another matter. There are times when it seems to me the KGB these days is not the cohesive force it used to be; then something happens which shows the apparatus is not completely moribund. The only thing you can be sure of is that there are a lot of people in Moscow who would like to silence Galina Kutuzova before she really opens her mouth."

"And if the KGB does decide to go after her, good old J.W. Ullander is going to find himself in deep shit because they will presume he must know where she is."

"That's the message I tried to get across," Ashton said.

"Yeah, well, I guess J.W. will have one eye over his shoulder from now on. I mean, after what you said to him, he's only too aware he could lead them to Galina."

"That was the whole idea. I'm hoping he won't go near her for the next day or so."

"You know something?" said Zale. "You British can be Machiavellian when you put your minds to it."

"You think so? Well, as long as it keeps Ullander out of our hair."

"We've still got Janice Xavier to contend with," Zale pointed out.

"I'm hoping that she won't be quite the same pain in the arse."

They reached the Y-fork at Cordes Junction where State Highway 69 branched off to Prescott in just under an hour and twenty minutes. Phoenix was sixty-five miles behind them now and they were more than halfway to Sedona. Provided they could maintain their present speed, Ashton calculated they should reach Ullander's lodge on the Munds Park Road by two in the afternoon.

"You're pretty quiet," Zale said, after a long period of silence.

"I was just doing a few sums in my head, trying to work out exactly when we would meet Starshii Leitenant Galina Kutuzova."

"Be more to the point if we discussed how we propose to interrogate her."

"What's wrong with the Mutt and Jeff routine? You can be Jeff, I'll be Mutt; I'm good at snarling."

"Okay. Who's going to open?"

"I am," said Ashton. "Whittle was killed on Friday the twenty-fourth of May by a bomb that was meant for her. I want Galina to explain why she spent the next fifty days waiting in Zürich before flying out to Montreal on Saturday July the thirteenth. That will be the litmus test; we'll know from the kind of answer we get whether the rest of her story is believable or not."

"While you're at it, you might ask her why she and Yuri Rostovsky were using that prostitute Tamara Chernenko as a go-between."

"Sure." Ashton consulted his map again, tried to work out which township would best suit their purpose – Williams, Flagstaff or Winslow. "First thing we have to do is move Galina to somewhere more private," he muttered.

"Did I hear you right?" Zale asked.

"I expect so. We can't leave her where she is. Ullander is a public figure, which means that both *The Republic* and the *Gazette* will have prepared his obituary in draft. If the editors don't know he has this retreat near Sedona, you can bet the newspaper proprietors do. Fortunately, the Kutuzova story has temporarily run out of steam, otherwise we would probably find the place crawling with reporters."

"I wouldn't put it past him to try and regenerate interest." Zale glanced into the rear-view mirror, then tripped the indicator and pulled out to overtake a slow-moving truck. "All he has to do is let it be known that she is being questioned by the Intelligence Services of the United States and Great Britain and the reporters will be up here in droves."

"Maybe you'd better forget the speed limit and put your foot down."

"And maybe you'd better figure out what we are going to do if she refuses to come with us."

"Don't worry," Ashton growled. "If necessary, I'll pick her up and carry her out of there over my shoulder."

Dyce wished he had stayed at home. Dedication, devotion to duty, job satisfaction; these were not the reasons why he had taken himself off the sick list. The three-day bout of flu was almost over and it had seemed pointless to stay in bed simply because he still had a sore throat, especially as Graber had dragged him into the office when he had really been feeling under the weather. The reason why he now regretted his somewhat quixotic decision was the double homicide which had occurred in Chandler, approximately twelve miles southeast of Sky Harbor International Airport.

The three men who had hit the liquor store on Sun Lake Road had chosen both the best and worst possible time to commit the robbery. Best because apart from the owner, his wife and a sales assistant, no one else had been present when they had walked into the single-storey building; worst because the country was in deep recession and trade was at an all-time low. Enraged to find the cash register was practically empty, they had forced all three to kneel down and had calmly executed the owner and his wife with a single shot through the head. The sales assistant had survived because he had seen what had happened to the other two and had deliberately slumped forward on to his face a split second before the gunman standing behind him had squeezed the trigger. The bullet had therefore struck him high up on the right shoulder, approximately one inch from his neck and had exited below the right nipple. That was how Dyce figured it, but he wouldn't know for sure until the doctors allowed him to question the survivor. The scene at the liquor store had sickened him; describing it again for Max Graber's benefit only impressed it more vividly in his mind.

"You're a great one for guessing, Lew," Graber said. "How the hell do you know the killers went away with empty pockets?"

"It's a pretty run-down neighbourhood, lots of retailers have gone bust, stores boarded up, that kind of thing. I don't think even the liquor store could have been doing a lot of business." Dyce took out a packet of throat lozenges and popped one into his mouth. "Something else, there was about twenty dollars on the floor around the bodies. Looks like they had forced the owner and his wife to eat some of the notes before they shot them. We'll know for sure when we get the results of the saliva tests."

"There were three armed robbers?"

Dyce nodded. "According to our solitary witness. He's a wino and not too sure which day of the week this is. He was resting up on the parking lot across the street and claims he saw three men get out of a beat-up Chevvy and enter the liquor store. Says they were in there about ten minutes, but he's pretty vague about that, like the descriptions he gave the first patrolman on the scene."

There wasn't much else Dyce could tell him. The alarm had been raised anything up to half an hour after the incident had occurred by a retired mailman who had wanted to buy a pint of bourbon. Two patrol cars had responded to the 911 and the mobile crime unit had arrived on the scene a few minutes before

Dyce had. The medical examiner and police photographer had not been too far behind him.

"And that's it?" Graber asked.

"So far. State police and Highway Patrol have been warned to look out for three men in a beat-up Chevvy, otherwise we have to wait on the mobile crime unit. Could be they'll lift some identifiable prints from the cash register and the dollar bills."

"Ullander's got the shakes," Graber said, abruptly changing the subject.

"Ullander? Oh yeah?"

"That guy from Washington you met yesterday went to see J.W. this morning. Had some Brit with him. Anyway, between the two of them, they scared the shit out of him. Seems they convinced him the Russians have sent a hit team after Galina Kutuzova. Insisted I call the Highway Patrol office in Flagstaff and have them check out his place on Munds Park Road where the Russian girl is staying with his secretary, Janice Xavier."

"It's got to be a publicity stunt, Max."

"He was worried enough to call his wife and warn her not to open the door to any strangers. Around noon she phones the office and tells him some woman reporter has been nosing around the neighbours . . ."

"Now I know it's a gimmick."

"I want you to get your butt over to Lincoln Drive and talk to the lady, see if we can put a name to this reporter."

"You're kidding . . ."

"I was never more serious," Graber told him.

"Yeah, I guess you are."

"Then what are you waiting for, Lew?"

Dyce left the office, went on down to the yard, picked up the unmarked Ford sedan and headed east on Van Buren Street. Switching channels on the radio, he retuned to Station KNLX in time to catch the one o'clock newscast. The armed robbery and double homicide in Sun Lake Road had grabbed the headlines, followed by the latest opinion poll which showed President Bush's popularity rating had taken another dip. Losing interest, he searched the waveband, picked up some country and western station and stayed with it for the rest of the way to Lincoln Drive.

Lois hadn't seen the reporter, didn't know which newspaper

she worked for and could only direct him to the neighbour who had met her. According to the latter, the reporter had introduced herself as Helen Teale and had produced a press card to prove it. Teale had claimed she was tackling the Kutuzova story from a different angle and wanted to know what local people thought of the Russian girl.

Two things made Dyce sit up and take notice. Although Helen Teale had spoken with what sounded like an English accent, she had been driving a Dodge with Arizona plates. She had also appeared to know that the Ullanders owned a cabin up Sedona way. Under the mistaken impression that she must have got the information from the family, Lois's neighbour had been happy to confirm this and supply the exact address.

Pushy, arrogant and lazy were the first three adjectives which immediately sprang to mind whenever Janice Xavier thought about the Russian girl. Of the many favours she had done J.W. over the years, acting as cook, housemaid and chaperone to Galina Kutuzova was proving to be easily the most demanding. It would have been bad enough keeping her company back in Phoenix, but up here in one of the loneliest places on God's earth, it was sheer unremitting hell. There were almost fifteen years between them and they had no interests in common. Furthermore, Galina smoked like a chimney, refused to do a hand's turn around the house and never stopped complaining about her cooking.

This was not the first time she had stayed at the cabin on Munds Park Road. In the late fall of '89, she had arranged to spend an illicit weekend with J.W. while Lois and the children were visiting her folks in Biloxi. J.W. was supposed to have joined her up in Sedona on the Saturday evening after attending a football game in Tucson which he had claimed would do him some good politically. But he hadn't been able to get away after the game and she had had to spend the night up there alone, scared stiff that some vagrant or drunk would break into the cabin.

Janice supposed she had only herself to blame for allowing J.W. to talk her into repeating the experience, but it was difficult to refuse him anything when he turned on the charm. And she could never forget how good, kind and thoughtful he had been when Neil had walked out on her five years ago. He had assigned one of the associate members of the law firm to handle the divorce, had got her the best property settlement and had then refused to charge her a cent. "One of the fringe benefits of working for Ullander, Power, Ironwood and Riker," he'd told her when she had protested he was being too generous. They had become lovers the following year, a liaison she had never regretted.

She was here with Galina Kutuzova because J.W. had asked her to do him one more favour and she happened to be in love with him; that was the bottom line. He had also assured her it would only be for a day or two until he could make other arrangements and had provided her with a Cellnet phone so that they could keep in touch. Remembering how frightened she had been the last time she had stayed at the cabin, he had lent her a .32 calibre Smith and Wesson revolver. The handgun was supposed to make her feel safe; unfortunately, there had been moments when she had felt like turning it on the Russian girl.

"I hate this place," Galina announced for the umpteenth time.

"I'm not exactly crazy about it either," Janice said tartly.

The cabin was too primitive for her liking; no running water, no flush toilets, no electricity. J.W. might like to draw water from a well, make do with a chemical toilet and generate his own power supply but she was essentially a city dweller at heart, not some damned pioneer.

"How much longer do we have to stay up here?"

In an effort to control her temper, Janice counted slowly up to ten, but it didn't do any good. "Until Mr Ullander can find us something more suitable," she snapped. "How many more times do you need telling?"

"I don't like your attitude, neither will your employer when I tell him how badly you have behaved."

"I'd save my breath if I were . . ." Janice began, then broke off to listen intently. At that precise moment, there was no sweeter sound to her ears than the crunch of tyres on the rocky track. "It must be them," she murmured.

"Who?"

"The two Intelligence officers Mr Ullander phoned me about." Janice got to her feet and started towards the hall. "You wait here."

"I intend to," Galina told her.

An officer of the Highway Patrol was the last person Janice expected to see when she opened the door.

"Mrs Xavier?" he asked politely, and touched his flat-brimmed hat.

"Yes. What can I do for you?"

"Are you okay, m'am?"

"You can see I am."

"Is something wrong?"

"Not a thing."

The broad smile which appeared made him seem even younger. "Mr Ullander just asked us to look in on you . . . see how things were."

"Oh, we're fine," Janice assured him. "Matter of fact, we are expecting an official from Washington and his British colleague. They should be here any minute now."

"I'll be getting along then."

The patrolman saluted her again, walked back to his car and made a three-point turn on the level bit of ground in front of the cabin. Janice stood there watching him from the doorway until his vehicle disappeared from view as it breasted the crestline to the road above.

Ashton looked back over his shoulder at the car receding into the distance. "Why do you suppose that Highway Patrolman waved to us?" he asked.

"Search me, maybe it was just a friendly gesture."

"Nice of him."

"We should be coming up to the slip road at any moment," Zale said pointedly.

Ashton took the hint and looked to the front. Around the next bend in the road he spotted what looked like a metal container on a stick by the roadside and suddenly realised it was Ullander's mailbox. "Fifty yards ahead," he said, "on your side."

"Got it." Zale glanced into the rear-view mirror to make sure no one was closing on him, then signalled he was turning left and drifted across the centre line.

The track dropped sharply away from the road and snaked down the hillside to the bungalow-style dwelling approximately a hundred feet below. Except for the stone chimney breast, gable end and slate roof, the building was constructed on the lines of a log cabin circa 1840 and was a good deal larger than Ashton had expected. He noticed there was an Oldsmobile under the carport adjoining the opposite gable end.

The woman who came out to greet them as Zale made a U-turn in front of the property was wearing a red and white gingham dress and beige-coloured moccasins. She was about five seven, had fair hair and was roughly ten pounds overweight for her height. Janice Xavier wouldn't see forty again and was covered in freckles, but this only became apparent to Ashton when he got out of the car and moved forward to introduce himself.

"And this is Mr Tony Zale," he added, "from the Defense Intelligence Agency in Washington."

"Won't you come in, gentlemen," she said in a pleasing tone of voice. "We've been expecting you."

"Yes. We were present when Mr Ullander spoke to you."

"I figured J.W. wasn't alone." She smiled. "Can I get you something to drink? Coffee? Orange juice? Coke? Seven-Up?"

"Thanks, but no thanks," Zale told her. "We've got a lot of ground to cover and not much time to do it in."

"I understand. You'll find Galina in the living room; I'll be in the kitchen should you need me."

Galina Kutuzova was not the same young woman whose photograph Ashton had seen in B Squadron, the 3rd Carabineers, eight long weeks ago. Her face was thinner, harder looking and the superfluous padding on her hips and thighs had disappeared. Her once dark hair had been cut extremely short and dyed a reddish brown.

"Simon Younger sends his regards," Ashton said, lying brazenly. "So would Bob Whittle were he still alive."

Galina stared at him, her eyes narrowing to pinpoints of hate. "I have nothing to say to you," she hissed.

"What about Mr Zale here?"

"Him neither."

"Bang goes your only hope of staying in America," Ashton said cheerfully.

"You obviously don't know J.W."

"You don't want to rely too much on Mr Ullander. He might win your case over here but you're not going to walk very far. You're an accessory to the murder of Captain Robert Whittle in Dresden on the twenty-fourth of May and the Germans have already applied for your extradition."

Another bare-faced lie, but Galina was not to know that. Taken aback, she instinctively looked to Zale for confirmation and got an affirmative nod.

"Your lawyer might be able to fight a rearguard action for a while, but in the end, Washington will deport you."

"He's right," Zale assured her solemnly.

"If you don't want to find yourself on a plane to Berlin, you have to convince us you are worth saving," Ashton continued. "Mr Ullander knows that; why else do you suppose we're here?"

Galina leaned forward, helped herself to a cigarette from the pack of Marlboro on the low table in front of her and lit it with a Zippo lighter. "What is it you want from me?" she asked.

"The information you and Yuri Rostovsky were proposing to sell to Colonel Lloyd Osmonde," Zale said.

"Provided we are satisfied it is worth having," Ashton added curtly. "First thing we want to know is why you spent fifty days in Zürich waiting for Rostovsky to join you when the KGB had already made one attempt on your life?"

There was a long pause while Galina concentrated all her attention on her cigarette, as if the glowing ember was the source of all knowledge. "There is an operation known as TRIP-WIRE," she began. "We were still microfilming the document when I had to flee the country. Yuri stayed on to complete the task."

"He wasn't exactly quick about it, was he?"

"The master copy of TRIPWIRE is lodged at Headquarters 6 Guards Tank Army. It wasn't easy for him to gain access after Colonel General Fedyanin had been replaced by Vitali Ilyich Lobanov."

"This was all prearranged, was it? You left Dresden like a scalded cat but faithful old Yuri knew what was expected of him without a word from you?"

"Of course he didn't. I left a message for him on the answering machine Tamara Chernenko shared with a Romanian prostitute called Janina."

"Who's Tamara Chernenko?" Ashton asked, poker-faced.

"Another prostitute, a Russian girl who sought the good life in the West and discovered the only way she could sample it was on her back."

"So how did you make her acquaintance?"

"I didn't." Galina stubbed out her cigarette, crushing it with angry force in a heavy cut-glass ashtray. "Yuri did. He was my case officer when I was given the green light to cultivate Simon Younger and we were running around West Berlin. Yuri got tired of following us from one night spot to another and looked for pleasures elsewhere. He found Tamara on Budapesterstrasse and took up with her." Galina shook her head at the wonder of it all. "He was a very handsome man, you know, a ram with all the charm in the world. He had only to smile and nine women out of ten couldn't wait to drop their pants."

"What about Tamara? Was she equally susceptible?"

"She was the dumbest of the dumb and so crazy about him she never cottoned on to the fact that he was using her. That was when we realised she would make the perfect go-between."

Ashton looked at Zale, raised an eyebrow and got a nod. Galina's explanation was as close to the truth as they were likely to get and he could see the American agreed with him. Leaving the other two for a moment, he went out into the kitchen and asked Janice Xavier to join them, then left it to Zale to explain why they proposed to continue the interrogation elsewhere.

"It won't be long before this place is swarming with reporters," he told her. "Once they arrive, we won't be able to do our job, which is why Galina will be leaving with us."

"I don't think Mr Ullander will be very happy about that," Janice said doubtfully.

"He'll be a darn sight more miserable if we take Galina to Washington," Zale said. "And we have the power to do that." He smiled. "Look, all we need is a few hours of peace and quiet. We'll have her back here long before dark."

"Where are you taking Galina?"

"We thought we would use one of the camp sites marked on the map – Navajo Flats?"

"Should be quiet enough at this time of the year with all the kids back in school."

"Good. If the reporters ask where we have gone, you don't know."

"Right."

"Are you going to let them get away with this?" Galina demanded.

"You bet I am," Janice said with feeling. "I could do with some peace and quiet myself."

CHAPTER 27

DYCE RAPPED the frosted-glass panel, opened the door and walked into Graber's office.

"Can you spare me a minute, Max?" he asked, then nodded to Assistant District Attorney Samuelson. "You don't mind me interrupting your powwow, do you, Bernie?" he added.

"Be my guest," Samuelson told him.

"Thanks." Dyce took out his notebook, flipped it open. "This reporter who was nosing around Lincoln Drive – her name's Helen Teale. She and her husband arrived in Phoenix sometime yesterday evening, rented a Dodge Spirit from Hertz and checked into the Paloverde Hotel. This morning, her husband takes off somewhere with the car and she spends a couple of hours sunning herself by the pool. He returns shortly before eleven, joins her at the pool, and guess what? Roughly ten minutes later, she takes the keys and drives off. It's like they were playing some version of musical chairs."

"How did you get all this stuff, Lew?" Graber asked impatiently.

"The neighbour she went to see on Lincoln Drive remembered her name. She also told me that Teale sounded as though she came from England."

The information had led him to ask the various agencies in town if a Mrs Teale from England had rented a vehicle in the last few days, and had learned that a Mr Eric Teale had hired a Dodge Spirit. The Hertz agency had also been able to tell him the name of the hotel where he was staying. With very few guests residing at the Paloverde, the hotel staff had no difficulty recalling him.

"The Teales are Irish, not English," he continued. "They do however live in London."

"You got that from the hotel register?"

"Yeah. They had just checked out when I got there. Only missed them by a few minutes." Dyce ripped a page from the notebook and placed it on Graber's desk. "This is the licence number of the Dodge."

"You reckon I should put out an APB on the vehicle, maybe pass the licence number to the Highway Patrol and State police while I'm at it?"

"It's up to you, Max. All I know is, this Helen Teale went to the Belmont Apartments on Thirty-Fifth and Dunlop Avenue."

"And exactly what am I supposed to read into that, Lew?"

"It's where Janice Xavier lives. The retired couple who occupy the apartment opposite hers told Helen Teale they thought she was taking a short vacation up Sedona way. She used that information to get the exact address of the cabin on Munds Park Road from the Ullander's neighbour."

"Sounds pretty ominous to me," Samuelson said quietly.

"It makes me nervous too," Graber admitted, "but you tell me what crime they have committed to justify an APB?"

"You stop them on any pretext you like," Dyce said. "Defective brake lights, malfunctioning indicators – take your pick."

"And after the patrolman has roasted them and they are squeaky clean? Where does that leave us, Lew?"

"No wiser, I suppose. But if the Teales are not who they claim they are, we may succeed in frightening them off."

"Do we have a description of them, Lew?"

Dyce ripped another page from the notebook and gave it to him. It read: Teale Eric. Male Caucasian, mid-thirties, height approximately six feet, weight 150 to 175 pounds. Colour of eyes – brown. Hair brown, brushed forward. Visible distinguishing marks – prominent cleft chin. Teale Helen. Female Caucasian, late twenties, height five six to five eight, weight approximately 125 pounds. Colour of eyes – grey. Hair dark and curly. Not unattractive and muscled like an athlete.

"This is the hotel staff again?"

"Mostly. Helen Teale's description was corroborated by the neighbours on Lincoln Drive and at the Belmont Apartments."

Graber eyeballed the phone, clucked his tongue several times, then lifted the receiver. "I guess it would do no harm to call the Highway Patrol office in Flagstaff again," he said.

*　　*　　*

293

Navajo Flats was situated on the east bank of Oak Creek some fourteen miles north of Sedona on State Highway 179. Up until Labour Day, the camp site had been crowded; now it was virtually deserted so that Zale didn't have to look very far to find a secluded spot where they could be sure of a little privacy.

"This picnic area will do us," he said, and pulled off the track on to a level piece of ground enclosed on three sides by scrub, juniper, fir and oak trees. "Got a table and a couple of benches. What more do we want?"

"Something to eat and drink," Galina told him.

"You have to earn your bread and butter," Ashton said. "If you don't, you go hungry."

They got out of the car and walked over to the benches and sat down, Galina on one side of the table, the two men on the other. Zale took out a small notebook, opened it at a blank page, then unclipped a ballpoint pen from the inside pocket of his lightweight jacket.

"Let's talk about TRIPWIRE," he said and smiled invitingly. "What exactly does it mean?"

"It's the codeword for the deployment of certain resources by 6 Guards Tank Army which can subsequently be used in either a defensive or offensive mode, depending on the situation."

"And no satellite can discover these resources? Isn't that what Yuri Rostovsky told Colonel Osmonde?"

"Yes."

Ashton gazed at her thoughtfully. "Would you say it was a highly secret operation?" he asked.

"Top Secret for High Command Eyes Only – there is no higher security classification than that in the Soviet Army."

"So how come a mere Starshii Leitenant in the GRU is privy to that kind of information?"

"The GRU unit in Potsdam has two roles; one is to monitor the activities of the British Arms Control Unit North West Europe, the other is to provide security advice to Headquarters 6 Guards Tank Army."

"That kind of job is done by NCOs of the Intelligence Corps in the British Army. They may advise Formation Headquarters how to safeguard classified material but they don't get to see the actual documents. So don't tell me it's different with you people."

"I would be lying if I said it was."

It seemed nothing he said was going to faze Galina or make her lose her temper. Her behaviour was contrary to everything he had been told about her character and was in marked contrast to the impression she had created little more than half an hour ago.

"It did, however, enable me to become acquainted with Colonel General Alexei Ivanovich Fedyanin," she continued. "Perhaps his name is not familiar to you, Mr Ashton?"

"Oh, I've heard of him all right." Fedyanin was the former paratrooper who had commanded 6 Guards Tank Army until relieved by Vitali Ilyich Lobanov on the third of June. Only fifty-three years old, he had made his name in Afghanistan and had been seen as a future Minister of Defence by Western observers.

"He was feeling low and vulnerable when I met him," Galina said.

"And you cheered him up?"

"He had lost his only son by his first marriage in Afghanistan; his new wife had remained behind in Moscow and was rumoured to be having an affair with the director of the Children's Theatre. He was drinking a lot and I came into his life at the right moment." She smiled lopsidedly. "I think part of the attraction for him was that he enjoyed the idea of screwing the granddaughter of General Nikolai Yakulevich Petrovsky, the former chief of the KGB's Armed Forces Directorate. Anyway, the general employed me as a supernumerary aide for a time, and that's how I got to hear about TRIPWIRE."

"For a time?" Zale picked up on her. "What do you mean by that?"

"I joined his staff in January 1990 and left towards the end of March."

"Did he fire you?"

"I got pregnant and had to have an abortion."

If her story was one big lie, Ashton thought, it was easily the most original and convincing one he had heard in a very long, long time. He did not have to ask Zale whether he believed her; he had only to glance at the notebook to know the American was hooked.

"That's a heart-rending story," Ashton told her acidly. "Now suppose you tell us what you know about TRIPWIRE?"

Galina raised her right hand, looked at Zale and rubbed the thumb across the fingers. "What's in it for me?"

"The choice between staying here or doing twenty years in a German prison."

"I wasn't asking you, Mr Ashton."

"I have to know what it is you're selling before you can put a price tag on it," Zale said tersely. "If you don't want to give me some free samples, we'll just forget the whole thing and you can take your chances with J.W. Ullander."

There was a long pause, then Galina smiled nervously and announced that she would prefer to deal with them.

The TV channel was showing an old 1949 black and white movie with Cary Grant as a male chauvinist French captain being chauffered around postwar bomb-shattered Germany in a motor-cycle combination by Ann Sheridan, the feisty WAC lieutenant appointed as his liaison officer. In the battle of the sexes, it anticipated *The War of the Roses* by over forty years, even though *I Was a Male War Bride* was the corniest title Janice Xavier could recall. The phone started ringing just as the boat they had borrowed from the army was about to be swept over a weir with them still in it. Aiming the remote control at the TV, she blanked out the screen before picking up the cordless phone which she had placed on the couch beside her. Although J.W. wasn't the last person she expected to hear, she was surprised that he should call her in the middle of the afternoon.

"I just wanted to make sure you're okay," he said. "Is that such a crime?"

"Of course it isn't, and I'm fine."

"Great." She heard him clear his throat, the way he always did when nervous or embarrassed. "Are Zale and Ashton with you?" he asked.

"No, they left shortly after two thirty."

"Uh huh." There was another pause and she could picture him frowning at the telephone. "An officer from the Highway Patrol will be dropping by the house . . ."

"He's already been here."

"Yeah? When was this?"

"Somewhere around two, a few minutes before Mr Zale arrived with . . ."

"He'll be back."

"I don't understand. Is something wrong, J.W.?"

"Look, I want you and Galina . . ."

"She isn't here."

"What do you mean, she isn't there?"

296

"Mr Zale and his English friend took her off to Navajo Flats in case the press descended on this place."

"Jesus."

"It's okay," Janice assured him hurriedly. "They're bringing her back here . . ."

"Forget Galina," Ullander said. "It's you I'm worried about. I want you to drop everything and get the hell out of there . . ."

"It's all right, J.W.; I can hear a vehicle coming down the track. It must be them – Galina and the other two."

"Well, you make damn sure before you open the door."

Janice told him to hang on, left the phone on the couch and went out into the hall. Through the window to the left of the door, she saw there were two cars – a Dodge and some other make she couldn't identify because of the dust cloud thrown up by the leading vehicle. Both drivers made a U-turn in front of the house and skidded to a halt. A man and a woman got out of the Dodge. A stocky dark-haired man wearing sunglasses alighted from the second vehicle, walked round to the back and opened the trunk. When he straightened up, he was holding a shotgun.

"Oh, my God," Janice said in a voice which did not sound as if it belonged to her.

The reason why J.W. had sounded nervous on the phone was now all too evident. Almost sick with fear, she ran back into the living room and picked up the cordless phone.

"They're here," she screamed.

"Who are?"

"I don't know." She pushed a hand through her blonde hair, grabbed a hank and almost tore it out of her scalp. "Two men and a woman," she sobbed. "One of them has a shotgun."

"Listen to me, Janice," Ullander said in a calming voice. "You're armed too. Now, sit tight, don't show yourself at a window and shoot the first bastard who attempts to break in. I'm going to call the police. Okay?"

"Yes."

She dropped the phone, grabbed her tote bag and somehow managed to loosen the drawstring with hands that wouldn't stop shaking. Her fingers sought the pistol grip of the .32 calibre revolver amongst the other hundred and one items, but the Smith and Wesson eluded them. Panic-stricken, she upended the bag and tipped the contents out on to the couch. Lipstick, purse, mirror,

297

comb, hairbrush, chequebook, tissues, sunglasses, shoehorn, but no revolver because Galina had taken it either while she had been talking to the Highway Patrolman or when she had answered the door to Zale and Ashton. Paralysed with fear, she stood there in the centre of the room like a rabbit caught in the headlights of an oncoming vehicle.

Stanford pumped a 12 gauge cartridge into the Remington semiautomatic shotgun, then moved quickly down the side of the house and tried the back door. Finding it locked, he used the butt to smash the kitchen window and chip the shards of glass from the frame. As he climbed inside, Stanford could hear a woman mewling like a kitten. He unlocked and opened the back door, then went on through to the living room, holding the shotgun in his right hand by the small of the butt, index finger curled round the trigger.

"Sit down," he told the woman. "Clasp your hands together on top of your head and don't move."

She backed away from him, her mouth working like a stranded fish. She bumped into the armrest, felt her way round the obstruction and sat down on the couch. Something brittle snapped in two under her weight.

"I've broken my sunglasses," she said, and burst into tears.

"Shut up."

"Who – are – you? What – do – you – want?" The questions were asked haltingly between muffled sobs.

"I told you to shut up, Mrs Xavier." Stanford prodded her in the chest with the shotgun, then backed off towards the hall, his eyes never leaving the faded blonde. "Come round the back," he yelled, "the door's open."

Janice Xavier was shivering as if the room temperature was subarctic. Her knees and thighs were pressed together, either to stop them trembling or in an effort to control her bladder.

"How do you know my name?" she whispered hoarsely.

"Never mind that. Where is she?"

"Who?"

"Galina Kutuzova. You'd better tell me before my friends join us."

"I don't know."

It was a stupid lie; he didn't believe her, neither did the other two.

The woman leaned over the back of the couch, grabbed a fistful of blonde hair and yanked Janice to her feet. Until that moment, the American woman had not been aware they were no longer alone. Shock, as well as the sharp stab of pain, made her cry out.

"We think you do," Helen Teale said.

She twisted the hank of blonde hair to get a tighter grip. With her other hand, she seized Janice's left wrist and forced her arm behind her back and then upwards until it came to rest between her shoulder blades. At the same time, she pulled her head back so that the American woman was forced to arch her body like a bow.

"Oh Jesus, that hurts," she gasped.

Stanford could have told her that the pain was only just beginning. When Teale took out his cutthroat razor and unfolded the blade, he walked over to the TV, punched one of the channel buttons at random, then brought the volume up to fill the room with the sound of some actor doing a hard sell on retirement homes in Phoenix. There was not the slightest chance that anyone would hear what was going on in the cabin, but he had no great desire to listen to Xavier screaming.

"Tell me where she is," Teale demanded.

"The police will arrive any moment. They were here earlier this afternoon."

She couldn't have seen the razor Teale was holding; Stanford thought there could be no other explanation for her stupidity. "Tell him," he pleaded silently, "make it easy on yourself. There's no point in prolonging the agony; get it over with because there is only one way the pain is going to end no matter what you do. Tell him. Tell him." But of course she didn't until Teale sliced her nose from the bridge to the tip and then cut each nostril with the precision of a surgeon.

There was a millisecond of silence before the pain got to her and she screamed like a wounded animal. "Two men called for her this afternoon; they took her to Navajo Flats."

The words came slowly as she alternately sobbed and half-choked on the blood flowing from her nose. Stanford did not want to hear the agony in her voice as she told them where the camp site was and how to get there, but there was nothing on any of the channels to drown it out completely. He did not want to see the dance of death either, but a terrible fascination made him watch as Helen killed her, right arm locked across Xavier's throat to provide a fulcrum for the left hand behind the American's head to push forward and snap her neck.

"We'll take the shotgun and go after her. You stay here and tidy things up." Teale grabbed his shirtfront and shook him. "Did you hear what I said?" he shouted.

"Yes, you want the shotgun," Stanford said, his voice all on one note.

"Come on, snap out of it. You're a Spetsnaz soldier, Nikolai Sokolov. Killing is your business, it's what you do best." Teale steered him through the hall and on out into the harsh sunlight, then opened the trunk of the Dodge and dropped a border spade and shovel at his feet. "There's some sort of flowerbed round the back," he said. "Bury her in that, the digging will be easier."

"If you say so."

"I do." Teale turned away from him for a moment, handed the ignition keys to Helen and told her to drive. "I'll take this now, Nikolai Sokolov," he said and prised the Remington semiautomatic shotgun from his grasp. "Soon as you have finished here, drive straight back to your motel. If you don't hear from me, check out tomorrow and make your own way home. Okay?"

Stanford didn't say anything, just stood there and watched them drive off. Teale had called him by his Russian name, not once but twice. If that wasn't a sign that the whole damned operation was coming apart at the seams, he didn't know what was.

The Highway Patrolman had been driving south on Interstate 17 when Flagstaff had put out an APB on a Dodge Spirit, licence number AZ 81–9637 and warned all officers to approach the occupants with caution. Four miles farther on when he had been approaching the roadside rest area at Banjo Bill, Flagstaff had asked for his location, then told him to check out the Ullander place on Munds Park Road. He had already been there once that day; this time he turned off Interstate 17 at the First Aid station and headed towards Sedona to approach the dirt track from the opposite direction.

The Oldsmobile he had observed earlier on in the afternoon was still in the carport alongside the cabin but there was another vehicle parked outside the front door. Although it wasn't the Dodge he had been warned to look out for, he was suspicious of the two-door Pontiac Grand Prix. Shifting the drive into neutral, he cut the engine and rolled silently and slowly to a halt. He was equally stealthy when alighting from the prowl car and deliberately left the offside door open. His right hand instinctively went to the .38 revolver in the leather holster on his hip and undid the retaining thong across the pistol grip so that there would be no obstruction in the way if he had to draw it in a hurry. The same instinct prompted him to circle the house and try the back door.

The man who was digging a trench in the flowerbed did not resemble the description of Teale, the male Caucasian who had rented the Dodge from Hertz. On the other hand, the Highway Patrolman was equally sure he wasn't Ullander's gardener.

"Hey there, fella," he said, "what do you think you're doing?"

It happened fast, so fast that he was taken completely by surprise. One moment the man in the trench had his back to him, in the next, he had whirled round and hurled the shovel at him like a goddamned spear. They were maybe twenty paces apart and he just had time to jerk his head out of the way, but the blade found its mark high up on the left shoulder, broke the collar bone and knocked him flat on his back.

There was no question of telling the bastard to freeze or any of that kind of chickenshit. Somehow he managed to draw the .38 from the holster and get himself into a sitting position before blasting the sonofabitch halfway to hell and back as he came charging towards him.

Galina was on her eighth cigarette and getting a little hoarse from talking. Zale had filled so many pages in his notebook, he was in danger of suffering from writer's cramp. What the Russian girl had told them was more than enough to disturb the air of complacent euphoria that had settled over Washington and London after the failure of the coup d'état in Moscow. And yet Ashton felt there were still some avenues which needed to be explored.

"After you fled from Dresden," he said, "you rang your mother, Lydia Petrovskaya. Why did you do that?"

"I don't know what you are talking about."

"Don't lie to me. I met your mother in Leningrad at the Gostinyi Dvor on Nevsky Prospekt and she told me you had phoned her from Zürich. There wasn't a lot you could say to Lydia Petrovskaya because you guessed the KGB had put a phone tap on her apartment, but you did manage to let her know that you had got out."

Most of it was based on guesswork but there was a kernel of truth in there, and Galina bought it.

"I wanted to let her know I was safe."

"What about your father? Why did you leave him in ignorance?"

Galina considered the question, chin cupped in the palm of one hand. Some way off, Ashton could hear a car moving slowly through the camp site.

"I am closer to my mother."

"So you told Simon Younger; but I think there is more to it than that. You were planning to defect long before Whittle got himself blown up by a bomb intended for you. And if things had gone according to plan, Lydia Petrovskaya would have slipped over the border into Finland on her way to join you in the West."

Ashton waited for her to say something. The car was much closer to them now but it was still grinding along at a snail's pace as if the driver was looking for a particular spot on the camp site and was deliberately keeping the vehicle in bottom gear.

"Oh, is it a crime to seek a better life in another country?" she asked.

"Of course it isn't; America would still be an underpopulated continent if it was."

"And you surely don't believe I would have deliberately left my mother behind, do you?"

"Yuri Rostovsky established your credentials with two photographs of your mother, one taken of her with your grandfather and Stalin when she was a child, the other with Andropov shortly after she had become engaged to be married. Aside from filial devotion, you wanted her to come out because she was supposed to bring the family album with her, which would really have increased your market value."

Again, it was pure guesswork, but as Wellington had observed a hundred and eighty years before, "All the business of war and indeed all the business of life, is to endeavour to find out what you don't know by what you do." In his words, it was called "Guessing what was the other side of the hill."

"What nonsense you talk," Galina said, but her voice denied it.

Ashton looked past her. A car had entered the clearing and had come to a halt forty yards away, pointing in their direction. The driver built the revs up, then allowed them to fall off.

"A Dodge," Zale muttered beside him.

At that particular moment, the vehicle reminded Ashton of a bull pawing the ground. As he watched, a man carrying a shotgun rolled out of the nearside door a split second before the Dodge leapt forward.

"Scatter," he yelled.

Zale dived to the right, Ashton to the left. Galina reached into her handbag and came out with the .32 calibre Smith and Wesson revolver she had stolen from Janice Xavier. Whirling round and clearing the bench with her feet, she crouched down, held the pistol in a double-handed grip, and aiming it at the driver, squeezed off three shots in what amounted to a burst of rapid fire. The windshield exploded like a bomb to become a crazy mosaic of diamond-shaped fragments of glass, but the Dodge came on, a ton and a half of irresistible metal. Breaking to her left, Galina fired at the other figure who was running towards her and was answered by two blasts from the shotgun.

Ashton saw her leap into the air like an ice-skater lifting off for a triple lutz and then go down hard, the revolver flying from her grasp. In that same instant, the Dodge ploughed through the table and bench seats reducing them to matchwood before ramming head on into a fir tree which stopped it dead. The bonnet sprang up, coolant spewed from the shattered radiator and the horn blared a requiem for an expensive piece of machinery which lasted until the battery finally shorted out. In the silence which followed, the offside door suddenly sprang open and a woman with dark curly hair toppled sideways out of the Dodge to hang there, restrained by the seat belt so that she was half in, half out of the car, her head dipping towards the ground, blood oozing from the neat round hole between her eyes.

The revolver was lying in the dirt some twenty odd feet from Ashton. Away to his right, Zale was on his feet hurling rocks at the gunman. Taking advantage of the distraction, he went after the revolver, completing just two strides before launching himself in a plunging dive. Landing an arm's length short of the Smith and Wesson, he scrabbled after it, wrapped his fingers around the pistol grip and while still in the lying position, snapped off a shot that went high and wide of the target.

There was no return fire from the gunman. He just stood there nursing the wound in his left side where Galina had hit him.

"It's over," Ashton shouted to him, "it's over, drop the shotgun." Something made him repeat it in Russian.

The man nodded as if he understood, then sank down on to his knees and rested his chin on the muzzle. Ashton saw him reach down the barrel towards the trigger and cried out, but some kind of fanatical pride made the Russian deaf to reason and his thumb slipped inside the guard and released the hammer. The lead shot blew away his jaw and exited from the back of the skull in a shower of brain tissue and shattered bone.

"Jesus." Zale stared at the bloody corpse. "Jesus Christ, what the hell did he do that for?"

"I wouldn't know," Ashton said, "and he's past telling you."

He got up, walked over to where Galina was lying flat on her back and crouched beside her. The pellets had only just begun to spread out when they'd hit and most of them had blasted into her left hip and upper thigh, severing the main artery.

"We need an ambulance, Tony, and fast. She's still alive."

"Yeah."

"So what are you waiting for? Take the car and get to a phone before we have another dead body on our hands."

Ashton removed his jacket, stripped off his shirt and ripped out a sleeve. A tie would have been handier, but he wasn't wearing one, and the sleeve had to serve as a tourniquet instead. He found a pressure point above the severed artery, wrapped the sleeve around her thigh and twisted the ends, tightening them until the blood stopped pumping out into the dust. Behind him, Zale scrambled into their car, gunned the engine into life and took off.

Galina looked terrible; her face was the colour of old parchment and was clammy to the touch. Her pupils were dilated, the pulse rate was feeble and irregular and she was barely conscious.

"I'm not going to die, am I?" she whispered in a rare moment of lucidity.

"Not you," Ashton told her, "you're indestructible."

But there were moments before the paramedics arrived in a Bell UH-1H helicopter when he doubted it.

CHAPTER 28

THE MIL Mi 24 helicopters were part of 6 Guards Tank Army order of battle. Known as the Hind-A by NATO, they belonged to the 10th Air Regiment based on Parchim, northwest of Berlin. In their assault role, each helicopter carried a crew of three and eight fully equipped troops in the main cabin. On the auxiliary wings there were four pylons for UB-32 rocket pods plus rails for a similar number of A2 Swatter antitank missiles. There was also a 12.7mm single-barrel DShK machine gun in the nose slaved to a remote-control sighting system. For the past week, however, none of the helicopters assigned to the TRIPWIRE verification team had been armed.

The number of Hinds committed to the inspection team had varied from day to day. At the start of the week there had been eight but as mission after mission had proved abortive, the number had steadily fallen to an all-time low of two. This morning, there were four helicopters flying in a loose star formation towards Neustrelitz, sixty-one miles north of Berlin. The additional Mi 24s had been put on to airlift Colonel General Lobanov and his operational staff as well as additional representatives from the Western Powers.

With his customary desire to seek the maximum publicity, the army commander had accompanied the inspection team to Grossenhain, Rodeburg and Pirna in the Saxony Länder, his complacent smirk becoming more and more pronounced as each TRIPWIRE site proved negative. He had put in an appearance on the second day when they had checked out a further four locations, this time in Thuringia. After that, Lobanov had let it be known that he had better things to do than participate in a wild-goose chase. His example had inevitably led to a corresponding reduction in the number of senior American, British, French and German observers. At rock bottom, the rump had consisted of eight

305

junior staff officers from 6 Guards Tank Army in one helicopter, Franklin, Ashton, Zale, Earley, Sergeant Norman and Dermot Capel-Tombs, an assistant undersecretary from the Foreign and Commonwealth Office in the other.

Not for the first time this morning, the Foreign Office man raised his eyes from the memo he was drafting on his lap to gaze at Ashton with what appeared to be studied indifference, unlike Head of Station, Berlin who, if looks could be said to kill, was getting ready to bury him.

"You've got a couple of good friends there," Zale said, leaning close to bellow in his ear in order to make himself heard above the roar from the two Isotov TV3–117 turboshaft engines.

"My fan club," Ashton shouted back, then turned sideways to look through the porthole window.

They were flying at an altitude of four hundred feet parallel to Route 96. Neustrelitz was the dark smudge he could see on the horizon that was rapidly drawing nearer; directly below, east and west of the main road, were scores of lakes characteristic of the Mecklenburg-Vorpommern Länder. It was, he decided, time to throw a spanner in the works. Leaving his seat, he opened the sliding door to the flight deck and told the ground engineer he wanted to use his boom mike and headset.

"Change of destination, Major," he cheerfully announced after the Russian had reluctantly surrendered his bone dome. "Neustrelitz is out, Neubrandenburg is in. Your new landing zone is grid reference 651392."

"But . . ."

"No buts, Major. Tell the other call signs and try to remember I'll be listening in."

Ashton switched channels from intercom to command net and waited for the inevitable protests. The other captains were not slow to voice their objections and he was equally quick to dismiss them. The diversion would put less than thirty miles on the round trip and with the reduced payload they were carrying, the Hinds were good for a combat radius in excess of three hundred. With a maximum cruising speed of a hundred and eighty-three miles an hour, the time factor didn't hold water either. That the Gaz jeeps would now be waiting at the wrong landing zone would of course be inconvenient, but as Ashton took delight in pointing out, it was hardly an insuperable problem. All the pilot had to do was call up the transport officer on the radio and give him the grid reference of the landing zone. Finally, he reminded all call signs that it was their own army commander who had directed that they were to take their orders from the inspection team. Thereafter, there were no further arguments and he returned to the main cabin.

"Seems to me we're changing course," Zale observed. "Could it be you're trying to pull a fast one?"

"I'd like to think so. I do know "Wild Boar" raised more objections than anyone else on the net."

"Wild Boar" was the call sign of the Hind transporting Colonel General Lobanov and his staff. Although the army commander hadn't spoken on the air himself, there was no doubting who had been prompting the pilot. All the same, Ashton wasn't sure whether he had succeeded in worrying the general or had merely annoyed him. He was, however, beginning to wonder if there had ever been a grain of truth in the information Galina Kutuzova had given them. The rigorous application of additional security measures after Galina had defected was not the reason why it had taken Rostovsky a further seven weeks to procure the rest of the information. The bastard had needed fifty days to manufacture a fake set of documents which he had then microfilmed for Lloyd Osmonde's benefit – that was the most likely explanation.

On the other hand, the Russians had been given ample time to conceal the evidence. A precious month had been lost while the Foreign Office had conferred with Bonn, Paris and Washington before seeking Moscow's agreement to a multinational inspection team. For security reasons, there had been no mention of TRIPWIRE during the negotiations and the FO had expended a considerable amount of time and energy devising a suitable cover plan. But any Russian staff officer with a modest IQ could add two and two and get the right answer.

In twenty-eight days, Commander 6 Guards Tank Army could have back-loaded enough ammunition to start World War Three. Or could it have been that simple? The weapons Galina had spoken of were so damned sensitive, it was unlikely the Soviet High Command would have trusted their emplacement to any run-of-the-mill unit. No, it was a job for highly motivated troops who could be relied upon to keep their mouths shut, and someone like Colonel General Vitali Ilyich Lobanov, a former chief of the Spetsnaz, would naturally

307

give the task to Special Forces. So would his predecessor, Fedyanin.

To deploy the weapons secretly would have been difficult enough, to withdraw them clandestinely without alerting the wrong faction in Moscow would be a nightmare. You would need people who had opposed Gorbachev and were equally at loggerheads with Yeltsin and the new régime. Finding the right men might not be easy and it could be that not all of the material had been removed yet. Ashton felt the helicopter lose height and thought it wouldn't be long now before they found out.

The pilot circled the immediate area as if hoping he could find something wrong with the landing zone which he knew had been picked off the map. The grid reference Ashton had given him was three thousand metres southeast of Neubrandenburg and well away from the lakes southwest of the town. The water table wasn't critical; the landing zone was in good, well-drained grassland. Ashton went forward to the flight deck to disabuse the major of any notions he might have to the contrary. He needn't have bothered; before he could relieve the ground engineer of his bone dome again, the pilot had picked his spot and put the Hind down. The other three helicopters followed him in.

The ground engineer came back to raise the upward-hinged window forward of the auxiliary wings on the port side. Ashton was the first out and walked erect under the still whirling rotor blades. Zale was close behind him, then Earley, Sergeant Norman and the two French observers who'd only joined them that morning. Dermot Capel-Tombs and a thoroughly disgruntled-looking Franklin brought up the rear. No one said anything until the whine of the turbo engines died away to nothing. Once he didn't have to compete with the noise generated by a couple of 2200 shaft horsepower Isotovs, Franklin didn't waste any time making his views known.

"Do you mind telling us exactly what we are doing in the middle of a field?" he asked acidly.

"Look around you," Ashton told him. "On your left is Route 96, goes all the way to Ruggen on the Baltic. Ahead is the railway from Neubrandenburg to Szczecin, Poznan and Warsaw. You've also got Route 198 on a near parallel course."

"So?"

"So both means of communication can be used as a main supply route in or out of East Germany."

Capel-Tombs consulted his map, then turned a complete circle. "And presumably we are now standing in the middle of a TRIP-WIRE site?" he drawled.

"It's one of the four grid references Galina Kutuzova was able to give us from memory."

"A few clumps of trees in otherwise open grassland – doesn't look very promising to me, Ashton."

"That has to be an understatement," Franklin said. "In my opinion, this is just one more example of her fertile imagination."

"If it is," Ashton said, "she certainly paid one hell of a price for it."

The surgeons had managed to save her life, but they'd had to amputate the leg and Galina was going to need a lot of psychiatric counselling before she accepted the artificial replacement.

"The jeeps are coming," Zale said in a low voice.

"So I see." Ashton left the group, walked over to where Sergeant Norman was standing and led him even farther away from the others. "I want you to stay here," he said, "while we take a look at the ammunition depot north of Neubrandenburg. Soon as we've gone, get your gear out of the chopper and start looking."

"How long will you be gone?"

"You can count on a minimum of two hours."

"Doesn't give me much time; it would take a thirty-six man troop a whole day to sweep this area."

"I doubt if the site's right out in the open. Go for the likely spots within striking distance of the supply routes which offer a certain amount of cover."

"Right."

"Just do the best you can." Ashton turned on his heel to rejoin Zale before walking over to the road with the rest of the entourage to board one of the waiting Gaz jeeps.

Sergeant Norman waited until the convoy had moved off before he collected his gear from the Hind. The mine detector he would be using was simply an improved version of the World War Two model which had emitted an oscillating note whenever the sensor passed over a buried metal object. To counter this, the Germans had developed a wood casing for the mine; in the postwar years, the Russians had taken the art of mine warfare a stage further, producing a munition that was almost undetectable.

With the aid of the ground engineer who insisted on helping him, Sergeant Norman slipped his arms through the web straps and heaved the battery-powered transceiver on to his back, then adjusted the headphones to fit snugly over his ears. He checked the detector, which resembled the brush and extending metal tubes of a vacuum cleaner, to make sure there were no loose connections and switched on the power supply. He looked round for the shovel that would be needed if there was a positive reaction from the sensor and saw the Russian had appropriated it.

"I go with you," the engineer told him.

"If you insist."

Norman studied the ground, looking for a possible site within a thousand yards of the road and rail links to Poland, and thought he would be better employed trying to find a needle in a haystack. "Go for the likely spots which offer a certain amount of cover" – Ashton's words. But the only cover was the isolated clump of trees well to the south of the landing zone and they were too far away to be of any use for an operation like TRIPWIRE.

"It is not a nice day, I think," the Russian engineer said in halting English.

Grey sky on a grey October day and a chill breeze coming all the way from the Urals, a foretaste of the winter to come.

"You can say that again, Ivan."

Sergeant Norman started walking towards the road and rail links in front of him, his new-found friend beside him. He had been there at the start of it all in Dresden and he would have liked to see it through to a successful conclusion, but life wasn't like that. There would be no neat ending, at least not here in the middle of nowhere.

At first, he thought the hollow was a large dried-up pond that had been used as a dumping ground for junk, then on closer inspection, it dawned on him that the hollow was a mass of interlocking craters. They were not as well-defined as they would have been forty-six years ago, but there had definitely been some sort of engagement in the area during the final stages of World War Two. The evidence was there when you looked for it – a few links of tank track embedded in the earth, part of a bogie wheel almost totally hidden by the grass.

Sergeant Norman fancied he knew what had happened. The Oder was only a few miles to the east, the last barrier before

Berlin. A number of Panther tanks or maybe 88mm self-propelled assault guns must have been lying there in reserve and the Red Air Force had found the panzers and reduced them to a heap of scrap metal. Since then, the ground had not been disturbed. Or had it?

His eyes went to a set of tyre marks that looked comparatively new. No more than five or six feet long and made by only one set of wheels. If they had laid a temporary matting roadway, he would never have spotted the tracks. But that was just what they had done, and one of the drivers had slipped off it when he had been reversing up to the dig. A crater bigger than the others; must have been made by a two thousand-pound bomb when it would have been something like twenty feet deep. Shallower now but still big enough for the purpose they'd had in mind. He swept the far wall of the crater with the detector, got a positive reaction and let out a whoop of triumph. It was now simply a question of digging, and the Russian caught his enthusiasm and went at it like a badger, attacking the bank with a shovel and hurling clods of earth over his shoulder. It took Sergeant Norman some time to persuade him they couldn't do the task alone.

The moment the jeep convoy rolled through the gates of the ammunition depot, Ashton knew he was faced with a hopeless situation. There was no question of making the inspection last even the bare two hours he had promised Sergeant Norman, never mind stealing an extra one. Every shed in the depot had been stripped clean, the doors left wide open so that anyone could see at a glance that there was nothing inside. Nevertheless, he had done his best to keep it going, much to the vast amusement of Colonel General Lobanov who had insisted they remove every drain cover and look inside to make sure they were not being used to store nerve agent munitions.

"This can't go on," Franklin said angrily. "The bastard is laughing at us. We have to call it off before we are made to look complete idiots."

"I agree." Capel-Tombs looked down at his spotlessly clean Wellingtons. "I realise you never expected to find anything in this location, Ashton, but clearly their general is right in maintaining that this was simply a storage facility for training ammunition."

Pompous, arrogant and insufferably condescending: there were other more forceful adjectives Ashton could have used to describe the Foreign Office representative, but they weren't printable. He wanted to tell Capel-Tombs not to be such an asshole but knew it would only be counterproductive. Earley, however, was under no such restraint.

"Training ammunition!" he exploded. "Jesus Christ, you've got to be out of your tiny mind. Look at the size of this place. You think they put in a branch line and a ramp long enough to take a thirty-car freight train just to rail in a load of pyrotechnics?"

"What does it matter now?" Franklin demanded. "The depot's empty, isn't it?"

He had a point, Ashton thought. No one could deny that and try as he might, he was unable to come up with one good reason why they should prolong the inspection of an empty, deserted ammunition depot in the middle of the Mecklenburg-Vorpommern Länder.

Lobanov hammed it up and expressed surprise that the British should want to leave so soon but was naturally only too happy to fall in with their wishes. The convoy formed up and moved off through the gates and on down the road to Neubrandenburg. The grey autumn sky matched Ashton's sombre mood. It was all very well Zale telling him he had given it his best shot and had been damned unlucky, but that was small consolation for failure. It took a small figure standing by the roadside in the distance to give him a lift.

"Who's that?" Zale asked.

Sergeant Norman rapidly coming into focus, large as life and twice as handsome. Sergeant Norman dancing a jig and punching a clenched fist into the air, a huge grin on his face that stretched from ear to ear.

"Pull up," Ashton yelled in Russian at the top of his voice.

The Russian soldier hit the brakes with a heavy foot and screeched to a halt. Taken by surprise, the driver of the following vehicle was slow to respond and rammed into them, with the result that Franklin pitched forward into the windscreen and collected a bloody nose. But Ashton was already out of the jeep and striding towards the hollow where a small crowd of Russian airmen were hunkered down, surrounded by discarded shovels.

"We did it, we did it," Sergeant Norman kept repeating. "We hit the fucking jackpot."

The entrance was waist high and just wide enough for a man to squeeze through on hands and knees. One of the Russians handed Ashton a flashlight before he crawled inside the shaft which led to a chamber that was only marginally bigger. The device was black, ugly-looking and roughly half the size of a dustbin. He stared at the munition, momentarily overawed by its lethal power, then recovering, he backed out of the chamber and handed the flashlight to Capel-Tombs.

"Here," he said, "you want to have a look?"

"What's in there?"

Ashton turned to Sergeant Norman. "You tell him, Sergeant; you found it."

"It's an ADM."

"A what?"

"An atomic demolition munition. The one in there can be set for either a five- or ten-kiloton yield."

"I don't believe it."

"You'd better," Ashton told him. "Sergeant Norman knows what he is talking about. He did a tour of duty with 33 EOD Regiment when he was a corporal and they're the people who've got the nasty job of defusing these things."

"An atomic demolition munition," Capel-Tombs repeated blankly.

Ashton smiled. "The likes of you and me would call it a mine."

"I still don't understand . . ."

"TRIPWIRE is about a different kind of minefield. Each one of these devices is an atomic bomb designed to achieve maximum fallout. They are armed and triggered by bouncing a command signal off a satellite. When one of these ADMs goes off, it is going to spread a load of contaminated spoil over a wide area, spoil that's emitting anything up to four hundred rads an hour. You drive through a contaminated area in a tank with a protective factor of twenty and you are still absorbing a dose rate of twenty rads an hour which is going to make you a very sick man."

Ashton didn't think it was necessary to spell out all the implications. Whatever else he might be, Capel-Tombs was not unintelligent and could work them out for himself. In a future conflict, TRIPWIRE could be used to delay the reinforcement of combat units in the forward area until the fallout had decayed to an acceptable level. Alternatively, the weapons system could be used in a defensive mode to prevent the resupply of an aggressor.

313

"TRIPWIRE." Capel-Tombs shook his head. "Whoever conceived the operation must have taken leave of his senses."

"Not necessarily," Ashton said. "If you were a seventy-year-old veteran like former Defence Minister Marshal Dmitri Yazov, you might feel that the only thing a united Germany had exported to Russia was war and death. He might have thought he was merely being prudent."

"Then we must be thankful he was dismissed before his men had time to plant more than one ADM."

"Is that going to be the official line?"

The complacent smile on Capel-Tombs's face rapidly dissolved. "I think you have a problem, Ashton," he said icily.

Maybe he did, but it was nothing like the one he was about to hand Lobanov. They might only have found one miserable 10KT ADM so far but there were a whole lot more, a complete barrier of them placed at tactical intervals throughout the old Eastern Zone of Germany and someone had to do something about it. Turning his back on Capel-Tombs, he advanced towards the Russian and shook his hand warmly.

"I can't thank you enough, Colonel General," he said in fluent Russian. "And I'd like you to know how much I appreciate all the help I have received from Lieutenant Colonel Alexei Leven. Without his invaluable assistance, we would never have found this ADM. You can be sure our Prime Minister will be writing to Mr Yeltsin to express his confidence that no unpleasant surprises will be left behind after the Russian Army has withdrawn from East Germany."

It was one small way of evening up the score for Whittle, and there were, he thought, at this moment in time, few greater pleasures in life than watching the sickly expression on Lobanov's face.